DRUID SACRIFICE

Down in the lesser hall she found the family and certain of Loth's closest friends gathered in noisy celebration, feeding on cold meats, but doing more drinking than eating. Some hailed her arrival with shouts, especially Owen ap Urien.

Her father, clearly much affected by drink, and seated, half rose as she came in, but staggering, sank back on the bench. He banged his tankard on the table-top for quiet, spilling mead.

"Ha, daughter!" he got out thickly. "You grace us . . . with your presence . . . at last! This, this especial night." He had difficulty with the word especial. "Come, you."

Set-faced, she moved a little nearer him. The queen came to stand behind her husband, looking more satisfied than usual.

"Tonight, I have . . . have good news for you, girl," the king went on, and drank. "Excellent news. One day you will be a queen. Queen of Rheged. Aye, Rheged. Queen Thanea!" He hiccuped. "Owen ap Urien has asked for you, for your hand in marriage. And I, have granted it. You hear? Marriage. You are to be this Owen's wife."

There were cries of congratulation from some of those around.

Thanea stood as though turned to stone.

Druid Sacrifice

Nigel Tranter

CORONET BOOKS
Hodder and Stoughton

First published in Great Britain in 1993 by Hodder and Stoughton
A division of Hodder Headline PLC
First published in paperback in 1993 by Hodder and Stoughton
A Coronet paperback
This Coronet paperback edition 1998

10 9 8 7 6 5 4 3 2 1

ISBN 0 340 59984 7

Printed and bound in Great Britain by
Mackays of Chatham plc, Chatham, Kent

Hodder and Stoughton
A division of Hodder Headline PLC
338 Euston Road
London NW1 3BH

To Lady Anne-Louise Hamilton-Dalrymple,
whose suggestion it all was

Principal Characters in order of appearance

Abbess Edana: Familiarly known as Monenna
Thanea: Princess, daughter of King Loth
Gawain mac Loth: Celtic prince, brother of Thanea
Owen ap Urien: Prince of Rheged
Queen Guanhumara: Second wife of King Loth
Loth: King of the Gododdin, of Lodonia, who gave name to
    Lothian
Mordred: Half-brother of Thanea and Gawain
Diarmid: Arch Druid
Fergus: A shepherd
Serf or Servanus: Abbot of Culross, and former prince
Gabhran: Bishop
Kentigern or Mungo: Son to Thanea
Nechtan: Mormaor or sub-king of Fortrenn
Eva: Queen of Nechtan
Finan: Son of above
Cara: Daughter of Nechtan and Eva
Morcant: King of Strathclyde
Felim: Arch Druid of Strathclyde
Fergus: Prior of monastery of Carnock
Arthur: High King of the Britons
Duncan: Druid of Airthrey
Guinevere: Queen of Arthur
Merlin: The High King's Secretary
Kessog: A druid of Arran
Lancelot: King of the Brigantes of Northumbria
Angwen: Miller of Cathures
Telleyr: Brother of above
Cadoc: Former Welsh abbot and monarch
Malduin: A druid
Nessa: Wife of Malduin
Ferchar: A senior druid
Cathal: An Irish bishop

Part One

1

The older woman spoke carefully, as well she might in the circumstances. "These men are not evil, even though they sin," she said. "They worship, even though mistakenly. We have to thank Almighty God for the sun, not to worship it, as these do. The sun is God's gift to us, to the whole earth, a blessing on all His creatures. But to offer sacrifices to the sun is wrong, folly – only to God Himself should we offer prayer and sacrifice. This harking back to the old religion is grievously mistaken, sinful."

The young women, almost a score of them, took that variously, some exchanging glances, some murmuring, some fingering the golden crosses which hung from all their necks, as though for reassurance. The one who had raised the matter, Anna, daughter of Conal of Pitcox, persisted – she was that sort of girl, bold-eyed, impulsive and good-looking.

"But Monenna, in Holy Writ they sacrifice. Sheep and goats and pigeons. Did not Abraham himself do so? A ram, was it not? But he was going to sacrifice his own son, Isaac? So can it be so wrong?"

"God taught Abraham better, Anna. But Abraham's sacrifice was made to God his Maker, not to the sun. If these druid priests were making sacrifices to their Heavenly Father, it would not be so ill. But not to false gods which, blessedly, our people have discarded for Christ."

"It is not only sheep and cattle, it is a woman!" That came out with a nervous giggle from another girl. "They say that there are to be *two* women so . . . used!"

That drew indrawn breaths.

"That is evil, uttermost evil!" Edana declared. Abbess Edana was a missionary nun from Newry in Ireland, of St Patrick's fellowship, come here to help convert, or re-convert, the Southern Picts, after they had resiled from the faith brought

3

to them by the blessed St Ninian a century before. The convent students – these were that, not nuns-to-be – called her Mo that is Beloved, contracted to Monenna, in their affection for her. "Men who can so treat women act like brute-beasts. Worse, since the animals, also God's creatures, know no better and do not seek to hurt. Here is shame, an outrage against the Most High." It was not often that Abbess Edaña spoke thus.

"Can you stop it, Monenna?"

"I can try."

"I do not think that you can," Anna asserted. "King Loth and the High Priest have ordered it. All nobles and men of substance are to be there. My own father. Most of our fathers." She glanced at the young woman sitting next to her, one of calm, serene beauty, dark-eyed, who so far had not spoken. "We will all have to be there, to watch."

"No!" That was part command, part pleading. "No, my dear ones – you *must* not go."

"My father has so ordered me. I think that these others will be so ordered also." Most of those present in that simple room were the daughters of the small kingdom of Lothian's nobles and chiefs.

"I will go up and see the king," the abbess said. "Pray God that he will heed me."

"I think not, Monenna!" Anna was in her element. "Not when it has been made so much of. And this Prince Owen come from Cumbria – the handsome one! It is to be a great occasion. The rising of Aries, at the Vernal Equinox tomorrow night. Midway between the solstices." Anna liked to display her knowledge, even of such non-Christian subjects.

"I will speak with King Loth. He may heed me. Or would I be best to speak with Queen Guanhumara?" It was seldom that the abbess showed doubt, at least before her students. And asking this question, she looked over at the quiet, dark-haired, dark-eyed girl beside Anna nic Conal.

That one shook her head, her customary serenity tinged with a hint of sorrow. "I cannot believe that she could, or would, change his mind. Not in this."

"You will know best, Thanea. I will go to him."

Although the girl did not speak again, she shook her head once more, and that was eloquence enough. And less than

4

encouraging. For, if anyone there was likely to know King Loth's attitude and likely reaction, his daughter would, for this was the Princess Thanea.

The implications of that were evident to all. Another voice spoke up, that of Eithne, daughter of Gabhran of Hailes, the nearest property to the north of this Traprain, and Thanea's closest friend. She was a red-head, warm of nature as of colouring.

"If we are *commanded* to attend, Monenna, what do we do, what do we say?"

"If I cannot persuade the king to halt this wickedness, at least I can beseech him not to insist on your presence," the abbess said. "I will pray. I urge that you all do so, also." She raised a hand. "But enough of this meantime." Recognising that the young women's heads would be full of this grievous and urgent matter, Edana curtailed the rest of the lesson on Latinity, and suggested that the girls should go outside to help her nuns at their work in the gardens and orchard, manual labour she held being good for the soul, especially for high-born young women who normally would be loth to soil their hands with the like. In late March outdoor toil was recommencing, and growth starting after the winter's sleep, to God's glory. She made the point that mankind could worship in this way also, by helping the plant creation to praise God the more fully. The Celtic Church was strong on outdoor worship and the oneness of creation.

So they all streamed out of that so humble little church with its reed-thatched roof, plain and dim interior and whitewashed walls of interlacing boughs, the intricate weaving of which, the over-and-under pattern, was reflected in the decoration of the golden crosses which all of the nobly born students wore round their necks.

The church and convent of Cairn Dinnes stood within green earthen ramparts – almost like a fort, for sadly it did require protection on occasion from the Norse sea-raiders who for so long had terrorised these coasts, the Norse Sea being but five miles away to the east, at the Tyne's mouth. Actually, the ramparts had been there before the church, for here had been a fortlet, outlier of the mighty Traprain above, Cairn Dinnes, the mound of the little fort. Now it was surrounded by gardens and orchards, cattle byres, poultry-houses and beehives, for the nuns were busy folk and produced much provender for the great fortress-city which soared above.

Inevitably, as the young women emerged into the slanting afternoon sunlight of an early spring day, their glances rose to the enormous whaleback hill which rose abruptly to the south-east of them, close at hand, indeed close enough to deny the convent the early morning sun. It presented an extraordinary sight, even in a land of hills, lifting steeply for a further five hundred feet and more, those green slopes at this side terraced by more ramparts of earth and stone surmounted by timber stockading, with deep ditches in front, half a dozen of these defensive barriers, through which a single climbing road picked its zigzag way to the summit. To the right could just be glimpsed, from here, the sheer cliffs which constituted its southern side. And up on top, unlikely as it would seem, high stone walls enclosed a city-cum-fortress, towers and roofs and gables of masonry and wood and Celtic hurdle-walled structures, whitewashed and gleaming in the sun, banners flying above all in the breeze, a sight to see indeed, the capital seat and citadel of Lodonia. This was now being known as Lothian, in honour of its present monarch, Loth mac Kynvarch, of the Southern Picts or Gododdin, as distinct from the Albannach, the main Pictish nation north of the Forth and Clyde estuaries – even though the Romans had called them the Votadini in their arrogant way of giving Romanised names to the so-called barbarian Celtic kingdoms. This citadel was such as to seem to dominate all, as well as hold the eye – and yet it was not infrequently on the defensive against the Norsemen, Saxons and Jutes, savage sea-raiders who sought their prey each hosting season along all the coasts of Britain.

The girls were somewhat slow to select which nuns' work they would go to assist, so preoccupied were they with discussing tomorrow's equinoxial celebration and its excitements – for not all of these daughters of the Lodonian nobility were as off-put by the ideas of druidical sun-worship ceremonies as was the beloved Edana. After all, their Christianity was, in the main, scarcely profound as yet, or wholly part of them, the long ages of pagan observance only fairly superficially overlaid. St Ninian had indeed brought Christ to the land, but only a century before, and his gallant mission had all too largely failed, or at least its effect deteriorated, and the druids, never wholly put down, had risen again. As witness tomorrow's events. The fact that these Pictish nobles were allowing their daughters to attend this Christian convent was not so much concerned with religion as with education, behaviour, training in cultural living, in the arts, reading, writing, embroidery, music, Latin and the like, at which the talented and devoted Abbess Edana was so able a teacher. Although it was for Christ's cause that Queen Anna, Thanea's mother, had encouraged the Irish missionary to set up her little church and convent here, it was for those other reasons that her husband, on her death six years before, had allowed it to remain. King Loth was a distinctly lapsed Christian.

Thanea and Eithne of Hailes went off together to their favoured garden activity at this season, pruning the apple, pear and plum trees and the berry bushes. The senior nun, Odora, was in charge here, but they needed no instruction.

"What will you do, Thanea, if your father says that you must attend tomorrow evening's rites?" the red-head asked. "Can you refuse the king?"

"I could refuse *a* king, perhaps – but not my father, I think. Monenna teaches us that we must obey our parents. At least while we are under full age. Yet not, surely, if it is against God's will? It is difficult. I will plead with him, if he orders it."

"Plead for me also."

"I shall, yes. For all of us."

"Some, I think, would *wish* to go! To see it all. Even though they know that it is wickedness. That Anna, for one!"

"Anna challenges always. But she is not unkind at heart. There is no real ill in her."

"I would not be so sure, Thanea . . ."

Presently the girls saw the abbess leave, to walk over to the base of Traprain Law and start the long winding ascent to the citadel.

"There she goes," Eithne said. "How successful will she be, think you? But – was she not going to pray about it, first?"

"Perhaps she will be praying as she climbs. She says that one can pray at all times and in all places. Climbing a hill may be as good as in a church."

Her friend looked doubtful.

They were still pruning the bushes when the girls saw two

7

horsemen coming down the same zigzag road which Edana had ascended. Soon it became evident that they were making for this Cairn Dinnes enclosure. As they rode up, there were interested, admiring and inviting looks, and even calls from some of the young women, Anna's as ever almost challenging. The two young men grinned and waved.

They made a contrasting but eye-catching pair, one fairly rugged, strong-featured, broad of shoulder and stocky, the other dark, tall, slender, with fine if rather hawk-like visage and a proud carriage, much more richly clad than the other. They both bore hooded hawks on their gauntleted left wrists. Dismounting, they exchanged pleasantries with the students they passed, but headed for Thanea and Eithne.

"Have you nothing better to do with your time than tend bushes, Thanea?" the stocky young man asked, but smilingly. "Your Edana woman could do better for you than this, surely? We saw her up at the palace, seeking word with our father." This was Gawain, Thanea's favourite brother.

"We do very well at this. Better than much that *you* spend your time on!" she returned. "Such as killing inoffensive little birds with hawks! You will eat these berries one day and enjoy them."

"*We* use slaves for such toil!" the other young man observed. "Not princesses. Why not come riding with us? I could take you up behind me. And Gawain this other? See some sport instead of grubbing in the earth." That was Owen, Prince of Rheged, of the Novantae – or, as he would have named himself in his Cymric tongue, somewhat different from their Gaelic, Owen ap Urien. Though they were in fact kin.

"Thank you – no," Thanea said, but not unkindly. "We are still at our duty, under the abbess's orders. She says that this can be worship also, you see."

"Strange worship! Scullions' drudgery, rather! *You* are under that Irishwoman's orders, are you? The king's daughter?"

"While we are in her convent here, we are, yes. And gladly. She is our mother-in-God."

The Cumbrian prince snorted. "We live otherwise in Rheged!" he declared.

Gawain, a friendly youth, one year younger than his sister,

changed the subject. "Our father requires that you come up to the palace tonight, Thanea. He is giving a banquet, in honour of Owen here, and you must attend. The others also, I would say. It will be a fine affair, with feasting, dancing and entertainers. We will show this Cumbrian that *we* know how to live, also! Now we go hawking for duck along the Tyne."

"Poor ducks! I cannot wish you good sport, for I love the birds."

"The hawks will enjoy it, however!" her brother pointed out reasonably, as the pair turned to stroll back to their horses.

"A banquet! And dancing and entertainers!" Eithne exclaimed, watching them go. "That will be good. Better than this other, the next night. I hope that I may come, also?"

"I expect that all will be invited. Monenna will tell us, no doubt . . ."

When the abbess came back down the hill, however, she had more on her mind than to retail the invitation for all her nobly born students to attend an evening's feasting – although she did pass on that call. Unhappily, she had to admit that she had failed to persuade King Loth either to cancel the following evening's ceremonies or to moderate their scope and sacrificial content, nor even that the young women would be spared attendance. All were to be there, an especial occasion, even herself, shame as this was. God preserve them all from the shame and contamination of it, and the horror. And forgive those who so rejected His holy commandments and Christ's teachings.

The students eyed each other.

They were all to go into the church again, and pray.

Later, all the girls climbed that hill, most chattering excitedly, however breathless with the exertion, although some were silent, to enter the great gates of the final barrier, the city wall, with their defensive timber breastworks. To any stranger it would be scarcely believable that a community, much less a city, could exist in such a position as this, on a hilltop. But it was a very special hill, however lofty and steep-sided, its summit almost a plateau, and comprising over forty acres, hardly level but its hummocks and outcrops and ridges adapted and trimmed to carry buildings innumerable. Threaded by streets and lanes, with open spaces, some of these were constructed of masonry, some of wood but most in the favourite Celtic tradition of wattle and daub, that is double walls made of interlaced sapling boughs to form hurdles, these infilled with stones and rubble, all whitewashed and clay-plastered, rising to gabled roofs of reed and straw thatch, mainly two-storeyed, some with wings and even small courtyards, these the town-houses of the nobility. As well as such residences, cot-houses and shacks, there were barns, storehouses, stables and cowsheds, all packed in rows and crescents and groupings as the plateau summit permitted. As well that it was necessarily a windy place, or the smells could have been on occasion intolerable.

The views from up here were breathtaking, near and far, over the sweeping descents to north and west, and the dizzy precipices to south and east. Lothian spread out below them, fertile and fair, the River Tyne winding its way far below, to the north, on its banks the properties of the chieftains, including Eithne's Hailes nearest, with farmeries spreading out therefrom, tillable land in long riggs or strips for good drainage, uncultivable slopes cattle-dotted. Far beyond the Vale of Tyne was another vale, that of Peffer, hidden by intervening lowish hills, and beyond that two more landmarks almost as prominent as was this Traprain; the conical and isolated steep green hill of Berwick Law, and further still the towering mass of the Craig of Bass, not so much a landmark as a seamark this, since it reared four hundred feet and more out of the waves at the mouth of the Firth of Forth. A dramatic sight indeed, three huge leviathans of a strange rock formation. And across the blue waters of the firth, the long vistas of Fife. Westwards, the Vale of Tyne reached, seemingly endlessly save where it was apparently blocked, a score of miles away, by another upthrusting and lion-shaped hill which was being named in honour of King Arthur, the smokes of Hedyn's Town and Travernent communities filming the clear air between. Eastwards, in just a few miles, were the great golden sands and wave-rimmed bar of Tyne-mouth, and then the limitless plain of the Norse Sea. And southwards, the hillfoot slopes rose and rose to Lothian's great enclosing barrier of the Lammermuirs, ranges of high grass and heather hills, the vast sheep-rearing terrain whence came most of the kingdom's wealth. No one living on Traprain Law, or Dunpelder to give

10

it its original name, could remain unaffected by the impact of those vistas wherever the eye turned.

Leaving Eithne at her father's house, Thanea walked on through the narrow streets, greeting folk, still climbing somewhat, for Loth's palace stood on the highest rock platform of all, near the southern precipice top, a fine hall-house of main block and two wings, high-roofed, its white wickerwork walling painted with the Red Boar's Head device of his line, banners with the same symbol flying on poles above. Its bare rock-surface courtyard, at necessarily differing levels, was lined with barracks, storehouses and stabling. Men carried buckets of water from the one deep hilltop well, always a vital concern up here, while others strolled and idled, and women spun wool and gossip, hung out washing to dry, and skirled laughter. All greeted Thanea respectfully.

Inside the palace the girl passed through the great high-ceilinged hall, where servitors were making preparations for the evening's banquet, and on into the family's private west wing. She was making not for her own bedchamber in the topmost attic storey, but for a lesser first-floor hall used as the royal household's withdrawing-room. But at the stair-head she met another woman, no servant this, but tall, handsome, imperious, perhaps twice Thanea's seventeen years, finely dressed and well made.

"Ha, Thanea, you have come, then!" she was greeted, but with no warmth. "We see little of you, these days."

"I am never far away," the girl answered. "And can come at need. I salute you kindly, Lady Mara." That perhaps was not strictly true, but it was well intended. Thanea could never bring herself to call this woman mother. To say queen would have been ridiculous, from her, and Guanhumara was too much of a mouthful. So Lady Mara it was. They did not get on together very well, stepmother and princess.

"You spend overmuch time with that Irishwoman, I tell your father," the queen declared. "She was here, but a short time ago, making insufferable complaints."

"Surely not insufferable? Edana is not like that. She is good, kind, and always courteous. And she had much to concern her, did she not? Where is my father?"

"He is . . . engaged."

11

"Then I must wait."

"Yes."

"He is here, in the house?" Thanea was speaking as she seldom did, in the convent or elsewhere, speaking like a princess. Probably she did not realise it; but that was the effect her stepmother had on her. "I will have word with him when he is free."

"He is with the Arch Druid Diarmid. Arranging tomorrow's great events." That was said strongly, almost defiantly, strangely from a queen to a young woman half her age. It was intended to hurt, certainly – but the way it was enunciated indicated that the speaker was not so sure of her position as she would have wished.

It was a strange, not to say strained, relationship between these two. Of course it can often be so with stepmothers and their husband's children. But this was more than that. A sense of inferiority held Guanhumara. She could forget and dispense with it normally, indeed acted frequently a deal more autocratically than did King Loth. But not with his children, the two sons and this daughter. Not only because they were the offspring of royalty and she was not, a smallish noble's daughter; but because her husband's first wife, the Queen Anna, had been the sister of none other than the great King Arthur himself, High King of the Britons, the hero of the Celtic peoples. So this slip of a girl was a niece of Arthur Battle-Leader, all but worshipped by Gaeldom, and this woman, Guanhumara, never able to ignore it. With Prince Gawain it was not so bad, being a man; but between two females it was dire, even though Thanea never consciously sought to trade on the relationship. She had not actually ever known Arthur ap Uther Pendragon – he was always much too busy fighting the Saxon and Norse invaders to go visiting kinsfolk.

Thanea went to her room. She heard men's voices coming from the lesser hall as she passed the door. Almost she went in there and then, but thought better of it.

Changed into clothing more suitable for a banquet, and looking notably fine even though she pretended that this was not her objective, she went downstairs again after a fair interval, and entered the lesser hall. Her stepmother was therein now, with two men, one of later middle years, the other young,

12

her stepbrother Mordred, and their father. The men hailed her arrival variously, the king assessingly, Mordred hooting. Gawain had still not returned from the hawking.

Loth was a big man, inclining now to stoutness, heavy of jowl but keen of eye, uncertain as to temper, sometimes amiable, sometimes irascible and harsh. Thanea was fond of her father, but had good reason to beware of his moods; they all had. She sometimes thought that Mordred had inherited their sire's less admirable side, Gawain his better nature. And herself, his daughter – what of her?

Now, at any rate, Loth was cheerful and in expansive frame of mind, and told his daughter that she was looking beautiful and liker her mother each time that he saw her, which was insufficiently often – a greeting which drew a quick frown from the queen. They were grouped round a well-doing fire of birch logs, for the March air still had a bite to it, especially up at this height.

"And what has your Irish priestess been dinning into your girls' silly ears today?" Mordred asked. He was of that sort, a scoffer.

"Much that you would be better of learning, brother," Thanea told him easily. She had been dealing with this kind of thing all her days.

Her father barked a laugh. "Swallow that with your wine, boy!" he jerked. "There are more foolishnesses than one! You saw Owen ap Urien, with Gawain, Thanea? What thought you of him?"

"I saw them only for moments, Father. He, the Cumbrian, is good-looking. But . . . appearances are not everything, to be sure."

"Ah! Do I hear criticism there? From our woman of experience! He will be King of Rheged one day." He glanced over as Gawain came in.

"I did not see, nor speak with him sufficiently long for judgment, Father. Nor do I seek to judge."

"Hear her!" Mordred exclaimed. "*She* does not seek to judge! She has been judging me since she could walk!"

"And you asking for judgment!" his brother declared, laughing. "Even I, who am no saintly Christian, have had occasion to judge you now and again."

13

Loth chuckled. "My loving family!" he said to his wife. "Where do they get it from? Not from a peaceable man like myself."

None commented on that.

"Wine, Thanea," the king went on. "Tonight's feasting I have ordered in honour of Prince Owen. You will enjoy it. And show some attention to our guest." That was clearly in the nature of a command. The girl did not welcome it, but did not say no. What she did say, however, took the more courage to enunciate.

"Tonight's celebration I may enjoy, Father. It is tomorrow's, which I hear of, which troubles me. And troubles others. Must you proceed with it? Make this . . . display? Of ancient pagan rites."

"It is the Equinoxial Festival, girl."

"Yes. But you have held such before, many times. But not as this is said to be. With offerings and sacrifices. Old evil superstitions, which surely ought to be forbidden."

"Hear her judging now!" Mordred exclaimed.

It was her father's turn to frown. "When I require my seventeen-year-old daughter's advice on what to do and what not, I will ask for it!" he declared. "This Equinox is especial. Last year's harvest was scanty, after a bad summer. This winter has been notably wild, much of the land is flooded. It is near to famine. The sun god has turned his face from us. Appeasement is necessary."

"There is no sun god," the girl said simply.

The queen spoke. "That could bring down further wrath upon us! It is . . . sacrilege, profanity. Thanea should never have been allowed to attend on the Irishwoman. Or the woman to remain here."

"She has her uses," Loth said. "But not in this. She will hereafter take a care to what she teaches. Or go! I told her so, this day. The Equinoxial Festival goes on."

"If it must, Father, make it less . . . wicked. Halt this of sacrifice."

"No."

"At least, then, spare us attendance at it. Myself, and the others at the convent. It is against all that we believe . . ."

"No, I say!" The king smashed down his fist on the table-top, those jowls quivering. "I will hear no more of this. You will be

14

there, all of you. The sun is not to be denied his due. To be spurned by such as you! It is enough. And, tonight, behave as my daughter should. My sons also!" And he stormed out of the hall, his wife after him.

Thanea looked at her brothers, sighed, and left to return to her own room.

The evening's banquet was well enough – although Thanea did wonder at the excellence and prodigality of the provision when there was all but famine in the land – a choice of soups, salmon and trout and sea-fish, chicken, duck, wild goose, beef, mutton, pork and venison, with honey-based sweets to follow. And the entertainment was as varied, music on lyres and lutes, acrobats, performing dancers and dogs. It was later that she found less enjoyable, when general dancing started, and she discovered herself to be very much Prince Owen's choice of partner. That was to be expected, of course; she had sat beside him at the dais-table, he was the guest of honour, and she was the woman of highest rank present – the queen was not dancing. And the Cumbrian was a good dancer, nimble on his feet and quite graceful. It was not his feet that she found trying, but his hands. He managed to find opportunity to touch and fondle her continually and fairly comprehensively, much more so than the reels and round-dances and flings called for, her heaving breasts and even buttocks his principal concern – and she was well made and shapely. This might be how they danced in Rheged, but she found it not to her taste; and she noted that when their gyrations and circlings brought them momentarily to other partners, his hands seemed to be much less busy. But it was difficult to reject his grippings and strokings in the circumstances of these so-active and energetic Celtic dances, which entailed so much whirling, skipping and arm-linking. Moreover, of course, her father had expressly ordered her to show especial attention to their handsome and so appreciative guest.

However, the very vehemence and vigour of their dancing allowed her eventually to plead weariness, exhaustion almost, and she declared it and announced that she would seek her couch. Owen accepted that readily enough, but announced that he would escort her to her chamber; and when she protested that this was unnecessary and that the night was young yet, and he could and should enjoy considerable entertainment still,

15

the prince would not hear of it, insisting that without *her* the proceedings would be dull indeed. Which might be flattering but was not what she sought.

Leaving the hall, she noted that the queen had already departed, and her father, drink-taken, had fallen asleep over the dais-table. Her brothers were still dancing, and few of her fellow-students seemed overcome with fatigue. Mordred leered at the couple as they passed out.

Climbing the stairs, Owen evidently felt that the girl's tiredness called for a helping hand; and he retained his hold of her right to her bedroom door.

There, however, she was firm, any weariness no longer in evidence. She twisted herself sharply free, thanked him briefly for his courtesies and, opening the door, got inside in one swift and complicated movement, half shutting the door again as she bid him a good night. As, even so, he took a step forward, Thanea slammed the wood firmly shut, and slid the bar into position.

Appreciation can be excessive.

The girl's prayers that night were fervid and prolonged.

Preparations for the Vernal Equinoxial Festival went on all next day, even though Thanea had nothing to do with them, despite being told that there was to be no convent attendance. It was, of course, one of the two occasions in the year when day and night were of precisely similar duration, and for those concerned with the sun, important. And was not the sun vital to all living things? This day, the sun, about to commence its new ecliptic pathway, was in a position to be approached. And approach was essential.

The procession moved out from the city at precisely one hour before sunset. It was led by the Arch Druid Diarmid with his priests and acolytes, horns blowing. Thereafter came the royal family, on foot, King Loth in front, alone, the three princes behind, with Owen, then the queen and Thanea, walking rather noticeably apart. The nobles followed on, their womenfolk in the rear, then the mass of the people, men, women and children, all attending at Loth's command. Thanea kept glancing back, to see if she could spot Monenna in the crowd, but could not pick her out.

They went down the steep winding road, to the monotonous

blaring of the bulls' horns. The sun was not actually in evidence, behind cloud; at least it was not raining.

At the foot of the hill they turned, left-handed, round the perimeter of the law. The light was beginning to fade. Thanea and the queen had not exchanged a word.

They had not far to go, a bare half-mile over cattle-dotted rolling grassland. As they curved round the base of the hill, the difference between its north and south faces became strikingly evident, all but sheer precipices of bare rock rearing at this side, a daunting prospect. The cliffs echoed to weird wailing notes of the horns.

Presently the procession came to a ditched-off area no great distance south-west of the cliff-roots, its wide moat-like barrier filled not with water but with cut thorn trees, to prevent cattle from entry, with a grassy causeway across, this barred by gates. And beyond rose a great stone circle, its thirteen monoliths, spaced regularly, rising upright like fierce fangs or the teeth of a huge dragon, a level table-stone recumbent within, to the south-east. Already a number of men were working there, in their long, dark brown druidical robes. The stone circle measured perhaps one hundred yards across.

The company now halted, the Arch Druid and his priests and horn-blowers to enter the circle, the king's party, backed by his nobles, to take up a semicircular stance on slightly rising ground close by to the west, the mass of the people ranging themselves behind. All were facing east. The horns were still wailing.

Thanea hated it, watched set-faced.

Clearly the Arch Druid was now in charge of all. He took up a position in the centre of the circle, and placed his minions beside each upright stone. After a little while, he raised one hand, and the horns at last fell silent. Then, after a quite considerable pause, he raised both arms high, and turning round, faced west. A single horn howled its command, and all present turned to face in the same direction. No sound now broke the hush, save for one or two children's high voices, which were quickly quieted.

For how long they all stood thus, gazing westwards, Thanea could not calculate, although it seemed a long time, silence prevailing, only a single curlew yittering its lonely call somewhere. Although all were staring, there was nothing to see, for it was

17

now greyest dusk and even the Lammermuir Hills' rampart had faded into the background southwards. Yet still they looked, waiting.

At last there was a single shout behind them, and a horn blared briefly. All turned again, eastwards. But not the druids. The priests and acolytes all fell on their faces. Only the man Diarmid remained standing in the centre of the circle. He was pointing into the west.

"The sun has left us!" he cried. "Call upon the mighty sun's mercy to return to us. Call! Call!"

The druids' voices were raised to lead, and all others joined in with varied cries and shouts and beseechings – all save the most confirmed Christians that is, Thanea amongst them. How the Arch Druid had estimated the exact moment of sunset, behind the cloud cover, she did not know – perhaps it was pure guesswork. But the gesture was there.

Another horn-blast gained him silence again. "The sun god makes his journey towards tomorrow, his chariot drawn by many horses," he called. "He goes to the invisible world wherein is the abode of the dead. Pray that, of his mercy, he will decide to smile upon us, and this land, when he returns. Meantime, pray that he keeps the moon goddess from harming us. He leaves the lesser deities, Thunderer, the sky-smith, lord of fertility; the sea god, with his trident, who supplies the sun's horses; the storm god, who does the sun's will with the weather; the corn goddess who controls seasons and harvests; the wolf god who will not steal our souls unless the sun permits. These, and many others. They are about us now in this night. We must placate them while the sun makes his far journey to the morrow. Pray to them also."

A varied murmuring arose at that, and continued.

More horn-blowing signalled a new activity, the lighting of fires, already prepared, around the stone circle, their timbers primed with fat to ensure swift burning and bright flame. These quickly illuminated the scene with flickering light and dancing shadows. From these fires the acolytes lit torches of resinous pine, and went to stand one beside each of the thirteen upright monoliths. The eerie spectacle was now visible to all – but only around the circle. The rest of the world might have been burned away.

18

Now the Arch Druid moved over to the recumbent stone – and everywhere a tension grew amongst the onlookers. "Manannan! Manannan!" he cried. "God of the seas. Heed us who crave your goodwill. We offer you our service and duty, you who are yourself the great servant of the sun. Accept our sacrifice, oh great Manannan of the trident." And he waved an arm.

Into the circle of firelight acolytes appeared leading two horses, one to either side of the altar-stone. No doubt they were male and female. Two druid priests stepped forward, bearing swords. From all round the circle horns blared. At the Arch Druid's signal the priests, obviously expert, raised swords in unison and with swift and vehement strokes slashed open the horses' throats. Even as the screams rang out, and the animals reared high, pawing the air desperately, the blood could be seen to gush out, black tides in the flickering firelight. Madly the creatures lashed and staggered and stumbled, held by the acolytes' long halters, and all around the people stared and exclaimed and shivered in reaction to what they saw and heard. The horns still blew.

One of the beasts fell, still kicking and twitching. Then the other fell. The priests moved close again, to slit up the brutes' bellies. The entrails burst out, heaving and coiling as though themselves alive. Torch-bearers came forward to light up the scene further, and the Arch Druid stepped forward also, to peer down at the moving, steaming masses, carefully considering. Then, straightening up, he made a brief cutting motion of the hand, and immediately the horns ceased howling.

"It is well, well!" he shouted. "The omens are good. Manannan is pleased. He accepts our offering. He of the sea-horses. Praise Manannan of the trident! Praise him!"

From hundreds of throats excited cries arose, some exultant, some heartfelt, some sobbing and choking.

Thanea had to swallow, determinedly, the sickness that surged to her throat.

Then Diarmid raised his arm again. "Thunderer, great Thunderer, we beseech *your* aid! Look down on us, god of fertility, the harvests and pastures. Give us of your plenty in the months to come, we beseech you. Accept, accept, Lord Thunderer."

This time it was a bull, black and heavy, and a cow, brown

19

and white, which were led to the altar-stone, no fewer than six acolytes having to lead the reluctant bull, and then to hold it approximately still with their halters, the cow much less difficult. The same grim process was gone through, the throat-slitting and stabbing. The cow collapsed almost at once, sprawling and jerking; but the bull remained standing, head drooping and swaying from side to side, but still maintaining its stance. The belly-slitters could go to work on the cow, but found great difficulty with the upright bull. There was a distinct hold-up, to the embarrassment of the priests.

The Arch Druid, however, only shook his head. "Thunderer doubts us, doubts the honesty of our worship and regard," he declared. "Oh, Thunderer, hear us! We own your power and splendour, under the sun. We call for your help. Hear us, Thunderer, and accept."

For moments there was a breathless pause, and then the bull's legs buckled under it and it sank rather than fell to the grass, massive dignity to the end. The shouts that arose were all but ecstatic.

Next to be placated was the corn goddess, and for her two sheep were considered adequate. These caused no trouble and were soon disposed of, not even baaing.

The appeasement of the storm god, who controlled the air and the winds, required fowl, poultry, hens, duck, geese, gannets and the like, and these, by their very nature, could cause difficulties in their dignified disposal – and dignity was important to the druids. So a device had been contrived, to cope. Reticules of netting had been made, and into these the birds had been imprisoned, still fluttering and flapping but secure, the nets carried slung on poles. Killing by throat-cutting, neck-wringing or stabbing would have been difficult also, so fire was used. Blazing torches were brought, to set beneath each netful, and the fowl, flap as they would, were duly burned to death. The problem was, of course, that the netting burned also, and the sacrifices could have fallen out and perhaps fluttered off. So acolytes had to hold iron grids beneath, a hot and awkward task which the priests themselves left to others.

This actually drew some laughs from the least reverent of the crowd, suitable or not.

But that did not last long. The most demanding and prolonged blowing of horns gained silence for the Arch Druid.

"Gods and goddesses!" he proclaimed. "The sun, in his majesty, your master and ours, journeys through his other world of the shades until morning. *You* can speak with him, we can not. But we would pay our deepest homage. Offer our worship. We call on you all, therefore, to tell him of it. Hail, the sun!" He gestured.

Out of the shadows they came, four dark figures and two light ones, robed priests leading two women naked, their bodies white even in the ruddy glow of fires and torches. Picking their way through the scattered remains of horses, cattle, sheep and fowl, they were brought to the altar. One was most obviously pregnant, the other younger and slim.

Diarmid, arms raised high, said something to them, and pointed. The slender one was picked up by the acolytes and laid on the altar, on her back. She made no evident struggle nor protest. Amongst all the enthralled and spellbound watchers there were murmurs and whispers, even some nervous giggling. Also questions as to identity. No doubt these were sinners, probably taken in adultery or refusing to obey husbands.

The Arch Druid himself now drew a dagger, and after holding it aloft and calling some incantation, plunged the weapon down between the girl's breasts.

The thin shriek, yittering almost like that curlew, rose high – and produced a choking, gasping reaction from the crowd. The young woman arched her back up, and the knife was withdrawn and plunged again. The screaming died.

Here, too, with the limbs still jerking, the stomach was slit open and the entrails, spilling out, consulted. Apparently satisfied, Diarmid drew back, waving.

Acolytes dragged the limp body off the altar, and others pushed forward the second woman. But she struggled now, and yelled, with a sudden access of strength. Haul and heave as they would, the men could not get the kicking, scrambling woman on to that altar. Possibly she was fighting for the babe's life within her. Frowning, Diarmid signed to one of his priests, with a down-slashing motion. The druid, still bearing the sword with which he had slain horse, cattle and sheep, slammed down

21

the flat of the heavy blade on the woman's head and, stunned, she sank to the ground.

Hoisted on to the blood-soaked altar thereafter without difficulty, hers was an easier death, unconscious, than that of her companion. The child within her presumably knew naught of its death either.

There was enormous reaction amongst the onlookers, almost hysteria, yells and cries, folk clutching and shaking each other in their wild excitement, in a frenzy over the climax of the entire occasion. Thanea was sobbing to herself, although her eyes had been shut towards the end, craven as she felt this to be.

The Arch Druid and his assistants were now leading the way in what amounted to a hymn of praise and acclaim to the sun, punctuated by single blasts of one horn in repetitive rhythm. Some of the great company joined in, but most were beyond anything such, shouting and cavorting in a sort of unholy glee brought on by what they had seen and experienced. Nobility and commonality alike, royalty not excepted, they embraced, waved and capered.

Diarmid and his druids were beyond all such folly. They formed up, leaving the fires but carrying their torches, to lead the procession back to the city, servants left behind to clear up the mess of carcases and entrails within the circle. But it is to be feared that it was a deplorably undisciplined procession, nevertheless, which began to follow them, scattered and noisy, dancing, skipping, playing the fool. Quite a large proportion of the whole, indeed, did not follow at all, or only so far, not a few, men and women, already on the ground and coupling, uncaring with whom they paired.

Thanea, desperately unhappy, stumbled along in the darkness, not waiting for any formal lining-up of the royal party. She soon found her brother Gawain beside her, and clutched his arm, unspeaking. But presently Prince Owen was at her other side, laughing, and quickly one arm was around her, the other hand feeling for her breast. Fiercely she thrust him off with her elbow, jabbing again and again. But still he laughed and groped, if not very effectively, as they moved over uneven grassland in the semi-dark. Gawain put one arm round his sister's shoulder, which helped.

That was a nightmarish journey back to the hilltop citadel;

22

but at the palace, Thanea escaped to her own chamber, and threw herself on her bed, weeping. She tried to pray, but failed miserably.

For how long she lay there she did not know, when a knocking sounded at her door and a servitor announced that the King Loth required the presence of the Princess Thanea in the lesser hall. She called back that she could not come, that she was unwell.

But before long the knocking resumed. The king *commanded* the presence of his daughter, and at once, she was informed.

Knowing her father's temper and how he could behave when roused, Thanea rose, sought to tidy herself and go as ordered – for she knew that she could well be carried down bodily if still she refused. Indeed, two servants were waiting outside her door to escort her.

Down in the lesser hall she found the family and certain of Loth's closest friends gathered in noisy celebration, feeding on cold meats, but doing more drinking than eating. Some hailed her arrival with shouts, especially Owen ap Urien.

Her father, clearly much affected by drink, and seated, half rose as she came in, but staggering, sank back on his bench. He banged his tankard on the table-top for quiet, spilling mead.

"Ha, daughter!" he got out thickly. "You grace us . . . with your presence . . . at last! This, this especial night." He had difficulty with the word especial. "Come, you."

Set-faced, she moved a little nearer him. The queen came to stand behind her husband, looking more satisfied than usual.

"Tonight, I have . . . have good news for you, girl," the king went on, and drank. "Excellent news. One day you will be a queen. Queen of Rheged. Aye, Rheged. Queen Thanea!" He hiccuped. "Owen ap Urien has asked for you, for your hand in marriage. And I, I have granted it. You hear? Marriage. You are to be this Owen's wife."

There were cries of congratulation from some of those around.

Thanea stood as though turned to stone.

"Go to him, girl!" her father said. "Do not stand gawping!"

"No!" That came from her, with a strange force, almost as a bark.

"Eh . . . ?"

23

"No, I say." That was more level, but sufficiently certain, in the negative.

Prince Owen did the moving. He stepped over to her, to make a little bow, not exactly mockingly but not far from it. "Thanea, my bride-to-be!" he said, grinning. "I have found a wife. At last!" He held out his arms in an elaborate gesture.

"No," she said again, and the words came out singly, emphatically. "I . . . will . . . not . . . wed . . . you!"

That tankard smashed down on the table. "By the sun and all the gods, you will!" roared King Loth.

Without another word, Thanea turned and ran from the hall – but not upstairs. She hurried out into the night's darkness.

Guessing that she would be followed and brought back, she darted into the first lane she came to, round the back of two houses and down another wynd. This brought her to the southern clifftop of the law. Here there was no need for a high enclosing wall, only a low dyke to prevent children from falling over. Hitching up her skirts, she clambered over this, and then crept down one of the many crevices which led down to the all but sheer drop of the precipice. Therein she crouched huddling, head in hands, hidden.

Long she stayed there, cold as it was, a young woman lost. Or not quite, for in time she found that she could pray, pray to the God of love and mercy, and Christ Jesus his Son, such a different god from those she had been ordered to worship that terrible night. Soothed somewhat, and even strengthened, she waited. And at length, when she calculated that all would have bedded down at the palace, she went back, watching for any who might intercept her. But none did, and she got up to her room and barred the door behind her.

It was long before she slept.

2

In the morning, although Thanea would have wished to go down at once to the convent, she guessed that her father would send for her. He did.

Although now sober, he was in little kinder mood than he had been the night before. But at least he saw her alone.

"You were an ill daughter to me, last night," he told her roughly. "Made me to look a fool and a weakling, before all. And then to bolt like some affrighted coney! Shame on you, girl!"

"I am sorry that I had to offend you," she said. "But . . . I cannot wed Prince Owen."

"You can. And will!"

"No, Father – I cannot. It is . . . impossible."

"It is my will, I tell you. I have given him my word. You will wed Owen ap Urien. He is a suitable match. Will one day be King of Rheged. It will serve our two realms well to be thus linked. And he is far-out kin, and desires you."

"I do not desire *him*!" She took a deep breath. "Besides, I am promised to another!"

He stared. "You . . . ! You are promised? You say that to *me*! How, how can that be? A girl of but seventeen summers. How say you that?"

Thanea had thought of this for half the night. "I am promised to God. To the true God, God the Son, Jesus Christ," she got out. "Vowed to Him, and Him only, Father."

The king's jaw had dropped, so shaken was he, finding no words.

"The Virgin Mary is the finest, the greatest, the most blessed amongst women. I, I seek humbly to be like her. Or as like such as I may be."

Loth found his voice. "By all the gods – are you run mad, girl? Bewitched? Here is folly, and worse – outrage! Crazy Christian folly. That woman Edana's work. She has been filling your

25

foolish head with her nonsense. You go no more to her. I will be rid of her. Send her back to Ireland."

"Be not hard on her, Father. This is of my own will, my own decision. *I* choose it so. Not she."

"It is not for you to choose, girl. Decision on your marriage is mine. You wed Prince Owen."

"I am sorry, Father. But that I will not do. I, I had rather be dead! And be with God that way!"

He clenched his fists. "If you do not obey me, you may be dead, indeed!"

She shook her head, silent.

Loth took a pace or two back and forward, seeking to control his anger. "See you, Thanea – I am your king as well as your father. I can compel that you do my will. But better that you see reason, use such wits as you have, act as a daughter should, as a *princess* should. Owen ap Urien is a fine young man, personable, royally born. We both descend from the great King Coel, High King of Britain. I say that you could not do better. He could choose from a score of princesses!"

"Let him so choose, then. But not me. I am not for him."

The king there lost his temper finally. Almost he struck her, so that she shrank back. "You will do as I say!" he shouted. "Do you hear? You will wed."

"No, Father. If I *am* wed, against my will and beliefs, I will flee from that man at the first moment that I can. Lose myself in the hills and forests. That I vow!"

"You, you . . . !" He grabbed and shook her. "Then to the hills and forests you will go! Daughter of mine or no, you will go. That *I* vow! Wed Owen. Or be cast out from here, from my house. Become a lost woman, a, a plaything for any man who finds you, a beggar for your bread!"

She shook her head, with sorrow but with no diminution of her resolve. "So be it," she said.

Cursing, he pushed her away. "Go to your room. Bide there. Do not leave this house. You hear? Your room."

"Yes, Father," she said, and turned to go.

Outside, there stood her stepmother Guanhumara. Almost certainly she had been listening at the door. Her look at Thanea was one of triumph. The girl guessed that she would be largely behind the king's harsh attitude.

26

She hurried upstairs to her chamber, desolate.

All that day Thanea remained alone in her room. No food was brought to her, no servant came with hot water to wash in, there was no communication with others. She prayed, but could not continue praying for long with any meaning to it. She questioned herself, of course. Was she justified in this disobedience to her father? Was her refusal to wed the Cumbrian right? Was her pride dictating her decision, not her duty as daughter, her acceptance of Christian behaviour? Yet, however she questioned, she knew, *knew* in her heart that she could not wed Owen ap Urien. The certainty was there. It was not that she hated him, or knew him well enough to hate. His behaviour towards her could have been that of any young lusty man who found her person to his taste. It was something else that held her back, exactly what she was not sure, but something imperative. She was not for him. This of being promised to Christ – she was all but ashamed of having used that excuse. Who was she to claim anything of the sort? It was but a device, however strong and sincere was her belief in God and His Son. Owen was pagan, like her father, to be sure, and to wed him was to commit herself to a pagan life. But was that consideration all that was behind her so determined decision? She did not know, she did not know . . .

It was early evening before there was any further development. Then a knocking on her door, which quickly became an angry banging, for the door was barred, left her in no doubt that it was her father himself. She drew the bar in its goose-greased slot, opened, and he stormed in.

"Have you come to your senses, girl?" he demanded.

"I am of the same mind, Father," she told him.

"Then hear this. I will not be mocked and made look a fool by any, in especial by my own daughter. I meant what I said to you. I dispossess you, Thanea. I cast you out. No longer will you act my daughter – which state you dishonour. You will be no longer the Princess of Lothian, for you shame me in front of all. Tomorrow I send you away from here. To the hills and forests you said that you would run to, from this Owen. You will go to Fergus of Johnscleugh, my furthest-out swineherd and shepherd in deepest Lammermuir, where the White Water is born. And there you will bide, tending swine and sheep, a

27

slave. You hear? A slave-woman. That is to be your fate, since you will not be Princess of Rheged! Tomorrow you leave this house for a swineherd's hovel in the far hills. That I swear. Unless you wed Owen."

The girl met the man's glare, and inclined her lovely head. "If that is your will, Father. I will go at your bidding."

"My *commanding*!" he shouted. And turning, strode out, slamming that door behind him.

Thanea drew the bar of it again, tears in her eyes.

Later in the evening another knock came to the door, just a tap this time. "Thaney!" a voice said softly.

Only her brothers called her that. But when she went to open, there was nobody there, only on the floor a loaf of bread and a beaker of wine. That would be Gawain. No doubt he had been ordered not to see her, but had shown his caring thus.

Despite her distress and the emotions churning within her, she ate hungrily.

She did sleep better, however, that night.

In the very early morning, before the palace and town were astir, Thanea was awakened by more rapping on the door and a woman's voice calling. When she rose, donned a bed-robe and opened, it was to find a servant-girl there, holding out a rough-woven, not over-clean, peasant's gown, shapeless and short of skirt, with a rope to act as girdle.

"You are to wear this, Princess. This only." That was nervously said, as she thrust the things out. "Men will come for you." And jerking an embarrassed bow, she hurried off.

Thanea eyed this symbol of her father's anger and hurt, and her glance went over to the garderobe where all her fine dresses hung. The ragged gown she had been given smelt as unpleasing as it looked; but, after a lip-biting pause, she put it on and tied the cord.

Two men were soon knocking at the door, members of the king's bodyguard. One pointed to the small bundle of belongings which Thanea had hurriedly gathered together.

"You may not take that, Princess," he declared. "The king's orders. Nothing to be taken."

"Surely some garb? A shift, a bodice . . ."

"Nothing." He looked unhappy, but firm.

Inclining her head, she followed them out and downstairs.

In the courtyard three horses, shaggy, short-legged garrons, were waiting, saddled only with sacking. No persons were visible. The younger man, glancing around and seeing no one, helped to hoist the girl up on one of the animals, much shapely white leg inevitably in evidence. The others mounted, and they rode off.

Down the hill they went, and at the foot turned left-handed as they had done two evenings before. Soon they were passing the stone circle of evil memory. Still some of the unpleasant litter remained, Thanea averting her eyes. They trotted on, fairly soon passing a single standing-stone which marked the grave of one of Loth's predecessors. Ahead of them commenced the foothills of the Lammermuirs.

Actually Thanea knew well where they were heading, for she had ridden these hills since childhood, far and wide. They formed a lofty barrier some twenty-five miles long by ten miles wide, separating the coastal plain out of which rose Traprain and Berwick Laws, from the Merse, the great downland of comparatively low ground which stretched northwards from the notable river of Tweed which marked the boundary of Loth's domains and those of the kingdom of Northumbria, the name Merse meaning march or border. These Lammermuir Hills, so called because they were the most renowned sheep-rearing area of all the Pictish lands, represented the main source of Lothian's wealth, wool. All the world needed wool, and these rolling heights of grass and heather were ideal for feeding and sheltering the hardy black-faced sheep, for there were innumerable hidden deep valleys and cleughs as they were called, usually grown with stunted hawthorn trees, which the sheep could seek in hard conditions of cold and snow, without having to be shepherded to cover, and where, unlike the swampy undrained tracts of the low ground, there lurked few predators, wolves, boars and the like. There were almost three hundred square miles of them. The names of the summits and ridges, and of the valleys themselves, emphasised their usefulness – Lammermuir itself, the moorland of the sheep; Tuplaw, tups being breeding rams; Rammerscales; Ewelaw; Wedder Law, a wedder being a castrated male ram; Hogcleugh, a hog a first-year sheep; and so on. These hills to which the princess was banished were not barren wilderness, but they held no population save for a scattering of shepherds and swineherds – for pigs also could pasture and root on the lower slopes, only there for they had not woolly coats to keep them reasonably warm on the chilly heights; these were not apt to be so very far removed from the wild boar from which they sprang.

The trio rode for miles, rising ground all the way, out of the foothill country where there were occasional small communities and scattered cot-houses, and a series of fortified areas, within ramparts, for the local folk to take refuge from raids by the invading Norsemen. But gradually these died away as the going became ever higher and steeper, until they came to quite a major fort, set on a mound partly artificial, within the jaws of a deep valley, almost a defile, and looking out over a vast prospect of the lower lands, to the sea and the firth and even over to the bounds of the Albannach kingdom to the north. This was White Castle, an important rearguard for Traprain. Here the riders paused, while the escort had a word with the captain of the fort, Thanea guessed about herself, for the men kept looking back at her.

After that they climbed ever deeper into the high hills, over lofty shoulders and heather tracks, dipping down into steep glens and narrow troughs where burns ran, and out again. Sheep were everywhere, with the early lambing already started.

About three miles beyond White Castle they came to Johnscleugh, a little group of thatched hovels set on a shelf of the hillside above a twisting, close-walled crease of the uplands, not much more than a ravine, down which a lively stream cascaded and splashed. It was noticeable that this burn was running southwards, for in their climbing and dipping they had in fact crossed the watershed, and rivers would from now on flow down to Tweed, not north to Forth. Fording this burn, the headstream of the White Water or Whiteadder as it was called locally, they climbed to the shelf above, threading their way past a herd of swine, snorting and rooting, lean and black of hide.

Their arrival was being watched by a little group, two men, three women, one with a baby in arms, and three other children, barking sheepdogs greeting them threateningly with curled-lip growls. Thanea saw the older man staring at her in wonderment. She raised a hand in salutation. She knew Fergus, the chief shepherd of this area, known as the Spartleton Edge.

"Princess!" he exclaimed. "Princess Thanea! What . . . ? How . . . ? Yourself, is it!" Almost that was a question.

"A word with you, man," the elder of her escort said quickly, dismounting. He led Fergus aside.

Thanea slipped to the ground, and went to the woman Duona, Fergus's wife, and her two daughters. They eyed her askance, in her frayed and ragged garb, rougher even than their own. They bobbed doubtful little bows.

She put a brave face on it, smiling, and reaching out a hand to pat one of the children's heads. "I hope that I see you all well," she said. And to the young man, "I see that the lambing has started. How goes it after the bad winter?" This was Fergus's son Dungal.

All were too astonished by her appearance to answer with any coherence.

She heard raised voices behind her, where Fergus and her escort seemed to be having words, the latter sounding threatening. She saw him grab the shepherd's arm and shake it. And when young Dungal ran to his father's aid, the other bodyguard dismounted, short sword drawn. The women exclaimed in fear, and the children ran off into a hovel.

Thanea went over to the men. "Fergus, do as they say," she urged. "It is at my father's orders. They only do as commanded."

"But, Princess . . ."

"Do not say princess. You are not to name her that," he was told. "She is no longer a princess. She is to be slave-girl to you. Treat her so. She is in disgrace. She is not to return to the city. You hear? A slave, to herd your swine. If she is allowed to leave here, *you* will suffer! Mind it. So says King Loth."

Silenced, the shepherd shook his head, bewildered.

Without further talk, or any farewells, the two bodyguards mounted and rode off, taking the third horse with them.

"Princess, what is this? Why does the king do this?" Fergus demanded. "Here is shame, wickedness. Have all lost their reason? You, high-born, and clad like the meanest servant . . . !"

"How I am clad matters not." Briefly Thanea explained the

31

situation, to the family's horror and distress. Duona, Fergus's wife, a practical woman, presently said that she would fetch food for the so-unexpected visitor, and soon reappeared with thick oatcakes, honey and a pot of goat's milk. Despite the orders, they all were calling her princess.

"You must stop naming me that," Thanea told them. "My father can be very stern, and if he heard that you were still so calling me, he would be very wrath. It could slip out, and be heard, and told to him. Call me Thanea – that is my name. And treat me as you are commanded. Lest *you* suffer."

All shook heads at that, but did stop saying princess.

Fergus conferred with his wife and the daughters, who it seemed had husbands out shepherding. They must make their guest as comfortable as was possible in their humble establishment. There were five huts, mere shacks of timber, turf and reed-thatch, windowless, with holes in the roofing for the smoke of central fires to escape – this in three of them. The other two housed poultry and goats. Fergus and Dungal went to work on the goats' one, clearing out the soiled reed-straw and bracken, with the women bringing buckets of water from the well to wash and scrub the interior, while the children were sent to fetch fresh straw and dead bracken to floor and line it all. Then other houses were robbed of sheepskins and woven matting, and three rugged plaids found for blanketing. Even some rather better clothing than she presently wore was produced for her. Thanea was greatly touched by this display of caring, and said so, pleading that they should not deprive themselves. She would do very well.

Left alone in her hut, however, she sat on her pallet of straw, and sank her head in her hands, less assured and confident than she had seemed.

After an interval thus she braced herself and went out to see Fergus, to learn what were her duties here. At the door of his hut she saw what she had not noticed previously, a small wooden cross affixed to the lintel. She heard the man's voice within, and called to him.

When he came out, she pointed. "Christ's cross?" she said.

"Yes, Prin . . . Thanea. We are Christians here, God be thanked."

"That is good, good. Myself, also. So we are one in that."

"My daughters' husbands are not, to my sorrow. So the children . . . !"

"I am sorry. But in time perhaps? This, this means a great deal to me, Fergus. All seems the more . . . to be accepted. Now – you must tell me what I am to do, how I may serve you. My duties."

"How can I give *you* duties, the king's daughter! It is a madness."

"But you must, my friend. It will be enquired into, nothing more sure. I am sent here to work and toil. I have disobeyed my father and must pay for it. He will require it of you. So tell me how best I may serve you and meet his demands. Tend the swine, he said . . ."

"No! Never that! Not swine. But . . . tending the sheep is none so ill. Now that winter is past. The lambing has started. See you, I think that I know what you can do. The old ewes know what they are at. But the hogs, breeding for the first time, can be difficult. Hide away under banks and in hollows and the like. Have their lambs there, at times but poorly. In especial if they have two. So those that have strayed to the far-out hills can come to trouble, both hogs and lambs. This you could do. Go looking for hiding hogs, and bring them into stells. None so ill work."

"But of use? I must be of use."

"To be sure. Necessary work. Many are lost thus each lambing. You can walk and climb well enough? We have no garrons here . . ."

"Always I have been a walker. And climbed. None who live on Traprain Law can fail to climb!"

"That is well. Tomorrow I will take you, show you."

"But – I have never seen a sheep lambing. Much less aided one . . ."

"It is not difficult. See you, Dungal is gone down to the main buchts, the folds, to aid Malcolm and Cormac, my daughters' husbands, at the lambing there. It goes on now. We will go down, before we eat. You will see how it is done. And tomorrow we will take to the hills."

So they set off slantwise down towards the valley floor, two dogs and one of the children with them, the baaing of sheep leading them on. Less than half a mile off, round a shoulder of

33

hill, they came to another and wider shelf, well above the flood-line of this Whiteadder, and here were the main Johnscleugh pens and folds, a series of stone-walled enclosures where five young men laboured amongst a multitude of loud-voiced and protesting sheep and busy barking dogs. Four of the men eyed Thanea with unconcealed interest; no doubt Dungal had informed them of something of the situation.

There were no fewer than five pens, or buchts as the men called them, on this valley shelf, all presently in use. In two actual lambing was going on, birth and delivery; in one ewes were recovering, with their new-born offspring; in another very pregnant ewes were waiting; and in the last, sickly lambs and those whose mothers had died giving birth were being tended. Great was the activity and the noise.

Fergus led Thanea around, instructing, the girl interested, even concerned. The birth process was normally not compli-cated, the ewes needing little in the way of assistance, the lambs astonishingly quick to get up on their wobbling, spindly legs to seek to suckle. But some had to be aided, ewes and offspring, and some sad lambs were born dead or dying. Only one mother died while Thanea was there; but there were other carcases laid aside – good eating, as one of the men pointed out. Fergus explained about the hazards, diseases which could affect the stock, weaken the ewes and so complicate birth: taid or tick, tape-worm, scab, foot-rot and paralysis which brought on chronic coughing. But on the whole this hill-stock was healthy, if on the thin side after the hard winter.

Thanea was particularly interested in the pen where prob-lems were being dealt with, the man Cormac in charge here, handling ewes, especially gimmers – that is two-year-olds – which had lost their lambs and were very doubtful about accepting others to suckle, usually where twins had been born, or where the mother had died. It seemed that the creatures, by smell, knew that these were not their own progeny and were reluctant to foster. Cormac was having to hold some down while eager lambs sought to suck. At Fergus's suggestion, the girl tried to assist at this process, and was most pleased when she got an unwilling ewe to allow feeding and even to show an interest in one of the little feeders. One suggestion, or solution, where the distressed ewe was particularly reluctant, was to skin her dead lamb and spread the pelt over the motherless one, when the scent seemed to engender acceptance.

When all returned to the hutments for the evening meal – the men to come back later, with torches, to finish the work for that day – Thanea felt herself to be initiated and accepted, spoken to casually, although Fergus was stern with one young man who had made a somewhat lewd suggestion.

Very much aware of the smell of the fleeces, eik as the men called the natural grease in the wool, and which clung to her, she found the meal to be very adequate, eaten off plank-beds used as tables in the largest hut. It was mainly mutton, needless to say, but preceded by a thick soup, and with cold wild duck, mallard, which apparently had been brought from an ice-house, no doubt in Thanea's honour. More honey and oatcakes followed.

Thereafter, thanking all for their kindness, the girl sought her couch in the goat-shed. It had been a long and stressful day, and tiring. But she found herself to be much less troubled and depressed than she had expected, nor uncomfortable, even though the hut still smelled strongly of goat, and the eik from the wool had not washed off from her person.

She slept without difficulty on her straw pallet, after a thanksgiving prayer.

Wakened early, to a substantial breakfast of porridge and more cold mutton, Fergus told her that she would require a dog for her day's tasks, and that he was going to give her the oldest and wisest of the many he possessed, Leot by name, a shaggy, grey-faced black and white creature, which she took to at once when it licked her hand instead of growling. Fergus also presented her with a crook-headed stick which he said that she would find useful, and a dagger-like sharp knife which she might have to use in awkward lambing – and which just possibly might serve a woman well against an evil-disposed man, not that there were apt to be many of such frequenting these empty hills. That somewhat sobered the distinct sense of adventure which she was experiencing in all this.

After the briefest of family prayers, from which Malcolm and Cormac absented themselves, she set off with Fergus and Leot for the high ground.

It seemed that the territory chosen for her to shepherd was

some three miles to the east, across the spine of Spartleton Edge, around the headwaters of a Whiteadder tributary, the Bothwell Water, the hillsides of Birk Cleugh, Crichness Law and Beltondod. One of the young men working meantime at the buchts, Murdoch, was resident shepherd over there, but had driven his main flock of ewes over here to drop their lambs, leaving the hogs, wedders and some gimmers to look after themselves. It was the odd hog or gimmer, pregnant and disturbed at being so for the first time, which might have strayed away to hiding. This was the problem, and Thanea's task to seek out. Leot would help.

They started climbing almost at once, through grass and faded bracken at first but soon into heather, no very steep slopes but fully a mile of it to the crest between what Fergus named as Lind Rig and Spartleton Law itself, this all part of the long ridge, or edge. The man had no cause to criticise the young woman's climbing; indeed in her eagerness to demonstrate her ability she found that she was outdoing his long but more deliberate striding, and soon schooled herself to his pace. They were passing scattered sheep all the way, hogs, wedders and gimmers; the tups or rams, Fergus mentioned, were now penned down in various cleughs, duties done for the season.

Up on the edge, the views were spectacular, ridge and valley, summit and corrie, seemingly to all infinity, a world of its own. But Fergus was pointing forward, eastwards still, with the immediate ground now beginning to drop again. Yonder was her territory, he told her. The nearest hill was Birk Cleugh Law, behind Spartleton. That was where they were heading. She would come to know this walk well.

Presently they were out of heather, where the grouse flew off protesting on down-bent wings, and down to grass again, Leot considering the sheep they passed with a knowing eye. Thanea was beginning to recognise gimmers and wedders and non-breeding ewes, which all had just been sheep to her hitherto. As they went, she told Fergus about the hateful sun-worship night at the stone circle, which he found as shameful as did she.

He was heading in especial today for an area of the Bothwell Water valley under Birk Cleugh Law which was apparently pitted with hollows and much grown with scrub birch, the sort of terrain to which first-lambing hogs were apt to gravitate to hide and shelter in their uneasy state. And here Fergus's experience certainly paid off, and surprisingly, for not only did they find three hogs, not together, one without a lamb, another with one, but the third with three. Triplets were highly unusual with hogs, and this creature clearly was unable to cope, the lambs looking very weakly. Fergus picked them up, gave one to Thanea to carry and took two himself, and going back to where the other two hogs were hiding, with the mother following baaing loudly, ordered Leot to herd the three adults and the one older, stronger lamb onwards, but unhurriedly. He was making for a stell, he said – that is one of the many circular stone pens they had passed dotted over these hillsides, quite small compared with the buchts at Johnscleugh. Into the nearest of these they put their charges, with a gate to prevent them from getting out. They would go down to Murdoch's hut and fold at Birk Cleugh, he said, empty at present, but where there was some store of bog-hay which they would bring back to feed these animals.

So soon Thanea found herself toiling uphill again, with a quite heavy netful of hay slung over her shoulder, Fergus carrying twice as much, back to the stell. On the way Leot, darting off, brought another ewe and lamb which he had scented in a gorse thicket, and this they herded on before them. She was a full-grown beast, not a hog Fergus said, which had somehow escaped the general round-up. And she might be useful.

What he meant by that Thanea discovered in the stell. If this ewe, with only one lamb, could be brought to suckle one of the triplets also, it might save a life. Thereafter the pair of them tried to achieve this, with only partial success, while Leot looked on interestedly.

They could not spend overlong at this, for the man had much more terrain to show his new shepherdess; but he thought that probably the older ewe would in time accept the extra lamb, hopefully before it died of starvation, for the mother certainly could not feed three. The supply of hay, so readily available, would help to satisfy the adults.

They moved off northwards now, up the Bothwell Water two miles, noting more stells, Fergus also pointing out a tall mound of stones on the top of a nearby hill which he named the Witches' Cairn, where he declared evil things had been done long ago, the hill being said to be haunted by the unquiet spirits of the dead.

Beltondod, behind the hill, was the limit of the ground Thanea was being allocated apparently, another hut, shed and fold complex, not presently in use save by some half-wild swine. Here they ate oatcakes which Fergus had brought, washed down with spring water, and rested for a little while. They had covered fully seven rough miles.

Going back almost directly westwards was easier walking although they had to rise high over the shoulder of Ling Rig, for now most of their way was on an ancient drove-road over which cattle were on occasion driven to markets at Dunbar and Innerwick on the coastal plain. Gimmers and wedders were to be seen all the way and, on the way down to Johnscleugh itself, a flock of goats. Thanea was weary but did not say so, with Fergus commending her pace and endurance.

She was glad of her substantial meal that night, more mutton, and did not long delay her bed-going, with no trouble in sleeping.

The following day driving rain persisted until noon and Thanea spent the morning being shown how to spin wool by Duona and her daughters, using not a wheel as she had seen at Traprain but a pirn, a bobbin which hung like a pendulum and was twirled round by hand, the wool carded or combed straight first. These hill-folk spun and wove their own cloth and made their own clothing. But after midday the weather improved, and the girl set off for the Birk Cleugh stell to see how matters went there, Leot alongside.

She found the triplets alive and looking stronger, obviously obtaining milk, another lamb born, and the two slightly older ones skipping about together. Feeling quite responsible towards the little creatures, she went on down to Murdoch's fold and carried up another bundle of hay. Satisfied, she returned to what she now had to consider home, by a circuitous route, feeling notably free, strangely. After all, this was all much less confining and restrictive than the quiet but firm discipline of Monenna's convent.

*　*　*

Thanea's freedom had its limits, however, as she discovered the next day. Before heading off, alone, on her survey of territory, she was bidden down to the buchts, to watch Malcolm and Dungal at the building of an extra fold or pen, dry-stone-dyking as the term was. Not that this was considered suitable work for a woman, lifting and placing carefully selected but heavy stones; but Fergus thought that it would be useful for her to see how it was done, so that she might be able to make small repairs to stell walls which had suffered damage, something which often happened. The craft, which in the past she had taken for granted, was indeed demanding but with its own fascination.

Presently she left them, with Leot, for the hill.

She was no great distance above Johnscleugh, just after the beginning of the heather, when the dog's backward glancing turned her own head. Horsemen were coming up after her, five of them. With no one else on the hillside, it had to be herself they were concerned with. She waited.

It did not take her long to recognise Owen ap Urien of Rheged, with four of his Cumbrian escort.

They rode up, and dismounted, Owen grinning. "So Thanea nic Loth acts the slut, the slave-woman!" he greeted. "Preferring this to being Princess of Rheged! By choice." He pointed at her. "Would I make so ill a man to bed with?"

"It was not that, Owen. But I am promised . . . otherwise," she told him.

"Better than myself?"

She bit her lip. "Other," she repeated. "*You* will find better to wed. Many to choose from."

"Perhaps. But you I wanted. I am on my way home to Rheged. But could not go without a sight of you. And to leave you with some token of myself!" Again that grin.

Thanea knew a surge of relief. She had been fearing that he was going to take her, take her with him, by force. With or without her father's approval. But her relief was short-lived, as he turned to his watching men.

"Take her! Take and strip her of her clothing," he ordered.

As she gasped, the four ran forward to grasp her. Leot, snarling now, snapped at one of them, and was kicked violently away but returned to the attack and was kicked again. Thanea had raised her shepherd's crook to defend herself, but had it grabbed away. Urgent hands gripped her, held her, while others tore at her short gown, wrenching, ripping it into shreds, the men shouting and laughing as they did so. Struggle as she would she could not prevail against them, the prince watching set-faced. The four dragged every scrap of clothing off her, hands busy on her body the while. In only moments she stood naked, trembling, but even so, head held high as she sought to ignore the men and stared at Owen.

His smile returned, wolfish now, as he considered her. "Down with her," he commanded. "And hold her out. Arms. Legs."

Only too eager, his men flung her to the ground, on her back, pinning her there in the heather, each taking a limb, holding her thus, legs wide, arms out, with all their weight and strength. And as she lay, Owen, opening his clothing, descended upon her, rampant, thrusting.

After a single cry she lay as still as his vehemence allowed; but by no means quiescent, for when in his vigorous riding motions his wet lips came down on hers she bit at them fiercely and he jerked back. But not out of her. That took longer, until he collapsed upon her. She tasted his blood.

His men were crowing and urging him on. Thanea's agony of the spirit was worse than that of the body.

When the prince arose off her, licking his bleeding lip, and stood back to stare at her, scowling, one of his men began to undo his own clothing, obviously preparing to follow his master's example. But the scowl became even more savage, ferocious, and Owen shouted, "Back, fool! Back, all of you! She is mine, mine only. Leave her."

Turning on his heel, and sorting his garb, he went back to his horse, kicking at the snarling Leot as he went. Without another word, or waiting for his men, he mounted and reined round, to ride off again downhill.

With disappointed glances at the hunched and naked young woman lying there, the four turned to follow their master.

For how long Thanea lay there, gulping, panting, quivering, she did not know. It was Leot's tongue, licking her, which roused her out of a sort of semi-coma. Shakily she sat up, eyed her bruised body and the dog's concerned eyes. Then, unsteadily, she got to her feet, and after standing, swaying,

40

went to gather together the scattered bits and pieces of torn clothing. Clutching it to her, no part of it sufficient to wear now as cover, she stood, alone, so very much alone and wishing to be alone. Water. She wanted water. To wash, to wash, to wash . . .

She recollected somehow that she had crossed a small burn not too far back, just where the heather started, and thither she picked her faltering way. The horsemen had disappeared beyond the curve of the hill. Leot, at her back, was whimpering.

She came to the burn quite soon and, narrow as it was, sought a straightish stretch where she could lay herself down in it to let the cold water flow over her and into her, the shock of it helping to gather her reeling wits in some measure. Long she lay there, shivering now, but seeking to feel at least a little cleaner, a little cleansed.

When she rose, by tying and knotting together pieces of her clothing, scanty as they were anyway, she managed to fashion some semblance of a garment out of them, enough to cover her breasts and stomach and groin. Thus clad, she made her way slowly down to Johnscleugh, dog at heel.

Fortunately the men were all still at the buchts, busy, and the women, appalled and horrified at what they saw and she told them, shooing away the children, quickly had her on to her couch, under the plaiding. They brought honey wine and insisted that she drink it, much of it, although she could stomach no food.

That wine, a sort of mead, was strong stuff and presently she slept, fitfully, Leot alongside.

3

In the days that followed, Thanea learned to live with herself
and the thoughts and pain of her ordeal. She told herself that
women had been suffering rape since men and women were,
and most probably had been little the worse in person and even
in mind. Her body did not take long to lose the hurt within,
although the bruising of her breasts and limbs took longer to
fade. She decided that what was required was activity, and
her lonely shepherding would best restore her to normal. The
menfolk were angry, shocked, and all sympathy, especially
Fergus who seemed to blame himself that he had not been
there to protect her – and he demanded to know why she had
not used the knife he had given her, in self-defence, and which
she had entirely forgotten. They did not want her to resume
her duties on the hill immediately, but she insisted that this was
best for her. The danger, after all, was past, and she enjoyed
the shepherding. And she had Leot for company.

So she resumed her daily tasks, sometimes Fergus with her
but more often alone, and encountered no hazards other than
those the weather and terrain provided.

It was fully a week after the attack on her that Thanea
came back to Johnscleugh, and news. While she had been
absent at Beltondod, the two bodyguards who had brought
her from Traprain had arrived again, to ask how matters went
with her, presumably on King Loth's orders. Fergus had not
known what to say, guessing that she might well not wish him
to tell of the rape, so shameful a matter. He had said that she
was well enough, out at her work on the hill, and proving good
at it. He had not said that she had done no swineherding.

The girl did not find fault with his reaction. She wondered
whether her father was in fact in any way concerned for her,
whether he had known that Owen was going to seek her out,
even guessed what might happen. Would he be wrath that his

outcast daughter had been so treated? Or would he consider it a fitting retribution? Would he still have some fatherly affection for his erring offspring? She just did not know.

Worse than questions as to her earthly father's attitudes and behaviour towards her was the question which on occasion recurred to worry her – that of her *Heavenly* Father. Could *He* be angry with her over her disobedience? Could the attack on her, the rape and humiliation, be His punishment? Honour thy father and mother, Monenna had taught her students. She had undoubtedly offended hers. Could God have chosen this retribution for her? Yet He was the God of love, as Christ had assured, the very soul and origin of all love. Could such Heavenly Father so ordain? At most times she could not believe it – but there were occasions when her faith was tested.

Testing of a different sort came to Thanea one day some weeks later. The lambing was over, and the helpers, other than the men of the family, dispersed to their own quarters and hutments in the valleys. The lambs were now out on the hills with their mothers, but still had to be watched over and inspected. Predators could attack them, eagles in especial. Few wolves frequented these high pastures from the low-lying woods and forests, but the hungry fox could on occasion be a danger. But the ravens and crows were the main menace, expert at seeking out the less well-doing lambs, pecking their eyes out and thus disabling them before killing and eating. Not that there was anything that Thanea could do against such, other than, like the male shepherds, make constant patrol and seek to keep odd ewes and lambs from straying far from the flocks and into remote and wilder areas. After heavy rains, too, when the burns and rivers rose in swift spate lambs and even sheep could drown. So wet weather was a problem as well as unpleasant, and it was important to keep the flocks to the higher ground at the very time when they tended to seek the lower, sheltered valleys.

It was on an occasion, after three days of rain in late May, that the girl, sent out to aid Malcolm at Birk Cleugh to ensure that the Bothwell Water valley floor was kept clear of sheltering sheep, found Malcolm himself absent, apparently upstream somewhere, but another man occupying his hut. He was of middle years, not a complete stranger, for Thanea had seen him once helping at a Johnscleugh lambing but had not spoken with him and did not know his name. She greeted him easily enough, however, enquired where Malcolm was, and asked whether the *down*stream valley had been inspected. The man said that he had just returned from so doing and was about to eat his midday bread. She could share it with him. It was in the hut.

But, once inside, he turned on her, to grasp her bodily and to tear at the neck of her gown. No doubt he had been informed that she had already been raped and thought to repeat the process. However, he was one man, not four, and she was now a more experienced young woman. Moreover, she had not forgotten Fergus's advice anent her knife. Elbowing the assailant away vigorously, she brought up a knee to his middle and, reaching down to her rope girdle, snatched out the weapon from its sheath there and pointed it at his throat. Hastily the man drew back, bent double now, and she ran out of the hovel, to where Leot was sharing some mutton bones with the other's dog.

"You try to touch me again and I will set my dog on you, oaf!" she exclaimed. "He is fierce. He has attacked men before you. Leot!" she called, and the animal came to her at once.

The man, still bent a little with the pain of her knee's thrust at his groin, stood uncertain, fists clenched.

She stepped over to where she had left her crook alean against the hut walling, and grasping it, waved it threateningly at the other, at the same time calling Leot's name peremptorily. The dog, sensing the enmity and challenge, growled deeply, stiffening.

That man promptly hurried back into the hut, and slammed the door shut.

Shaken, but with some feeling of satisfaction also, Thanea turned to walk upstream beside the swollen brown-stained waters. She would find Malcolm and tell him that his assistant was a rogue.

She did not locate the shepherd, who was presumably up in one of the hidden valleys, but when she got back to Johnscleugh she told Fergus, who swore that the man, apparently named Drost and a sort of itinerant helper from the Edenshall settlement to the south, would never again be employed by him. And if he saw him, he would teach him a lesson. Almost smugly, Thanea declared that perhaps she and Leot had already done that.

The girl's relationship with Fergus's family was now more than just friendly, warm indeed, warmer and closer than she had known at Traprain since her mother had died, even Dungal and Cormac treating her like a sister, and Duona insisting on mothering her. Herself friendly by nature, she responded gladly.

With the early summer blessing the Lammermuirs and their denizens, the birches feathered with green, the young bracken uncurling on the hillsides, and the wild flowers smiling colour to the sun, Thanea's appreciation of it all became tempered with the awareness of a different sort of burgeoning. Slight morning sickness was the first warning of it, and recognition of some change in her normal bodily functions. It did not take her long to perceive the significance of this. She was pregnant. Owen ap Urien had indeed left her something to remember him by.

Shaken, she was of course prey to varying emotions, alarm, concern, dread, and yet a sort of wonder that there should be a new life developing within her. Was this more of God's dealings with her? His judgment? Or His punishment? Or His purposes? Whatever the answer to that, this problem would demand some solving . . . An unmarried mother . . .

Thanea did not tell her friends at Johnscleugh. No doubt they would learn the truth before very long. And there was always the possibility that she was mistaken.

But as the weeks wore on she knew that it was no mistake. Her condition might not yet be apparent to others, but it became very much so to herself. She was still able to roam the hills, even to enjoy the summery delights and the sense of freedom they engendered. But she felt her person to be heavier, to be less nimble on her feet, to tire more quickly. Foolishly she hoped that it was not evident to others.

It was mid-August, and the sheep-shearing and wool-baling proceeding when, alone one evening with Duona, that woman took the opportunity to speak of it.

"You are with child, Thanea," she said. "You must know it, I think. *We* have guessed it for some time."

The girl nodded, dumbly.

"We grieve for you. It will be . . . difficult. How feel you?"

"I am well enough."

"Aye. But in your mind?"

"It, it must be God's will."

"Yes. That is the best way – God's will. It will be about Yuletide?"

"About that, I suppose."

"Will you bide on here? It is scarcely the place for a princess to give birth. Will you go back to your father's house at Traprain? To be attended by those skilled in the matter?"

"I think not, Duona. No, not there. You know the punishment for unwed mothers! I must think on this. I will not be of much use at the shepherding, the last months. And I cannot just sit about, idle. In winter . . ."

"You could spin. And weave. And sew. We will aid you, gladly."

"I thank you. But . . . no, I will think on this . . ."

Thanea did indeed consider the matter, the more so as her girth grew thicker, her breasts swelled somewhat and her condition became apparent to all. She was afraid that her father would send again to enquire of her, and that the pregnancy would be reported to him. She was fairly certain that he would be the more affronted, angry, not accepting or forgiving. The druids were very harsh against unmarried mothers, an offence against the sun, it seemed, for some reason. She would have wished to go to Monenna, who would understand, but that was not possible. And Monenna might no longer be at Traprain. Then it occurred to her – there was another nunnery in this part of Lothian, at Whittingehame, in the skirts of Lammermuir none so far away, a small place which had survived when greater establishments had been put down in the relapse to paganism. Her mother, Queen Anna, had taken her there as a child, but she had never been back since. She might go there to have the baby. The nuns would not cast her out, nor tell her father. That is what she would do.

Towards the end of October, then, when the tups were mating with the ewes, and she was fairly big with child, Thanea said farewell to the family at Johnscleugh, uncertain indeed as to her future but promising to come back, God willing, all much concerned for her. Fergus had shown his concern by going

46

down to a low-country farmery at Cranshaws, to the south, and bringing back two garrons so that the girl would not have to walk the difficult ten miles across the hills to Whittingehame, for they must not go by the more direct route, by White Castle, where the captain thereof might well consider it his duty to inform King Loth. With the few belongings which she had accumulated, she was helped up on to the horse's broad back, after an emotional leave-taking. Fergus in attendance, and Leot running behind, the man's parting gift to her, they set off north-westwards.

After a mile up the infant Whiteadder, they left that valley to climb up by a corrie called Tavers Cleugh, which led them over the shoulder of quite a high ridge between Bleak Law and Rangely Kipp, on deer and sheep tracks now. Still westwards, presently they descended a tumbling stream towards another shepherding community called Snowden. But they avoided this, wishing to keep their travel as secret as possible. Down the Papana Water they again avoided a community, Garvald, *garbh-allt*, the rough stream, and a mile or so further to the north reached their destination, the little convent of Whittingehame, hidden away in open woodlands.

The establishment, a dozen thatch-roofed, stone-walled huts and a tiny church within grassy ramparts, was smaller than Thanea had remembered it as a child and, sadly, declining still further, for there were only six nuns, and all now elderly. As was to be expected by its name, it was dedicated to the Virgin Mary, for Christian church names with White in them, or Whit, always so referred.

The old chief nun Maura greeted them warily at first, but learning Thanea's identity, quickly changed to friendly concern. She had heard of the princess's disgrace and banishment – all Lothian knew of it by now – but had not known to where she had been sent. Given details, she saw the girl's ordeals as a sacrifice for Christ's cause, and was entirely accepting of the idea that she should remain at the convent until her child was born, and thereafter if so she wished. The necessary secrecy she agreed to also; indeed she wished it that way, since she did not want to antagonise King Loth and his druids, who could so easily decide to turn them out of their little nunnery. The princess could have one of the unused huts, and she and her nuns would care for her. Maura was a little doubtful about the dog, but on Thanea's pleading, let Leot stay when Fergus took his leave.

Parting with her friend was sad for the young woman, but he promised to come and see her frequently, so she must not feel abandoned by her adopted family. He assured her that none of them would tell the king's emissaries, if they came again to Johnscleugh, where she had gone, merely that she had left them of her own will.

The other nuns, none much under three score years, were much stirred by the princess's arrival, and fussed over her with much exclamation, a notable excitement in their enclosed and disciplined lives. They cleared out and furnished, after a fashion, a hut for her, and even found Leot an interesting addition to convent life.

So Thanea and the dog settled in, gratefully.

She found that, with All Hallows festival approaching, there was just then much preparation by the nuns, for this was a very special occasion for them, the feast of the Blessed Virgin Mary herself, and all martyrs. One of the requirements therefor, seemingly, was a multitude of candles, and in the making of these Thanea was glad to help, for she had no desire to sit idle, and this was no time of year for working in the garden or orchard. The candles were made from beeswax, and the nuns tended many hives, or skeps as they called them, made out of plaited straw. The process demanded the draining of honey from the combs, and then the melting down of the cell walls in hot water, direct heat having to be avoided. The wax thus produced had to be strained, a difficult task, reheated, and then poured into moulds contrived out of hollow bones in two parts tied together but which could be separated later. Wicks, made of plaited flax, grown in the nuns' garden for this purpose, were hung centrally from a hook at the top down into the moulds, to be carefully held vertical while the wax was being poured in. When set, the bone halves were detached and the resultant candle taken out, warmed again in hot water to soften it so that it could be rolled into smooth and regular shape. The wax was used also for dressing leather and as a base for ointments. So the bees were important in the nuns' lives.

Thanea became quite expert at this manufacture. It was two

days later, when she was bringing more honeycombs from the skeps in the orchard, that three men drove up on a cart laden with cut timber for the nuns' fires. At sight of her they stared, not to be wondered at perhaps, to see a very pregnant young woman in an establishment of elderly nuns. She greeted them but did not engage in any converse, not wishing to become involved in explanations. Later the sisters told her that the men came once a month with fuel, from Garvald, one of them however a stranger this time.

It was All Hallows' Eve when the blow fell. A group of armed men of the king's bodyguard rode up to the nunnery, to announce that they were informed that the former princess, the woman Thanea, had left her place of exile without permission and come here. They were to take her back, not to Johnscleugh but to Traprain.

There was no refusing them, of course. The chief nun, sorrowing, said that the stranger with the wood-cutters must have recognised Thanea and reported the matter to the king's servants. Sadly, the girl had to say farewell again, and mount a horse behind one of the riders. Leot had to be held back from running after them, after his mistress had patted his head.

It was no lengthy ride from Whittingehame to Traprain. At the citadel, Thanea was taken not into the palace itself but shut up in one of the courtyard outbuildings. She feared greatly. None of the men had spoken with her on that ride.

She was left alone for a considerable time. Then her father, stepmother and Diarmid the Arch Druid arrived – and from the first glaring inspection of her person, and lack of answer to her greeting, she knew that she could expect no favours, perhaps no mercy.

"So! It is true!" Loth got out, after a moment or two. "Slut! Beyond all that you have done, you would present me, *me* the king, with a bastard! It shall not be, I tell you! I will have no bastards in my family."

"You should have told that to Owen ap Urien, Father," she answered him.

"Silence, whore!" he barked. "*You*, you have given yourself to men. Who knows how many. You have disgraced my name and fame. You are of all creatures most shameful, unworthy to

49

live. You *shall* not live! And that bastard within you shall not live, to be called grandchild of mine. You hear? You die. And it with you." And without waiting for any answer from her, Loth swung about and stormed to the door and out.

The others followed, unspeaking, and the door slammed shut.

The girl sat down on the straw – for this was the store for stabling – and buried head in hands. No tears came; she was beyond tears. And she was not taken by surprise. She had more or less anticipated something like this, on the ride hither. She was going to die, yes. She could, she must, bear that ordeal, as so many had had to do before her. But . . . stoning to death! For that was the penalty demanded by the druids for unwed mothers. *Stoning!* Slow agony. Could she face that? She would have to. God give her the strength – if God had not indeed deserted her. It seemed that He had.

Long she sat there. It took the stirring within her to remind her that it was not only herself who was to die. The young life there was condemned also. So cruel, cruel. And her own father commanding it. The hurt of that was sore indeed.

Darkness fell and none came near her, no food nor drink brought her. Outcast.

Off and on that night she slept uneasy and awakened, slept and wakened. She tried to pray, but found herself only repeating words, all but meaningless. Wherein had she so greatly sinned . . .?

In fact she was asleep when they came for her in the morning, some of the bodyguard, including the pair who had taken her to Johnscleugh. Grasping her, they took her out of the palace yard and up to the very highest point of that great rock. There the Arch Druid waited, with a small crowd. There was no sign of her father or stepmother. Nor of any of her brothers.

Beside Diarmid was a trolley, one of the many used for dragging wood up from the forests for the citadel's fires. Men were sorting its ropes.

One of the bodyguard holding her pointed to this. "Your chariot to the netherworld!" he said, with a guffaw.

Another, one of the Johnscleugh pair, was less unkind. "You were to be stoned," he whispered. "But none of us was prepared to cast the first stone. So – this!"

The ropes ready, and Diarmid pointing, they took her to the trolley and forced her to lie on it, on her back. They tied her securely. She knew now, of course, her fate. She was almost relieved. She was to be thrown over the cliff on this carriage. At least that ought to be a quick death, a deal quicker than stoning.

The Arch Druid, seeming impatient, intoned a declaration to the sun, very brief. Then he gestured towards the cliff edge, leading the way to the exact spot chosen, no doubt at the very sheerest point of the precipice. Creaking, the trolley was trundled thither.

Thanea had not spoken throughout. Nor did she now. What point was there in words? Save in prayer. If only she could pray. She could try, her last effort in this life.

At Diarmid's shouted command the men pushed the trolley forward, forward. Its front wheels went over the edge, and it tipped. But the undercarriage caught on the rock lip, and it hung thus. Eyes tight closed, fists clenched, the girl held breath, no prayer forthcoming. Then the men behind gave the extra lift and push, necessary to slide it over.

Thanea was not unconscious, yet she was aware of nothing then, no feeling of falling, no rush of air. That is, until she knew a terrible jarring shock and then another and another. The pain of it was beyond all bearing, and her body knew it. Oblivion . . .

Thanea nic Loth was not dead. When consciousness of a sort did return to her and her eyes opened, it was to light. She was not sure of anything but that, only light. Not even pain just then. Was this death, she wondered, after moments of awareness? It was light, light after darkness. Was this the next world reached? Then she realised that, out of the light, a face was peering down at her, a face that she recognised. It was that of Monenna. And Monenna surely was not dead? Then Eithne's face was there also. Thanea recognised that she could not be dead. And with that realisation came pain, comprehensive pain. She closed her eyes again. The darkness had been better.

When she returned to consciousness of a clearer sort, she was able to take in details, although the pain was still there. She was being untied from the broken wreck of the trolley. Monenna and some of her students were clustering round her, seeking to raise her from the broken timbers, men standing behind them watching. Beyond, she could see the soaring face of the precipice thrusting high.

She perceived that Monenna was speaking, repeating. "It is a miracle! A miracle of God! A miracle!" Some of the girls were touching her, stroking her hair. Herself, she could find no words.

Then she was aware of something almost unbelievable. The Arch Druid was there, pushing forward to stare down at her. And Monenna was waving him away, commandingly, as though some common intruder, telling him to be gone, that Almighty God had taken Thanea into His especial keeping, and the heathen murderers should look well to themselves lest Christ-God struck them down in His anger. And Diarmid accepting it, or at least turning away, and leaving.

Monenna indeed seemed to be in charge. She ordered some of the men to go and fetch a litter. No, not a horse, a litter, a hand-litter. The princess could not mount any horse. Nor could she walk. A litter to carry her. Quickly. Men, seemingly afraid of her now, or of her potent God, so evidently involved here, hurried off.

Thanea was only partly, intermittently, able to take all this in, a mixture of wonder and pain preoccupying her. The pain seemed to come from all over, her head, arms, legs, body. Then a kicking within her informed that her child had survived also, and she knew a great warmth of gratitude.

She found her voice at last. "What . . . ? What . . . ? How . . . ? I live! I live!" she got out.

"God be praised, you do!" Monenna cried. "A miracle. A blessed and miraculous deliverance, Thanea. God has saved you. For His own purposes."

The girl turned her head to gaze up at that fearsome precipice, speechless.

It was Eithne who elaborated. "We saw it all, Thanea. We knew, were here, to watch. To, to cherish you when, when . . ." She shook her head. "This cart they tied you to, when it fell, hit an elbow of the rock, and was thrust away, off, on a different course. Not straight down the cliff. It went sideways, hit other parts on a less steep course, was flung this way and that. We saw it. But there was no mighty drop . . ."

"All the way," Monenna took up the account, "it was guided. Guided by God's own hands. Its course directed so that it missed the dire falls which could have killed you, *would* have killed you. Oh, praises be! You are to live, Thanea!"

Blinking, she sought to absorb it all. More kicking within her reminded her. "The child. Within me. It is alive also. I feel it."

Monenna was calling for water to bathe the bruised and bleeding brows, cheeks, arms. There must be water somewhere hereabouts, at the cliff-foot.

"It . . . the child . . . it is not coming? You do not feel birth coming, Thanea?"

"I do not know. But I think not. It feels no different. Kicking, yes – but it did that before."

"You have no pains?"

"I am all pains. But not there."

"My poor lamb. Can you stand?"

Supporting her, they raised her from the wreck of the trolley. But when she tried to walk she would have fallen in a swoon had they not held her up. So they sat her down again, and one of the girls arrived with wet cloths to bathe her sores.

How long they were at this Thanea did not know, in her present state. But it must have been some considerable period, for it gave time for men to arrive with a litter, a stretch of hide on poles, presumably obtained up at the citadel. On this she was laid, and four men raised it up to carry her, Monenna and the girls alongside.

They had not gone far when who should come hastening but her father, brother Gawain and Diarmid again. They stopped the bearers to stare down at her, silent.

Thanea mustered a faint smile.

Gawain reached out, to touch her head. She shrank from the pain of it, but smiled again nevertheless.

Loth was not smiling nor touching, but frowning. "It is beyond belief," he muttered.

"Not so!" Monenna declared. "Almighty God in heaven took charge of her. Thanea's Heavenly Father is kinder than her earthly one!"

Loth looked at Diarmid, who shook his head. "A mischance," he said. "It may be that we chose the wrong death, displeasing the sun. It could be that the morning, early, was not the time, the sun new-risen from the eastern sea, the sea god, Manannan, offended."

"What now, then?"

"We must consider well."

"Consider well indeed!" Monenna said. "God the Father, the God of love, has spoken. Repent you, and turn to Him, the Lord of all."

"Quiet, woman!" the king jerked. "Or it will be the worse for you." To the litter-bearers he said, "Take her back. Up to the stables. We will consider. Take her up. And send these women away." And he turned to stalk off whence he had come.

Gawain looked down at his sister, pityingly, but followed his father, as did the Arch Druid.

So, at the start of the climb to the citadel, Monenna and her students were sent off to their convent at Cairn Dinnes, and Thanea was borne uphill, flanked by men of the bodyguard, all these now eyeing her warily, all but fearfully.

In the palace yard she was taken back to her hay-store, set down, still on the litter, and left.

Scarcely able to believe that it was not all only some dream, she lay and thought and thought. Had she indeed now to thank her God? Or was that premature . . . ?

They came for her about noon, Diarmid and two of his druid priests.

"Get up," she was told peremptorily. "You are to be given to Manannan, of the sea. The sun has rejected you. Manannan will take you." One of the priests stirred her aching body with his foot.

She sought to rise, but had to be aided up, however roughly. Standing, she swayed dizzily, not only from her sore body but from her empty stomach, for she had not eaten for two days and nights. They half carried her outside.

There a group of garrons were standing, two of them linked together by an oxhide to form a berth, a horse-litter. Getting Thanea up into this was difficult and hurt grievously. Diarmid, his priests and some of the bodyguard mounted and they moved off without ceremony. None of her family was present, although perhaps some watched from the palace windows.

It made an uncomfortable journey for the girl, her two garrons not being used to working together failing to harmonise their trotting, pulling apart or closing together, sometimes one ahead, sometimes the other, with the oxhide litter pulled this way and that. Thanea had to cling to it tightly.

They went downhill again, beyond the foot of the law to the nearest ford of Tyne at Hailes. Then up the long slopes to the north, to surmount a flat-topped ridge which separated this Vale of Tyne from another shallower but wider, the Vale of Peffer. From this summit they could see the Norse Sea to the east, at no great distance, and the Firth of Forth to the north, another five miles. Thanea, knowing that she was going to be sacrificed to the sea god Manannan, concluded that it was to the latter that she was being taken, or they would have turned off down Tyne earlier. She felt strangely unconcerned now. Presumably she was to be drowned. But after the dire precipice experience, she doubted whether this could be as grim.

They rode down to ford the Peffer's swampy banks near Prora, a place she knew well, for this was a famed hunting-ground for wild boar and the marsh deer, the bogs and scrub woodland having to be carefully negotiated however or the horses would have sunk deep. Then on down the north side of Peffer, a sluggish stream, the name of which oddly meant fair or beautiful, on slightly higher ground now. She reckoned that they must be heading for the great Aberlady Bay where the Peffer entered the Forth estuary. Thanea knew enough about that wide but shallow bay to wonder whether indeed drowning could be her fate, for only at fullest tide would the water be deep enough to drown in, unless she was held down bodily.

Presently they did reach that bay, and proceeded along its shore to its western horn, the tide half out. The Peffer clung to this side, leaving vast levels of mud-flats and sand stretching eastwards to sand-dune hills. Where the stream actually reached and breached the sand-bar at the bay-mouth was a small fishing-haven and a few cot-houses, from which their arrival was watched with interest. Here the party halted, and dismounted, Diarmid going over to one of the watchers, who bowed respectfully, and giving his orders. The man hurried off.

Thanea was roughly assisted down from her litter.

Soon the fisherman was back, almost hidden under the bulk of a coracle which he bore on his shoulders, a small boat constructed of waxed hide stretched over a frame of saplings, used for one-man inshore fishing and the like. This, instructed, he took down to the river's edge and said that he would go back for a paddle.

"No paddle!" the Arch Druid said briefly.

The girl now understood. She was to be cast adrift on the outgoing tide in this coracle, without means of directing it, to let the sea take her. She might drown eventually, if she did not starve to death first; but that, possibly, would not be for some time.

Diarmid ordered her to be taken down and put in the boat. He raised a hand.

"You, shameless daughter of the mighty Loth, we now

56

commit to Manannan, god of the sea, to work his will upon. Go – and trouble the sun and his lesser gods no more. Go!" And he gestured to his men to push the coracle out from the shingly bank.

Sitting in the cradle-like craft, Thanea looked at them, almost wonderingly, asking herself how men, much less her father, could do this to any woman who had never harmed them. But she did not look for long, for the light boat at once caught the Peffer's current which, allied to the outgoing tide of the bay, swirled the all but circular craft round and round almost dizzily. She clung to the sides to keep her balance.

Quickly the coracle went dancing out, heading for the gap in the long sand-bar where the stream entered the outer bay, marked by white rollers. Without a paddle to steer it, would the boat survive in those breakers? Would she drown swiftly, after all? That might be the objective. No human hands needed to soil themselves, to hold her down.

But the coracle proved to be more buoyant and seaworthy than might have been expected from its frail construction and shape. When carried into the rollers it jerked and spun and whirled, but did not capsize, only a little spray coming inboard, the girl clutching the framework.

There was some fifty yards or so of this rough water where the fresh water mixed with salt ebbed over the shallows of the sand-bar and met the incoming waves of the estuary. It made a bumpy, rocking passage, but the craft survived it and was swept on into the very different, slower and less jabbly motions of the Firth of Forth.

For All Hallows' Day the weather was reasonably good, dull and grey but with only a light wind from the east. The seas were long rather than high and with few white crests now. On these the boat rose and fell comparatively gently, and Thanea relaxed somewhat.

Out here it was difficult to judge movement and speed, other than the swaying motion. But by gazing fixedly at points on the shore she had left, she could discern that she was drifting east by north on the fairly strong outgoing tide. And thither lay the Norse Sea.

The girl sought now to compose and settle her mind and spirit to accept this new situation. Should she expect God to deliver her again? Or was in fact the cliff escape pure chance? If she was now heading, however slowly, for the open sea, how would her end come? Would a storm drown her? Or would she suffer a slow death by starvation? Could she face that? It would be wrong, sinful, to cast herself overboard. Would it be an agonising end? She did not know, she just did not know.

Then a kicking in her belly reminded her that she had to think of two now, not only herself.

It did not take her long to realise that she was drifting quite fast, as the coastline slipped past and she identified landmarks, Gulyn Point, St Patrick's chapel, the offshore islands of Eyebroughty, Fetheray, Craigleith and the mighty, towering Bass Rock with its halo of circling seafowl. She perceived something else – that she was drifting *north* by east, for the said southern shoreline was becoming ever further off. Indeed her course seemed to be set directly for the large and cliff-girt Isle of May, out beyond the mouth of Forth.

This recognition sparked off a sudden new gleam of hope. Suppose she was to be cast up on that? Did not drift past it. Was that possible? In all the wide sea it was not likely, yet it looked as though she was heading thither. Was there any way whereby she might somehow steer this craft, lacking a paddle? Would some of her clothing, hung over the side, help to influence the direction of drift? Even try to paddle with one hand? Would that make any difference, out here amongst the ocean's waves? She could scarcely think so. And yet . . .

Soon she was really hoping, for the coracle did in fact seem to be proceeding almost straight for the island which, she guessed, could be almost a mile in length, and lay broadside-on. Was she not doomed to die, after all? Another escape? Could it be . . . ?

Gazing, the Isle of May became a symbol of hope – for, despite all her summoning of resolution and courage, she desperately wanted to live.

Would she be able to live on the May? So far as she knew, it was uninhabited. Would there be anything for her to survive on there? Plants? Seabirds? Rabbits? Eggs? Would there be fresh water? She knew how to make fire, by using stones, flints to make sparks into tinder, dry grass and the like. She could perhaps find a cave? Or build a shelter. There appeared to be no trees on the island. Could she survive here . . . ?

And then, with the cliffs of the May, white with seabird droppings, soaring less than a mile in front, and the boat seeming to be bobbing directly to them, Thanea's hopes were dashed. She realised that not only was she getting no nearer but she was actually receding. Spirits plunging, she recognised that it was the tide. The tide had turned. It no longer ebbed. And, flowing, it would carry her away again. The Isle of May was not for her.

Thanea's disappointment was slightly tempered by perception that this rising tide would now carry her coracle in the other direction, up Forth instead of seawards. Would this have any great effect on her fate? She might not drown in the Norse Sea, but she could drown or starve equally surely in the sixty-mile-long estuary. How far had she come from Aberlady Bay? She did not know, but guessed nearly a score of miles. It had been around half-tide when she was launched. So it had taken perhaps six hours for her to drift thus far. Twelve hours, and the tide would change again. She might ground first. Could she hope for that? Would the tide flow at the same speed as it ebbed? Twelve hours. Perhaps thirty–forty miles. So long as she did not ground in Aberlady Bay again. Although no one would now be looking for her there . . .

It was getting dark, and she was cold now, cold. And hungry as she had never been before. And bruised all over, aching. Could she sleep?

Time, Thanea was learning, was of variable perception. It could pass swiftly or slowly or not seem to pass at all but to stand still. The hours that followed seemed indeed timeless. There was no way of judging them. Once darkness fell there was no view save of flowing, dipping waters, and even these vague, uncertain, hissing, mesmeric, and added to by the swaying motion of the coracle, sleep-inducing. Undoubtedly the girl slept, off and on, although she felt that she did not. Strangely that feeling of cold faded, as did most other feeling, blessedly. Undoubtedly the strains of the last days were telling, and her body's reaction was kinder than men had been.

It was first light when she was fully aware again. So she *had* slept, and deeply. The dawn showed the loom of land on both sides of her now, clearly much closer at hand than hitherto, especially on the right, the north side. So she was well up Forth. Still the coracle was moving westwards – so the tide had not yet turned again. Where was she? She had sailed up Forth with her brothers, more than once. But she did not recognise any landmarks. Only, she could see that the estuary was narrowing noticeably still further not so far ahead. There were low green hills on both sides, well back from the shores, higher to the south.

She was cold again now, and all of her aching, stiff with her crouching posture in that confined space, dizzy with weakness.

Presently she saw that there was a small island immediately ahead, low, grassy. Was she going to ground on that? But no. The tide was taking her north of it. She now perceived that there was a low headland reaching out at the side, featureless, little more than a sand-spit but quite long, forming a bay beyond. Between islet and spit the tide carried her, not more than two hundred yards from the northern shore. But no, the coracle did not ground. Into the shallow bay it bobbed.

There was less than a mile of bay, sufficiently shallow for her to see the sand beneath the water. Halfway across, Thanea perceived life, moreover. Two men were wading in the shallows, garments kilted up, dabbing downwards with sticks. She was going to pass within a few hundred yards of them. She knew what they were doing – spearing flounders, using their bare feet to locate the wriggling fish, and then to stab at them with spears. They had bags over their shoulders. Fishers. They must see her. She began to wave.

The men gazed at her, no doubt astonished. However, she was too far out for them to be able to reach her. Biting her lip, she drifted on, but slowly, as they stared after her.

She hoped now that she might in fact ground on the western horn of the little bay, although it could scarcely be called a horn, so minor was it compared with the other end. There was less than half a mile to go.

And then she realised that in fact she was not going to reach it. The coracle had become stationary, swaying on the waves but no longer drifting forward. Was this something to do with currents in the bay? Or – had the tide turned again?

Wondering, she sat. Was she once again going to be carried away eastwards down the estuary in her endless ordeal? If it was to be that, would she not be better to throw herself overboard? It was not very deep here; she could see the bottom sand. Too deep to wade, though. Could she swim, in her present weak and awkward state? It would not have to be for long, perhaps only a few hundred yards, before it shallowed sufficiently for her to wade ashore. Better that than to be carried off again, seawards.

She had decided that this was what she must attempt, when she recognised that the coracle was indeed moving again, slowly eastwards – but, praises be, swinging slightly landwards. Some trick of the tide in that sheltered bay seemed to be pulling the craft nearer to the shore. If this continued, she might not have to go overboard, at least not to swim. The water was definitely shallowing beneath her.

Thanea was so taken up with watching the depth of water and the direction of drift that she forgot about those two flounder-spearers. That is, until they shouted. Looking over her shoulder, she saw them not fifty yards off and wading deeply towards her, habits hitched high. With a great surge of thankfulness she perceived that she was probably going to be rescued, at least from this part of her troubles. She turned round to hold out her arms to the men.

Then she noted something else. The fishermen's garb was dark brown, and fair quality, habits, and moreover both wore crosses on chains round their necks. They were Christians, almost certainly monks. The girl, weak and light-headed as she was, almost swooned away in her joyous relief. Churchmen!

Soon the men were grasping for the coracle, putting their fish-spears into it and starting to drag it towards the shore, bombarding her with questions. She was too overcome with emotion to answer them with more than incoherent, gasping words. But they pulled on to the beach, mystified but active in their help.

They dragged the coracle right on to the sandy strand, and rising stiffly Thanea was aided to step out, dizzy as she was. Strangely, the firm land set her reeling again, all but falling, after the long hours of the sea's motion. Her rescuers, seeing it, and her condition, took an arm each in support, dropping

61

down the skirts of their habits and collecting their spears from the coracle, which they pulled higher. Then, pointing inland, they led her slowly up from the beach.

Now she saw that some way inland, on a grassy shelf above the sands, was an establishment of some sort and of some size, indeed looking like a larger version of the Cairn Dinnes convent, houses and huts within earthen ramparts. But what took and held Thanea's reeling attention was the tall wooden cross which rose beside the largest of the wattle and daub buildings, Christ's cross. She was being brought to a church. God, dear God, had not forsaken her, after all!

Scarcely able to walk as she was, she actually pressed forward, with those supporting arms, in a state bordering on delirium.

She was vaguely aware of developments, surrounded by men, monks assuredly, exclaiming, questioning. She could only shake her head at them, trying to smile, no intelligible explanations forthcoming. Then, with the small crowd drawing back a little, she found herself confronted by a big man of middle years, dressed simply like the others but with an undeniable air of authority, his cross larger and of gold.

"Here is the Abbot Serf," she was told. "Serf. Servanus. St Serf himself. Our abbot."

She scarcely took it in, so bemused was she. She stared, lips trembling, and tears filled her eyes. She could only shake her head again.

The big man, although of stern features, considered her, reached out to grasp her shoulder, and smiled – and it was a warm and kindly smile.

"Daughter!" was all he said.

That one word demolished the last of her used-up reserves of strength. Thanea wailed out a choking cry, and pitched bodily forward against the abbot's chest, her legs buckling under her.

But she did not fall, for Serf's strong arms held her up. She knew no more – save of an all-embracing peace.

5

When next Thanea was fully conscious of herself and her surroundings, she was aware, again, of the peace first of all. Then of, and contributing to it, the situation in which she found herself. She was, in fact, in bed, unclothed and in comfort as far as her bodily state allowed, alone in a small whitewashed chamber, simple, austere, but adequate, with a little table beside her bed on which was a beaker of milk, a platter of cold chicken legs and another of oatcakes with a honeycomb. Also a little silver bell. A form, a sheepskin on the floor and a pottery bowl in a corner completed her sanctuary's furnishings. She knew a great content.

But she did not lie overlong savouring it, for she was aware of a great hunger. That food . . .

It did not take her long to wolf down the provision supplied; she could indeed have looked for more. Then she lay wondering, wondering . . .

In time the door of the hut opened and a face looked in, to disappear again. And soon thereafter the Abbot Serf arrived, alone. He came to look down at her.

"So, daughter," he said, "you have slept long. You were, I fear, very weary. And distressed?" That was in the nature of a question.

"Yes. I was, yes," she agreed. "I, I was weak. With hunger."

"With more than hunger, I think. But – you feel better now? You have eaten, I see."

"I thank you. I thank you for this, this care."

"It is little enough. And you in need. And with child. May I know who you are to be in such sore straits? Alone, and adrift on the sea."

"I am Thanea nic Loth," she said simply.

"Loth?" The big man stared. "Not *King* Loth? Of the Gododdin, surely . . . ?"

"The same," she said. "I am his daughter."

"Daughter of Loth! In this state! A princess! I thought that you were well born, despite your clothing. But . . ."

"It is true." She sat up and, the blankets slipping down and revealing her bare bosom, she sought to cover herself somewhat. "My father has cast me off. Would have no more of me. Named me harlot and whore. I am not, I am not! Set me adrift in that coracle for his sea god Manannan to take me. After seeking to kill me over a cliff." That all came out in a rush. "I am not. No harlot. I was raped . . ."

Shaking his head, the Abbot Serf reached out to press her naked shoulder back gently. "Lie quiet, daughter," he told her. "Do not distress yourself further. You are safe now. Lie there. Tell me what you would have me to know, but be not concerned over the telling. All will be well now. You are in God's good keeping."

"Yes. Yes. I know it now. I should never have doubted. I was weak . . ."

So she told him her dire story, or most of it, Monenna's teachings, her father's paganism, the arrival of Prince Owen, the sun-worship and sacrifices, the decision that she should wed the prince, her refusal and the consequences, her reduction to slave status, her rape, her shepherding, her recourse to the nuns of Whittingehame, her removal therefrom, the condemning to death, the ordeal of the precipice and then this casting adrift in the coracle. It all poured out. The abbot had drawn up the form and sat listening, grim-faced.

When, choking with emotion, she finished, he took her hand. "Girl, girl," he said, "here is sin and shame almost beyond belief. And a father's doing! King Loth is to be utterly condemned. And yet, and yet – he must be forgiven. If that is possible. By you, his daughter. For that is Christ's way, His teaching. Love, forgiveness, always. The sin condemned but the man forgiven. Clearly he is under the evil spell of the man Diarmid, the sun-worshipper. Yet even he should be forgiven, for he does worship, even though false and cruel gods. Can you forgive, Princess?"

She swallowed. "I can try."

"Yes. You see, Thanea, Almighty God's hand must be in this. By no other means could you have survived, to reach me here,

64

you and your child within you. God must have a purpose for you both. Satan may have been behind King Loth and the druids. But Satan has been vanquished in this, glory be! For God's good purposes, of that I am sure. For you are safe here now. None will reach to harm you here. We, at the abbey of Culross, are not in your Gododdin realm. We come under Alba and the Mormaor of Fortrenn. The mormaor is not Christian, not yet. But his wife is, and he respects me. I baptised his child. He finds me useful. So – you will stay here meantime, for so long as you wish. King Loth will not know that you have survived – and I shall see that none will tell him. We will not call you princess, but only Thanea. When your time for delivery comes, we will find women to attend you. No more fears, therefore."

Thanea clutched his hand in gratitude and relief. She had heard of this Serf or Servanus and his monastery of Culross in Fothrif of Fife, a high-born follower of the Church St Ninian had founded in these Celtic lands but which had sadly been so largely engulfed by paganism. Monenna had spoken of him with something like awe, calling him saint, although she had never met him. Extraordinary that in all the sixty-odd miles of the great Forth estuary which separated Lothian of the Gododdin from Alba of the Northern Picts, or Cruithne, her coracle should have brought her to Culross. She could no longer doubt the divine guidance.

"Oh, you are good, good!" she exclaimed.

"I am not good. Only God is good. I but seek, unworthily, to know His will and do it. When is your child due, think you?"

"It was at the end of March when, when Owen ap Urien raped me. That is seven months past. So – it could be Yuletide. Earlier perhaps."

"Yes. Perhaps you will emulate the Virgin Mary herself! Bear your child when she did. That would be a joy, would it not?" He eyed her keenly but kindly.

She shook her head uncertainly.

"Thanea, nighean," he said – that is, daughter, "this of the child? How do you think of it? Begotten as it was by a cruel and savage man? Do you dread it, the birth? More than any young woman at a first child? How see you it?"

"I, I do not know. To bear Owen's seed! Yet . . . he is mine also. And has shared all the hazards with me. Endangered

65

as I was. Yet still he moves within me. I cannot hate him . . ."

The man smiled. "I see that you think of it as a man-child! But – it is good. You must not mislike him, nighean. No fault lies with the child. He is innocent, and deserves, needs your love, whatever the father's sin and guilt. You have both come through great dangers, been preserved as by miracles. Who knows for what purposes perhaps. Love the child, girl. Look with joy to his birth, not dread. Never that. You have not been brought this far for no purpose."

She nodded.

"Feel safe, secure here. This will be your home for so long as you desire it. We have no nuns here, so you will be the abbey's only woman! But there are women nearby, in the village. I will see that some come to attend you. Fear for nothing. Rest as you require. But when you are rested, you will find sufficient work to do. You must not feel estranged. We are all God's servants, and we will cherish you. Is there aught that you want? Now?"

She did smile then. "Yes. You are kind, kind. But – I am still hungry! A little more food . . . ?"

"Ha! That is an excellent sign. Good. You shall have it. When last did you eat?"

"I have forgotten. But it seems long!"

Serf left her then. By the time that a monk arrived with more provender, Thanea was fast asleep again.

The next morning when she wakened, it was to find women's clothing at her bedside, simple but a deal better in quality than the rags she had been wearing when she arrived at Culross. Whoever had brought them had been thoughtful enough to ensure that they were sufficiently wide about the middle to encompass her increasing girth. There was food again, and warmish water in a basin. Washing first, and grateful to do so, then eating and donning the clothes, Thanea ventured outside.

It was to a cold morning's scene of activity, even though the early winter's day was yet young. The Celtic Church was a very practical one, concerned with works equally with prayer and teaching, recognising worship as to be evidenced in deeds and daily living as well as in words and meditation.

66

Thanea had found this principle in Monenna's convent and in the Whittingehame nunnery, to be sure. Here and now the worship appeared to be the building of a new and large house.

The girl, distinctly shy in the circumstances, although as a princess shyness had been trained out of her, went to watch, but at a distance. Fully a score of men were at work, including Abbot Serf himself. Some were lopping and trimming the green boughs of trees, saplings. Others were pleating and entwining these together, interlacing them, a task which called for strong hands and arms and considerable expertise. Some were hammering and nailing the interlaced boughs into frameworks to form hoardings. Others were trundling up barrow-loads of small stones, gravel and shell-sand from the beach. Serf was superintending the placing and digging-in of the upright sapling hoardings, two at a time some two feet apart to form walling for the house, this to be infilled with the rubble and stones. Half a dozen of these frames were already in position, upright, constituting most of one side of a fair-sized building.

The young woman's presence was quickly spotted, although the monks, young and old, were careful not to stare. Soon the abbot came over to her, to enquire how she felt this morning, and to hope that the clothing obtained was not displeasing to her. She thanked him for all his forethought, declared that she was well, and said that she wanted to help. What were they building here, and what might she do to aid in their work?

Serf explained that this was a hospice they were erecting, for travellers, where they might offer hospitality to wayfarers, especially seafarers, something much required hereabouts. As to her helping them, he looked doubtful. But she assured him that she was strong and knew how to use her hands – the convent and the shepherding had taught her that. Could she not select and trim saplings, to start with? She had seen this done often.

So, eyed interestedly by the other workers, she set to with a small axe to cut off small branches from the pile of green wood gathered, and to make heaps of the different thicknesses of trimmed boughs. She found monks coming to assist her, but assured them that she did not require help. Thanea, however humble-minded and friendly she was determined to be, did not realise that her king's daughter's upbringing was apt to reveal itself.

Men were arriving all the time with cartloads of wood and stones. The most difficult part of the process was the emptying of the infilling rubble down between the upright hoardings, for their height, of course, demanded step-ladders be used, with men having to climb up with loads of stones to throw in, a slow and wearisome task. Thanea did not offer to assist in this.

Actually, she soon tired, however willing a toiler. Perhaps this became evident, for presently Serf came to her and said that he thought that she had done sufficient in her present state. She asked what else, of less heavy labour, she might do, asserting that she was used to working with bees, wax and candle-making, also weaving, knitting and embroidery. This was not the season for garden and orchard work, but surely there was something that she could effect?

So she was taken to a shed where the honeycombs were stored, and there, able to sit, she worked away quite effectively. A monk brought her a brazier of glowing charcoal to keep her warm.

Towards midday a bell rang, and she went out to see what this signified. She found workers going into the little church for worship of a different kind. Following them in, to kneel at the back, she listened to a short service of readings, prayers and psalm-chanting, conducted not by Serf, but by a senior monk, the abbot worshipping amongst the rest. Thanea noted that the candles flickering on the altar were not so well made as were her own, lumpish and with the wicks burning askew and dribbling wax in consequence. Here was something to which she *could* usefully contribute.

After the service it was meal-time, and she went to eat in the kitchen building. Deliberately the young woman did not go to sit beside the abbot, not to seem presumptuous, but chose to eat with the elderly monk who had taken the service and who introduced himself as Bishop Gabhran. It seemed that Abbot Serf had two bishops under him at Culross – and others in his abbeys and monasteries elsewhere, at Burntisland, Carnock, Airthrey and other places in Fortrenn, for he was the most important churchman in the mormaordom. Thanea was insufficiently versed in Church matters to understand that, unlike the Romish Church, the Celtic one was abbatial, monastic, not hierarchic, and bishops served under abbots but with

68

their own distinctive duties and offices. They were, in fact, the *ministers*, where the abbots were the monastic authorities and mission-leaders. Most abbots had been bishops before they were raised to abbacies.

After eating an ample meal, Serf demonstrated his authority by ordering the girl to go and rest for an hour or two.

Then it was back to candle-making. It gave Thanea real pleasure to go, presently, back to the church and to substitute fresh and carefully wicked and rolled candles for those guttering there – and when evening prayer took place, to have the fact noted and herself congratulated and thanked.

She retired to bed that night more satisfied with life than she had felt for long.

So the days passed at Culross and became weeks, and Thanea found herself fitted into the life and rhythm of the abbey with a minimum of difficulty. There were certain problems, of course, for any woman in a man's establishment, especially a pregnant one, but the monks were consistently helpful, tactful and understanding, indeed interested in her condition and eager to see the outcome. Serf was quite frequently absent, with his other charges to keep an eye on, but the girl made an especial friend of Bishop Gabhran, finding him a gentle, kindly man of whom she could feel less in awe than of St Serf – not that the latter sought to awe, but his personal authority could not be ignored even by a one-time princess.

She got to know some of the women of the nearby fishing-village, but was aware that here she was not accepted quite so fully as at the abbey. This was understandable. She was a stray female, with child, unknown as to background and this not explained, clearly having no husband and taken into a male company to become part of it, where they themselves were not. So most kept their distance, the more so when some of their menfolk made lewd comments. But when, on one occasion, St Serf himself came with her to introduce her to the village midwife, jeers and jokes ceased, and the women became more respectful, if still not very forthcoming. The abbot's authority told here, as elsewhere.

The midwife, Seana, experienced as she was, asserted that Thanea would come to her time in mid-December.

It was at the beginning of that month that Serf mentioned that he had news of the great Arthur, High King of the Britons, and Thanea's uncle. He was coming east on a visit to King Loth. The Mormaor Nechtan of Fortrenn had sent to inform him, Serf, and requested that he should go and see Arthur, there to seek his aid on Nechtan's behalf to restrain raiding bands from Strathclyde from harassing the western Fortrenn lands of Strathearn and the Mounth of Teith, this having become a grievous nuisance. Nechtan did not want actually to invade Strathclyde in retaliation, which could result in major warfare; much better if Arthur, who was High King of all the Britons and therefore overlord of the King of Strathclyde, would use his influence to have the raiding stopped. Arthur was a Christian, and might well better heed Serf than any pagan messenger. And Serf knew King Arthur.

Thanea was much interested, naturally. Why would the High King be visiting her father, with whom, since his lapse from Christianity and the death of Anna his sister and Thanea's mother, he had not been on the best of terms? Serf did not know that, but guessed that it might well have something to do with Saxon advances into the Anglian kingdom of the Brigantes, south of Tweed, and the Cheviot Hills, bordering on Loth's territories, of which he had heard. He revealed that he, Serf, had links with Arthur through his mother, Alma, a Cruithne princess from Galloway in Strathclyde. He also admitted that he felt uncomfortable about visiting King Loth's court in the circumstances, and wondered how he would conceal his anger at that man's treatment of his daughter – for of course he must not indicate that he knew that she was alive.

Thanea sympathised, but said that he must not let her affairs complicate his mission. She would dearly have liked to have her brother Gawain know that she had survived, but recognised that this was too dangerous to be considered.

When she learned that Serf intended to set out next day across Forth in one of the abbey's boats, she summoned up courage to ask him if he would, in fact, tell someone of her safety and present whereabouts – the nun Maura at Whittingehame. She could be trusted, surely, to keep the secret, especially under the abbot's strict orders. It took the girl not a little resolution to tell Serf why she wanted this done and to trouble him with her purpose – but she was encouraged thereto by the fact that that man was notably fond of the animal world. He had a pet sheep, which he had saved and nurtured as a motherless lamb and which now, when permitted, followed him about like a dog; also a tame robin, which liked to sit on his shoulder. So she ventured her extraordinary request. She had left her dog Leot at Whittingehame. He had been her faithful and constant companion, and had tried to save her from the rape. If St Serf could bring him back to her . . .

The abbot patted her head. "Nighean," he said – he always called her that now, pronouncing it Nine, "it will be my pleasure. Any friend of yours is a friend of mine. I will be glad to call at Whittingehame nunnery. And if your Leot is still there I will bring him to you."

Thanea burst into tears. She recognised that she was in an emotional state, something to do with her condition, no doubt.

In the days which followed, during Serf's absence, the young woman recognised more than that. She was aware that the child within her somehow seemed to have dropped lower, causing additional inconveniences. Walking became less easy and she often felt new movements and contractions. When, a little alarmed that the baby might be in some trouble, she told the midwife Seana, she was assured that this was normal, and represented the infant's changing of position preparatory to a head-down delivery. Two weeks now, perhaps . . .

Reassured, she began to count the days.

Then, after a week, Serf returned, with Leot trotting at his garron's tail. It was all dramatic and astonishing, for the girl was sitting in the candle-shed working by the brazier when the dog came bounding in, knocking over a trayful of melted wax pans, indeed all but knocking herself over in his so vehement joy, paws up, to lick her face, yelping and whimpering, tail and whole hindquarters wagging. Presumably he had obtained and recognised her scent – a thought that one could smell sufficiently for that – and come hurtling in. When Serf appeared at the open door, Thanea was all but having to protect herself from the effusive and continuing canine affection. Not that she complained, the joy reciprocated, although Serf was somewhat concerned for her safety.

When matters calmed down somewhat, the girl was given a report. The dog had still been at Whittingehame, and the nuns had been sorry to see him go, although he had told only Maura why he was taking him, and to whom, she sworn to secrecy. As to what had happened at Traprain, he said that he had managed to hide his feelings towards Loth, and had not seen the Prince Gawain. He had consulted with King Arthur, who was there to co-ordinate his various sub-kings' strength against the Saxon hordes who were invading the Anglian lands north of Diera and York, and so threatening the Celtic areas across Tweed. Arthur had agreed to warn young Morcant of Strathclyde, at Dumbarton, to control his people better or suffer his displeasure. Arthur was a fine man, a good and devout Christian as well as a great warrior and leader of all the Celtic peoples. Thanea should be proud to be his niece. So the excursion to Lothian had been a success.

The young woman told of her developing condition and its signs. No, she was not afraid of the birth pangs; after what she had been through, this most natural woman's experience should not alarm her. *Should* not . . . !

Eight days later, early in the morning, her pains started. She had had warning beforehand, with backache and a show of blood. So she was not taken by surprise. But the dread and tension were not to be denied. She rang the bell which Serf had provided, and the night-duty monk was not long in appearing. Leot, at the bedside, growled at the man's arrival. He said that he would go for the midwife.

In mid-forenoon, after a labour which Thanea was assured was unexceptional, although she found it taxing enough, her child was born – and, she was informed, normal and without blemish; which added mental relief to physical, for she had not been able wholly to banish fears that, owing to all the stresses and upheavals which the little creature had been through within her, he might have suffered some physical harm.

For *he* it was indeed, a man-child, as somehow she had known it would be. All dreads past when she heard the first crying, Thanea sank away into thankful sleep, with Leot licking her hand.

6

Serf, sharing the bedside with the dog, was all congratulation and acclaim – a Yuletide birth, like the Virgin Mary's. Who could tell what their Heavenly Father had in store for this lusty-lunged newcomer? What was nighean going to call him?

The proud mother admitted that a number of thoughts had occurred to her on this subject. There was Fergus, the shepherd who had befriended her when she so required a friend. There was Gawain, a family name, the brother of whom she was most fond. There was Serf himself, who called her nighean, his daughter. She hesitated a little. There was even Leot, her other friend here. Leot was a good man's name, after all . . .

"You could not call your son after a dog!" the abbot protested.

"Not *after* the dog, no. But Leot is the same name as Lot and Loth. Only differently spelt. There have been great men of the name. Is there not a Mormaor of Mar of that name? Or is he dead? This Leot was my companion when I was carrying my son, all those months on the hills; and sought to save me from Owen. And now Leot guards the boy as though he was his own."

"M'mm. Nevertheless, fond as I am of God's animal creation, I could scarcely christen your son with your dog's name, nighean."

"Not *after* Leot," she insisted. "But . . . perhaps you are right. I would have liked him ever to remember Leot, that is all."

"I see that, yes." Serf stroked his chin. "See you, there could be another way. To keep the memory without so naming. If you called the child master or friend of Leot? Something of that sort. Ceann-Leot? No, master of Leot sounds arrogant, as though lord of some man of the name. But . . . master of the *dog*? Ha, there *is* a name, Kentigern – that is, the

73

Hound-Master, he who keeps the king's hounds. How would that serve?"

"Kentigern? Kentigern!" She savoured the sound and meaning of that. "Yes, Leot's little master. That would sound well. Kentigern! Good – Kentigern it shall be. I like that. I thank you . . ."

"I have never christened a child with such a name, or such *reason* for a name, before. But then, this is a very special infant, is it not? How feels it to be a mother, nighean?"

"I do not know fully, yet. But I am grateful, and proud. I have a son. He is born out of wedlock – but he must not suffer for that."

"He will not. I am no prophet – but I make bold to foretell that your young Kentigern will be a prince amongst men. And a much better prince than his father, or his grandsires indeed, both of whom are kings!"

Thanea recovered quickly, with no complications, and was able to take part in the Christmastide celebrations. The baby prospered, with Leot in constant attendance. The child was duly baptised Kentigern; but such a resounding style hardly suited such a tiny scrap of humanity, and Serf began to refer to him as Mungo, which meant manikin; and the by-name was taken up by the monks and even by Thanea herself. The entire abbatial establishment adopted the infant as its own, something highly unusual in monastic quarters.

The girl, for her part, found herself wholly accepted also, and grew to look on Culross Abbey as her home, with no desire to leave and find another. After a month or two, with young Mungo flourishing and no problems developing, however, she did recognise that she ought to speak to Serf on the subject, however unwilling she was to contemplate any departure. His reaction, when she did, was very positive, like most aspects of the man.

"Why leave us?" he demanded. "You are happy here, nighean, are you not? And we all much enjoy your being with us. And Mungo *belongs* here, does he not? Your coming to us has been, I say, a godsend. Why leave? Aye, and where would you go?"

"I do not know. Some nunnery, perhaps. I could not go back to Whittingehame. But another? Although – they would not

74

take in me *and* my child, I think, without me telling why and who I was."

"No. That is not to be thought of. If not in a nunnery, how would you live? And where? Casting yourself adrift on a different sea! No, no, nighean – you must bide here, where you have been sent. And you are useful. You brighten our lives."

Thankfully she accepted it, and the subject was not raised again.

Leot settled in at Culross entirely well also. It was amusing that when the dog was not on duty with little Mungo, he was quite often to be seen keeping company with the tame sheep; they walked together like old friends, to Serf's delight.

Thanea was never idle. Looking after Mungo took up more of her time than she would have thought. But she found a sufficiency of duties for herself in the establishment, which were appreciated. The candle-making, important as a source of income, for supply to the neighbourhood, as well as for the abbey's own use, was now left entirely to herself; and this entailed, of course, much work with the bees. And the honey was important also, for sweetening, cookery and honey wine. As spring advanced, the garden and orchards demanded much attention, at which she was quite experienced; and the abbey had its own flock of sheep and herd of cattle, where she and Leot could help. She could spin wool and weave cloth. Moreover, she discovered in herself quite a talent for painting and illustration, especially in the traditional Celtic designs and symbols which had always fascinated her; and Serf was glad to use this for the decorating and enhancing of prayer- and psalm-sheets and holy missals. The young woman felt, as time went on, that she was earning her keep.

Nevertheless, Thanea did know bouts of a sort of restlessness, especially when, in May, the cuckoos began to call their haunting, repetitive invitation to roam. Perhaps it was in her blood, the legacy of a long line of sub-kings and warriors who had always roved afar. Brought up in the Lammermuir foothill country, she had been used to freedom to walk and ride with her brothers and friends, and even alone at times, for who would attack a princess? Now, on occasion, distances called. The baby, of course, was a tie, if a beloved one, but the urge was there. She did go sea-fishing in a boat with the monks, taking the child with her, which helped. But still those cuckoos called and called . . .

Serf was often absent, superintending his other monastic centres, and after his return from one such, in June, Thanea involuntarily came out with her envy for his freedom to travel. Eyeing her keenly, discerningly, the man questioned.

"You feel held here, nighean?" he wondered. "Like some penned ewe with a lamb? You, used to a less enclosed life than an abbey's?"

"It is foolishness," she admitted. "I am so happy here, everyone so kind. Yet sometimes I find far places calling. Not to go to bide in, only to visit, to see, to travel. Can you understand it?"

"I can – for I know it well myself. Only I can indulge myself, aye and call it my duty!"

"Yes. And I have Mungo, which should content me."

"He ties you, yes. But he is now of six months and sturdy. He could travel with you, on a horse, in your arms. No?"

"I would think so, yes."

"We could contrive a sling of sorts to bear much of the weight, ease the carrying. You could try that."

"That would be good. But where could I go? Round and about Culross?"

"You could come with me on some of my shorter journeys. See you, I go to my little monastery at Kinghorn soon. A score of miles. Could you, with Mungo, ride so far? Near four hours. With a babe?"

"I would think so. That would be most kind. We could try it. Try the riding and carrying first . . ."

So the thing was attempted. They made a sling out of plaiding which, when hanging round Thanea's neck, cradled the baby comfortably and securely whilst leaving the girl's hands free to control the horse. She had always been a good horsewoman, and found the burden and the motion no problem. She took to riding around the Culross area frequently, and Mungo obviously found no fault, gurgling happily when he did not find the trotting movement rocking him to sleep.

His mother knew a considerable sense of freedom in consequence.

* * *

Two weeks later, then, they set off, Serf, Thanea and Mungo, with Leot at heel, on two sturdy, stocky garrons, long of mane and tail. They rode eastwards, round Torry Bay to Kinniny Point, which by now the girl knew well. But beyond was new to her, a coastline of shallow coves and beaches, a few backed by low sand-dunes, where oyster-catchers waded and knots and dunlin flighted. Serf sang as he rode, for he had a fine and tuneful voice, and Thanea joined in where she could, picking up the lilt if not the words. Mungo added his own burbling contributions.

They came to a fishing community, which Serf named Rosyth, where they paused, for there were a few Christians here. What these thought of the abbot's present company was anybody's guess. Thereafter they turned inland, to cut across the base of a thrusting peninsula projecting more than a mile out, which very considerably narrowed the Forth estuary here, practically halving it indeed. Beyond they came to another bay and fishing hamlet, Inverkeithing by name, where there was a tiny and humble church which Serf had established, and where he held a brief little service for such of the folk as were not away fishing and did not remain unbelievers. They were halfway to their destination now, the girl learned, as they were provided with cold fish and oatcakes. Mungo here got his sustenance also. Thanea was long past any embarrassment at breast-feeding in front of others.

Serf explained that because of the Mormaor Nechtan's respect, he was permitted to play the missionary anywhere in Fortrenn, and he had had considerable success, especially along this seaboard, where fisherfolk seemed to be more receptive of Christ's teachings than the herdsmen and farmers inland – this, he imagined, because they were more apt to be endangered by storms and hazards and so felt the need of divine protection.

They rode on, Mungo asleep.

Round the wide but shallow loop of another large bay, Dalgety, they presently came to a haven amongst fine woodlands at the head of a long stretch of the most brilliant white sands Thanea had ever seen. She said that she would enjoy bathing here – but this was scarcely the time. The village was called Aberdour, with the Dour Burn entering the firth here.

Now they had only another mile or two to reach the Ross

Point of Wester Kinghorn, where the monastery was sited on a grassy shelf near the shore. It was a modest enough place compared with Culross, six monks and as many trainees under an aged priest who was all but blind, but who appeared to be competent enough and obviously beloved of his little flock.

Serf's welcome by all was touching, his authority by no means inhibiting fond regard and affection. Thanea and her child were accepted because of this, she and Mungo being introduced simply as God's children in especial care. A somewhat weary Leot was not neglected.

They were to spend the night here, and a couch was found for the young woman in an empty hut within the enclosing green ramparts. After a meal, Serf was to interview the novices and to examine them as to their readiness for promotion to fuller status. It was a fine July evening, and Thanea took child and dog, to sit above the beach and gaze out southwards.

This was something of a bitter-sweet experience, for it was the first time that she had been able to see her hills of home. The Forth here was some seven miles wide, and almost directly opposite she could see the distinctive and prominent lion-shaped hill which was being called after that lion amongst men, her uncle, the High King Arthur, rising out of Middle Lothian. But much further off, to the south-east, she could make out the long skyline of the Lammermuir Hills and, if one knew just where to peer, it was even possible to distinguish the hump-backed silhouette of Traprain Law, darker against the green background. That would be fully thirty miles away.

She wondered and wondered anew at her strange fate and the extraordinary sequence of events which had brought her here, with her child, cared for and respected even – and yet barred from ever returning across this water to her home and family, outcast, believed dead on one side of Forth, and cherished on the other, that water down and up which her coracle had drifted. Why her, Thanea nic Loth?

It had been Serf's intention to return to Culross the next day. But it transpired that one of the senior monks had gone on a brief mission inland to a little group of Christians in the Dunearn Hills some miles away, taking two of the novices with him, for experience. They were expected to return on the morrow. They would be greatly disappointed not to see, and their progress not

78

to be considered by, Abbot Serf. That man, ever concerned for others, felt that he must stay and give them the opportunity the others had had. So he would delay departure. Meantime, he suggested to Thanea that they might visit his diseart, some eight miles further along the coast. This was his quiet sanctuary, for occasional retreat. All Celtic missionaries had these lonely places, often on little isles, to which they could retire for contemplation, prayer and spiritual renewal. Serf's was no island but a cave above the shore.

Thanea was nothing loth.

They rode by clifftops to the opening of a wide, shallow bay or crescent of shore, with the hilly land drawing back from it, which Serf named as Raith. Part-way along this they passed a community, part fishing but mainly concerned with farming and pasture inland, at which the abbot ruefully admitted that he had had no success with his Christianising efforts. But he would continue to try, although not today. Beyond, a couple of miles, higher cliffs began to rise again, forming the eastern horn of the bay. Here, after a mile, a prominent, upthrusting rock represented the site of an abandoned Pictish fort, some of the defensive ramparts still evident. Raven's Craig it was called, apparently. And a little way below it a narrow, steep and winding track led down the cliff, no place for horses. So they tethered their mounts on a grassy shelf where there was ample grazing, and Serf, taking Mungo in his arms for safety, led the way down, concerned that Thanea might feel dizzy on that precarious descent above the waves, although she assured him that she had a good head for heights.

Two-thirds of the way to the rocky foot, without mishap, Leot bringing up the rear, they came to another lesser shelf, pink with wild thyme, no more than four feet wide and still some fifty feet above the shore, along which they came to the opening of a cave in the red sandstone cliff. The entrance was fairly narrow and not high either, but it opened out considerably within. Serf ushered Thanea in, with something almost like pride.

She was fascinated. The cavern's interior showed the evident handiwork of man. Clearly the almost ruby-red sandstone was soft, and apt for carving and excavation; indeed amongst the first items to catch the girl's eye were a mallet and iron chisels for stonecraft and mason-work. Benches had been cut in the walls, wide enough to lie upon; and near the entrance was contrived a shelf at chest height, obviously an altar, for above it was carved a cross within its circle representing eternal life; and at the side a bowl scooped out, for holy water. Elsewhere round the walls was more carving, of typical Celtic interlacing design, with decorative birds, animals and symbols. Thanea was loud in wonder and admiration.

The abbot was distinctly like a boy in his demonstration and explanations. He had done it all himself, he declared, over the years. There was more to do yet. Here he could worship God undisturbed and undistracted, with his heart and soul yes, but also with his hands and wits. Also his eyes, for the outlook from the cave mouth was glorious. He had chosen this cavern carefully. This entire coast, from here eastwards for some miles, was honeycombed with caves in the soft sandstone, indeed it was known by the name of Wemyss, from *uamh*, a cave. This one had the advantage of its fairly narrow entrance, which could be hung with a sheepskin curtain to keep out wind and rain. Moreover, there was a crack in the roof, which he had widened into a chimney to carry away the smoke of a fire, the flue opening on to the cliff-face above. See – there was the fireplace. And driftwood gathered from the shore below. And, best of all, at the very back, deep in, was fresh water trickling down, where he had fashioned another bowl to catch the good water. And the beach was rich in mussels, cockles and the occasional oyster. He could dwell here for days at a time, in his diseart.

Thanea, entranced, said that she had never seen the like, and announced that *she* would love to roost in this eagle's nest of a place – although she realised that this could not be considered in a saint's holy place and hermitage. The man admitted that they could hardly dwell together here, but said that she might come here on her own, with Mungo, on occasion if she so wished, and if she did not mind the loneliness. She would be safe enough, for none of the local folk ever visited it. Indeed, he confessed that, apart from Bishop Gabhran, she was the only person whom he had ever brought here.

She was the more appreciative.

They went and sat on the stone bench at the door, looking out, the girl cradling Mungo in her arms, Leot peering downwards. The vista was indeed spectacular. Here they were directly opposite Aberlady Bay, a dozen miles away to the south, from which her coracle had been cast off. The Lothian coastline was spread before them, fully forty miles of it, from beyond Arthur's Craig on the west to the Craig of Bass and the conical Berwick Law on the east, with all the intervening islands and the hinterland of hills, the Pentlands, the Morthwaites and the Lammermuirs. Nearer at hand, this Fife shore held its own challenges to the eye, although, placed where they were, down a cliff, these could not be so extensively seen. And Serf pointed out the pink thyme, the silver eyebright and the yellow bedstraw and other flowers which managed to grow from crevices of the rock, and to the seabirds which huddled on ledges and projections, kittiwakes, guillemots, fulmars and various gulls, all beautiful in their own perfection. God loved beauty, and ordained it for His own joy, whether men saw it or not.

They ate the provision the Kinghorn monks had given them, washed down with ice-cold water from the rear of the cave, Thanea feeding Mungo, who had grown restive. Then, after a prayer before the little altar, and the renewal and blessing of the holy water stoup, they climbed up that track again to the clifftop, and the garrons, for their return journey.

The child loved being carried on horseback, the motion always producing cries and chuckles of delight until sleep overtook him.

Thanea realised that she had never been so happy and fulfilled in all her life.

Part Two

7

Kentigern's childhood was probably all but unique, reared in a community of monks, one infant with one woman – and one dog. But it was a happy, advantageous and educative one, rich in love and affection, but disciplined also, the boy's mental and spiritual development matching the physical.

Thanea herself knew a great fulfilment as she watched him grow, accepting her responsibilities but gladly embracing the joys of motherhood. And Serf was as good as any grandfather to him, while the monks vied with each other in replacing the family which he was not to know.

He grew and developed apace, and was clearly going to be of a determined but sunny nature.

For her part, the young woman developed also, for after all she had been only in her late teens when she came to Culross, and there is growth of various important sorts to be looked for after that. Her dire experiences admittedly had matured her early, in some respects; but as well as parenthood, the monastic life, the emphasis on religion and worship, and above all the prevailing climate of love, kindness and selflessness, much moulded the further fulfilment of her character in a way which would have been unlikely indeed had she continued to live the life of a princess at Traprain. Very quickly she came to recognise her good fortune, her gain instead of her loss.

Not that she spent much of her time in such introspection – she was far too busy for that. What with mothering, bee-keeping, candle-making, mead-distilling, gardening, fruit-preserving in the various seasons, spinning, weaving, knitting and embroidery, and exercising her talent in painting and illustration, she was seldom idle. Her forced training as a shepherd served the abbey in good stead, for she persuaded Serf greatly to increase the small flock of sheep, sending them to pasture on the hilly ground known as the Uplands of

Devilla, nothing like the Lammermuirs but fair feeding-ground nevertheless, amongst whins and scattered hawthorn trees, hitherto little used save by deer. And this, in a year or two, much added to the abbey's income, enabling Serf to take in and train more monks, and to build additional little churches in the Fothrif and Ochil Hills area. Also it took Thanea away from the monastic premises quite frequently, to look after *her* growing flock, which helped to counter any feelings of restriction in the monkish disciplines. And she continued to accompany Serf on his tours of inspection and supervision to his many mission stations and little Christian congregations, some quite far afield in the Fortrenn mormaordom, northwards and westwards as far as the Firth of Tay and the wide strath of Earn, in which lay Forteviot itself, the mormaordom capital. On these sallies they did not always take young Mungo who, once breast-feeding was past, could be left perfectly happily in the care of the monks and Leot.

It was on one such journey, to Dunning in Strathearn on the far northern slopes of the Ochils, that Serf announced that he would like to pay a visit to the Mormaor Nechtan and his Christian wife, Eva. There were rumours rife that the High King of the Britons, Thanea's uncle, Arthur, had fought another great battle against the Saxons; and Nechtan would be apt to know the truth of it. And the abbot liked to see Queen Eva occasionally, to encourage her in her efforts to bring up her children in the Christian faith, contrary to the druidical urgings of her husband's advisers. He had baptised her first child, a son; but now there was a daughter, and Nechtan was doubtful about letting her be turned into a Christian. So he would wish to win him over in this matter. The problem was, now, could Thanea appear at Forteviot with him without revealing her identity? Not that there was much coming and going between Fortrenn and Lothian, for they were in quite different Celtic high kingdoms, Lothian part of Arthur's Brythonic empire, based on Carlisle in Cumbria; and Fortrenn in the Gaelic high kingdom of Alba, based on Inverness. Nevertheless, there could be the risk of word getting from one to the other, especially on a matter so extraordinary as the survival of King Loth's daughter.

Thanea well recognised that. But she did not want to restrict her protector's plans and wishes. Could they not go without revealing who she was? Just say that she was a Christian woman whom he was sheltering?

Serf looked doubtful.

"Why not say that I come from a nunnery on the other side of Forth? Which is the truth – Whittingehame. Come on some mission. Yes, that is it. Say that you have brought me, a woman, that I might perhaps be of some use to this Queen Eva, as to her children's instruction in the faith. Another woman. Would that not serve? Help her, perhaps, as a man could not?"

"Ha – that is a notion, yes. Call you by another name . . ."

"Yes. You name me nighean – so make it Ninenna, a nun in training. Say that I have a child of my own, but am now committed to God's service. In penitence. Which is truth also . . ."

So it was agreed.

Forteviot was in fact not far off, only four miles or so from Dunning, where the Water of May joined the Earn, easy going after the Ochil Hills they had had to cross to get here. As they rode, Serf explained to the girl the differences between the Brythonic and Albannach high kingdoms, both Celtic but having their own systems of government and their own traditions from far back. He, Serf, knew it all well, for he was of both, his father having been a Brythonic sub-king, and his mother a Cruithne from Galloway; Cruithne was the true name for the inhabitants of Alba, although the Romans had called them Picts because they used a pictorial or symbolic language instead of a written one.

The main difference between the two regimes was that the Cruithne succession to kingship and lordship was matrilineal, that is, through the female descent. The rulers were men, yes, but they succeeded through their mothers not their fathers. Which was why Mormaor Nechtan was more concerned that his daughter should not have the doubtful stigma of Christianity, as his son was seemingly to have, for eventually the girl's son would be Mormaor of Fortrenn. They used the term mormaor, meaning great lord, rather than king, although kings they were, sub-kings like his own father, Proc of Cantyre. They were called the *ri*, under the High King, the *Ard Righ*. There were always seven of these in Alba, Fortrenn the most southerly, Ross the northernmost, with Moray, Buchan, Mar, Atholl and Angus in between. The High King was appointed by the *ri* or sub-kings, always of the royal stock, his seat at Inverness in Moray. He was the equivalent of King Arthur of the Britons, whereas Nechtan was of Loth. Unfortunately, Christianity had not reached Inverness, and none of the mormaordoms had embraced the faith; indeed Fortrenn, in allowing him, Serf, to missionarise here, was the most hopeful, this because he was useful to Nechtan as a go-between with the Britons, especially the Strathclyde ones, who could be very troublesome for Fortrenn.

Thanea knew some of this but not all; and she had not realised that Serf was himself a prince, his father having been the Brythonic King Proc of Cantyre.

They came to Forteviot, near the abandoned Roman camp of the same name. From any distance, it did not look an impressive site for a capital city, unlike Traprain on its whaleback summit. But the fact that a Roman camp had been placed here spoke for itself, and closer inspection showed that, in fact, marshland and flooded ground can be just as effectively defensive as can rocks and cliffs. For here, where the Water of May came rushing down from the Ochils, to join wide Earn, and was often in spate, a flood-plain had developed; and contained in this, and the rivers, was Forteviot, to be reached only by easily defended narrow causeways of stone. The town within covered only perhaps fifty acres, although there were farming and pasture communities around, behind the marshland.

The newcomers were duly challenged at one of the causeway-heads, but Serf's announcement that he sought the Mormaor Nechtan gained them entry. Within its timber stockading, the little city was not unlike Traprain, only more level, with narrow streets and wynds and the usual wattle and daub whitewashed housing.

It did not take them long to reach the palace, a typical wooden hall-house, the tallest building there, with banners flapping lazily in the breeze – and by that time they had picked up a tail of interested children and barking dogs. They were informed by house guards that Nechtan mac Cormac was out hunting, but that Queen Eva was within.

They were ushered through a great hall and into a grass-grown courtyard behind, where fruit trees grew and where a woman sat at ease, stitching at an embroidery frame, a toddling girl played with a puppy and a boy of about four years swung on a rope hanging from a tree bough, a pleasing domestic scene.

The woman was pleasing of aspect also, not beautiful but quite comely, fair-haired and plumpish. She glanced up, with a quick smile at Serf, and rose. "Abbot Serf! How good! Here is joy!" She looked at Thanea questioningly.

"Queen Eva, God's blessing upon you. And these little ones. I rejoice to see all appearing in good state. I was at Dunning and thought to visit you and the mormaor. Here is one, Ninenna, who has come to Culross from a nunnery in Lothian."

"A nun? I have heard of nuns, but never seen one." She considered Thanea interestedly, question still in her eyes.

"I am not yet a nun, lady," the young woman said. "But a believer, a penitent. Abbot Serf most kindly allows me to accompany him, on occasion. That I may speak perhaps with the women, where that may help in spreading God's word. Speak with some understanding of women's needs and, and difficulties. For these are not unknown to me!"

"Ninenna has had a child. Born out of wedlock," Serf added. "So she is not ignorant of problems. And wishes now to aid others. So she travels with me, usefully."

The queen absorbed that, but found another smile. "We women have our problems, yes." She turned. "Come, Finan. Greet Abbot Serf. And here is Cara. Has she not grown?"

The children were introduced, and themselves introduced the puppy, which Thanea picked up and allowed to lick her face, which pleased the youngsters. They all went within, to give the visitors refreshment.

When Serf began to question the queen as to her husband's present attitude to baptism for the girl Cara, Thanea asked the young Finan whether he had the wherewithal to draw or paint pictures. She was led off upstairs to an attic chamber which served as a playroom, followed by the pup, and there employed her talent for illustration in entertaining the pair by sketching animals and birds, some in the traditional Celtic designs, and even the puppy itself, this on a smooth slate and using a pointed splinter of the same. She was entertained, in turn, by the youngsters' efforts at copying. By the time that they were summoned downstairs for the evening meal, she had established a happy relationship with the children at least.

The mormaor had returned and proved to be a stocky, square-built man in his mid-thirties, dark, with a somewhat brooding and anxious look to him. But he greeted the young woman civilly enough, and indeed eyed her in assessing and not unflattering fashion – for she had lost none of her good looks. He and Serf seemed to be on friendly terms, although he was obviously not of an effusive nature. There was no difficult nor strained atmosphere evident.

The meal over, very much a family occasion, and the queen taking the children off to bed, the others moved over to the lesser hall fireside – for it was late autumn and the evenings held a chill. It was clear that they were going to spend the night here. Thanea wondered whether she was intended to remain with the men; but it became evident that this was so, Serf continuing to include her in the conversation, and Nechtan himself handing her a tankard of honey wine. They quickly reverted to the subject of Arthur mac Uther Pendragon.

It seemed that there had been a major battle, and not so very far away, in the Brigantes' kingdom of Bernicia near where King Lancelot had his seat at Bamburgh some way south of the Tweed. This was now an Anglian kingdom, but Lancelot had had a Celtic mother. The Angles, of York, Deira and Bernicia, were not now the principal enemies of the Celts, as once they had been; it was the fierce and aggressive Saxons, a Germanic people, who were the menace. They had conquered most of the east of southern Britain, formerly all Celtic land, and now they were ever probing northwards, raiding the Anglian territories equally with the Brythonic, Welsh and Cornish. They were scarcely yet a menace to Alba, but that would undoubtedly come, for they were great seafarers and could land in Fife or Angus just as easily as they could in Bernicia or Lothian. Hence Nechtan's concern.

The warrior Arthur had won this latest battle apparently – he had the reputation of winning all his battles, after having been victorious in no fewer than twelve, after the famous Badon

Hill a score of years earlier; but with these Saxons, winning individual battles did not imply winning the ongoing war. Indeed it seemed that no sooner were Lancelot's foes driven off than another threat had developed far to the south-west, in the Lancaster area where Cumbria met Wales, and Arthur had had to march off forthwith to counter that.

"These Saxons are devils!" Nechtan declared. "Will they never be content with what they have gained? All these raiders from the east, the Angles, the Jutes, the Goths and the Norsemen are bad enough. But the Saxons . . . !"

"They have the lust for power as well as for lands," Serf said. "It is well that we have Arthur, you in Alba as well as his own kingdoms."

"I know it. But I would be the more thankful for him if he would keep some of his own kingdoms in better order! Strathclyde in especial."

"You are still suffering from their raiding?"

"Yes. But a month ago they were back over in my high ground to the west, the Mounth of Teith, burning, slaying, stealing cattle. It is beyond all bearing."

"I spoke with Arthur on this, at Traprain. And he promised to caution Morcant of Strathclyde, who is a hothead, it seems. He would do so, I believe, for Arthur wants no trouble with Alba, you may be sure. But there has been so much of threat from the south . . ."

"And now he has gone further south still, to this Lancaster. So these rogues from Strathclyde! I would lead a force of my own to their land, to punish them, teach them a lesson. But I do not want to create war between the Albannach and one of Arthur's kingdoms. It could lead to that. This Morcant . . ."

"It may not be *his* doing. He is young, and may not have sufficient hold over his people near your borders. The raiders may be petty chieftains acting on their own."

"It may be so. But he is responsible. My friend, will *you* go to see Morcant? Reason with him. Urge him to act, to control his people."

"*I* go? Why? Why should he heed me? He is no Christian. He need fear nothing from me . . ."

"You are known. Your nephew is King of Cantyre, to the

north of Dumbarton. Morcant would not wish to offend Cantyre. *And* Fortrenn. *And* Arthur!"

"M'mm."

Thanea had listened to all this with interest. Now she ventured comment. "I have heard that Morcant of Strathclyde is a strange young man. Very fearful. Not of hurt or battle or the like, but of evil spirits. Of cursing. It is said that his father, Coledoch, died of a curse. And the son fears it."

They eyed her questioningly.

"Coledoch was cursed by some witch. For some hard deed of his. She laid the curse on him that he would not succeed his father as king. That was old Morcant Bulc. And he did die, to leave this *young* Morcant to succeed his grandsire as King of Strathclyde. It is said that he therefore greatly fears curses. There may be other reasons. So . . ." She looked at Serf. "Could you not visit him, and threaten him with a curse, a *Christian* curse, if he does not better control his people?"

Both men stared.

Belatedly it occurred to her that she perhaps had spoken unwisely, especially when she perceived Nechtan's searching gaze. This indicated that she knew more of King Morcant than did her hearers. And that could be dangerous, revealing something of her true identity. There had been talk about it all at Loth's court; but that connection was to be kept secret. Had she spoken unadvisedly? But she had to go on now, having got this far.

"Abbot Serf, your name will be known to Morcant, even though he is no Christian. Your name is famed. And your nephew King of Cantyre, neighbouring kingdom of Strathclyde. He would heed the threat of a cursing from you."

"Christ's servants do not go in for cursing, Ninenna."

"Not evil cursing. But a warning of God's wrath if he does not do better."

"What excuse could I give, for that? To reproach him of this, of his people's raiding. As a Christian. Scarcely God's especial concern!"

"St Patrick," she said simply.

"Ha! Patrick!"

Nodding, Thanea turned to Nechtan, who might well not know of the story of St Patrick.

"Patrick was a Strathclyde man, his father one of the converts of the great St Ninian, who first brought Christianity to these lands more than a century ago. To Candida Casa, at Whithorn in Galloway. That mission failed, when Ninian died, and your druids regained all. Or almost all, for some remained faithful. Including Patrick's father, a shepherd in the hills east of Dumbarton. One day, when still a youth, out herding, raiders from Ireland took Patrick and carried him back to Ireland. There he grew to manhood. But his faith survived. Eventually he escaped and went to Gaul." Monenna had told all her students this story many times, for she was from Strathclyde herself. "In Gaul Patrick entered a monastery and became a priest. When fully grounded he came back to Strathclyde, to his own folk, as missionary. But he was driven away by the then king. So he sailed over to Ireland where he felt that he was needed. And there he was more successful. He won over large numbers to Christianity, and in time founded the Church in Ireland. They look on him as *their* saint. But he was a man of Strathclyde."

"And so . . . ?" the mormaor wondered.

"If St Serf was to go and say that God held Strathclyde guilty of driving out Patrick. Say that perhaps that was why Morcant's father died, not because of any witch's spell. And now this. You see, Patrick's birthplace was in the very hills which lead up and over to your Mounth of Teith, and where he set up his mission before being driven out – that would be by Morcant Bulc's father. They are still called the Kilpatrick Hills, where his cell was. These raiders must cross and recross them to descend upon your lands. So here is excuse enough for our Christian God's displeasure."

Serf was looking at her now in obvious admiration and something like wonder. Nechtan's gaze was wondering also, but more questioningly.

"How come you to know all this, young woman?" he demanded.

She cast a quick glance at Serf. "There is talk of it in Lothian," she said. "In the nunneries. Of Morcant and his fears. And all Christians know of Patrick." She hoped that sounded convincing.

The abbot came to her rescue. "Ninenna is well informed.

We Christians teach our young people. This of St Patrick is well thought on, it seems to me. And my own teacher in the faith, St Palladius, was taught by Patrick."

"Then you will do it? Go to Dumbarton and speak with this Morcant?"

"Well . . ."

"I would reward you well."

Serf stroked his chin. Naturally he did not wish to seem to be bargaining. On the other hand, Nechtan's rewarding could be valuable for Christ's cause.

"It is late in the year, winter almost on us. The hill passes will soon be closed by snows. A long journey. And I have much to see to at my missions." Reluctance was evident.

"You could have *further* missions. I could grant you leave to spread your faith in new parts. Since your Christians do not appear to hurt my rule."

"That would be good, yes."

"It can wait until the winter is over. There will be no raiding in the snows. So when spring returns . . ."

"Very well." Serf gently pressed his advantage in this. "I have wished to teach the Gospel in the Loch Leven area, north and east of Fothrif and the Ochils. My Bishop Gabhran comes from there, Kinross. If he could set up a church there . . . ?"

"You may do so, if you bring me back Morcant's pledge to halt his raiders."

"And your daughter, the Princess Cara? May I baptise her? Your queen would have it so."

"I cannot accede to that without my druids' agreement, since of her will come rulers of Fortrenn. I will speak with them. But . . ."

They left it at that.

Soon they were rejoined by Queen Eva, who declared that Ninenna had endeared herself to the children and that her drawings were now in bed with them both, uncomfortable as slates were as bedfellows. Her sketchings were admirable. Thanea said that if they could find her colouring matter, she would do better in the morning.

Serf told their hosts that the young woman was doing much decoration at the abbey and illuminating documents and their copies of the Gospels; which led to a discussion on Celtic design, Pictish carvings and symbols, a sufficiently safe subject as far as revelation of identity was concerned. And presently the queen led her upstairs to a bedchamber not far from the children's room. There they talked for a little, the older woman asking about the child which Abbot Serf said she had had. Thanea had to be careful what she said about that, not mentioning rape but indicating that the pregnancy had been unwanted. The queen nodded understandingly, and Thanea thought it wise to add that she was well born but considered to be disgraced, so she had come to the Church in penitence.

This was accepted, and Eva left her, with a kiss.

In the morning, Serf announced that he intended to stay at Forteviot for another day. He admitted to Thanea that it was because of her St Patrick suggestion that he was doing so. That Nechtan was eager for this Morcant visit was obvious, and her proposal had made it all a practical gesture and with a possibility of success. The mormaor was more concerned over this cross-border raiding than might have seemed likely. This, it transpired, was because he was a peaceable man and there was pressure growing on him from his fellow-mormaors to the north to join in warfare against the Scots of Dalriada who were proving difficult neighbours to Alba in the north-west, having recently taken over the great island of Mull. Nechtan was counselling peaceful representations instead of war to the High King Fergus in Inverness. But if he himself was to go in arms against Strathclyde it would be as good as condoning the battle strategy. He could hardly refuse to join his more warlike colleagues if he did this. So the notion of Serf's mission to Morcant much appealed. And for his part, Serf saw the possibility of using the promise of it to help the Christian cause, here in Fortrenn. He had asked, as part of the price, to be allowed to address the druid council here, in the first instance, to try to get them to agree to the baptism of the little Princess Cara; but further to accept, not Christianity itself, too much to hope for, but that allowing the faith to spread would not injure Fortrenn – and who knew, the Church might gain the advantage in this. St Ninian had always said to use the pagans' need to worship to advance God's purpose, wherever that was possible; for all worship was better than none, the recognition that there were higher powers than man's. So there was to be a meeting with the Fortrenn druids that day.

Thanea was glad that her suggestion anent Patrick had sparked off this initiative. She would have liked to attend the druid meeting herself, but recognised that she could hardly so request. The Albannach system of succession might be matrilineal, but it was very much the men who ruled, and women were expected to know their place. So she wished Serf well in his efforts, and went to spend the day with Queen Eva and the children.

In the event, perhaps she achieved more than she could have done with the druids, for she and Eva got on very well, friendship burgeoning. They were not so far apart in years, and their upbringing had been fairly similar, Eva being the daughter of the Mormaor of Buchan, a younger daughter, and an object of criticism for her embracing of Christianity. As young mothers, they had much to discuss and relate, and their affection and respect for St Serf was an added bond; also they shared the abbot's fondness for birds and animals.

Their visit to Forteviot proved indeed to be beneficial as well as productive of friendship. For Serf managed to convince the Fortrenn Arch Druid, a less extreme character than the Lothian one, that druidical traditions and values would suffer no handicap by the princess being baptised a Christian, like her brother, that *she* would not rule Fortrenn and her offspring would nowise be committed to that faith; nevertheless, that Christianity might well make a useful contribution to the mormaordom's welfare, without necessarily requiring any yielding up of principles on druidism. This acceptance could clearly assist Serf's opportunities.

So the pair of them returned to Culross well pleased, leaving behind goodwill and a promise to visit Strathclyde when spring conditions made travel reasonable through mountainous country, the passes snow-free, the rivers fordable and the valley floors drained as to their bogs and floods. Without being actually stated between them, it was more or less assumed that Thanea would accompany the abbot on this difficult and different kind of mission. He was beginning to appreciate that he had possibly acquired a useful collaborator.

8

That winter saw Mungo developing from infant into little boy, with his own quite definite character, sunny and cheerful but positive, determined even and yet sensitive, more easily hurt than alarmed. Highly sociable also, as was not to be wondered at, being adopted by all the abbey's inmates so that he had a large family even though he had no other children to play with. Leot, the sheep and the robin were his playmates when the monks failed him, and a fondness for animals was very much part of him. He seemed to be able to communicate readily with creatures which were only dumb in that they had no speaking voices. He could be naughty too, of course, and Thanea did not fail to discipline him on occasion. He loved outdoor activities, especially the shepherding, even in hard weather, able to walk quite remarkable distances on his short legs. Serf's Christmas gift of a pony added to his mobility. This he named Marc, for some reason of his own, and Marc quickly became one of the quartet of Mungo's close friends, with Leot, Cora the sheep and Rua the robin.

So Thanea, and even Serf, was apt to move around with a tail of adherents, four-footed as well as two. Indeed dissuading Mungo from accompanying the abbot and his female coadjutor – for more and more Serf came to recognise the advantage of having Thanea with him on his missionary rounds, as able to reach the women better than he could do – on their journeyings around the Fothrif and Ochils area became quite a problem, especially with a sheep, not to mention a bird, eager to come along too.

At least there could be no question of this when, in April, immediately after Serf's birthday celebration, the promised mission to Strathclyde was embarked on – even though there was likewise no question but that the young woman should accompany him thereon, her usefulness acknowledged and her company enjoyed. These two had developed a rather wonderful relationship, not exactly like father and daughter, nor leader and assistant, but trusted colleagues with a personal fondness and understanding. Their different sexes did produce slight problems on occasion; but with each other there was no real difficulty, accepting one another's differences, attitudes and appreciations, mental and physical, as natural — whatever others might conjecture about their association. Serf was a whole man, and Thanea knew that he found her person as well as her personality attractive, and was glad of it, for she was all of a woman herself, and did not seek to hide it. On occasion they had to be very close, and came to accept it without embarrassment.

This aspect of their relationship would necessarily be fairly prominent on their journey to Dumbarton, for it entailed travel of over seventy or eighty miles, and this over wild and empty country, largely trackless save those of deer. There was a choice of routes. In essence they would have to cross the watershed between the firths of Forth and Clyde, at the very waist of the land, but this was complicated by the terrain itself. The Carse of Forth, beyond where the estuary narrowed to a fordable river, was a vast and undrained moss, fed by many tributary streams from north and south, this huge marshland a world of its own, impassable save by its own wild four-legged or web-footed denizens, and stretching for over twenty miles westwards, and five miles across, ending eventually in the mountain mass around Ben Lomond. So travellers from Fife and Fothrif had to go north of this, or south. The latter demanded following up the Forth estuary to the Snawdoun of Stirling and fording the suddenly narrowing river there, and afterwards journeying westwards through the hills of Gargunnock, Fintry and Campsie and then crossing the wide strath of Blane into the Kilpatrick Hills of Strathclyde. This was probably the most direct route, if that description could be applied at all. The northern approach would be by the Mounth of Teith, the River Teith being the Forth's greatest tributary, indeed, as a river, greater than the Forth itself. This would bring the travellers to the mountain area known as the Levenachs, or Lennox, flanking the long Loch

Lomond. Skirting this, they would come to the Kilpatrick Hills from the north instead of the east.

Serf decided that they should use this northern route. He thought it wise to try to visit some of the areas where raiding had taken place, to learn details if they could, and possibly even names, to put before King Morcant. He pointed out to the young woman that there could be danger in this journey through country where unruly men dwelt and ill deeds could be done. But Thanea was not to be put off.

So they made their farewells, telling Mungo and Leot to look after Marc, Cora and Rua, and were on their way, the weather showery but reasonable.

They rode along the shore of the estuary westwards, past Longannet Point, whereafter it quite suddenly began to narrow considerably to merely a wide river. They deliberately avoided a community on rising ground inland here, where Serf said that worship of Manannan, the sea god, was practised; they had Manannan's stone in the centre of the village. He had tried to make converts here, but without success, indeed his life had been threatened. Thanea was glad to be spared any further contacts with the sea god, to whose mercies she had been committed at Aberlady Bay – although in fact perhaps he had not done so ill by her, since she had survived! But she wondered why the sea god should be especially worshipped here, at a considerable distance from the sea? Serf said that he thought that it was because hereabouts was where the tidal sea-water reached and prevailed against the fresh water of the River Forth, and so the god fell to be placated lest he proceed further upstream, to the people's hurt. There was a similar spot on the Tay, to the north, beyond Perth, called Scone, where a like place of worship had been established.

They did not exactly follow the river-bank hereafter, for it began to loop and coil in great meanders through a low-lying flood-plain, but cut across these necks of land on the firmer ground, although in the general direction of the river's course. Soon they could see, far ahead, a great rock towering out of the river's levels. This Serf declared was the Snawdoun of Stryvelyn, or Stirling, site of a former great Pictish fort and citadel, a very strategic place which the Romans had named Mons Dolorum because they could not take it; but King Arthur had done so, and then demolished the fort, that it should no longer be a threat to his kingdoms. The abbot hoped that they might get at least that far before nightfall.

They had to go quite some distance inland, presently, in order to be able to ford a fair-sized incoming river which Serf called the Black Devon, why black he did not know but Devon was merely another rendering of their Celtic word for river, *avon*, of which there were many versions throughout the land – such as A'an, Allan, Almond, Awe, Afton, even Deveron, corrupted by local speech differences. In Wales, he was told, they had many rivers called Afon; and even lands now held by the Angles and Saxons had Avons and Alns, reminders that all had been Celtic territory once.

Thus the man whiled away any tedium in their journeying, to Thanea's appreciation as well as her edification.

They did better than reach Stirling that night, riding on until they came to another tributary entering Forth, this one the Allan. There was a community here, called Alauna, important in Roman times to guard the ford, but now much decayed, still necessary however, for this river was apt to flood, coming from the Ochils' high ground to the north, and travellers often had to wait. So Serf was able to find them accommodation for the night, primitive and not over-clean but at least a roof over their heads, for they had to share the same shack. There was simple food, and hay for the horses; and they paid in candles, having brought a good supply of Thanea's handiwork with them, wrapped up in the blankets they would use when there was no overnight roofing – although in fact they used their own blankets here also. Candles were a useful means of exchange, for everyone needed them on occasion, and they were often in short supply.

Side by side on the earthen floor they slept, uncomplaining.

Next day they had not far to go before they reached the River Teith, which thereafter they would follow up for many rough miles. This was a major stream, and Serf was mystified as to why it was considered to be a tributary of Forth, since it was the larger and brought down a greater volume of water; and why the eventual firth was called of Forth not of Teith. Its headwaters area, a score of miles ahead, was known as the Mounth of Teith, mountainous as distinct from hilly as on the other southern route to Strathclyde, and a deal more of a challenge to travellers. But it was there that the raiding had taken place which was worrying the Mormaor Nechtan, this being the highest part of Fortrenn, not populous but fair cattle country producing a hardy breed of beasts.

So up Teith the pair made their way, north-westwards, finding it actually easier going than on Forthside, this because it did not wend its way through low-lying flood-plains but ran a much more direct course through rising country, less than straight admittedly but on much firmer ground. By Keir and Inverardoch and the Doune thereof they went and on to Coilechat, the Wild Cats' Wood, climbing steadily all the time, the blue mountains now looming ahead. There were villages of cot-houses and small farmeries, and at these Serf began to ask whether there had been any Strathclyde raiding. All had heard of this, but the attackers had not come so far down as this, the gods be praised. Higher in the Mounth it was, beyond the Pass of Torrie, where the mountains began, these the more easily reached from Strathclyde by those evil ravagers.

On they rode until the land grew steeper and the river-banks began to close in on them, this some fifteen miles from Alauna. And at a cowherd's shack, where river and track entered scarcely a gorge but a narrow rift in the hills, the Pass of Torrie so called, they gained the first sure information as to the raiding. None so far ahead, three or four miles to the south-west, leaving this river, was Loch Rusky, beneath the heights of Ben Gulipen and Ben Dearg. Here were the communities of Letter Rusky and Letter Gulipen. These had twice suffered raids, the cowherd told them, and were much afraid of more. Indeed the folk there had plans to move up, with their beasts, into the hidden mountain corries, for fear of further assaults.

So, in late afternoon, having threaded the pass, the couple abandoned the Teith and climbed out of its valley to mount the hillsides, southwards now, open country although dominated by high peaks and ridges to the west. They went by deer tracks through the heather.

They had no difficulty in finding what they sought, at any rate, for quite soon they came in sight of a sheet of blue water ahead, not large but very evident, squarish and less than a mile across, which could only be Loch Rusky, scattered hawthorn and birch surrounding it. Sturdy small black cattle began to dot the slopes.

As they neared the loch, they could see a settlement to the north of it, the blue smoke of household fires rising above. This presumably was Letter Rusky, letter meaning a slope and rusky a morass. Closer scrutiny showed blackened walling and roofless shacks and hutments, and alean against these roughly built timber shelters people were watching their approach warily – although one man and a woman could represent little threat, surely.

Serf, necessarily good at greeting and reassuring folk, quickly dispelled any doubts as to their goodwill, announcing that they came from the Mormaor Nechtan at Forteviot, their purpose to enquire into the damage done by raiders. That soon loosened tongues. Dismounting, they received a flood of eloquence as to the shameful wickedness of the Strathclyde raiders, women declaring that they had been humiliated and raped, their children abused, men attacked and wounded, cattle stolen and houses burned. For no reason. They were greatly fearing return raids at any time now, with May the First, Beltane, the feast of Baal the god of fire, almost upon them, and the passes clear of snow. These savages could come back. Was the mormaor going to come to their aid?

Serf explained that he was a Christian, and on his way to see King Morcant, at Nechtan's behest, to protest.

Being made welcome, the travellers decided to stay the night here, even though the accommodation was primitive, to say the least. But they fed well, on beef, with salmon from the loch.

Their questioning elicited information such as Serf sought. Yes, they knew who the raiders were, or some of them. They came from the East Lennox, the Strathendrick area, Drymen and Gartocharn. They had taken three of the young women away with them, and after some weeks, two of these had managed to escape and found their way home, ravaged as they were. These brought the word. The leaders of the raiders were two brothers, Lonan and Drust mac Bran . . .

"Bran!" Serf interrupted the recital. "Bran was the brother of Coledoch, that I know. Morcant's father. If it is the same

102

Bran, then these are cousins of Morcant's own." He exchanged glances with Thanea.

Their hosts did not know as to that, only that the brothers Lonan and Drust were chieftains of some sort, and evil.

The visitors slept that night knowing that they had at least some details to put before King Morcant. But if indeed the chief culprits were the king's cousins, would this make their mission the more difficult?

In the morning they went over to the other community, Letter Gulipen, only a mile or two away and nearer the mountain-foot, being escorted by some of the Rusky men. Here they actually met the two young women who had been abducted, misused and managed to escape, one most evidently pregnant. Their stories were grievous and evoked much understanding and sympathy from Thanea in especial. These confirmed that Lonan and Drust were high-born, with quite large hall-houses and many men. They were cruel. The women did not know whether these two were cousins of King Morcant, but said that they did go quite frequently to Dumbarton, the Strathclyde capital.

Distressing as these victims' stories were, it was something else which seemed to be affecting their fellow-villagers more directly. This was not only the damage done and cattle stolen, but a desecration of a different sort which the raiders had committed. In their burnings and spoliation they had set alight the hut, under its sacred oak tree, which was the shrine of Gualpian, the torturer, the dire god after which the mountain, and their village, was named Gulipen; and the carven stone therein, to the god, had been blackened and damaged. This was greatly worrying the villagers; indeed they were wondering whether to leave the area and set up a new community somewhere more distant from the shadow of this mountain – for Gualpian was a very fierce and jealous god and they greatly feared his wrath, that they had not better protected his shrine. Living as they did directly under his frowning escarpment they were now in constant dread.

Serf sought to reassure them, saying that the true God Almighty was a god of love and caring. He recognised that it was of no use just to declare to these people, without considerable preparation, that these pagan deities were in fact

103

non-existent, for this they would nowise believe. Converting to Christianity was not achieved overnight. But he did seek to convince them that this Gualpian would not harm *them*, innocent of offence as they were. Perhaps one day he, Serf, would come back here and seek to convert – but this was not the time for it.

Leaving their goodwill, and some candles, behind them, the pair proceeded on with what would almost certainly be the most difficult part of their journey, west by south over the Mounth and through the trackless mountain country to the head of Forth and beyond. Had it not been for the vast mosses of Poldar and Gartrenich and the rest, with the large Loch of Menteith in their midst, they could have journeyed almost due southwards and reached Strathendrick and the Kilpatrick Hills more or less direct; but those Forth flood-plains were impassable, so they must keep to the mountains.

They made very slow progress now, following twisting glens and over gaps amongst rock and heather summits, rising high. As the crow might fly they covered only six or seven difficult miles – but they were no crows. In all that day's riding they saw only one habitation of man, or a *former* habitation, for the cowherd's dwelling of Tombae was burned and abandoned. But the vistas gained at least were enchanting, peak and ridge seemingly to infinity, and the herds of deer seeming to drift across it all to rival the cloud shadows doing likewise. Following the instructions from Letter Gulipen, they managed to keep approximately on course; and thankfully, in early evening, they saw the width of the Forth valley opening before them, and worked their way down to the village of Aberfoyle, where that river had narrowed to little more than a burn.

Here they found the same tale of disaster and rapine, these folk that much nearer to the raiders' home grounds. But the visitors were kindly enough received, fed and sheltered.

That night, in their blankets before sleep, Thanea told Serf what she had been turning over in her mind all that day.

"This of the torture god, Gualpian," she said. "Could we not use this against Morcant? Who is superstitious and fearful of curses? He may not be greatly concerned over threatenings in the name of our Christian God, but this of his people defacing the shrine of the torturer might well hit him sorely. What of a curse in *his* name?"

"Nighean, I cannot take the name of a pagan god to use! It is . . . impossible! I can not, even so to prevail on the man."

"*I* can!" the young woman declared. "In the cause of these poor injured and harried folk. Surely, if it would be effective, then Christ God would not judge it so ill?"

"It would go against all that I hold and have taught."

"Yet it might serve a great good."

"I cannot think it right to do ill that good may follow, lass."

"Did not St Ninian worship God in stone circles? Because it was there that the pagans did their worshipping."

Serf shook his head. "That is different. He did not *use* the names of pagan gods."

They slept on it.

The next day's journey was a deal easier. They rode due southwards now, skirting the mosses to the west, by the higher ground of Gartmore, to the Kelty Water and across this to Gartclach and Gartachoil – most of the names hereabouts seemed to start with *gart*, which just meant enclosure – and so down to Strathendrick. They were now into the Strathclyde kingdom, and must go warily. Probably they were in no greater danger here than in the wilds of Fortrenn; but they *felt* that they were on enemy territory and wanted no complications before they saw Morcant. So instead of going on down the River Endrick to the Vale of Leven and so to Dumbarton, by which way they would pass Drymen and Gartocharn of the raiders, they chose to strike off up the tributary Water of Blane, near Gartness, and so to the Kilpatrick Hills, a longer and more difficult route but safer perhaps.

On the way, Serf spoke of St Patrick and his extraordinary life, to have been so ill-used and rejected and then to be responsible for the conversion of an entire nation and become the saint of Ireland. How often must his faith have been put to the test! A lesson and example to all lesser missionaries indeed! How puny *his* own efforts, in comparison! Thanea knew only what Monenna had told her of Patrick, when she had taken her students to see St Patrick's Well, on the Lothian coast at Gulyn, not far from Aberlady Bay; that his badge was the trefoil or shamrock, signifying the Holy Trinity,

105

and that he had founded three hundred churches in Ireland. Did Serf know where in these Kilpatrick Hills the saint had come from? Her companion admitted that he did not. But perhaps they could ask.

Thus far they had come less than a score of miles and not in difficult country. But they would not get to Dumbarton that night, through these uplands. So they might have time to make some search for Patrick's birthplace. Serf decided that it would be sensible in the circumstances, although perhaps less than heroic, to hereafter describe himself as the Prince Servanus, uncle of the King of Cantyre, rather than any Church missionary, Thanea agreeing.

They reached a sizeable community called Carbeth, on the shore of a small loch, and here sought directions as to the best route to Dumbarton. The Prince Servanus was told that the shortest route was through the hills, due westwards, but that the kindest road was on southwards down this valley for another five miles, then turn west on the lower ground at Baljaffray, to make for Duntocher and the Clyde shore. On adding that he wondered where the renowned Christian St Patrick was born in these parts, Serf was looked upon more suspiciously; but a woman, sniffing, told him that there was an old man at the village of Cochno, who was said to be one of these Christians, and who claimed to have known the man Patrick. Receiving directions as to the whereabouts of this Cochno, the couple were on their way.

They found the village without difficulty, this also with its loch, this being a notable area for small lochs; and asking for the Christian called Ferchar, were directed to a broken-down cot-house where an ancient man was plucking a chicken. When they told him that they were Christians also, and were seeking St Patrick's birthplace, he was eager to tell them all he knew, even though, being toothless, his gabbled speech was difficult to understand, especially the word which he kept repeating and which sounded like bannertaven, but which after repeated enquiries they established as Banavem Taberniae, an extraordinary name indeed which meant nothing to the hearers. However, the old man was able to describe where this odd-sounding place was located, almost on the bank of the Clyde itself, many folk now just calling it Kilpatrick.

Their informant, when he learned that he was speaking to one St Serf, of Culross, was all but overcome with excitement, and his gabble the less understandable. But they did gather that this strangely named house had been quite a large one, Patrick not really being a shepherd's son as they had thought, his father actually a Roman official at nearby Dumbarton, or at least an official of the Roman occupation. When the invaders had eventually left Strathclyde, Patrick's father had retired into the hills and kept a few sheep, which was no doubt how the shepherding story came about. The old man himself had been converted to Christianity in his youth by Patrick, before the saint was driven out to Ireland.

There was still some three hours of daylight, and this alleged birthplace was apparently only about four miles away. So thanking their friend, and giving him a couple of candles, they were directed to ride on a mile to an abandoned Pictish fort and then to turn due westwards, making for the Clyde where it began to widen to an estuary. Where their track reached salt water, there was this Banavem Taberniae of the saint – at least, this was what the visitors *thought* were their instructions.

In the event they found the place readily enough, the ruined skeleton of a fair-sized house, which had obviously been pillaged to provide materials for the group of shacks which now surrounded it. The position was pleasing, with the Clyde here perhaps a quarter-mile across and rapidly widening to the beginnings of a firth. Looking on westwards, five or six miles ahead, they could see a great upthrusting rock which seemed to rise out of the Clyde itself, and which was undoubtedly Alcluyd, or Dumbarton, the dun or fort of the Britons. They could probably have reached there before darkness; but they were unsure of their reception at Morcant's town and palace, and there might be gates shut at dusk. So they sought overnight accommodation at the shacks, and were allotted a chamber which smelled as though it had formerly sheltered a goat. But of princely birth as they both might be, they were not off-put; and after a simple meal of soup and porridge, went to pay their respects to St Patrick's memory.

In the wrecked and ivy-grown ruin, Serf said a prayer of gratitude for that renowned missionary's life and achievements, and that they themselves might seek humbly to follow his lead in however minor a fashion.

They returned to their odoriferous hut, the man declaring that the strange name of the place was possibly a corruption of Latin, not to be wondered at if Patrick's father had indeed been a Roman official. It might well be *benevolus taberna*, meaning a kindly and benevolent house or booth. Not that this was important, but the matter challenged him somehow.

In the morning they set off along the coast to Dumbarton, after seeking to wash and tidy themselves as best they might. As they drew nearer to the great rock they perceived that it was not just a steep conical hill, like North Berwick Law, but in fact had double summits, separated by a deep cleft. Despite the steepness and height of it all however, almost the entire rock appeared to be covered with building, in stone and timber, houses, ramparts and stockades, unlikely a site as this might be.

The rock, however dominant, was not alone in catching the visitors' eyes. It was not an island, as it had seemed from a distance, but occupied a little spur of peninsula. Landward of this and along the coast westwards stretched quite a large town, indeed the largest Thanea had ever seen, much larger than Traprain or Forteviot; houses and shacks, sheds and barns, with jetties and piers of stone and timber projecting into the firth's waters to provide safe anchorage for shipping. Clearly this Alcluyd – for that would be the town's name, Dumbarton referring obviously to the rock, with its dun or fort – was an important place and no doubt a great trading centre, by all that shipping. Which did not cheer the visitors, since it would probably mean that its ruler would be the more arrogant and difficult to deal with.

As to procedure they decided that it might be wise to make enquiries in the town before presenting themselves at the fortress-palace, for some guidance on Morcant's whereabouts, habits and attitudes. Their arrival created no especial interest, indeed there seemed to be few people about. Their dress was sufficiently plain and travel-stained to attract little notice. They were looking for some larger house where they might find a townsman of some standing to advise them, when they heard an unmistakable sound ahead of them, the rhythmic clash of cymbals. To Thanea at least that was an ominous sound, connected with pagan worship.

In the centre of the town a river, quite large, reached the Clyde, and a raised and wide causeway of stone linked the two sides. This is where the people were waiting, on this east side mainly, and looking northwards upriver. And coming down towards them on this river-bank was a procession, from which the cymbal-clanging emanated.

Asking what this meant, they were told that this was the monthly ceremony of petition to the sun, to Manannan the sea god and to Lug, the fertility god, it being the Eve of Beltane, the first day of May. The plea was that the gods would not allow the salt water of the estuary to reach further up this River Leven than the place of Dalfarg, that it did not flood and destroy the fertile oat-growing lands above, on which all men depended for their daily bread. This service was held just when the rising sun appeared over the eastern hilltops. Now here were King Morcant and the druids returning from their supplications.

Serf and Thanea dismounted, to wait and watch.

Presently, pacing in dignified fashion to the beat of the cymbals, came the official company, led by banner-bearers, with the Arch Druid and his minions following on, carrying their curious symbols; then, alone, a young man richly clad and with a golden torque around his neck, who could only be Morcant, with a file of nobles and great ones bringing up the rear.

The visitors eyed the king keenly, assessingly. He was tall but slightly built, all but reedy, with lean sharp features, keen darting eyes and a pointed chin. He did not look the easiest person to deal with. And clearly this was not the moment to approach him.

They watched the procession head on for the great rock citadel. At least they knew now that the man they sought would be at home.

They waited for a while at a dockside inn, to give time for Morcant to breakfast. Then, leaving their horses, they set out for the fortress.

Approaching it, the entire complex of rock and its clinging buildings seemed the more extraordinary, reminding Thanea rather of the mighty Craig of Bass at the mouth of Forth, with all its gannets' and other seafowl's nests festooning every ledge and crevice from top to bottom. Houses and erections of every sort and size perched and huddled anywhere, and in the most unlikely positions, the building of which must have presented problems and dangers indeed. There were stockades and walls at various stages almost to the top, with fortified gates in them. The largest of the buildings, presumably the palace, with banners flying above, seemed to be set within the very cleft between the twin summits, at hundreds of feet above the estuary's waters – the occupants thereof presumably developing notable leg muscles in their surmounting of the ascent. The wonder was how the Romans had ever managed to capture this place, unless they starved the defenders into submission by prolonged siege.

At the lowermost gatehouse and bridge across a deep moat, the visitors were challenged; but the announcement that it was the Prince Servanus of Cantyre come to visit King Morcant, although producing stares, gained them admittance. Thereafter, they commenced the climbing of a thousand steps cut in the solid rock.

They had to pass three more gatehouses as they mounted, but they encountered no difficulty other than breathlessness and aching tendons, long days of riding scarcely preparing them for this.

How to explain Thanea's presence had been much exercising them both. There was unlikely to be much communication between the kingdoms of Lothian and Strathclyde, but it was just possible that word of this visit and her true identity might get from one to the other. Yet her presence here would look less strange if her high-born rank was known, especially, as she pointed out, her link with King Arthur, Morcant's overlord. A princess-niece of Arthur would perhaps impress; but the name Thanea was unusual and could cause questions. Serf said if only she had had a second name . . .

"I have not. But I did have a pet-name. My brother Gawain used to call me Eunach, that is Little Bird, when I was a child. He still calls me that, on occasion – or did! Eunach. Would that serve?"

"Eunach? The Princess Eunach. Why not? I need not say

110

whose daughter you are. It may be assumed that you are from Cantyre, or even Dalriada, to the north. Yes, Eunach, my daughter-in-God."

At the final gate, before the tall hall-house palace, they were kept waiting while guards went to enquire whether King Morcant would see them. Now that it came to a confrontation, Thanea felt distinctly nervous.

It took some time for the required permission of entry to arrive. They were then conducted not into the hall-house itself but to a lesser building behind, wedged between stacks of rock. Here they found Morcant awaiting them, with the Arch Druid. They would have preferred to see the king alone.

They received no smiling welcome; but then Morcant did not look much of a smiler. "Did I hear aright? You are from Cantyre?" he asked.

"Not *from* Cantyre, but *of* it," Serf replied. "I am Servanus, uncle to its king. And this is the Princess Eunach. We come from the east, from Fortrenn."

The young man stared, with those hot eyes. "Fortrenn. What brings you to Dumbarton, from Fortrenn?"

"No joy, King Morcant. But a necessary mission. On behalf of the Mormaor Nechtan."

"That . . . man!"

"Yes. Your neighbour. And neighbours should live in amity, no?"

Morcant glanced at the druid but gave no sign of sending him away. "Well?" he demanded. Clearly the visitors were to be offered no hospitality, as was customary.

"What we have to say, perhaps, would be best in your ear alone, King Morcant."

"The Arch Druid Felim will stay." That was abrupt.

"As you will. Nechtan of Fortrenn has had occasion to protest to you in the past, over raiding of his lands of the Mounth of Teith, from Strathclyde. But the raids continue. He is much troubled over this. But he does not wish for war . . ."

"He is wise in that, at least! Strathclyde would grind him like corn in a mill!"

"Not, I think, if the other Albannach mormaors supported him. As is mooted. But – it is not our mission to make

111

such threats. But to urge that you have this raiding halted, nevertheless."

"*I* halt it? *I* do no raiding."

"Your people do. As their king, you can and should halt it. Your simple duty, is it not?"

"Who are you, man, to come and teach me my duties and affairs? If some nobodies go ranging those wild hills, what concern of mine is it? They may be from anywhere. Not necessarily from my Strathclyde."

"They are not nobodies from anywhere, King Morcant. We know who they are. They are in fact of your own kin, Lonan and Drust mac Bran. From Drymen and Gartocharn."

"Idle tales!"

"Not so. Some women whom they abducted and took back with them escaped from Drymen and won home. *They* have reason to know the truth."

"You cannot hold me responsible for the like. I have more important matters to attend to."

"Your High King Arthur accepts your responsibility. Did he not send to warn you?"

That obviously shook the younger man. He looked at the Arch Druid again, and chewed his lip.

"I myself spoke on this to King Arthur a year ago, and he was concerned. He wants no trouble with the Albannach. He has overmuch else to deal with. And this could lead to such trouble."

"You build a mountain out of nothing! Here is folly."

"Folly, yes – but for you, King Morcant. For it could bring about your very downfall."

"Downfall! Me? Morcant of Strathclyde. Have you lost your wits, man? Over a few women and cattle!"

"Over a king's failure to control his people. That is how Arthur sees it. As do others in high places. And in the *highest*!"

"What mean you by that?"

"I mean that we are servants of the Most High God. Christians. Whom Nechtan has entrusted with this mission – although he is no Christian. And what you do, or fail to do, is against God's will."

"Christians!" the king scoffed. "Believers in idle fables. Well seen how *you* believe these tales of raids and the like since you believe in this false nonsense from a far-off land. When the true gods are all about you!" And he turned to the druid again.

That man made his first contribution. "Mistaken foolishness!" he agreed. "Which could provoke the gods to grave punishment."

"You think that Almighty God and His son Jesus Christ will not punish especial transgression against Himself?" Serf asked sternly. "When your people have desecrated the memory of his great servant St Patrick."

His hearers stared.

"All this raiding has been done across the Kilpatrick Hills, where God's especial servant was born, he who brought Christianity to all Ireland. It is an especial territory. Through it raped women and stolen cattle have been led. Think you that you will be forgotten and forgiven if you do not repent of it, and swear to halt all further raiding?"

"Empty babblings! How dare you come here and make such fool's threats to *me*, the king!"

"I dare because I am sent, Morcant. Heed, and think well. Lest I curse you in Almighty God's name!"

"You cannot do that . . ."

"I can. And will. That is why I came. And you have had sufficient cursing in the past, have you not? Did not your father Coledoch die of it? Do you wish to follow him?"

"That . . . was a witch. An evil witch . . ."

"And think you that God in heaven, the king of kings and lord of lords, cannot curse more direly than some wretched witch?"

"Pay no heed, King Morcant," the Arch Druid said. "These would but cozen you. Their false god has no power against you while our potent gods, from the great sun downwards, protect you. As *I* invoke them to do."

The king, who had been looking uneasy, those pale eyes darting, nodded reassurance. "Fool!" he jerked. "You cannot hurt me with your idle threats. Begone before I have my men teach you a lesson!"

Thanea thought that it was time that *she* made a contribution. "King Morcant, hear *me*! And I am niece to King Arthur. Not only have your people offended our Christian God but they

113

have grievously insulted one of your own. Does Gualpian the torturer mean nothing to you?"

That had its swift effect. Neither of the pair spoke but they eyed her almost askance.

"Amongst their savageries, your shameful kinsmen attacked Letter Gulipen, beneath the shadow of the torturer's mountain, Ben Gulipen. And there they burned the shrine of Gualpian and defaced his monument. The torturer, I think, did not get that name for nothing! I say that you should beware, King Morcant!"

There was no question as to the impact that she had made. The king's hand went up to his mouth and the druid looked unhappy.

The young woman went on. "This day you have been praying to the sun, to Manannan and to Lug. Did you remember Gualpian, their fellow-god? I say that you should have done. For the people of Letter Gulipen beseech him daily, for vengeance. What, think you, will the torturer contrive for you if you do not swiftly seek to placate him, punish his offenders and stop the raiding?"

Morcant was clearly now much upset, and getting little help from his Arch Druid. "I . . . do not know," he got out.

Serf added his voice. "Will you have me curse you in the name of God Almighty? As well as this of Gualpian? Say now!"

"No! No — not that."

"The choice is yours. Yea or nay! Your sworn word. Or . . . !"

"Yes. I give it. My word. The raiding will cease, the raiders be punished. By the gods, I swear it."

"That is as well. Do not forget this day, King Morcant. Or . . ." He left the rest unsaid.

There was nothing for them to wait for now, no point in prolonging so uncomfortable an interview. Without any more formal leave-taking — and still no offer of hospitality — they bowed briefly and left the pair standing.

As they descended all those steps, Thanea observed that, sadly, it seemed that the pagan deities were still more effective in St Patrick's birthplace than the true God he had so bravely proclaimed and preached, Serf ruefully having to accede to it. The time would come, however, that *he* swore . . .

With nothing to delay them now, and the day still young, they decided to set off for home forthwith, and by the shortest route – that was by the Kilpatrick Hills again and then the Campsie Fells and Fintry Hills, and so along the south side of Forth to Stirling, and across there, two days probably instead of four.

Despite Serf's reservations about using the heathen god for their purposes, they were reasonably satisfied with their mission. The abbot was admiring of his companion's handling of Morcant mac Coledoch, at least. And that man had not asked *who* Princess Eunach was . . .

9

Mungo was five, and growing apace, in character as well as in body, a happy, lively, friendly boy, full of energy and ideas, some of them demanding. He liked people, and showed it, and his fondness for animals was a notable part of him, to Serf's joy. Leot, Cora, Rua and Marc the pony were his constant companions, and he seemed to be able to communicate with these in extraordinary fashion.

It was with the robin that an incident came about which was to have a profound influence on the boy's development. It was the beginning of the lambing season, and he had accompanied his mother to the higher pastures to bring down the pregnant ewes and gimmers to the lower ground nearer the abbey, where lambs would be safer from predators, eagles, ravens, foxes and the like. They and their baaing flock, Leot in busy attendance, were still about a mile from their destination when who should arrive, to come and perch on the boy's shoulder, but the little redbreast, come a long flight for so small a bird and one no longer young. Presumably it had heard the baaing from afar and had come to welcome its friends back. Mungo was, of course, delighted.

But his delight was short-lived. For when, after a little, Rua soared up on its swooping flight, over the flock, to pay its respects to Leot rounding up straggling ewes, a shadow came over the pleasing scene, not a cloud shadow but from above nevertheless, in the shape of a kestrel. The hawk came circling over, hung for a few moments on winnowing wings, and then dropped down like a plummet on Rua hovering above the dog. There was a small explosion of feathers and a furious barking and leaping from Leot. The hawk flapped up and away, empty-clawed.

Thanea and Mungo had seen the hawk and its stoop, horrified, saw the impact and heard the barking which drove off the predator. The boy, shouting his anger and concern, leapt down from his pony and ran through the flock of sheep to where Leot had halted. And there, on the ground, lay the pathetic little victim, wings outspread, still, the dog sniffing down at it.

Crying its name, Mungo knelt to pick it up, gently. It remained motionless in his hand. Weeping, he raised the little creature to kiss it.

Thanea came up, sad, to grip her son's shoulder, murmuring her sorrow and sympathy, and saying that it was a shame indeed, but a quick and painless end for the tiny creature. But her son was not murmuring. Stroking the bundles of feathers he was almost shouting again, face upturned.

"Dear God, dear God!" he cried. "Why did you let it do it? Why? To Rua. To poor Rua. You should not, God – you *should* not!"

"Hush, Mungo, hush! You must not say that . . ."

"I must. I shall! God let that wicked hawk kill Rua. It is wrong, wrong!" He held the little bird up towards the sky, accusingly. "See what it did to Rua!"

Thanea stroked her son's head, shaking her own.

Quivering with emotion Mungo waved Rua about, seeking for words. At length he got them out.

"Dear God, you were wrong! But – you can do anything, everything. You can make Rua live again. You *can*! Oh, dear God, make Rua live again." Staring down, he willed that bundle of feathers to live, to stir.

And it did. A faint and feeble tremor moved in his hands. As he caught his breath another stirring occurred, and one of the outstretched wings closed slowly in on the little body.

"Look! Look!" the boy yelled. "See – Rua *is* going to live again! God, God has heard me!"

"Oh, Mungo, how good. Rua was not really dead. Only stunned. That is splendid. Not dead at all."

"Yes, it was! Rua *was* dead. But God has heard me. God has done it, made Rua live again. Because I asked him. Heard me up in heaven. Oh, I will be good, now!" A brief pause, and amendment. "I will *try* to be good now. I promise . . ."

The robin folded its other wing, and opened its eyes. The boy raised it to kiss it again.

"See what God can do. If he will. I did it: I got God to save Rua. I will tell St Serf." Mungo always gave the abbot his saintly title. "Look, it's getting better."

The bird was indeed perking up in the boy's hands, with Leot coming to nose it.

Thanea nodded now. "Perhaps you are right, Mungo, my dear. We will ask St Serf. See – we will make a sort of nest for Rua in your coat, and you can carry it home."

"Was that not good! Did I pray well?"

"M'mm. I do not know that I would say that, my dear! You spoke to God rather . . . harshly! But you *did* speak to Him . . ."

"And He heard me!"

"Yes. Well – the sheep are straying. Leot must see to them." And she gestured to the dog. "Come, Mungo, back to the horses . . ."

Holding the robin as though it was the most precious item of creation, the boy paced slowly off in triumph.

Serf, when he heard the story, was glad indeed, but careful in his comments, confining himself to saying that God was good, loved all his creatures and heard prayers. When Mungo protested that God would not love that wicked kestrel, the man asserted that, yes, He would. The kestrel was one of God's creatures too. No doubt it did its Maker's will in its own way. It made a mistake in attacking this especial friend Rua, perhaps. But we all make mistakes sometimes, and hope for forgiveness. So the kestrel must be forgiven too.

Mungo was very doubtful about this, but did not contradict the abbot, whatever he had said to God. And he insisted that Rua *had* been dead, and had been brought back to life by prayer.

Serf said later, to Thanea, that they should not seek to disillusion the boy about the bird not really being dead. Who were they to say that miracles could not happen? And Mungo's belief would strengthen his faith hereafter. Let them seem to accept it.

Rua, after a couple of days being unusually inactive and subdued, quickly returned to normal behaviour, spry and cheeky as ever. As for Mungo, he suffered from no doubts, but was warned not to boast about it all. He did wonder whether

Rua would grow new feathers to replace those it had lost in the attack. He hoped that God would see to that.

Once the lambing was over and the little creatures big enough to go back to the higher pastures, Thanea, as shepherdess, was more free with her time; and Serf decided to take her with him again to visit Mormaor Nechtan at Forteviot. He had not forgotten that man's promise, that if he managed to stop the Strathclyde raiding, he would be allowed to pursue his missionary activities around the Loch Leven area. They had heard nothing from the mormaor since their return from Dumbarton, and did not know whether indeed the attacks had been halted and Morcant's promise fulfilled. So they would go to discover the position.

On the way, Serf wished to visit an old friend and helper, one Fergus, who had assisted in founding a mission and small monastery at Carnock, near to Stirling, but who had unfortunately become hopelessly lame and unable to travel and act the missionary any more. But he still ran the monastic establishment after a fashion, and Serf liked to see and encourage him on occasion.

Carnock, although of the same name as a village near Culross, was on the far side of Forth, so that a round-about journey there was involved, up the estuary to the first crossing, at Stirling, and then south-eastwards for about six miles. But they ought to manage it in a day.

They did so, and reached Carnock as dusk was settling on a strange land of level marshes and pools, burns and runnels, seeping waters everywhere, all flanking the Forth on this side, and really only a continuation of the great flood-plain to the west, although the high ground of Stirling came between. It was no ideal place to plant a monastery, but the only location that the local chieftain, a pagan, would allow, and that on condition that the brothers kept certain areas ditched and drained for his cattle-grazing. The peewits and curlews were calling, calling their lonely evening cries as the travellers threaded the marshes.

They were warmly welcomed by what had become a distinctly aged community, but none the less friendly for that and eager to inform the abbot of their continuing endeavours for the faith. Old Fergus was a sad sight, but by no means pathetic, crippled and drawn yet uncomplaining, and only concerned that he was not able to do more in his Master's cause. Thanea told him the story of Mungo and the robin, and the old man was much intrigued, chuckling and rubbing his hands. Serf warned her afterwards that this was how legends and fables were born.

The monks entertained their guests as well as they could out of their modest resources; and asked Serf if he could not find them some young men, novices, to come and aid their work here. The abbot was doubtful as to possibilities, but would do what he could.

In the morning they rode back across Forth and thereafter northwards, past Alauna, to round the western shoulders of the Ochil Hills, and up Strathallan, to reach Forteviot, as before, by Dunning, a fair day's riding. They were well received, warmly by Queen Eva and the children, civilly by Nechtan, who was glad to tell them that he had had no reports of raiding – and undoubtedly he would have done if there had been any.

Serf described their journey and visit to Dumbarton and Morcant's reaction, rather emphasising the threat of *Christian* cursing as distinct from pagan, for obvious reasons, Thanea finding no fault. In announcing the girl's part in it all, Serf felt that it was necessary to reveal now that she was King Arthur's niece, the Princess Eunach, although he had called her Nighean or Ninenna. Eva welcomed this revelation and her husband accepted it without comment.

It did not take Serf long to broach the subject of expanding the area of his missionary endeavours; and Nechtan redeemed his promise, agreeing that the abbot could seek to proselytise in the Loch Leven neighbourhood if so he wished, so long as, in his teachings, he reminded the people of their loyal duties to himself, their mormaor. Serf assured him that his Christian converts would make better and more reliable members of the Fortrenn community so long as they were not expected to take part in pagan rites. The queen supported him in this.

Eva and Thanea, as before, got on very well together, indeed they were becoming friends, so much so that when, next day, Serf would have been on their way south, the queen persuaded him to stay a day or two longer, that she might enjoy the Princess Eunach's company further. The abbot acquiesced, admitting to Thanea privately that he was glad of this association in that it might not only strengthen the queen's faith but perhaps encourage her to work quietly for her husband's conversion, which he thought might be a possibility.

So they spent a pleasant couple of days at Forteviot, as guests, and the cause of Christian mission none the worse for it.

When they left, Eva suggested that they should come back soon, and that Thanea might bring her little son with her, to make cause with her Finan and Cara. She had been enthralled by the story of Mungo and the robin.

They did not return as they had come, but struck southeastwards through the eastern end of the Ochil range, less high than the other extremity. They had to climb considerably nevertheless, by cattle and deer tracks, to the headwaters area of the River Devon which they had crossed at its lower stages on a previous journey. They followed the rapidly growing stream down into what became Glen Devon, with Thanea asking when and why the river became the *Black* Devon? Serf said that they would ask at Kinross.

There was quite a large community at the head of Loch Leven, where Bishop Gabhran had come from, and where it was hoped to start the new mission. It lay about five miles from where the Devon emerged from the hills before bending abruptly westwards.

Leaving the river at length they rode eastwards, over comparatively level ground, and presently saw in front of them a great sheet of water, blue amongst green braes, which was Loch Leven. Serf said that it was heart-shaped, perhaps four miles in length and three in breadth, and dotted with islets. It was the largest lake anywhere south of the mountains.

At the north end of this was the sizeable community of Kinross, largely of fisherfolk, for the loch was celebrated for its great quantities of salmon and trout. Here, amongst the cottages, huts, and smoke-houses for preserving the fish, they sought out Domangart, a brother of Bishop Gabhran, who was one of the village's elders, and a Christian.

Domangart was glad to hear of Nechtan's permission to proselytise, and was hopeful as to results. He had sought to

121

spread the word, in a small way, over the years, and many were not unsympathetic towards the Christian message. There were no druids here, and there should be little active opposition – although whether there would be many actual converts was another matter.

The pair decided to spend the night at Kinross. They had Domangart call a meeting, by the lochside, and practically all the population came down to it, men, women and children, an undoubted event in their less than exciting lives.

Domangart introduced the abbot as Prince Servanus of Cantyre, and Thanea as Princess Eunach, a niece of the great King Arthur, which helped to gain a respectful hearing. Serf then addressed them, simply, quietly, not at all dominant nor princely, any more than challenging or fiery. He spoke of love and caring, of family life and daily work, of relations between men and women, of those with plenty and the poor and needy, the sick and the aged. Then he went on to mankind's need to worship, to realise that there were powers greater than man's. But worship should be heartfelt, without fear or threat, without other sacrifice than one's own personal interests, prides and time. This was where the Christian God Almighty, as revealed by Jesus of Nazareth His Son, was so different from the pagan gods, from the sun downwards. He was the God of love and kindness, of hope and cheer and friendship, not of doom and pain and terror. He had created all things, the sun itself, the moon and stars, not as lesser gods but as inanimate things to serve His own good purposes. There *were* no other gods, these but the inventions of foolish men, no Manannan, no Lug, no Gualpian, no Baal. These were but names, representing men's terrors and fears, sacrifices to them pointless and abhorrent to Christ God. So – let them all ponder on this, and he would come back another day and tell them more, teach them God's ways, and try to help them see how it all could greatly improve their lives in this world and ensure them a better life in the world beyond the grave.

He then asked Thanea to say a few words.

This was that young woman's first real missionary effort, and she was grievously aware of her inadequacy for the task despite all Monenna's teachings. She declared that she would speak especially to the women, but that since women were necessary

122

to men, and men to women, there might be something for men to think on also. Women were as much God's creation as were men, and they had responsibilities such as men had not, in the bearing and rearing of children in particular, on which the very continuation and future of mankind rested. So let none undervalue their part. They could, and should, pray to God equally with their menfolk, and teach the little ones to pray also. *She* had a little son, aged five years, and was teaching him about the good, kind God – and she told them the tale of Mungo and the robin, addressing herself particularly to the children there. That she had general and fascinated attention was clear, even though some of the men grinned with scorn rather than wonder, which made her question whether she had been wise in mentioning this, and glanced at Serf. But that man smiled and nodded.

She did not say much more, except to add that her uncle, King Arthur, was a strong Christian, and that all should be grateful that he was so, and was, in faith, protecting all these northlands from the Saxon heathen invaders.

Afterwards the couple moved amongst the people, answering questions and showing their friendship. Thanea found herself besieged by children exclaiming their comments anent robins and birds and animals generally – so much so that, later, Serf had to admit, with head-wagging, that probably she had made more impact that evening with her story than he had done with all his talking. So much for the exposition of doctrine!

They learned, incidentally, that the Black Devon was so called for no better reason than that its waters were particularly peat-stained.

Next morning, promising to return before long, they were on their way, with about thirty miles to cover to reach Culross, by the Cleish and Rescobie Hills and the other Carnock. On the way down Loch Levenside, they noted a quite large island at the south end, green and tree-clad. Serf, pointing, said that there might be the place to establish a little monastery, should their efforts at mission in Kinross bear sufficient fruit. Monasteries should be near enough to centres of population, but apart, their Church taught, the monks available and accessible but yet able to withdraw

123

for contemplation and their private devotions. This island might serve.

Thanea was longing to see Mungo again.

10

It was months later, autumn, before, making the same return journey down Loch Levenside, Thanea asked Serf whether he had remembered to ask Mormaor Nechtan if he might use that larger island to the south for a possible monastery site; to be told that, yes, he had permission. This visit to Forteviot and Kinross had been delayed, for the abbot had much to do otherwise, the superintendence of his quite numerous monastic outposts and other missionary efforts, the main Culross community itself demanding much of his time, with the training and confirming of novices and the everyday duties entailed in managing quite a large company of his fellow-men, Christian or otherwise. The pair had at length gone up to Forteviot, taking young Mungo with them, there left Thanea and the boy for a week, on holiday as it were, while Serf went back to Kinross to proceed with his mission, happily with considerable and heartening success. So now Mungo was riding his Marc with them, and their travelling in consequence somewhat slowed. The boy had enjoyed himself at Forteviot, with the mormaor's children.

The inevitable happened. Mungo, on talk and sight of that island, pleaded, indeed demanded, to be taken out to visit it, all this association with royalty, and his own princely blood perhaps, telling. Surely they could find a boat and go to it? His elders did not, in fact, put up much resistance, Serf himself not averse to a brief inspection, the young woman nothing loth. So, instead of proceeding on southwards, they turned round the foot of the loch looking for some house or hamlet where they might borrow a boat.

They had to go quite some distance, for this end of the loch was low-lying and marshy, undrained, unsuitable for human habitation. They had to cross, with some difficulty, the River Leven which here emerged from the loch to flow eastwards through Fothrif and Fife – Thanea telling Mungo about that other River Leven which they had had to cross by a causeway at faraway Dumbarton, and what these names, Leven, Devon, Avon, Allan and the rest meant – before almost a mile up the far side of the loch they came to a small village, this called Portmoak, and as its name implied, another fishing community. Here they had no difficulty in finding a small boat, a coracle, to take them out the quarter-mile to the island, the boy asking to be allowed to try his hand with the paddle, with wet results.

Not only Mungo was greatly taken with what they found on the island, they all were. It was heart-shaped, like the loch itself, almost a mile long, with its own little bays and headlands, its minor heights and valleys, even its springs and a burn, a little paradise. Mungo raced about it all, pointing and shouting and laughing, and Serf, although less vocal, was almost equally delighted, all but claiming it as his own already and declaring what a diseart it would make. He amended that presently however, saying that it was just too attractive and enticing. That was not what disearts were for, sterner conditions required for due and concentrated communion with their Maker, not enjoyment of the senses. Thanea said that she did not see why. Was not appreciation of God-made beauty and excellence conducive to communion? They taught that God was kindness and love, and beauty too. Why the need for sternness?

The abbot asserted that some sternness was necessary because of *man*'s aptitude for ease and lukewarmness in his devotions. He knew himself how, in such a small earthly paradise as this island, he would enjoy it all so much that his religious disciplines, which were part of the need for disearts, would suffer. No, it was not a matter of scourging himself, but of necessary self-denial. Nevertheless, the man went ranging that island to find the ideal place to establish his desired cell.

Indeed they spent so long on that gem in the loch that they had to spend the night at Portmoak before heading into the wilderness of the Cleish Hills. And all this talk of disearts impelled Thanea to raise the subject which had been on her mind for long. When was Serf going to take her to spend some time at his cave diseart up the Fife coast? He had said that he might, one day. He had gone off there a few times for the required contemplation and spiritual refreshment, but he had never suggested that she accompanied him. She would not intrude unduly on his solitude and devotions. They could take Mungo, and she and the boy could leave him frequently. She wanted her son to grow and develop unconstrained by the monastic restrictions, good as these would be for him eventually. But a child should not be too confined.

Serf commented that his cliff-face cave was scarcely the safest place to take a child. Thanea said that she would look after her son. They could use one of the cliff-*foot* caves if that was advisable. But she dearly wanted to be part of a diseart vigil, even though it could be only something of a pretence for her.

The man acceded. He was due to have a vigil before long. They would all go – but on condition that she left him alone for periods.

When they left Portmoak, and Mungo waved goodbye to the island, they promised each other that they would be back, and before long.

The diseart visit took place a couple of weeks later, with the Culross brothers getting used to losing their abbot, Thanea, and son fairly frequently, although Cora and Rua were less resigned to it. In this case Leot came along also, trotting behind the horses, to be protector of Mungo and his mother when Serf required privacy, or such was the excuse.

They had to call in at the coastal mission stations on their way, this keeping in touch with his so-scattered flock one of the abbot's major preoccupations. The small boy inevitably aroused much interest and comment – and Mungo reciprocated enthusiastically, introducing Leot to all, and making new friends. He took part in the brief services, singing psalms heartily, and improvising his own words or just adding la-la-la.

He was greatly excited, of course, when they came to the cliffs and caves at Wemyss, and here had to be physically restrained – although he had already been duly warned as to dangers and the need for the utmost caution. Leot proved valuable here, for the dog was very wary of the heights, keeping well back from dizzy edges, this ensuring that Mungo did so also, the boy much concerned with protecting and reassuring his friend.

Two-thirds down that cliff, in the main cave, he was enthralled, exploring, exclaiming at its features, even though not so much interested in the views as was his mother. They held a little service of re-dedication, to indicate that this *was* a vigil, and then Serf took them down the rest of the way to the beach, by a very devious descent in the cause of safety, Leot whimpering and Mungo patting comfort. Here they examined three more caverns, one quite large, and selected the middle one for occupation by mother, son and dog, an L-shaped one, and dry, to leave the higher eyrie free for abbatial devotions. Serf did bless this one for them however, declared that they would be safe enough here, but that if there was the least hint of intrusion, they were to shout. He would hear, above, and be down to them promptly.

They were left to their own devices.

There was a much more exciting seashore to explore here than that at Culross, which was estuarine and fairly muddy, whereas at Wemyss there were rocks and reefs, sand, pebbles and seaweeds, innumerable different kinds of shells to collect, little crabs, starfish and odd items of flotsam. The myriad lugworm casts intrigued Mungo, but dig as he would he did not unearth, or unsand, any of the worms, to his mystification.

The feeding situation was less satisfactory. Diseart vigils were not the occasion for any sort of feasting, indeed fasting was apt to be the rule; but Mungo was developing a hearty appetite and saw no virtue in starving. Thanea had brought some simple provender, but the boy had heard that shellfish were good to eat, indeed had sampled some at the abbey. Unfortunately his mother was uneducated in this matter and unsure which were edible and which were not. Taking no risks, she said that she would ask St Serf on the morrow.

So they ate bread and honey that night, washed down with water from a burn.

Actually, Serf came down to say goodnight, by which time Mungo was asleep at the back of their cave. He explained to Thanea about mussels and cockles and how to eat them, doubting whether they would find many oysters here. She forbore to ask him how his vigil went, knowing herself to

128

be incapable of that sort of wordless adoration which seemed to be required in it, but respecting those for whom this was possible.

Long she sat alone in the cave mouth thereafter, gazing out over the darkening sea towards the now invisible Lothian coast, thinking long thoughts and wondering. What was her future? And Mungo's? Had God sent her to this entirely new and full life of His set purpose? What was happening over there, at Traprain? What of those she had left? Gawain, the brother whom she loved? Mordred whom she loved less than perhaps she ought? Monenna and the young women who had been her fellow-students, many probably married by now, and probably to pagans? And her father? What of him? Was she failing in her daughterly duty in her attitude to him? He had tried to kill her, yes. But was not that out of some mistaken conviction that not only did she deserve it but that her death would in some way placate the pagan deities he believed in, and so help others of his people, the monarch thinking of his wider duties? He must have had some very strong reason for doing as he did to his only daughter, however mistakenly. Was *she* at fault in judging him harshly? Herself a Christian. Forgive, Christ said . . .

It did not occur to her, there, that she was perhaps keeping her own sort of vigil and worship.

The next day she and Mungo went further eastwards along the shore, and presently came to an area of mussel-beds, where they set about gathering a great haul of the shellfish, which they found difficulty in transporting back without container until, for want of better, Thanea took off her skirt to make a sack of it – to her son's glee, who had been reared to be frank and natural in such matters. He offered to take off his own tunic, carefully embroidered by his mother with Celtic decoration, but it was too small and not the right shape to be of much use.

Thereafter they went up to Serf's cave, risking reproof, but were kindly received, the abbot genially commenting on shapely legs. He provided his cooking-pot from its recess, and filled it with water from the trickle at the back, devotions being deferred meantime and replaced by much splitting open of mussel shells and scooping out the contents into the pot. Then Mungo demonstrated his expertise in making fire with flint sparks into tinder, and blowing into flame, for the abbot's store of driftwood. Soon they had mussel stew bubbling, bread being added to turn it all into a kind of soup – which Mungo at least declared delicious, even if his mother was less enthusiastic. Fasting, like devotions, was deferred; but Thanea asserted that surely using God's gifts thus was a form of worship also?

They left Serf in peace, if with full stomach, and went to explore inland.

The following day, the abbot, an energetic saint rather than a contemplative one, decided that some action was called for. He had heard that there was a quite large community at Innerleven, at the mouth of the same river which flowed out of Loch Leven, its course eastwards all this way. They would go on to Innerleven and prospect its possibilities for establishing a mission there, then return for one more day of the vigil.

So they rode off along the coast the five or six miles. But at the river-mouth village they found the climate scarcely apt for even tentative missionary activities. The folk were in a state of great alarm. The barbarous invaders had landed, the Saxons. And none so far away.

Questioning elicited that a large Saxon fleet of longships had appeared off Fife Ness, some twenty miles to the east, and had landed a large host at Crail where there were shelving sands. They were ravaging and slaying inland from there, north and west. With no army to oppose them, they could overrun the land of Fife. They could be here, at Innerleven, in a matter of days.

This was dire news indeed. These Saxons represented ever-present menace – as King Arthur had reason to know, having spent the last twenty years resisting and repelling them. But hitherto they had confined their assaults to the Brythonic kingdoms of the south and west and the Anglian lands of Deira and Northumbria. Minor raiding *had* occurred on the coastal acres north of Tweed, to King Loth's alarm; but never large-scale invasion. This report might be exaggerated, of course; but these fisherfolk here would not be likely to name a few raiding vessels a large fleet. And if there was indeed a major force, it must have greater ambitions than merely local pillage and rape.

In the circumstances, Serf forbore from any missionary talk, and said that they should head back for Culross forthwith.

On the way home he discussed with Thanea the possible consequences. The Saxons were warriors, much more so than the Angles who had preceded them, and with an all-consuming ambition to take over lands and build some sort of empire of the north. The fact that they had landed in force in east Fife, if true, was significant, and must mean that they had territorial designs. This was a comparatively unimportant part of the mormaordom of Fortrenn. Were they aiming at that? Fortrenn? Thus far they had not really threatened Alba. Or might it be Lothian itself that they coveted, a richer prize? By making a base on the eastern peninsula of Fife, they could menace Lothian's fertile heartland much more seriously than by invasion of its cliff-girt and rock-bound coast to the south. Either possibility was grievous.

They returned to the abbey in anxious state.

And there they found a messenger from the Mormaor Nechtan awaiting Serf. He came to ask the abbot's help. Nechtan knew of the invasion of his land and was much perturbed. His information was that after the Saxon force had landed, most of the ships had sailed off, round Fife Ness, northwards, presumably making for the Tay estuary. That could mean that the invading army was also heading that way, overland. He feared that Fortrenn was the objective, that the Saxons were now turning their aggressive intentions to Alba. He, Nechtan, was mustering his forces. But unfortunately he· had sent a contingent of his best fighting men to aid in the Albannach endeavours to recover the great island of Mull in the Hebridean Sea from the Dalriadans who had occupied parts of it. So he was in no state to repel a Saxon army successfully. King Arthur, Arthur the Saxon-Slayer, and Loth of the Gododdin, should take a hand. For they also were threatened in this. Would Prince Servanus go to his Christian friend Arthur and urge him to act? And quickly, for haste was vitally necessary. It might seem strange for the Picts to be seeking the help of the Britons. But if the Saxons overran Fortrenn, or part of it, most surely it would not be long before they turned their attentions southwards across Forth, to Lothian, or south-west to Manau and Strathclyde.

Serf could not reject this plea from the mormaor, with whom he so desired to remain on friendly terms. Especially as it was to his own advantage to have Arthur take a hand, in that the Saxon threat applied to Culross as well as elsewhere, of course; the abbey could be endangered, the invaders no respecters of Christianity. Also he felt that it would not be impossible to convert Nechtan himself to the true faith eventually, and this service he could render him might greatly help.

So – he would be off, seeking Arthur. The problem was, where to find him? The High King could be anywhere over a great area of the Brythonic kingdoms, from Wales in the south to Strathclyde in the north. But in the circumstances, he might well be at his own capital of Carlisle. For if this was indeed a major Saxon venture, and at this season of the year, it was likely that they would not be invading elsewhere at the same time and dividing their forces. So Arthur might be having a breathing-space. He, Serf, could try Carlisle, then.

Thanea suggested that he went to see her father first. After all, if a large fleet had sailed up the coast to Fife, it almost certainly would have been seen from somewhere in Lothian and reported to Loth. Her father could well be already on the alert, concerned. He might even have sent word of it to the High King, Arthur, for support in case of invasion of his own territories. For that matter, Arthur himself would probably be well informed as to the matter, his spies always on the lookout. It could be that Serf would not need to go all the way to Carlisle. His task might be, rather, to persuade her father, and Arthur, that just to remain on guard to protect Lothian was not advisable, but that they should actually themselves cross over Forth and assail the Saxon rear, and thus aid Nechtan *and* themselves.

The abbot admitted that this was good counsel. He would go first to Traprain. But, in the interim, he was concerned over the safety of those here at Culross. What if the Saxons swung westwards, or some of them? They were only twenty miles away, after all.

Thanea thought that any attack here was unlikely at this stage. If most of the ships had sailed north to the Tay, it was surely probable that the Saxon host would head that way also, and not be diverted to random raiding, Fortrenn and Forteviot the target. But if there was word of raiders coming this way, they could go into hiding. Where? An island? There were numerous islands in the Forth estuary – but the longships

132

could reach them. What about their little chosen island in Loch Leven? No sea-going vessels could reach that. They could all go and hide there. It was nearly a mile long. There would be room for all the abbey's people, for a short time. Would that not serve, if it came to flight? A sanctuary indeed!

Serf was doubtful, but could think of no better refuge. But – God would surely look after them. They must have faith . . .

He was off at dawn next morning, a man with much on his mind.

11

In the event, the abbot was back at his abbey sooner than expected — and found all in order there and no panic. He brought heartening news. Thanea's assessment of the situation had proved fairly accurate. On arrival at Traprain, Serf had found all there mustered for war and in a state of readiness, only awaiting the arrival of King Arthur himself, the Saxon invasion of Fife known to all, and recognition general that Lothian might well be threatened next. The High King had arrived the day following, to take charge. He had not required the Mormaor Nechtan's appeal for help, for he had come prepared to cross Forth and assail the Saxon rear. He had sent for King Lancelot of the Brigantes to join them, from south of Tweed, and that young man had arrived the same evening, with a sizeable force to add to the rest. They were awaiting Urien of Rheged, and meantime collecting shipping from all the Lothian and Forth havens, mainly fishing-craft necessarily, to transport what would be a major host across the ten miles of estuary mouth from North Berwick. So all was as well ordered as was possible. The Saxons were going to be at the receipt of some of their own treatment.

Thanea was relieved, and hoped that Arthur's army would not be delayed in crossing Forth, a great undertaking in small boats. For Forteviot was none so far north-west, and she was anxious, in particular for Queen Eva and her children.

Serf said that at least Nechtan and his people were advantaged in knowing the territory, where the invaders would not, and could select the best ground to try to hold up the Saxon advance. He, Serf, was uninformed as to the lands of northern Fife and the eastern approaches to Forteviot; but there were bound to be areas of marshland, difficult river-crossings and the like, where a lesser force could restrain a larger, and at least give time for Arthur's host to catch up.

At Culross all they could do now was to pray, and wait for news.

There followed a tense few days. Serf sent out some of his young monks north and east, to try to gain and bring back word of events. The abbot instituted continuous prayer sessions, day and night.

In the end it was not his monkish scouts who brought the news, but fisherfolk from the mission station of Rosyth, who had learned it from others of their kind – for the estuary was full of the boats which had ferried the army across, and agog now. There had been a great battle at a place called Abernethy, where the River Earn joined great Tay, and the Fortrenn forces had held up the Saxons. There King Arthur had caught up with the invaders, as they were awaiting their ships to take them round behind Nechtan's men across the marshes. Instead, they were caught between the two hosts. There had been great slaughter, and the Saxons, or some of them, had taken to their longships indeed, but to flee. The invasion was over.

The prayer services at Culross turned into thanksgivings.

It was only a few days later that the abbey had visitors. There was alarm at first when two longships of the Saxon type, high-prowed and sterned, with thirty-six oars and a square sail, appeared in Culross Bay and beached. But no crowd of savage invaders came ashore, only a small party of finely clad although armoured men, obviously chiefly, and with no swords drawn, nor axes and spears in evidence. Serf, eyeing them as they came stalking up from the shore, let out a shout.

"Arthur!" he cried. "Arthur! Great Arthur! God be praised – Arthur himself!"

Thanea, standing behind, drew a quick breath. But it was not at the announcement of that renowned name, impressed as she might be; it was because, just behind the tall leader of the group was her own brother, Gawain.

Uncertain what to do, she hesitated, scanning the rest of the party for identities. Her father? Mordred? No – there was no one else that she knew. Would Gawain recognise her? It had been almost six years. And he would be thinking her dead . . .

Serf strode forward to greet the High King, arms outstretched.

135

Arthur was a big man in more than his deeds and fame, tall, broad-shouldered, powerfully built, and handsome in a square-featured way, his bearing quietly authoritative, anything but arrogant. Now in his forty-seventh year he looked every inch the hero-king he was. Yet his slow smile was almost gentle, his speech easy, natural.

"Servanus, old friend!" he said. "We could not sail up Forth in our captured ships without calling to see you. God has been good to us, and we would say a thanksgiving with you. Or *some* of us!" And he smiled wryly, with a jerk of his head backwards at some of his party, presumably pagan.

The two men clasped each other.

Thanea, head down, had drawn a little way aside, not knowing what to do. Gawain, eyes on the High King and Serf, was not looking at her. Should she hurry away, before she was recognised? The visitors might only be here for a short while, and for a brief service in the church. Yet, despite it all, one part of her wanted to run forward and throw herself into her brother's arms. Could she? God guide her . . .

Whether it was God who guided her, or merely Mungo, was open to question. For her son came running from wherever he had been playing, calling aloud, not to his mother or Serf, but to the sheep Cora, and the robin Rua which was hovering above, Leot in attendance. This unusual assortment inevitably drew all eyes; and, since the boy made directly for his mother, Thanea also came in for attention. There was no avoiding it now. She turned to face her brother.

She saw him staring, eyes wide, lips parted, a shaking hand rising to point. And abandoning all reserves and caution, the young woman exclaimed, "Gawain! Gawain!" and ran forward, to throw herself bodily into his arms.

What followed was beyond all words, their own or in the telling. Clutching, all but wrestling with each other in their overwhelming emotions, the pair gasped and panted, tried to speak but could not, while all around them gazed, astonished.

Again it was young Mungo who effected some change in the situation, not prepared just to gaze like the others. He went to grab and tug at his mother's skirt, demanding attention – and inevitably dog, sheep and bird with him, which did little to lessen the concern of others. For once the High King Arthur was not the centre of attraction.

Thanea, blinking away tears, and seeking to smile instead, detached herself from Gawain's convulsive embrace and reached to stroke her son's fair head.

"Gawain – here is Mungo. Or Kentigern. Mungo – this is the Prince Gawain, my brother." Which introduction did not greatly clarify the situation, for most there.

"Eunach! Eunach – you, you *live*!" her brother got out. "You live! You are not . . . you, you survived! The sea. You were not . . ." He still clutched her arm. "We . . . I believed you dead. Dead! Dear God – here is wonder! Wonder!"

"Wonder, yes. God saved me. And Mungo. My son. Oh, Gawain – I rejoice! I could not tell you. I could not send message. In case our father . . . ! The boat drifted here. St Serf took me in, cared for me. Kindness. And Mungo was born . . ."

Mungo demanded attention. "Cora has a sore foot," he declared urgently. "See – she does not walk well. She drags it. Poor Cora. Her foot."

"Yes. Poor Cora. But later, Mungo. Not now. Prince Gawain is your uncle. My brother. Greet him kindly."

The boy was more concerned with the sheep. "Cora is *hurt*," he insisted. "Look – her foot . . ."

"This, this is Owen's child?" Gawain said, wondering.

"Who else? He, Owen – he is not here?" That question held a note of alarm.

"No. He was with the host, yes. But has now returned to Rheged with his father. We go to Manau, and then, by Rheged, to Carlisle."

"He, Owen, must not know. *Must* not!"

"No. Oh, Eunach – *our* father!"

"Where? Where is he? He must not know, either. You must see that, Gawain." She shook her head. "You will not tell him?"

"No. I *can* not, lass. But . . . perchance he knows now, nevertheless. *Now!* Eunach, our father is dead. Slain in the battle by the Saxons."

They stared at each other.

"Dead! Father, dead. Slain. Gone to . . . to God!"

"We must hope so. Pray so."

Thanea did not, could not, weep for her father, for Loth. But she could sorrow that he had died an unbeliever. Would he learn better now? Would his soul survive and know truth? In pain? Or would God's mercy prevail?

Such questioning was not to be pursued there and then, with Mungo tugging at one side and a new voice speaking at the other. Serf had brought King Arthur over to her.

"Thanea, girl," he said, deep-voiced. "Gawain's sister. *My* sister's daughter. I once saw you, as a child. I have heard your sad tale. And now – this! *Your* son, here. New kin for me! A fine boy. Servanus has told me. Thanea, I salute you!" And he bent to kiss her brow, bent although she herself was tall.

"I, I thank you, my lord King. And, and uncle," she got out, finding difficulty with words, still.

Not so her son. "Cora has a sore foot," he reminded loudly, almost reproachfully, to all.

Smiling, the High King stooped, to pick the boy up. "Your name, lad?" he asked.

Serf answered for him, Rua now perched on the abbot's shoulder. "We named him Kentigern but call him Mungo. He rejoices us all. He has many friends, this one. And not only of mankind, as you see. God will be his friend always also, I think, I believe. Thanea teaches him well."

"I am glad. I can see it." He still held Mungo. "Now, friend, let us to our thanksgiving. We cannot bide here long. I must be in Manau, at the Snowdoun of Stirling, this night. Where is the church?"

"Yonder, Lord Arthur. But – you have time thereafter for some small refreshment, I think? No? Your unbelieving friends can go to eat now. And we will join them shortly." And Serf pointed the way for the others.

"They can come with us," Arthur said. "Let them see how we thank *our* God for victory, where their many gods have not helped them! Who knows – it may yet help to turn their hearts." And still with the boy on his broad shoulder, he turned and headed where Serf indicated, towards the little church with its surmounting cross. They were followed by the entire party, also the sheep and the dog, Mungo beckoning. Gawain and Thanea walked together, arm-in-arm.

138

What followed was scarcely a service, but it was certainly worship, brief prayer, vehement praise and loud singing of psalms, Mungo beating time. Thereafter all went to partake of the provender the monks had been busy providing, the boy still concerned about the sheep's foot, but being told that it would not suffer by waiting until the visitors had gone.

Sitting together at table, Thanea plied her brother with questions as to their father's death, what went on at Traprain, especially what of Monenna. And, of course, Mordred.

"Monenna is banished," she was told. "Soon after you were . . . sent away. She went first to Whittingehame, and then we know not where. The nuns at Whittingehame said that she spoke of making for St Ninian's shrine at Candida Casa in Galloway. Whether she did or no, who knows? Her students were dispersed. The girls are mostly married now. Your friend Eithne to Murdoch of Ystrad. I think that she is happy enough."

"Poor Monenna! She was so good, so kind. Why did she have to go?"

"Our father was angry with her. She reproached him over what he did to you. He said that she was having a bad influence with the other girls. The druids indeed would have burned her! So she had to leave. These last years our father was ever more under the sway of Diarmid, the Arch Druid – who all but rules the kingdom now. All traces of Christianity to be put down. I have had to hide my faith much, God forgive me!"

"I am sorry. You have been grievously unhappy. You *must* have been."

"I have spent much time with our uncle, King Arthur. My father could not prevent that. I find him, Arthur, all that our father was not, great, noble and strong in the faith. I am proud to be his man."

"I understand that. But – that will all be changed now, Gawain? Now *you* will be King of Lothian."

"No. Not so, Eunach. I have no wish to be the king of a heathen realm. Perhaps I may be weak. I do not see it in me to be able to turn Lothian back to Christianity, much as I would wish it. I need a leader, such as Arthur, not myself to be the leader of a kingdom. I will stay with Arthur. Mordred can have Lothian."

She looked at him, wondering. "You, the elder brother, to give up the throne to Mordred! Your birthright!"

"Aye. You think me feeble, Eunach? Perhaps I am. I know myself, see you. I can make a fair assistant to Lothian, where I would not make a strong monarch for Lothian and the Gododdin. And Mordred wants the throne, where I do not. So he has gone back to Traprain, to take it. I go with the High King, and can serve better with him. Can you not see it?"

"It may be that you are right. But Mordred is pagan. And can be fierce. Lothian will never return to Christ under him."

"Would it under *me*? With Diarmid and his druids gripping all. Mordred may even keep *them* in their place! Not bring Christianity back, no – but not let it be druid-ridden, as now."

She wagged her head. "Mordred as king! What does Arthur say to that?"

"He will seek to keep Mordred in order, as High King. And Mordred is a fighter. He may serve better than I would, in supporting Arthur against the Saxons."

Thanea sighed. "What would our mother say, I wonder? I so often think of her. If only she had lived, so much would have been different. God works in strange ways, does he not? But Serf would say that is wrong thinking. That *we* know so little, and the Creator knows it all. So who are we to judge? I try not to judge. Judge our father. Or even Owen ap Urien! I try."

"You are made of better stuff than I am, I think!" her brother said. "Me – I would slay Owen – if I dared! For what he did to you."

"No, Gawain. For, look what in fact he has done. Mungo, my son, and *his*, is my joy and delight. Serf is my guide and dear friend. I am happy here, with a part to play, possibly even a little part in God's purpose. Happier, I believe, than ever I could have been at Traprain. And all because of what Owen did to me!"

"Yet I prayed that he might die in that battle! Where so many died. For the Saxons are terrible fighters. But he did not, and is gone back to Rheged with his father."

"God's mysterious ways again . . . !"

With Arthur rising from the table, they left it at that.

All Culross Abbey's denizens trooped down to the shore,

even the hobbling Cora, to see the visitors on their way up Forth for Stirling, Gawain promising to come and see his sister again soon; also, at her urgent request, not to let her survival be known to others and so possibly get to the wrong ears. He was sure that King Arthur would be equally discreet.

After the waving goodbyes, the preoccupation was the serious matter of medicating a sheep's left forefoot.

12

As it transpired it was some considerable time before Thanea saw Gawain again. King Arthur and his lieutenants were kept busy going to the aid of the Welsh princes who were suffering repeated Saxon inroads, while Lancelot of the Brigantes also needed help against raiding along his Northumbrian coasts. Not that time hung heavily at Culross, for they all were very active there also, not so much at the abbey itself but in the superintendence of the various mission stations; in especial the establishment of the little monastery on the island in Loch Leven, from which to missionarise Kinross. This island was Mungo's idea of heaven, and although Thanea was glad to help Serf, where she could, at his teaching and preaching, especially to the women, she spent much time on the island, already being called Serf's Isle, with Bishop Gabhran, whose monastery this was to be, and a few monkish builders. She took on the duty of clearing an area for the necessary garden, and then digging and turning over the sandy soil, quite heavy work at which Mungo assisted after a fashion, although the little bays and coves and woodlands, with their multitudinous water-fowl and bird-life, drew him away. He made an especial friend of a bald-headed coot, which developed a taste for oatcakes, and had to be sought and fed each day.

The proselytising at Kinross went well, to Serf's great satisfaction.

Almost more pleased, however, although he told himself that it should not be so, was he over the conversion of Mormaor Nechtan, who, after Arthur's victory at Abernethy, allowed himself to take Christianity really seriously. Serf, while admitting to Thanea that the winning of a battle should not be the deciding factor in a man turning to Christ, was nowise going to refute Nechtan's new belief that it was the Christian God who had contrived the victory and so saved Fortrenn from the Saxons. With a newly baptised ruler, the mormaordom suddenly became much more accessible for his missionary efforts. So it was all activity.

Thanea and Mungo, in consequence, saw much of Queen Eva and her children. Their friendship developed.

It was Eva who was in fact responsible for a quite major venture. She was so thankful at the victory over the Saxons, and her husband's conversion, that she wanted to show her gratitude to God in tangible fashion, in more than words. She wanted to perform a missionary effort on her own, in some measure, now that Fortrenn was open for Christianisation, nothing very large of course, for she recognised her limitations, but something, as a gesture, to try to turn one or two other souls to Christ. And this suggestion rang a bell with Thanea. She had never forgotten how she had used the pagan god Gualpian the torturer to threaten King Morcant of Strathclyde into halting the raiding into Menteith, and Serf's doubts over the matter. She had, indeed, been rather ashamed of it all, and promised herself that she would try to redeem her lapse one day. Just assisting Serf in his various efforts was all very well, but some effort of her own was called for, she felt. Now, linking this with the queen's urge, she proposed that they should make it a joint enterprise. That they should go together to the remote part of Fortrenn, the Mounth of Teith, where she had helped the inhabitants in the name of Gualpian, and there try to redeem herself by teaching them who was the true God. They would be grateful for her service rendered, and with their queen taking the same message, ought to be the more readily convinced. It was a fairly long distance to go, but not so far from Forteviot as from Culross.

Queen Eva enthused.

So did Mungo, who had been listening attentively. He would go too. And tell these people how God had brought Rua back to life. The other two children clapped their hands. They also would be missionaries.

It had not occurred to Thanea that they should take the youngsters on such lengthy travel into wild country, nor to Eva either. But on urgent and very persuasive pressure, and on consideration, they came to the conclusion that it was quite feasible. The queen always rode the land with her own small guard, so they would be safe enough. If Nechtan would agree . . .

The mormaor, amused, made no objections, so long as they had a sufficient escort. After all, they would not be leaving Fortrenn, and his children were good on horseback – they had to be.

So it was agreed. At the beginning of May, the Beltane festival period again, they would make a two-family mission westwards.

The sun smiled on them, at least – however contrary to sun-worship was their errand. On a day of filmy high clouds, the birches showing young green and the cuckoos calling, Thanea and Mungo set out for Forteviot, with Serf's blessing. Mungo had wanted to take Rua with them, declaring that it could make the journey perfectly well, flying occasionally but sitting on shoulders most of the way. But his mother had drawn the line at that. Rua was getting old, for a bird, and this would be too much for it; they did not want it dying of exhaustion, did they? Besides, Cora and Leot needed its company, would be lonely without Mungo *and* the robin. At least he, Mungo, would have Marc the garron with him.

They left Forteviot next day accompanied by an unusual retinue of six fierce-looking horsemen, armed, the children vocal in the extreme. Thanea wondered whether there had ever before been a Christian mission composed like this. From this Strathearn their route was by Dunning and Auchterarder to the Allan Water and down this to the Doune of Menteith, and thereafter up Teith, the same way that Serf had taken those years before. Strangely, perhaps, the party of eleven did not travel so speedily as had the pair previously. With a queen and children unused to improvised quarters, they had to halt at Lanrick, four miles up from Doune, for the night. This was a fair-sized community with a chiefly hall-house, where, surprised as the owners were to see her, their mormaor's wife was made welcome. They had heard of no more raiding from Strathclyde into their hilly lands westwards.

With only three miles to go upriver to the Pass of Torrie next day, and then another four south-westwards over the hills to Loch Rusky, they were at Letter Rusky before noon, the children finding it all a great adventure, especially when they set up herds of deer drifting off over the heather.

At Letter Rusky they found only the one stot-herd's cabin occupied, and learned that the previous inhabitants, with those of Letter Gulipen, had removed eastwards a few miles, to a location where they could no longer see Ben Gulipen, at Ballanucater – this not so much because of any fear of renewed raiding but because they dreaded the wrath of the torturer. Not that they themselves were responsible for the violation of Gualpian's shrine, but the angry god might not discriminate between guilty and innocent men. They would be happier out from under the frown of his mountain.

The travellers were given instructions as to where to go. Thanea at least thought the news encouraging. If these folk were frightened over the hostility of one of their terrible heathen deities, they might well be more prepared to seek the protection of the kinder Christian God of love.

They found Ballanucater without difficulty, by the side of a stream flowing out of small Loch Dhu, about two miles from Loch Rusky. Here the two Letter communities had set up a joint village around a shepherd's hut and barn. Alarm at the appearance of the mounted and armed party was very evident, but Thanea was quickly recognised and fears allayed. They were distinctly overawed when they learned that their queen and her children were amongst the visitors, and that these intended to lodge meantime in their humble dwellings. They set about preparing quarters to the best of their ability; but Thanea assured them that their requirements were modest indeed, clean straw in two barns being adequate, one for the escort. Mungo proved to be a real asset here, swiftly making friends, seeking to help by carrying straw, laughing and shouting and thereby helping to put the villagers at ease, his two young friends seeking to follow his lead. Very quickly he was reciting the Rua legend to all who would listen, *his* mission begun at once.

Eva had brought food, cold meats and bread in quantities, with plenty of men and horses to carry it, so that they would not too greatly strain their hosts' resources.

That very evening, Thanea and Eva gathered all together at the burnside, men, women and children. The queen had said

145

that they came amongst them with an important message, on an especial errand which all must listen to carefully. Although not sternly announced, this did hold a queenly if not autocratic note to it, which Thanea felt to be scarcely the best approach. So that when it was her turn to speak, she adopted a rather different style.

"You will mostly remember me, Thanea, who came to you those years ago with Prince Servanus, whom we Christians call St Serf," she commenced. "We prevailed upon King Morcant of Strathclyde to stop his men raiding your homes and herds. We believe that there has been no more raiding since then. Is this so?"

There was nodded acceptance of that.

"That is good. We were glad indeed to be of some service to you, who had suffered much. But Queen Eva and myself, with our children, now come to you offering what we believe to be a still more important service, for the benefit of you all. We understand that you have moved to this place from your old homes because of fear that Gualpian the torturer, under whose mountain you lived, might vent his anger upon you for the defilement of his stone and shrine there, even though this was done by the Strathclyde men and not yourselves. Here, where you cannot see Ben Gulipen, you feel the safer. But we have come to remove altogether any such fears, and many another fear likewise. Do you understand?"

She was gazed at wonderingly, doubtfully.

"We are Christians, you see, and *know* that you have no need of these fears. Christ God has already aided you. It was He who stopped the raiding, not Serf and myself. The Almighty is the God of love, not of hatred, fear and threat. He sent His only Son Jesus Christ into this world to become a man and die for all men, so great was His love. Your pagan gods are otherwise – or as you believe them to be – harsh and cruel and vengeful. But, in fact, they do not exist. We realise that you will find it hard to accept. But these, Gualpian, Lug, Manannan and the rest, are but of men's imaginings. Because you *think* that they are there, and the druids proclaim it and sacrifice to them, they are – but only in your minds. Even the great sun, which is sinking yonder," and she pointed westwards, "even the sun is no god, has no life of its own, only a kindly heat and light

146

maintained by Christ God to comfort and warm you, and help your corn to grow and your beasts to prosper. This is our message to you."

The stares were as wondering as before, but unconvinced.

Thanea recognised that probably she had said enough, for a start. Much more would undoubtedly only confuse and fail to sink in. She looked at Eva, who nodded.

"Go now, and think on all this," she went on. "Consider well. Talk of it amongst yourselves. Ask yourselves what good, or even harm, Gualpian or any of the others has ever done to you. You have never seen him, or any. Only *men* have harmed you. You believe only what you have been told by men, druids and their like, who are themselves ignorant of the truth. You have no need to live in fear when you can live in love and kindness. Go, think on it. And tomorrow we will talk more."

"*I* prayed to God and He made Rua my robin live again," Mungo added, as finishing-piece to cap it all.

The queen said that she wished them all very well, a good night under God's good care, and ears ready to hear more, and minds to understand.

Later, with the children bedded down in blankets on the straw, Eva complimented Thanea on what she had said, and confessed that she could not have done it nearly so well. Next day they must speak of everlasting life hereafter, in eternal love, which *she* had always found to be the most enheartening aspect of Christ's teachings.

In the morning they advisedly did not plunge into more teaching but sought to turn their hands to work which helped the villagers. In this, Thanea and the escort found themselves to be better qualified than were Eva and her youngsters, who had never had to work. The guards helped with the new hut-building which was proceeding, cutting sapling boughs to make the interlaced frames to form walling, and digging rubble and small stones from the burnside for the necessary infilling. Thanea spun wool and did some weaving, while Eva ran honey from combs into pots, making a sticky business of it which demanded much hurrying down to the burn to wash herself. The children played with the local youngsters and enjoyed themselves. This partaking of the village life was

147

undoubtedly beneficial, causing the visitors to be accepted and their teachings therefore to be the more heeded. While the women forbore to mention the subject of belief throughout, no such inhibitions constrained Mungo, who clearly was going to waste no opportunities. His version of the Gospel message might be limited and personal, but it was pressed home at any and every opportunity.

It was afternoon before his elders thought the occasion ripe to proceed, and got most of the community assembled. On Eva's urging, Thanea led off. She began by asking how many of her hearers had thought at any length on what had been said the evening before – to be rewarded with quite a few nods, some more embarrassed than enthusiastic. She did not pursue that line meantime but said that Queen Eva wanted to talk to them about eternal life, that is, life after death, which was a central feature of Christ's teachings. The druids taught of this, in some measure and circumstances, but far from comfortingly. The queen would tell them differently.

Eva was more diffident now, realising that Thanea had the more effective and interesting approach. She said that the druids held that there *was* life after death, for some, but that it was full of hazards, punishments, reincarnation in animal form, and the like, the soul often in torture. Christ the Son taught quite otherwise, that God the Father, being love personified, His kingdom hereafter was fair and joyful, wherein men and women, children too, could fulfil themselves as perhaps they had not been able to do in this life, and go on to ever fuller living, richer, where there were no oppressors, no fears, no pains. They all had to die some day, so it was good to look forward to this better life.

She obviously made an impression with this, her hearers eyeing each other.

Thanea took it from there. "Christ taught of more than eternal life," she said. "More than the *next* world. Of making a good and satisfying life in this one. And He did more than teach and talk. He healed the sick and gave sight back to the blind, helped and fed the poor and needy, forgave sinners and rebuked the wicked. But even to these last He offered forgiveness if they repented of their evil ways, all showing the kindness of His, and our, Father in heaven. And He loved children, always sought out children as especially favoured of God. And animals too. He said that His Father fed the birds of the air and the beasts of the field – "

"Rua!" Mungo had to interrupt here, loudly. "My robin! And Leot and Cora and Marc! My friends, dog and sheep and horse. Yonder is Marc! They are loved too."

This unscheduled interjection gave the Princess Cara a fit of the giggles, which in turn set off her brother. Mungo, urgent as he was, could not keep a straight face thereafter either. This inevitably reacted on the village children, and the entire company. Clearly further preachings would best be postponed.

However, three people came up to Thanea thereafter, a youngish woman, a man and a little girl. After some hesitation the woman informed that she was one of those who had been abducted by the Strathclyde raiders, and abused, but who had escaped and won back to Letter Gulipen. This was her husband and the child born to her. She and her husband were prepared to believe and accept the Christian message.

In an emotional reaction Thanea threw her arms round the woman and hugged her. She had made her first converts.

She wished that there was some action which she might take to celebrate this event, some gesture of welcome to Christ's Church, the company of the faithful, some thanksgiving. She could not admit nor baptise, to be sure; only a priest might do that. But some little ceremony seemed to be called for.

Discussing it with Eva, they decided that a little service at the burnside would not be presumptuous nor out of order, not exactly baptism but indicating the washing away of paganism. From some of the lengths of the sapling boughs being used by the barn-builders they fashioned a rude crucifix by binding two pieces together crosswise, the one longer than the other; and planting this in the ground beside the stream, they called for as many as would come to watch.

Practically all there did come. Not only so but the couple concerned, with their little daughter, brought another woman with them to be made Christian. This proved to be the other escaper from the Strathclyde raiders – a fact which greatly touched Thanea, that it should be the principal sufferers from persecution who had first turned to the faith of love.

149

So, when all were gathered, Thanea said a prayer thanking God for these former pagans now turned to Him and His loving care, after their ordeals at the hands of savage men. Now they would be received into the company of the faithful, and their lives transformed and made fuller, joyful. Then she and Eva, also the children, kicked off their shoes, and the women hitched up their skirts and waded into the burn, beckoning to the new converts to follow – however unqueenly a proceeding this might be. This was not Christian baptism, they emphasised, but a symbolical washing away of past sin such as they all had committed, even the best of them.

They washed themselves in the water, the children splashing about merrily and soaking themselves and the others; to such effect that the village youngsters ran in to do the same, shouting happily. Entering into the spirit of it all, if scarcely its spiritual significance, many of the adults did likewise, so that the stream, apparently known as the Rednock Water, was soon full of cheerful folk in holiday mood, up and down. Mungo conceived it his duty and opportunity to race amongst them all, splashing them liberally in the name of the better life. If it was an unusual introduction to Holy Church, it was at least memorable and positive.

Out on the bank again, Thanea reminded them that this was not true baptism – the significance of which she sought to explain – saying that one day St Serf would send an ordained priest to administer the proper rites; but meantime these four could consider themselves Christians, and must try to live the Christian life. Next day they would have another talk, before they left for home.

That evening, while they were putting the reluctant children to bed, another four of the villagers came to them to announce that they also were prepared to turn Christian, one of them an old man, the father of their first convert, this greatly heartening the tyro-missionaries. So next morning there was another burnside initiation ceremony, with more wadings and washings. Eva had her doubts about all the hilarity generated, but Thanea thought that the good Lord would understand and accept. After all, who were we to assume that the God who made us all did not possess a sense of humour Himself?

Instead of a teaching session thereafter they asked the folk for questions, and held a very profitable hour or so trying adequately to answer the many queries so haltingly put to them, some fairly far removed from normal Christian dogma. Quite a number of their hearers, without actually committing themselves, indicated that they would think further on this matter, and perhaps when the promised priest came to baptise, they would give him their decision.

Mungo was somewhat scornful at such cautious reaction, but his elders were otherwise, prepared to calculate their mission a success, however inadequate their efforts. At midday they set off on their return journey to the Teith and on to Forteviot. The village children ran along beside their horses for quite some distance in friendly farewell. What the armed escort thought of it all was not vouchsafed – but the queen hoped that perhaps some of the men might themselves see the light as a result.

Serf, in due course, heartily agreed that they should consider their mission a success, amused as well as impressed by the details he was given. He promised to send one of his younger priests to Ballanucater of the odd name forthwith, to confirm and continue the good work.

13

Word reached them at Culross that summer and autumn of King Arthur's victories on a wide variety of battlefields, largely on the Welsh marches but also as far south as Cornwall, all against the Saxons and their Jutish allies. They heard of no Celtic defeats; yet as a continuing war rather than just a series of battles, victory seemed to elude the High King, for the Saxon outbreaks went on over great areas of Celtic Britain, with the south-east lands, as base, firmly in their hands. Serf was worried. So long as they had Arthur, the planted seeds of Christianity might be fairly safe and bear fruit; but if he fell, and the Saxon hordes triumphed . . .

They learned also, from nearer at hand, that Thanea's brother Mordred was proving to be a strong but harsh King of Lothian, imposing his own will rather than the Arch Druid's, but his subjects being little the better for that. After the Abernethy battle, when apparently he had been very critical of the Lothian contingent's war prowess, he had decided to train an army of his people to be an effective fighting force. This news at first had been greeted with a fair amount of approval, the assumption being that it was to be used to fight and contain the Saxon threat; but when it transpired that bands of his Gododdin had been raiding over Tweed into the Northumbria of King Lancelot, that produced a different reaction. It looked as though Mordred was aiming to be a warrior king. His neighbours perhaps should beware. Loth, at least, had not been one for conquest. Such tidings must be disturbing to Arthur, who had sufficient to worry him, without trouble with one of his sub-kings.

Word of all this reached Forteviot also of course, and Nechtan shared Serf's concern. Alba, in the past, had been fairly free from external assaults, save for Dalriadan inroads in the Hebrides, however much internecine unneighbourliness there might be between the various mormaordoms; but the Saxon invasion, culminating in the Abernethy battle, made it clear that Fortrenn, the most southerly of the Albannach kingdoms, was vulnerable to attack from that direction. And with Serf ever widening his missionary efforts therein, he shared this concern. He was much at Forteviot, and Thanea and Mungo apt to be with him, to mutual satisfaction.

It was on one such visit almost a year to the day after the Ballanucater episode, at the Beltane festival, that Nechtan told Serf that the Fortrenn Arch Druid, Maelcon, was having trouble with one of his own subordinates, the Druid Duncan of Airthrey – and on account of this man's alleged leanings towards Christianity. He was, apparently, neglecting his druidical duties and had more than once visited that odd little monastery at Carnock, near to Stirling – where old Fergus was prior – and this was angering the Arch Druid, for Airthrey was a significant place for their religion, site of especial observances on Dumyat, the sacred mountain of the Ochils. It was some time since Serf had visited Carnock, preoccupied with all his new endeavours; so he decided to call on this druid, Duncan, and on Fergus, on their way back to Culross. Needless to say, Thanea and Mungo went with him.

The long range of the Ochil Hills stretched westwards by south from near the Tay almost to Stirling, some twenty-five miles, separating the wide straths of Tay and Earn from the plain of Forth, a wide upland barrier, scarcely mountainous but many of the summits lofty. This hill, Dumyat, which Nechtan had mentioned, was by no means the highest, but it was the most striking, shapely and outstanding, catching the eye from a wide area to the south. It was almost at the very western end of the range, not far from Alauna, overlooking the Allan Water's junction with Forth; and was held to be especially important for worship for some reason, Airthrey, this Druid Duncan's establishment, being at its very foot.

From Forteviot, therefore, the trio made their way south-westwards down to Strathallan, and followed the Allan Water some score of miles, by Balhaldie and Ledcammerach to Alauna itself, still a sizeable town although no longer so important since the Romans had departed. Turning eastwards here, rounding as it were the westernmost shoulders of the Ochils, they quite quickly came to Airthrey, under the conical and challenging Dumyat. The sacred nature of the site was made very evident to visitors by no fewer than three stone circles in the vicinity, and a number of other incised standing-stones.

They found the druidical settlement not so very different from their own abbey of Culross, save for the giant monoliths instead of crosses, a group of whitewashed and colourfully painted houses and huts and barns, within grass-grown ramparts. By this time it was early evening, and they found Druid Duncan and his acolytes at supper.

Serf's name was, of course, known to this Duncan, and the visitors were more warmly welcomed than was to be expected by Christians, old Fergus at Carnock, who all but worshipped his abbot seemingly, having passed on something of his admiration to this man. Immediately places were made for the trio at table, Mungo attracting almost as much interest as he himself evinced in all that he saw, in particular the golden collar and bracelets which Duncan wore, and the life-sized stone statue of a naked woman, painted all black, which dominated the dining-place, and from between whose legs issued a serpent. Inevitably pertinent and searching questions followed.

After the meal, an excellent one, better than the monks went in for, when they could be alone with Duncan, Serf explained that they were on their way to Carnock monastery, which he had heard that the druid visited on occasion; and this being unusual for a druid priest he, Serf, had wondered and so called.

The other, a man of middle years, powerfully built and with a great shock of iron-grey hair and intelligent features, accepted the visitors' interest quite readily. He admitted frankly a growing curiosity over the Christian faith, saying that he had been suffering a disenchantment with many aspects of druidism for some years, and feeling that there must be some better form of worship, some truer and more attractive beliefs than these. He had eventually gone to the old priest, Fergus, at Carnock, which was the nearest Christian establishment to Airthrey, and questioned him. The answers he had received gave him much food for thought, and he had gone back. He had not yet decided to turn Christian, and give up his present

154

position; but he had learned much which intrigued him, much that made him further question druidical practices. He had much yet to learn as to the faith of this Christian God, but what he had discovered, he favoured.

Serf, of course, was more than ready to teach him more. He thought, and said, that probably the best course was for Duncan to relate some of his disenchantments with the druidical beliefs and observances, and afterwards he would tell him the Christian reactions and attitudes thereto.

And so they listened to a great deal about druidism and pagan theology, some of which they already knew, or Serf did, but also much that was new to both adults – and Mungo needless to say listening agog, his interjections having to be much restrained. They learned that the druids sought to foretell the future by, for instance, impaling sacrificial victims, and watching their agonised convulsions. Also by shooting arrows at selected innocents and counting the number of hours these took to die. That they practised divination by the flight of birds, and by the croaking of ravens and the chirping of tame wrens – this having Mungo interested. They recited magic poems to create storms. They used sorcery and hypnotism, also necromancy, to conjure up illusions. They chewed raw horseflesh in front of idols – which was why that black woman's statue was there where they fed, she representing a goddess. Druidesses appeared naked at special celebrations, all painted black.

Amidst many head-shakings and exclamations from his hearers, Duncan hastened to add that not all druid customs were cruel and fearsome, although much undoubtedly was. For instance, in their sun-worship they had children to dress as different kinds of flowers, and dance. They imitated bird-song in their music. They held the oak and mistletoe as sacred. They divined by sneezing, and calculated the passage of time by nights rather than days . . .

Thanea took Mungo off to bed after sufficient of this, in a spare hut provided, leaving Serf to amplify the Christian reaction to at least some of all this. Her son, all too wide awake, took a deal of getting to sleep that night.

In the morning Duncan took them round the stone circles and carved monoliths nearby, explaining their significance, especially how the circles were lined up for sunrise and sunset at the solstices, and with astonishing accuracy; how the astronomical, horometrical and astrological calculations were arrived at, and the intersecting lines plotted and diagrams drawn into the earth. This, while fascinating to his elders, did not greatly interest Mungo, although he did find the curious carvings and symbols on the stones to his taste, requiring reasons and explanations. But when Duncan pointed up to Dumyat and said that on its high summit there was a great cairn – where he himself would wish to be buried one day – and from which could be lined up more than a score of other stone circles, nothing would do but that they should climb up and see this wonder, hills anyway always a challenge to the boy.

Thanea was not averse, having been reared on top of Traprain Law, and with the Lammermuirs all but her playground; indeed she wondered if her son's conception in the said hills might perhaps account for his love for climbing. And Serf, in his fondness for the boy, although he declared that he was getting too old for this sort of thing, did not really demur, since they had the time, with only about a dozen miles to go to Carnock for the next night. Duncan clinched the matter by announcing that he went up to the hilltop at least once every week, his favoured pastime.

So off the four of them went, on horses to Blairlogie, a hamlet nestling in the foot of a corrie of the hill, and leaving their beasts there, started the climb. Duncan pointed out landmarks and features of interest. He explained that the name Dumyat was a corruption of Dun Miod, meaning the fort or castle of a vow, its summit cairn the sacred place where vows had always been taken to the sun god. When they reached this they would see why it was thus specially chosen.

The climb was quite taxing on account of the steepness of the ascent, the defiles and corries to be encircled and what almost amounted to cliffs to be scaled, much to Mungo's joy if not to his mother's, who had difficulty with her breathing, this despite the druid assuring them that he was taking them by the easiest route.

When they eventually reached the top, it was to appreciate that Duncan had not misled them. The cairn, a great mound of stones culminating in a pillar-like monolith, and surrounded by a wall of stone and turf, was impressive. Sundry privileged ones were buried therein, they were informed, in chambers hollowed out.

But it was the prospect which gripped and enthralled the visitors. Few viewpoints, even in this land of hills, could surpass this, surely. Because Dumyat thrust some way out, southwards, from the mass of the range, its comparative isolation and height ensured almost all-round vistas. Serf agreed with Duncan that they could see at least a hundred-mile stretch from the Norse Sea beyond Fife Ness on the east, to Ben Lomond and its mountain neighbours on the west. Southwards the Lammermuir, Morthwaite, Pentland, Campsie and Fintry Hills limited views to a mere fifty or sixty miles. And northwards, only the Highland Line giants far beyond Tay, Strathmore and South Atholl, made the horizon. Perhaps ten thousand varied, colourful and anything but square miles were outspread for their delectation that early May day. Small wonder that the druids named it sacred to the sun.

Duncan pointed out the locations of innumerable stone circles, only a few of which they could actually distinguish from this height, but all sited accurately to link up with each other in relation to the sun's seasonal variations, an astronomical and geodetic wonder, and tribute to at least that aspect of druidical culture, indeed science.

Mungo was more interested in other summits positively waiting to be climbed, but Serf said that he must be satisfied with this one, for they must be at Carnock by nightfall.

On the way downhill Thanea took her son some distance ahead, to enable Serf to continue his theological discussion with the druid – this to some effect, for when at length they said their farewells and left Airthrey, the abbot confided that this talking had been very profitable and that he had high hopes of Duncan's conversion. This would be a major success, and could set an example for other moderate-minded druids to follow. Much of the credit, of course, must go to old Fergus at Carnock, who had laid the groundwork.

Crossing Forth below Stirling they made their way south-eastwards around the meanders of that great river to the little monastery in the marshland. They found Fergus perhaps a little more crippled and going slightly blind, but otherwise much as before, and greatly delighted by their visit. He was glad to hear of progress with Druid Duncan, and said that he had hopes for another druid priest at nearby Plean, who was in fact a kinsman of Duncan. If the latter did indeed embrace Christianity then Fergus thought that the other might well do so also. Which would be a great lift for the faith in this Manau kingdom, and perhaps further afield as well. If they could win over a number of druids . . .

Serf was generous in his praise; but it was Mungo who had the old man slapping his bony knee in joy, with his version of events and progress, his simple acceptance of miraculous aid clearly appealing to the ancient, so that youth and age forged a fine accord and mutual enthusiasm. Getting the youngster to bed that night became something of a prolonged campaign for his mother, Mungo expert in delaying tactics and religious interests and questions.

The boy was disappointed that they did not remain longer at Carnock than the one day. But Serf had his programme to adhere to. That man often admitted wryly to Thanea that all his duties of visiting, ordaining, inspecting and the like did prevent him from the fullest exercise of his main task and calling, the conversion of unbelievers to the true faith. At times he felt frustrated. She sympathised, but suggested that leadership was also a God-given talent, not possessed by most folk, and as necessary for the furtherance of Christ's purposes as was teaching and preaching.

They headed back for Culross by Tullibody and Alloway, where there were other missions to administer.

14

Mungo was twelve before he saw his uncle, Gawain, again, and his mother her brother. This was mainly because that man was so busy supporting *his* uncle King Arthur all over Britain; and also because Thanea suffered a quite serious illness, which left her weak and unfit for travel for quite a lengthy period. Much vomiting and severe stomach pains produced dizziness and inertia. Oddly enough, after some time, she came to be treated by none other than Duncan from Airthrey, a druid no longer, who had now embraced Christianity. He proved to have a talent for treating the sick with herbal remedies and potions, allied to pressures on selected areas of the body and sundry exercises. He said that he thought that her trouble stemmed from a disorder of the kidneys. Had she ever suffered an injury to these parts? Some violent blow? A horse's kick, perhaps? Thanea admitted that, as she put it, she had fallen over a cliff about a dozen years before. Could that have had anything to do with it? If so, why no ill effects until now? Duncan said that this could well be the cause, damage often delayed in its consequences. He prescribed and concocted a potion made from tormentil and lady's-smock, and a dietary regime, which the young woman followed religiously.

Serf, of course, was much concerned, and attentive; while Mungo positively besieged their Maker with clamant, all but accusatory, demands for betterment, asserting that God obviously required frequent reminding as to His duties.

However that might be, Thanea did make a fair recovery, although it took a long time before she was fully back to her normal health and strength, or nearly so, and could resume her accompanying of the abbot on his journeys, and her visits to Forteviot.

It was her thankfulness for recovery which, in the end, and in round-about fashion, brought about her reunion with her

159

brother Gawain – this allied to Serf's own gratitude for his missionary successes, especially with the Mormaor Nechtan and the druid, which opened up much wider possibilities. It had, apparently, always been his desire to make a pilgrimage to the shrine of St Ninian, at Whithorn in Galloway, he who had first brought Christianity and the Gospel to this land about a century before, and in whose footsteps he, Serf, all unworthily sought to tread. He had always seemed to be too busy to make this long journey; but now he felt that he could make the time. With Thanea likewise-minded, and now able to go, he thought that it might be possible, despite the distance, if they did not hurry overmuch.

There was a problem, however, where Thanea was concerned. Whithorn, and Candida Casa, where Ninian had established his first monastery and base, was in Galloway – and Galloway was in the kingdom of Rheged, where Urien was king and Owen prince. Owen presumably did not know that Thanea had survived, and had his son. But . . .

Serf thought that if they went anonymously, quietly, they ought to be safe enough from intervention. Galloway was a large land of long peninsulas and great bays, and Whithorn at the tip of one of the former. They need not go anywhere near to Dunragit, the capital of Rheged. Indeed if they went south-about into Arthur's kingdom of Cumbria, they could probably avoid travelling through Rheged altogether, and reach Whithorn by boat across Solway, from the Carlisle vicinity.

This was agreed.

The three of them left Culross on their one-hundred-and-fifty-mile journey on Midsummer's Eve, with an extra horse to carry provisions, blankets and gear. They rode by Stirling, to get across Forth, halting at Carnock for the first night. Then on southwards for the River Carron, and over the higher ground beyond to reach Slamannan for the second night, Serf anxious not to overtire Thanea. Needless to say, Mungo demanded to know why this place was called after Manannan, the sea god, like Clackmannan so far away from salt water, to be told that this was a different derivation altogether, really the *sliabh* or moor of Manau, the kingdom.

They bedded down in a shepherd's hut.

Here they were indeed on the border of Manau and

Strathclyde, and onward they would be in the latter for much of their way, this the largest of the Brythonic sub-kingdoms. But after that episode with King Morcant, they anticipated no problems.

They were making now over the high desolate moorlands of Shotts and Dungavel for the Clyde at Lanark, which they reached after a rather depressing ride, the featureless landscape not being improved by drifting thin rain. Serf reckoned that they were still not halfway to their destination, and he was anxious about Thanea and how she was standing up to this continuous travel. She was able to reassure him.

From Lanark they followed Clyde up to its very head-waters on the lofty Tweedsmuir, where the two other great rivers of Tweed and Annan were also born, a strange circumstance, one running to the Norse Sea, the others to the Firths of Clyde and Solway. Down the last, the Annan, they progressed, to reach Moffat.

The River Annan, in its lower reaches, formed part of the border between Strathclyde and Rheged. They held to the east side, in kinder weather now, making for where the Dryfe Water and the oddly named Water of Milk joined Annan. This was pleasing country, the hills low, rolling and green, rich in cattle.

The last night of their journey was spent at Gretna, where, at the mouth of another great river called Esk, they at last reached the Solway Firth, a strange, wide estuary, so shallow that much of it was dry sand when the tide was low, save for the many rivers which drained into it from the high grounds to the east – Nith, Liddel, Esk, Eden and the others further south. Navigation here demanded knowledge and expertise, and the travellers would have to find reliable boatmen if they were going to sail to Whithorn.

It was only some dozen miles from Gretna to Arthur's capital of Carlisle, less as a bird might fly, but the distance increased by the need to find fording-places over the many rivers and streams. They soon could see the city ahead, a great spreading place, quite the largest that even Serf had ever seen, but not distinguished by any dominant rock fortress like Stirling, Dumbarton, Dunedin or even Traprain. As they drew near they could see, towards the northern end, on slightly higher

161

ground above a sharp bend of the River Eden, an extensive range of buildings above which numerous flags and banners flew, no doubt Arthur's palace. Once inside the city walls, for this they made. Whether the High King would be there was problematical; from all accounts he seldom was, these days.

In fact he was not, but was only temporarily absent, being down at Bowness on the Solway shore superintending repairs and renewals of his fleet, which had been much in use recently for his various campaigns; but he would be back in the evening.

Meantime the callers met Queen Guinevere, famous in her own right, not only for her good looks but for her reputation as a warrior queen and battle-leader, worthy mate for her husband. Thanea at least was a little daunted by the thought of meeting this formidable aunt by marriage; but as it transpired, she need not have been.

Guinevere proved all that she was renowned to be, but kindly and friendly with it, not in the least frightening nor domineering – although perhaps she could be if the occasion warranted it. She was beautiful, tall and of a magnificent figure, with plentiful hair the colour of ripe corn, brilliant greenish eyes, a wide mouth and a ready smile. Half of Arthur's court and aides were said to be in love with her, why it was not hard to see.

She was in her orchard garden gathering flowers when they arrived, and she received her visitors graciously, warmly, when she learned their identity. Her husband had told her of them all, she declared, and that in most admiring terms. Her niece she was delighted to meet, complimenting Thanea on her appearance and saying that she knew something of her dire story, told her in confidence by Arthur. Prince Servanus, of course, was renowned, and his efforts in Christ's cause praiseworthy indeed. Mungo she took to immediately, and he to her, so that he was treating her like an old friend within minutes. Altogether they made excellent company.

When Arthur returned with his assistants, he too was warm in his welcome and, when he heard of the object of their visit, declared that he also would go to Ninian's shrine. He had been there before, of course, more than once, but not in recent years with so much else demanding his attention. They would go

162

together, Guinevere adding that she would go also. They would make it a family pilgrimage, go in the royal barge.

Gawain was with his uncle, and rejoiced to see his sister and nephew. He seemed to have matured considerably since last Thanea had seen him – perhaps she had done so also? She felt that he would make a good king for Lothian. Was that possible? He said that he did not think that he could, or should, unseat his brother now, even though Mordred was proving a hard ruler, and becoming something of a problem for Arthur. For himself, he was better as he was, as his uncle's aide and left hand.

The visitors met, for the first time, the two sons of Arthur and Guinevere, Lohot and Amhar; and perhaps unfairly, thought them both to be rather feeble offspring of such a renowned couple. They were now in their later teens and, although well developed and quite good-looking, did not sparkle nor have much to say for themselves. That, to be sure, could be the lot of the progeny of highly distinguished parents.

Amongst others, they met a much more remarkable man, of early middle years, the High King's secretary, called Merlin. He was darkly slender, saturnine of feature and obviously highly intelligent. He by no means thrust himself forward in that company, but he stood out nevertheless, and clearly Arthur relied on him for much. Strangely, Mungo did not like him, from the first, which was unusual for that friendly youngster, declaring that that man gave him shivers down his back.

The visitors enjoyed a feast that night, so very different than had been their eating of late – although it might be that the High King's court always dined like this when he was at home, Mungo announcing loudly that he had never before eaten thus, to the amusement of all.

In the morning they discussed the pilgrimage. Arthur said that he could not go that day, for he had a meeting with two Welsh princes who were seeking his authority to unseat their half-mad father who was misruling their kingdom. But they would all go the day following, and hope for good weather for their crossing of the Solway, for despite its shallowness, or probably *because* of it, strong seas could suddenly spring up and make sailing uncomfortable as well as dangerous.

So Gawain took charge of the visitors that day, showing them over the city and its immediate surroundings, proudly exhibiting many of the trophies of war and items of interest which Arthur had collected, in the gaining of some of which he himself had had a part. They enjoyed it all, a change from constant travel. And in the evening, Guinevere made an excellent hostess.

On the morrow, then, it was an early start, partly on account of the tide but also because they had a fifty-mile sail ahead of them and, sailing west by south, with the prevailing winds against them, it would be oar-work most of the way. Quite a large party rode down to Bowness, where the Romans had had a camp and harbour in the mouth of the Eden River, all navigation hereabouts having to be from such places. Here, and at Cardurnock on Moricambe Bay, Arthur's fleet was based, and there were quite large communities of seafaring folk. The company, as well as Arthur, his queen and two sons, and Gawain, included Merlin the secretary, Manus the chaplain, an expert on Ninian and his sanctuary, and two of the lords. Also two of Guinevere's musicians.

The royal barge proved to be a sizeable sea-going vessel, with no fewer than sixteen oars, each manned by two rowers. It looked somewhat ungainly, despite colourful painting, carved figureheads and banners, for it had to be wide enough to carry horses – not that they would require mounts on this occasion, barefoot walking being apparently part of the pilgrimage routine. Mungo was much excited.

Embarking, with the tide two-thirds full, they were pulled out into mid-channel at once, to gain depth of water, before turning westwards for the firth. Thereafter they had to follow a zigzag course down the channel, unseen but known to the shipmaster. And even beyond the Eden mouth, with seemingly open water, their twisting progress had to be continued, for they were still in fact necessarily following the river's course for miles out, as would have been only too evident at low tide. Explaining this to Mungo, Arthur pointed out that although this strange shallow coast had its difficulties and problems, it was why his capital, Carlisle, sat fairly secure where it did, from seaborne invaders who did not know these complicated waters. And of course the high hills to east and south added their own protection.

They were between the headlands of Skinburness on this Cumbrian coast and Southerness on the Galloway shore, some nine miles apart, before the careful navigation could cease and they could head westwards across the firth on a direct course. They had already come some fifteen miles, with another thirty-five to go – but it had taken them almost half of the time that they would use to do so.

Now, with plain uninterrupted rowing, the sail of little use to them in the contrary breeze, it was time for the musicians to play their part to while away the time, for there was little to see, the coastline to the north being undramatic. Accompanying the rhythmic creaking of the oars, they produced a haunting repetitive melody on pipe and harp, to which the oarsmen, or some of them, joined in at grunting, jerking intervals, as did some of the passengers less gaspingly, led by Guinevere and Mungo. Arthur pointed out the headlands of Balcary and Borness and the Galloway Isles of Fleet, unimpressive landmarks as these might be. But the further Galloway coast they were making for was different, he said.

Mungo wanted to know why it was called Galloway when it was the kingdom of Rheged? He was told that the two were not exactly the same. Urien's realm of Rheged did not cover all Galloway; that name referred to the *people*, and should really be Gallwyddel, the land of the stranger Gaels, so called because they had long before come over from Ireland and spoke a different version of the language. The Romans had called them the Novantae, just as they had called the Gododdin of Lothian the Votadini. Mungo was little the wiser.

At length, after three hours of this, they could see something more worth looking at, and this straight ahead, a varied coastline of cliffs and creeks, rocks and headlands, backed by low hills. This was the Machars peninsula, they were told, a score of miles of it, at the southern tip of which was Isle of Whithorn, their immediate goal.

This Isle of Whithorn was scarcely an island by normal standards, just a detached hummock of rock and grass separated from the rest of the peninsula by a little moat of water which could be waded over. But its western side formed a sheltered haven, and round to this the barge pulled in, and all disembarked.

On the summit ridge of this isle was a small ruined building of stone, roofless now but the walls complete, which Mungo, assuming it to be Ninian's chapel, ran to inspect. But Manus the chaplain said no, although this *was* connected with the saint, some suggesting that it was the first place he built, to lodge in, before he moved inland to Whithorn itself to set up his church and monastery. That is where they would go now. The custom was that the pilgrimage should be made barefooted, but it was three miles inland to the shrine and village, and most pilgrims made only the last half-mile unshod. All there agreed that this was sufficient – except for Mungo, who had his shoes off there and then, and ran ahead joyfully.

Without any steep hills, the ground rose fairly rapidly through cattle-dotted slopes. Presently they could see the whitewashed houses of the township, the boy pointing, as though their guide. But before they reached Whithorn he had halted at an isolated monolith at the pathside, inscribed with a cross above a circle, and the Ch R monogram. He demanded to know if this was Ninian's grave, but was told that it was not, that it represented the tomb of one Latinus and his daughter. Who was this Latinus? The chaplain did not know. Oddly, it was the man Merlin who spoke up.

"That is the oldest Christian monument in all Britain," he mentioned, almost casually. "It was there when Ninian came."

However undramatically stated, that announcement had a marked impact on his hearers, even Arthur himself looking a little uncomfortable at his secretary's statement, and perhaps at the slightly sarcastic way he said it. For, of course, if this was true, then it scarcely tied in with the tradition of Ninian being the first to bring the faith to this land, if this Christian monument was there when he came.

Manus frowned. "That is mere conjecture," he objected. "And even if it is so, it does not lessen Ninian's achievement in *converting* so much of the land to Christ."

Smiling with a sort of wry amusement, Merlin shrugged. "If the folk were not converted first, before, how came it that

166

Ninian made *his* pilgrimage to Rome, and there was turned into a bishop by the Pope?" he wondered.

The chaplain was looking upset when the High King intervened. "We are here to pay tribute to Ninian's great service to Christ's cause," he reminded. "Not to argue over dates and details. Let us on to his shrine."

Serf nodded. "So say I."

But not far from the first of the buildings they came across another standing-stone beside the track, this also having a circled cross, with a Latin inscription beneath.

"This is St Peter's Stone, erected by Ninian in honour of the apostle, after his return from St Peter's shrine in Rome," Manus said.

They all glanced a shade apprehensively at the secretary to see if he had any contrary opinion about this one. But it was Mungo who spoke.

"Why put it here?" the ever-inquiring boy demanded. "Not in his, his place yonder?"

"Perhaps he did not want Peter to seem to compete with himself?" the secretary suggested. "It was to be Ninian's place, not Peter's!" Clearly that man, with his Welsh accent, was something of a sceptic.

Guinevere it was this time who changed the subject. "This is where we take off our shoes." And she stooped to do so.

"I do not think that I like that man," Mungo confided to his mother in a penetrating whisper – and although Thanea shushed him, Serf gave an affirmatory nod.

All barefooted then, even Merlin, and picking their way the more carefully now, they came to Whithorn.

They saw a small community of the usual whitewashed wattle and daub houses, and a little way apart, within grass-grown ramparts, a stone building rectangular on plan and plain but with a cross topping one gable.

Chaplain Manus stepped forward to address them all, but carefully aimed his remarks at the High King, to ensure no interruptions from Merlin.

"Sire, here is Candida Casa and Whithorn, where the saint laid the foundations of Christianity in this land," he declared, all but defiantly. "Ninian is himself worthy to be called an apostle of Christ, not just a disciple. He sought to convert

167

whole nations, caring nought for scorn, hatred, hurt or danger. He gave his life that men might have the chance of salvation. If comparatively few so chose, and of these many relapsed, Ninian's name and fame live for ever."

"Why did he die?" Mungo demanded.

"Why, boy? That you must ask the good Lord."

"I will, yes."

Thanea laid a hand on her son's arm.

"Ninian belonged to this land. Rheged. And now Rheged is pagan again. Apostate! The shame of it . . ."

But Mungo was not to be silenced. He had been journeying for a week to see this wonder, and was all but bursting with questions. "Why is it called the White House?" he demanded, pointing at the church. "It is not white. It is the only one that is not! All these others are white . . ."

"It is a misunderstanding," the chaplain told him, less than patiently. "Candida Casa, in Latin, means not white but luminous, shining, the house of light, the light of the world, Christian light. But the local speech here makes it *whit aern*, or Whithorn, and so it has become the White House."

"It is not really a house at all, is it? It is a church. I do not think that it is a good name."

"A church is the house of God, boy." Manus was showing signs of exasperation. Probably he would not have gone thus far had the interrupter not been of the High King's kin. "Ninian was born in these parts, of the royal line. That would be about the year of our Lord 370. He went to Rome as a young man, and came back in 397 to start his great work, this when the Romans were leaving Britain. On his way home he stayed for some time in Gaul, with St Martin at Tours, and learned much from that great man." Glaring at Merlin, he went on. "Contrary to the suggestion that he wanted this church and monastery to be named for himself, he dedicated it to St Martin, who he learned had died soon after he left Tours . . ."

Mungo was beginning again when his mother restrained him. "I want to know about St Patrick," he protested to her. "He has said nothing about our St Patrick!"

"That was later, Mungo . . ."

Manus went on. "Ninian set about his task with great courage and determination, travelling the land. At great risk to his life.

And here, at Candida Casa, he set up a school, a college, a place of instruction in the faith. Here he converted and taught many famous saints: St Drayne; St Finnian of Ireland; St Mahee; St Palladius . . ."

"Palladius! That was the one who taught Abbot Serf!" That was a shout.

That man nodded, smiling.

"Let us go on to the shrine itself," Arthur said.

Still barefooted they made their way past the scatter of houses, eyed interestedly by the local inhabitants and barked at by dogs, to the plain little church. There was not a great deal to see remaining here, save for some gravestones, and these, although carved, being unnamed, there was no knowing which was Ninian's own – a fact which Manus did not fail to point out to Merlin as refutation of any self-glorification suggestion. He added that this sanctuary had suffered pillage and defacement at the hands of pagans, and the renowned library of illuminated gospels, psalms and sacred writings dispersed who knew where. Fortunately St Finnian had copied some of these documents while here, and had taken them back to his monastery at Moville in Ireland, so something survived.

Serf said a prayer before the plain stone altar, and, Guinevere leading, with strong support from Mungo and accompanied by the musicians, they all sang a psalm. There did not seem to be much more to be done, although Thanea thought that they had come a long way for this – but told herself that this was unworthy thinking.

However, Arthur declared that there was a really more striking and personal link with Ninian about four miles away, on the west coast of the peninsula, the saint's diseart, a cave where he went alone for prayer, reflection and renewal. This inevitably had Mungo vocal about Serf's cave on the Fife coast, with details as to plenishings, water supply and even mussel stew, this variously received. The High King added that it was quite a long way to walk, and thereafter back to the barge at the isle. He proposed that they returned as they had come, but with their shoes on, and then took the barge round the headland to the cave. He assured them that it was an interesting place.

This met with general approval, although the Princes Lohot and Amhar showed little enthusiasm.

On the journey back, Gawain recounted some of his adventures on the campaigns against the Saxons, and had his nephew enthralled and wondering whether he might go and do likewise when he grew up — not so very long now?

There was ample food and drink on the barge, and of this all were glad to partake as they were rowed on westwards, round the cliffs of Burrow Head and on up the rock-girt coastline beyond for some three more miles until they came to an inlet, too small to be called a bay, where the quite lofty cliffs drew back a little. Into this the barge nosed its way carefully. Ahead of them, they could see the yawning mouth of a cave.

The landing here was difficult, amongst rocks and the surging tide, and the two women kilted up their skirts and waded precariously ashore, however many offers were made to carry them, Guinevere declaring that she would sooner trust the sea than some of the gallant offerers, especially the Lord Perceval who pressed most urgently.

The cave was larger than Serf's one, and deeper, darker, although it did not have the spectacular views. But there was a sufficiency to see, carvings on the walls, an altar, stone bench cut for sleeping on, catchment-basin for water, a fireplace, shelves hewn out. If it was remarkably similar to Serf's own refuge, that was not to be wondered at, since conditions and requirements were the same.

Here most of them could feel more of the presence of the man they had come to honour. Another prayer was offered up, another psalm sung, and Serf gave a brief address on the problems facing missionaries, other than merely the reluctance to believe on the part of the hoped-for converts, stressing organisational and institutional duties which were so apt to take over from successful evangelism.

Then Thanea suggested to Mungo that they should go out and collect wild flowers growing on the ledges and in the crevices of the cliff, to make a wreath or just a posy, as a little tribute to leave behind them, a notion which Guinevere applauded, and came to assist.

They found wild thyme, crow's-foot trefoil — or creepie-craw-taes as Mungo had learned to call it — harebells, yellow ragwort and clovers, even some splendidly blue viper's bugloss, sufficient, with twisted grasses, to form into two wreaths of

170

a sort; and these they left, one on the altar and one on the sleeping-bench.

After a final salutation, they all re-embarked with a great splashing. It was late afternoon by now, and they had that quite long voyage back. But now they had the breeze behind them and could hoist the square sail as well as row, so that they went at perhaps twice the speed of the outward journey. They were back in Bowness and Carlisle in time for a late supper. In between bouts of music and singing, the man Merlin demonstrated another side to his character when, at Arthur's invitation, he recounted various strange tales of the supernatural, messages and communications which he said that he had had from persons afar off, even from the dead, ghostly sightings, levitation of inanimate objects and the like. Mungo very doubtfully wanted to know whether these were miracles; but Manus muttered about wizardry, devil-worship and druidical practices.

The Culross party spent one more day at Carlisle before heading for home. They left with Arthur's suggestion that Prince Servanus might consider one day paying a visit, as missionary, to the Isle of Arran. It would be, in fact, a lesser journey for him than that of coming here, and none so far from Serf's father's kingdom of Cantyre. That large island had been granted to him years before by Comgall mac Fergus, King of the Scots of Dalriada, who found it very difficult to preserve from attack and invasion by the aggressive monarchs of Strathclyde, to which it was all too close, and separated from the rest of Dalriada by Cantyre. The Irish St Brendan had done a great work of Christianising there, but had returned to Ireland a few years ago, leaving no adequate successor. He, Arthur, had dedicated it to Christ as a holy isle; but with so much Saxon-fighting to be done, he had neglected it, indeed had not visited it for years. If Serf found abbatial duties and cares interfering with his desired missionary urgings, how thought he of a high king's responsibilities, as against his personal wishes? Would he try to make time to visit Arran?

Serf promised to bear this in mind.

15

Mungo was fifteen before the projected visit to Arran materialised. Not on account of any reluctance on Serf's part, but merely because a man cannot be in more than one place at one time. With all Fortrenn now to be Christianised, not to mention parts of Manau, the Apostle of the Ochils, as Mormaor Nechtan was now calling him, had his hands full. Thanea, now accepted by all as assistant missionary, usually accompanied him on many of his rounds, and Mungo was seldom left behind. The question had come up, more than once, as to Thanea's status in Church matters. Serf thought that she ought to be ordained into some recognised ministry. She could hardly be a prioress, which implied leadership of a nunnery, mother superior similarly. Deaconess also would not be quite right. And the style of nun itself did not appeal to that young woman, who felt that it could be restrictive. Indeed, she elected to remain as she was, just a helper and companion. And, after all, she had a son born out of wedlock, which surely debarred her from any degree of holy orders? Serf thought that that could be got over, but did not insist.

She and Queen Eva, moreover, had established quite a well-doing mission of their own, aimed at womenfolk and children in the main but by no means ignoring men; and Eva's rank and title served adequately as sufficient authority for them both. They did not limit this activity to Ballanucater and the Mounth of Teith area, where they had started, but took on the western and upland parts of Fortrenn as their especial responsibility, and with a fair amount of success, little populated as this territory was. Serf had to send his ordained priests after them, to be sure, to baptise and make, as it were, official; but the real work was done by the two women, with Mungo's enthusiastic assistance and, to a lesser extent, that of Eva's Finan and Cara.

During this period Mungo suffered two dire blows, the deaths of Leot and the robin. Leot, of course, had been a mature dog when first he had adopted Thanea; so it was something of a wonder that he had survived thus long. Not that this consoled the boy, who had more or less assumed that his animal friends were immortal. Serf sought to comfort him by pointing out that the Celtic Church held that creatures loved by men would also be loved by the God of love, and would survive death. So Mungo might well catch up with his Leot again one day. As for Rua, it just disappeared; and when after some days of anxiety there was still no sign of the little bird, Thanea warned her son that he must be prepared for it never coming back. That took a little accepting; but a day or two later Mungo announced that since God was obviously much interested in Rua, He had one day just ordered it to go on flying upwards and upwards to heaven, in order to save it from becoming old and tired on this earth. This probably was as good a way of dealing with the loss as any, and neither Thanea nor Serf sought to question it.

At least Cora the sheep remained meantime.

It was a strange circumstance which in the end spurred on Serf to make the Arran visit, despite all the other calls on his time – word of Mordred, Thanea's brother. It seemed that Arthur had decided to answer an urgent call from the Celtic people of Brittany, or Britannia Minor as the Romans had called it, in Gaul, who were being grievously raided and oppressed by the Franks, to the east. They were looking on him as saviour, his reputation as a warrior king now farflung. Leaving his own kingdoms for what might well be a lengthy campaign, he had been concerned that the Saxons would take advantage of his absence to attack in more concentrated fashion. He had left Queen Guinevere as regent, but felt that she might require support and backing of a military sort. And of all the sub-kings, Mordred mac Loth had proved to be the most effective fighter and general, however harsh a ruler. So he had appointed him to be deputy commander, in effect as co-regent with the queen.

Serf, for one, very much doubted the wisdom of this, as did Thanea; but presumably the High King knew what he was doing. Mordred was pagan and ambitious; if by any chance Arthur did not return . . . ?

Such thoughts prompted Serf to seek a belated fulfilment of his promise to Arthur anent a visit to Arran, St Brendan's isle, just in case a new regime made such a thing less practical. Mordred might be in a position to stop it.

At the beginning of August then, in that year of 533, with Thanea's health holding up and Mungo all urgency, they commenced this very different sort of pilgrimage from the last one, for St Brendan this time, and to seek to continue his work, not just to celebrate it – as far as they knew he was still alive, at Clonfert, in Ireland's Galway. Different as it was, however, they started out by the same route as heretofore, spending the first night with old Fergus at Carnock, and proceeding on by Slamannan to Lanark in Clydesdale. There however they changed course, to ride down Clyde to where the River Aven entered it, and to turn up this – Mungo observing that most of the rivers in the land seemed to have names like this, a point further stressed when, after climbing out of Strathaven over the Corse Hills, they came to the Annick Water, down which they headed westwards, making now for the Firth of Clyde. It was at the Blackshaw Hill ridge, after a night at Dalry, that they first saw Arran, its mountains soaring blue across the dozen miles of firth, to the boy's excitement. He was going to climb those, he declared, all of them, wonderful mountains.

They took their way downhill now right to Farland Head, which Serf had been informed was one of the best places to find a boat to take them across to Arran. There would be innumerable fishing-havens along this stretch of the Firth of Clyde coast; but since they would have horses to transport, they would require a scow to do so, and these were less frequently available. Farland Head, above Ardneil Bay, apparently was the harbour for these, the crossing here at its shortest.

They found two or three of the wide flat-bottomed craft moored below the headland here, and men prepared to ferry them over. But, bargaining over the cost, they came to the conclusion that they would save both time and effort if, instead of just making the dozen-mile crossing, they got the shipmen to take them right round the head of the great island and down the far side, by the channel or sound which, it seemed, was already being called after St Brendan and which separated Arran from Cantyre. Serf knew this sound of old, of course, having often sailed it in his youth; but he had not realised that Brendan's monastery had been established on that less populous side of Arran.

So they set sail due westwards, with the horses, Thanea exclaiming at the obvious size of the island ahead, which stretched southwards as far as eye could see, a score of miles long, Serf said, by half that across, a province in itself almost. It was the mountains which preoccupied her son, quite the most spectacular which he had ever seen, if not the highest – although, rising all but from sea-level as they did, they seemed lofty as well as majestic. He wanted to know which was the highest – they seemed to be endless – and in what order they would climb them; and had to be reminded that mountain-climbing was not really the object of the visit. One particularly attracted his attention, shapely indeed and coming to a recognisable nipple-like point. Asking its name of the shipmaster, he was told Cioch na-h-Oighe, the Maiden's Breast. Mungo made no comment. Further on, passing the upthrusting headland which marked the very northern tip of the island, very dramatic, this was described to them as the Cock of Arran – and again the youngster forbore remark. Thanea noted this, and recognised it as a sign that her son was growing up, and was finding some embarrassment in such physical nomenclature, for hitherto he had been frankness itself about such things, and interested. She perceived it with something like a pang; his childhood and boyhood had been such a joy for her. Would this change to young manhood be as rewarding?

Down the west side of the great isle they turned, with the lengthy peninsula, almost fifty miles of it, which constituted Cantyre, Serf's birthplace, only five miles away. They soon passed a large inlet or deep bay which was named Loch Ranza and then the mouth of the major glen of Catacol piercing deep and steeply into the mountains, before proceeding on down a challenging cliff-girt coastline, with the hillsides coming right down to the shore, mile after mile, with few signs of human habitation. At last, after almost a dozen miles, the hills began to fall back and the land open out, with houses and communities beginning to be seen, although even here the mountains dominated, not far off. Where a large river, the

Abhainn Dubh or Black Water, came into a bay, their scow drew in, and here they found a harbour, the first they had seen. Their shipmaster, as they landed, pointed southwards to where, less than a mile away, they could see on slightly rising ground a cluster of buildings. That was St Brendan's cashel and monastery, they were told, although he had dedicated it to St Patrick, his predecessor and exemplar – Kilpatrick.

Mounting, thither the trio rode, Mungo wanting to know whether Patrick had in fact ever been here? Serf admitted that he did not know, but thought it likely, none so far from Dumbarton by boat.

They found the cashel a rather sad place, only three fairly elderly men in possession, and giving little impression of vigorous mission, the premises wearing a neglected look. Serf remarked that this was the ever-present danger for Christian endeavour, when an energetic and vital missionary departed and left no similarly enthusiastic successor in charge. He sometimes worried about this for his own foundations, Mungo declaring strongly that *he* would see to them.

The visitors learned that there were some half-dozen cells or little churches scattered over the island, established by Brendan, but that the faith was waning and paganism waxing. These brothers sounded sad about it, but clearly saw it as no fault of theirs. They did what they could, but . . .

Serf, avoiding outright condemnation, was less than sympathetic; Mungo was scornful.

They started a tour of the island the very next day, to judge the position for themselves, a major operation in itself, for Arran covered two hundred square miles even though most of it was mountain and hill. They took the youngest of the three brothers, one Seumas, with them as guide; it was perhaps typical of the situation here that they had no horse at Kilpatrick, and the newcomers had to go down to the nearest farmery at Auchavoulin to hire one for him.

Having seen from the boat the uninhabited nature of this northern coast, they elected to go southwards first, necessarily still holding to the shoreline. It took them three miles or so of pleasant enough riding, however unprofitable, to reach the first little community, where the Sliddery Water reached the sound. This was to be a day of exploration, not teaching, so they did not do more than say to the folk that they would be back bearing the Christian message, before passing on.

Two miles further, with the coastline beginning to bend round eastwards towards the southern foot of the island, they did come to a little village, with its church empty and bare, although Seumas said that occasionally they held a service there. This place had been called by Brendan after the Virgin Mary, Kilmory. Serf said a prayer therein; and Thanea and Mungo pulled wild flowers to leave on the altar.

Strangely they found another little chapel only a mile away on the clifftop. Seumas did not know why this had been established here, so near the other, but thought that it might have something to do with St Brendan having a diseart or refuge in a cave of the cliffs below. Anyway it was never now used. Another prayer and floral tribute, and they rode on.

This southern end of Arran was, although not mountainous, almost as spectacular as the northern extremity, this because of the enormous precipices rimming it, and the jagged reefs and skerries below, on which the seas surged and foamed white. Here was no chapel, but relics of the earlier folk, Picts; a stone circle, cairns, a fort and standing-stones – these still tending to send shivers down Thanea's back, but which greatly interested her son. Looking at him inspecting these, she wondered, as she had done so often before, at the fate which had made her a sacrifice to what these represented, and Mungo, the Christian enthusiast, to be the result. With God working His will in such curious ways, was there any *need* for Serf and such as herself to struggle so on His behalf? Should they perhaps not just leave it all to Him? Then a glance at their companion, Seumas, reminded her what neglect of Christ's cause could result in. As frequently, she prayed silently to be forgiven unworthy thoughts.

Rounding Bennan Head, they commenced their northwards travel, and with some dozen rough miles covered, Seumas, unused to horse-riding, already beginning to show weariness. But Serf was in no mood to yield to such feebleness, and they pressed on. They passed more burial cairns, pagan monuments and stone circles behind another headland, Dippin – clearly druidical worship favoured such prominent and outstanding sites – and eventually reached another of the chapels, which

Brendan had dedicated to the renowned woman saint of Ireland, Brigit or Bride. This was amongst more stone circles at the head of a great bay, which was part-closed by a spectacular isle, really just an isolated mountain-top soaring from the waves, Seumas calling it Mullach Mor, Mungo eager to explore and climb this challenging feature.

They were now entering the most populous part of Arran, where the hills drew back, and there was almost something of a coastal plain and gently rising ground into which rivers emptied themselves. At Invercloy, on the large Brodick Bay, there was quite a township, but strangely there was no chapel here – or not so strangely perhaps, since here was the abode of the island's chief druid, and Brendan had found the greatest opposition to his teachings. Serf took note.

They were still only halfway up this eastern coast. It had never been the intention to try to get round the island all in one day. It seemed that there was a major track back to the west coast from here, up a glen called Shurig and over quite a pass through the mountains, this much used for communication between east and west, some nine miles. Seumas was torn between desire not to go any further and to get out of his saddle, or to head over the hills for home. No such question troubled his companions, who were used to much longer riding than this. They turned their beasts' heads westwards, for Kilpatrick, it still being only early evening.

This cross-island road proved to be more than just a con-venience, for it was very scenic, especially in the steep high pass, dotted with burial cairns, and with a former Pictish fort dominating the further mouth of it, with fine views. Down the Machrie Water beyond they went, Seumas thankful presently to see his cashel home ahead.

Before bed that night they discussed what their programme should be. This visit was not intended to be anything in the nature of a major campaign but, as it were, a showing of the Christian flag and an indication that Brendan's work was not forgotten, and that King Arthur was concerned for the welfare of his island. Some teaching and preaching were called for, but encouragement of the faithful should be the prime objective rather than new conversions. Seumas had indicated that the chief druid was fairly new, and less hostile than had been his predecessor; and Serf had a notion that it might be worth while to call on him and seek, scarcely his co-operation, but at least no active enmity. After that conversion of Duncan of Airthrey and what had followed, he had come to the conclusion that he need not always be in head-on collision with the druids. They were all worshippers, after all, and there might be advantages in a policy of gradualness. Thanea was less hopeful – but then she had had dire experiences at druidical hands.

Mungo did not fail to remind them that there was a host of splendid mountains waiting to be climbed.

Next morning, then, being Sunday, they held a service at the cashel's little church, the three brothers, plus Mungo, having been sent around the neighbourhood to ask the people to attend, the boy at least all enthusiasm, declaring that they *must* all come. So successful was this summons that, although the intention had been to hold the service in the church itself, far too many turned up and the devotions had to be held outside. Probably more folk came out of interest in the newcomers and their intentions than out of the urge to worship, as a change in their everyday routines, but come they did. Serf tailored his devotions to simple essentials, and in his address told them that King Arthur, even though at present far away in Gaul, was not forgetting them on St Brendan's isle and was concerned for their continuing faith in Christ. It was on the High King's urging that they had come here.

Later, they set off on the cross-island road again, dispensing with Seumas's services this time. They had no difficulty in finding the druid, Kessog by name, a youngish man, good-looking, who greeted them warily. Such was the character of the island people that he knew already of their coming and that they were Christians.

Serf was determined to be friendly and to put the other at ease as far as was possible, while explaining that they had come at the behest of the High King, an authority which the druid could not question. He mentioned St Brendan's work and said that he hoped that the Christian and druidical communities did not clash here, for of course they had much in common – an attitude which obviously surprised the younger man. St Serf went on to elaborate on mankind's essential need to worship, and the recognition of higher power than their own. This worship surely should be based on respect and love rather than on fear.

The druid did not challenge that, but remained guarded.

Thanea recognised that this interview might well go on for quite a time, and that she and Mungo would be unlikely to have anything vital to contribute. And with her son's eyes ever turning towards those towering mountains to the north, she put forward the suggestion that she and Mungo might leave the two priests to their deliberations, and go climb one of those mountains – knowing that Serf was less than eager to do the like himself.

That was well enough received; indeed the druid demonstrated his first signs of enthusiasm, declaring that he too enjoyed climbing mountains and felt that he was nearer to his great god, the sun, on a high summit amongst the winds than anywhere else. He did not actually offer to come with them, although Thanea got the impression that he would rather have done this than remain to argue religion with Serf; but he volunteered the information that the highest of all the Arran mountains, Gaoithe Beinn, the Mountain of the Winds, was only some four miles away, and that they could reach its foot, up Glen Rosa, on their horses quite quickly and conveniently, although the climb thereafter would be taxing for a woman.

It was interesting if communication with the druid was to be established through love of mountains.

So they left the two men to their discussions, and made for the mouth of this Glen Rosa, which they could see yawning not far off. Indeed they could glimpse their goal itself, or the topmost tip of it, towering up behind a lesser hill, looking nearer than any four miles. Mungo was in such a hurry to get started that he would have had his horse cantering had his mother not restrained him.

The twists and turns of the river and glen did make for delay, but presently it straightened out into what amounted to a defile with very steep sides, so steep that even the high summit of their mountain was lost behind the intervening escarpment. It looked as though the most challenging part of their climb would be the surmounting of this immediate obstacle of soaring rock and scree.

For quite a long way it seemed just too steep for Thanea

to assail, whatever her son said, and they rode on and on looking for a more practical ascent, Mungo most evidently being patient. But the druid had been right, and it was fully the four miles up before they found something in the nature of a corrie, a recess in the escarpment face, down which cascaded a foaming burn, more waterfall than stream, and Thanea recognised that she could probably use this in the nature of a step-ladder, difficult as it still might be. They tethered the horses at the burnside and commenced the ascent, Thanea's skirts kilted high, and tied so. She told Mungo that he could go ahead at his own pace, but to wait for her within sight; she was not going to hurry.

That was a demanding climb indeed, even for the boy although he pretended otherwise. Often they had to be in the burn itself, and not complaining of the splashing water to cool them. Much of it required handwork as well as foot, and even knees. At its head the corrie was all but perpendicular, and they had to trend away right-handed for a considerable distance to win out of it.

When they at length achieved this it was to find themselves on a lofty northern shoulder of the mountain, still with a long way to go to the summit, but no more cliffs to negotiate, rocky and still steep as it was. Mungo, although breathless, was loud in acclaim, declaring that all would be simple now, just steady climbing. But Thanea was already preoccupied over the problems to be faced in getting down again, certainly not relishing returning the way they had come.

She tried not to let this thought spoil her enjoyment and sense of triumph at the top, at length, which was as breathtaking as had been the getting there, the prospects stupendous, the sense of height dizzy-making, the winds buffeting. They could see, it seemed, almost to infinity, over the firth far into mainland Strathclyde and down to Galloway; and in the opposite direction across the Sound of Brendan right over the Cantyre peninsula to the Hebridean Sea and its islands. But it was nearer at hand that mostly held their gaze, the thronging multitudes of Arran's other peaks, ridges and ranges, uncountable, from here seeming to be a different world altogether, detached, serene, and unconcerned with the paltry affairs of men.

They did not linger there for long, for the wind was chilly on their heated persons; and anyway they felt that they could not leave Serf for overlong. From up here however they could see that the most suitable way down, and possibly the best way up, would be by a northern spur of the mountain, even though that was the reverse of the direction they wanted to follow.

In fact, this descent was considerably easier than Thanea had feared, and would have made a much better ascent, although it brought them down into Glen Rosa fully a mile further up than where they had left their horses. Mungo was triumphant. He had conquered Arran's highest.

When they got back to Invercloy, they found Serf still in the druid's house, now in amicable converse about King Arthur's campaigns and the Saxon threat – although Kessog was more concerned over the Norse raiders, who were apt to terrorise these Hebridean coasts. He was greatly interested in Mungo's almost step-by-step account of the ascent of Gaoithe Beinn, saying that they should have gone up by the way they had come down, but asserting that it was not the *most* challenging of the Arran climbs, a peak called Cir Mhor, the Great Comb, claiming that distinction, steeper and more isolated although a few feet lower. This of course had the boy agog at once, demanding where and how – and when? The druid said that it was perhaps more difficult of access, and the route up involved; but Mungo was not to be put off, and his questioning ended with Kessog offering to act as guide, to the boy's delight.

Serf, noting all this with a mixture of amusement and calculation, by no means sought to dampen the ardour, in fact all but encouraging this development of mutual enthusiasm, clearly seeing it as a means towards closer co-operation, if not friendship, with the druid. It was agreed that, two days hence, the weather being propitious, they would all make the attempt on Cir Mhor.

On the way back to Kilpatrick, Serf, enlarging on how he had got on with Kessog, explained that he had distinct hopes for that man. Being young, he was not so deeply committed to all the practices of druidism as were many; also being of high-born stock, he could relate to Prince Servanus of nearby Cantyre. He was, too, in a different position from the other druids Serf had had to deal with, in that this Arran was not a kingdom under a

182

pagan ruler whose views had to be considered, but a property of the Christian King Arthur, so that he was not under the usual pressures for pagan conformity. This mountaineering interest could be a valuable link.

Thanea said that she liked Kessog, and did not think that he would ever be a cruel druid. Were there others on the island?

Serf said that apparently there were two others, both older but both junior to Kessog. He did not think that they would represent much difficulty.

The day following, the trio went southwards, to do some mission work at Sliddery, Kilmory and Kilbride, the last reached by another cross-island roadway which cut off the southern headlands. This made a busy day, but all felt the better for it in their minds, even though Mungo's thoughts were apt to be on surmounting physical rather than spiritual difficulties. Not that they met with many of the latter. On the whole, Brendan's work appeared to have lasted fairly well.

Prayers for good weather, that night, were fervent.

The great day dawned hazy, with high cloud, but all were convinced that it would remain fair, Mungo up at first light and eager to be off. They crossed the pass to Invercloy, and found Kessog ready and waiting. They noted that he had a rope circled round his middle, like a girdle, which he said might just possibly come in useful – a suggestion which two of his hearers found just a little alarming.

The druid had his own horse, and they set out, as before, up Glen Rosa. Actually they went on almost to the corrie where the horses had been left on the previous occasion, but turned off into another and larger corrie on the other side of the glen, recessed into the opposite escarpment. The lower slopes of this were not so steep as on the east side, and they were able to ride some way up before leaving their beasts tethered.

This was Coire Daingean, they were informed. But they were not going to try to follow its stream up for, as they could see, it became no more than a prolonged waterfall down sheer cliffs at the corrie's head, hardly surmountable. Instead, they would climb left up a shoulder, steep but not impossibly so, and working up and around this would bring them eventually to their ridge.

Eyeing their proposed route, Mungo was not exactly scornful

but indicated that this was less of a challenge than had been the other day's climb. He was told to wait.

Serf found it sufficiently demanding, at any rate, fit as he was for his years. They took their time about it, Thanea glad not to have to try to keep up with her son, Kessog all gallant attention to her. When they reached the summit of that shoulder, it was to discover a second escarpment ahead, and this with no convenient corrie to assist them, and steep, steep, horseshoe-shaped. There was nothing for it, they were told, but to scale it as best they could. But now they could see what Kessog had meant by challenge, and also why the mountain bore the name of a comb. This ridge above them was serrated in an extraordinary way, being a series of minor peaks and pinnacles stretching along northwards for fully a mile, to end in the main soaring summit, the teeth of the comb. Thanea for one eyed that jagged ridge askance. Were they going to have to traverse that? All those tortured ups and downs!

For the next half-hour she had little opportunity to worry about that further trial, so preoccupied was she into getting up to it, a clambering, edging, creeping, and clinging progress over the rock face. She was helped, to be sure, for Kessog constituted himself her guide, support and encourager, close to her all the way, hoisting, holding, pulling her – and clearly enjoying the process. As well that she had never been coy nor prudish about bodily exposure. She felt that probably Serf required the druid's assistance fully as much as she did, but that man restricted his succour to herself. She was worried about Mungo's safety also, although the boy seemed to have a natural aptitude for this rock-climbing. He led the way, she and Kessog followed as best she could, and Serf brought up the rear.

At length, shouts ahead proclaimed that Mungo had reached the top and that he was even more than usually excited at what he was finding up there. And when, presently, she and Kessog, he still clutching her, were able to join the boy, Serf still a fair distance behind and labouring, she too was lost in wonder. For what had seemed from below merely a serrated ridge now proved to be almost a prolonged knife-edge of bare granite, with the other side falling away quite as steeply and immediately. A narrow walkway, if that it could be called, worn by wind and weather, surmounted this extraordinary spinal crest, while all around was space and sky and wind.

Thanea clung to her supporter, calling urgently to her son to be careful, not to stand so near the edge, her heart in her mouth as she saw that they were obviously intended to go on along that tightrope of stone, up the first of the pinnacles ahead – since there was nowhere else to go save back whence they had come. Waiting there for Serf, Kessog explained that this long ridge was A'Chir, the Comb itself, with the great peak at its far end, Cir Mhor. They would go right along the crest, rising and dropping, all the way to that thrusting summit. She was not to fear – he would hold on to her.

Serf needed something of a rest when he reached them, but seemed less daunted by the prospect of that ridge-walk than was Thanea. Yet she had always thought herself good on heights. Part of her trouble was seeing Mungo darting about and peering over the very edge, this turning the stomach within her. He seemed impervious to vertigo.

When they set off, the first few minutes were a test indeed of faith and courage; but gradually she was able to accept the situation, not take every step as a hazard, and even to look up occasionally to admire the tremendous vistas – always with Kessog's hand gripping her or his arm about her. She had opportunity, also, to recognise that even druids could be as human as other men.

How many pinnacles and apexes and cornices they surmounted and descended on that traverse even Mungo did not count, but before the last of them Thanea was feeling the exhilaration of it all, Mungo hoarse from shouting, exclaiming and laughing joyously. Kessog was going to be a hero for him from now on, undoubtedly.

The mountain-top itself, when they reached it, in consequence proved to be something of an anticlimax, shapely, pyramidical and vehement as it was. Its views were not so extensive as from Gaoithe Beinn, for that higher summit blocked out eastwards prospects, and there were another two high and massive peaks to the west. Anyway, the climbers' eyes were apt to be drawn back to the dramatic ridge of A'Chir which they had bested. Even if she never climbed another mountain, Thanea had that to her credit.

Descending the far side of Cir Mhor was far from tame, for here too there were precipices and screes to negotiate, some almost perpendicular; and here Kessog's rope came into use, as a means of preventing slipping and unsteadiness resultant from tired muscles, even though the druid's more personal aid was much in evidence – and gratefully received.

They eventually got down to a sort of small watershed where the rivers Rosa and Sannox were born, and had to plouter now across peat-bog and heather to make their way southwards. But soon the Rosa made them a valley to follow, and they could walk fairly normally. Half an hour of this, and two of them admitting to weariness, they reached their horses.

The day was not over yet, for Kessog invited the trio to have a meal with him in his house – where he turned out to have a good-looking young woman servant or housekeeper, who soon proved as effective as she was decorative. Thanea, smiling to herself, suffered some diminution of attention; but when, after an excellent repast and easy converse, the druid saw them off on their way to Kilpatrick, he contrived something of a bear's hug by way of farewell. By this time Mungo had ensured that they would have another expedition two days hence, this time to that strange mountainous island, Mullach Mor, which part-blocked the large bay to the south.

Riding back over the pass, Serf remarked on Kessog's advances towards Thanea, and wondered whether she objected? She assured him that she did not, that he was quite a personable young man, and herself, she hoped, a normal young woman. She would not let it go too far, of course. But might it not help in the process of the hoped-for conversion? Serf coughed, but did not deny the possibility.

They made a missionary journey to the northern parts of the island next day, which Serf felt they had rather neglected, underpopulated as it was. According to the Kilpatrick trio Brendan had established only one chapel up there, also dedicated to his heroine St Bride, at Loch Ranza; but there was a holy well, site of a miracle, which he had blessed at Tonregethy on the north-west coast.

So the missionaries proceeded up that western shore of the sound, which they had seen hitherto only from the boat which brought them here, a quite lengthy ride with not a great deal to attract the attention, for the hills here came right down to the coast, precluding inland views, and the cliffs they passed were not spectacular. Their eyes were apt to turn westwards, to the long outline of the Cantyre peninsula four or five miles away. Thanea had not failed to note Serf's fairly thoughtful looks in that direction ever since they came to Arran, although he had made no especial comment. Now she thought to ask him how did he perceive that land of his birth? And did he intend to pay it a visit while they were so near?

The man was slow in answering. No, he said, he had no thoughts of going over there. He had no love for Cantyre, only unhappy memories. He did not detail what those memories were, but said that his nephew ruled there now, and they had never been friendly. He had paid only the one visit in the last twenty-five years, and it had not been a success. Cantyre had not reverted to paganism as had Lothian, Manau and Strathclyde, but the Christianity which survived was of a very doubtful and decadent sort, in his opinion. He had indeed taken a vow not to return – which was perhaps wrong of him; but he felt strongly in the matter – and there was so much more worthwhile work awaiting him elsewhere. He added that the far west side of the peninsula was the more populous area, his nephew's palace, his own old home, down near the southern tip of the mull, at Dunaverty. This seeming remote part was in fact much nearer to Ireland, a mere twelve miles, than to any other part of the mainland of Dalriada, Strathclyde or Alba, and most of the links were with that country.

Thanea recognised that her friend was entitled to his private reservations, and did not press the matter further.

At Tonregethy they found a tiny fishing-haven, and were directed to the holy well, reputed to be efficacious in the treatment of skin ailments. Mungo tried washing in it and drinking some, but announced no improvement of a couple of pimples he had developed on his forehead – and was advised to give it time. They were also taken by the fisherfolk to a little burial ground, where Brendan had interred two of their number and where others had been buried since. Here Serf conducted a brief service, and they moved on.

Loch Ranza provided a very different scene, a large bay or

sea-loch thrusting half a mile into the joining of two major glens and dominated by fairly tall mountains. It supported three separate communities of fishers and farmers. Most of the menfolk were absent on their various activities, but a sizeable congregation of women, children and oldsters were persuaded to come along to the chapel of St Bride. This gave the impression of being little frequented, although here too the burial ground adjoining was clearly still being used. The service here produced satisfactory reactions, and Serf and Thanea had much question-and-answering to deal with afterwards, which was a hopeful sign. Thanea noted here, as she had done elsewhere on this Arran visit, that Mungo was less forward in his involvement and contributions. She wondered if this was just part of his growing-up process – and hoped that it did not signify any lessening of his so eager faith.

They had by now come seventeen or eighteen miles from Kilpatrick, and were faced with the question of whether to return as they had come or to take the somewhat longer route back by the east coast and so to Glen Cloy. The local folk told them that there was a short-cut through the hills up Glen Chalmadale here; and Mungo, ever urgent for new scenes and activities, rediscovered enthusiasm. So they headed on south-eastwards, up the left-hand valley, a long ride rising quite high before they sighted the Firth of Clyde. Thereafter they rode downhill to reach eventually a larger river mouth and bay, which they discovered was the same Sannox which they had been at the birth of the day before, under Cir Mhor. There was a small community here, with a haven; and another at Coire nan Larach further down, at each of which Serf said a few words to such as could be assembled, at short notice, on Christ's message and also on King Arthur's interest. Another seven miles took them to Brodick Bay and Invercloy.

Mungo was for visiting Kessog again, but his elders thought it better not to. They would be seeing him on the morrow, and it had been a long day, almost fifty miles of riding before they won back to Kilpatrick. They were not all fifteen-year-olds.

In the morning an early start, with cloud low in the pass, had them wondering. But Kessog was all optimism, and said that it would remain fair. The main matter was that it was not windy, for of course they would have to go by boat to this Mullach

Mor isle, and it having no harbour or boat-strand, choppy seas would make landing there difficult. He was in good spirits, and obviously had been looking forward to the occasion almost as much as had Mungo.

So they made a cheerful party as they set off southwards for the bay with the island, a mere five miles. Serf took the opportunity to point out at the other Kilbride chapel they passed, amongst all the stone circles, something more of Christian doctrine and aims, the druid showing interest at least.

At the bay beyond the prominent Claughlands Point, their destination looked suitably spectacular and inviting, soaring from the waves like some sharp-snouted leviathan, the columnar sandstone cliffs seeming like the straining muscles of the neck. It was less than two miles in length and only a half-mile in breadth, they were told, yet it rose as high as many of the inland hills, and this from sea-level. Kessog had conducted sun-worship services on its summit – although before very small congregations, for not many were prepared, or able, to climb to the top. This sounded somewhat ominous to Thanea; but at least the druid had not brought his rope with him today, which was something.

They rode right round the bay to its southernmost headland, under the shelter of which was a group of fishers' houses, where the necessary boat could be obtained to take them over the mere quarter-mile passage to the isle.

They had to choose a landing-place, for there was no recognised strand, although, as Kessog put it, some spots were worse than others. Even though the day was calm, the tide surged sufficiently to make disembarking something of an adventure in itself, much to Mungo's glee. They tried two or three possible ledges and inlets before they found a place where the boat could be held approximately steady and they could land without disaster, wet as Thanea's skirts became.

The ascent, the druid said, was best attempted from this southern end, where it was steep but without actual cliffs, save for the rocky escarpment near the top, just steady climbing. That was one way of describing the situation, apprehensive visitors decided.

Steady climbing proved something of a misnomer. By fits

and starts, pausing for breath, picking devious routes, seeking handholds as well as footholds, they worked their way upwards, Kessog never leaving Thanea's side and declaring that there was no hurry, unnecessary assurance as that was. She wondered that practice did not seem to make for easier going; after all, this was the third major climb they had made in a few days. Seemingly not however, for her muscles seemed to ache the more, and her breathing was the less controlled. Sometimes she actually had to hold her heaving bosom in check – however much Kessog would have preferred to do it.

But at length they reached those topmost crags, to find Mungo already scrambling up like any spider and shouting back instructions as to how it was to be done. Kessog chose an alternative route for his charge, but even this was almost too much for her. She debated with herself whether women were intended to be scalers of heights, physical or spiritual. But were the heights necessarily for scaling? Might not caring and appreciative attention to the lower ground be as productive, if not more so? The *views* of the heights might well be sufficient. Adequate for most, and sometimes even more productive, contemplation and imagination the contribution? She must ask Serf – who also was labouring.

The summit, attained at last, did rather tend to cancel out her doubts and questions, so rewarding and stimulating were the prospects and sense of accomplishment. This was not just a repetition of the other days' experiences. The sea here made an extraordinary difference, its level plain seeming to emphasise the majestic upthrust of their tower, the lack of any nearby competition likewise, the crown of the eminence so limited.

Very clear to perceive, from up here, was the reason for the comparative choppiness of the water in the seemingly sheltered bay, Kessog explaining. Some trick of the prevailing south-westerly wind, aided no doubt by the mountain mass to the west, caused a continual swirling and downdraught round this Mullach Mor, which whipped up the seas so that they were often rougher in the bay than in the firth outside, and from above could be seen to be so, the wrinkled effect pronounced.

The same wind made it chilly, and they did not linger, their guide taking them on down the opposite, northern side. This in fact proved to be less fierce at first, so that they wondered why they had not come up this way. But halfway down they had to make a major diversion to avoid cliffs and, strangely, in the opposite direction to what was required, eastwards, this so that they could reach almost shore-level and thus work their way round the coast to get under the said cliffs. They were making for the cave, Kessog said.

This, they discovered, was a large cavern facing the bay, and dedicated to the sea god Manannan, information which had the visitors raising eyebrows. With a glance at Serf, Thanea decided that there could be no harm and that there might possibly be good, in telling the druid of her experiences in Manannan's territories. Briefly she recounted the circumstances of her coracle voyage and adventures at sea, and how her prayers to God had been answered, ending in asserting that Manannan, if he indeed existed, was clearly subservient to their Christian Father in heaven. Kessog listened attentively and seemed impressed. He said that they, on Arran, being surrounded so completely and closely by the sea, paid considerable respects to Manannan. Could *their* God be his superior? Rather than the sun?

That simple question represented something of a triumph for the others. Here was the druid acknowledging that the sun was perhaps not supreme, that there could be a still higher power, this a major step towards his conversion.

Serf seized his opportunity. The sun, he declared, obeyed laws, did it not? None could deny that. It rose and set at given times. It was less prominent in winter than in summer. It could be obscured for days on end by clouds. If it was supreme, as the druids taught, it would not have to obey its own laws. A law-giver does not have to abide by his own orders. Yet the sun did. So there must be a higher authority which ordered the sun, or it would not have to hold to set courses and never deviate.

Kessog nodded thoughtfully.

As for Manannan, Serf went on, the seas also obeyed laws. The tides ebbed and flowed in regular order. No amount of praying to Manannan could alter that. It was the tide turning which had saved Thanea. The sea-water was salt and could not be made fresh. Manannan could not change that either. But it was not the sun which so ordained. The clouds rained down *fresh* water. So sun, clouds and sea came under a higher power.

The same applied to all the other pagan deities. Friend Kessog must see it.

Mungo added his contribution about birds and animals and their love for humans. Which hating, terrible god gave them this ability to love?

In the cave they found sundry carvings incised on the walls, fish and seabirds and the intricate interlacing of what presumably were seaweeds, all apparently ascribed to Manannan. Mungo found a sharp stone and went to work to obliterate one of the fish, and then to chip and scratch a representation of Christ's cross within the circle of everlasting life, telling Kessog that this was for *him*, to ensure his better life hereafter, climbing the heavenly mountains. He, Mungo, might join him in that, too.

Thereafter they explored the perimeter of the isle as best they could considering that so broken and awkward coastline, discovering two wells of fresh water in the process, this all taking some time. Then it was back to their boat and so to the horses, and a return to Glen Cloy for further hospitality from Kessog and his laughing housekeeper.

They left, all convinced that the druid was not far from becoming a Christian, Serf saying that he would have one more session with him, and seek to baptise him – only one, for he feared that they must return to the mainland in a couple of days, his wider responsibilities calling. They would have been gone almost three weeks by the time that they got back to Culross. No more mountaineering, it was to be feared.

The following evening there was joy at Kilpatrick. Kessog had embraced the true faith, indeed had been baptised already. Not only that, but he had agreed to seek to convert his two assistant druids, and to try to maintain Christianity on the island. He would endeavour to retain his druidical status meantime, and use it to bring others to the true God. This might be possible, for he was in a very special situation for a druid, Arran having no arch druid over it, an independent province directly under a Christian high king. He was hopeful that a policy of gradualness and merging of the two religions might bring worthwhile results. Serf had encouraged him in this conception.

Two mornings later, then, Kessog accompanied them down

to the haven in Brodick Bay, where there was a scow to ferry them and their horses over to the Strathclyde shore. This actually was the principal harbour for Arran, the one they had arrived at, on the west coast, being only the most convenient for Kilpatrick. The new convert had another suggestion. If they hired the boatmen to take them not just across to Farland Head but north-eastwards to a haven called Largs, considerably further up the Strathclyde coast, they could save themselves at least a day's journeying by heading eastwards, north of the way that they had come, by Renfrew, and crossing the River Clyde at the first fordable point after it ceased to be an estuary, thereafter making for Slamannan and Stirling. The trio were surprised at Kessog's knowledge of the mainland, but he said that he had twice attended a druidical instruction centre at Airthrey under the sacred hill called Dumyat, near to Stirling. This of course produced much exclamation, and considerably delayed their departure.

The actual leave-taking was quite emotional, all promising, God willing, to return one day and renew their association – although their friendship would endure even if that proved impossible. Thanea received a final and comprehensive hugging, and Mungo even had to blink away tears.

They sailed away from Arran and its mountains on the south-west wind, hearts full.

The route Kessog had outlined for them proved to be a success, saving them many a weary mile, their crossing of the Clyde much further down than formerly, near in fact where the fresh water gave way to salt, where they found the first fording-place for horses, this at a village called Cathures. They would remember this, for future reference.

Oddly they had cause to remember that name and place very shortly afterwards, for, reaching Carnock for their final stop before Culross, and telling Fergus there of the success of their visit to Arran, the old priest informed them that he in fact had been born on the bank of Clyde at Cathures, and had, with his parents, joined Christ's Church there, at a little chapel established by St Ninian. In due course he hoped to be buried there, beside his parents and a brother.

This talk of burial was played down, of course, but note was taken.

They found only minor problems awaiting the abbot at his abbey next day, with further praising God therefor.

Part Three

16

Thanea, celebrating her thirty-fifth birthday in the year 536, and therefore halfway to the three score years and ten which was mankind's allotted span, had to recognise that she was no longer a young woman, even though she felt no differently than she had done ten and more years before. Serf assured her that she looked no different either, but no doubt he was prejudiced. And she had her son ever before her, to emphasise the situation, now almost eighteen years and a young man, childhood and youth behind him. To be mother of such was a joy, but also a reminder of her age.

Mungo's development was, nevertheless, all that she could have hoped for. He had quite quickly outgrown the rather awkward stage of embarrassments and young male inhibitions. His was now a most frank and open nature, lively, friendly, an enthusiast but a caring one. And physically he was good to look at, tall, broad of shoulder, almost handsome in a strong-featured way, a determined jut of chin tempered by an ever-ready smile, and dancing blue eyes beneath a shock of fair hair. His faith was stronger than ever, but more controlled and directed. He was now Serf's right-hand man, Thanea content to be the left. He was eager for the day when he would be ordained priest, which Serf said could hardly be before his twentieth birthday.

Serf himself was ageing inevitably but was still fit, hale and active, coping with his widespread responsibilities like a man of half his years, but concerned for the future of it all.

As well he might be, for the situation prevailing was scarcely propitious for Christianity, as for much else. King Arthur was still away in Gaul, staying there much longer than had been intended, where the heathen Frankish threat was ever-increasing, with the Roman withdrawal, and the danger to the Celtic peoples there dire. And in his absence, there was great trouble at home, especially for Christians. Serf had been right in judging the appointment of Mordred as commander, and in effect co-regent with Queen Guinevere, as a mistake. Mordred, although effective in keeping the Saxon threat at bay, was proving no kindly ruler and, being pagan, Christians suffered even more than others. He was reputedly at constant loggerheads with Guinevere, and having control of the armed forces was in a position to enforce his will. This situation concerned Serf indirectly because, although Fortrenn remained unaffected, under Nechtan, Mordred acting the high king and behaving savagely encouraged other pagan sub-kings, such as those of Strathclyde, Manau and Cantyre, to misbehave also, and this had repercussions over wide areas.

The situation was complicated by developments in Northumbria where, at Bamburgh, Lancelot was King of the Brigantes. Encouraged no doubt by Arthur's absence, an Anglian chieftain called Ida had attacked and succeeded in ousting Lancelot, who had now taken refuge in one of his remote houses in the Cheviot Hills, called Yetholm, while the invading Ida ruled from Bamburgh, calling himself King of Northumbria. Lancelot, while not a Brythonic sub-king of Arthur's, was his friend and ally, and had been protected by him; whereas Mordred had been the reverse, and raided his territories. It was unusual for the Angles to emulate the Saxons like this, and further evidence that the warrior High King was much needed at home.

Nechtan was concerned about all this also, his mormaordom being too close to these unsettled areas for comfort. Thanea spent much time with Queen Eva, and they continued with their own missions to the Mounth of Teith and thereabouts, but always these days with apprehension as to what might be their converts' fate – although Mungo asserted stoutly that God would look after them.

Serf had an unexpected visit from no less than Kessog some eighteen months after their return from Arran, and he at least brought good news, the Christianisation of that island proceeding apace and no hostile gestures coming from Strathclyde or Cantyre. He had come, not only to report progress to his mentor, but to try to see that other former druid, Duncan of Airthrey, in the hope that they could together work out a detailed programme for his system of gradualness, an amalgam of the better aspects of druidism and the Christian faith, with the latter gradually taking over. It was working on Arran, but Kessog recognised that conditions there were unusual. He thought that Duncan, who had been an arch druid and an important one, would be the one to consult.

So they had taken their visitor to the little isle in Loch Leven, where Duncan had succeeded Gabhran as prior, with responsibility for the Kinross and Ochil hillfoots area, and there they had had a highly profitable exchange of ideas, Serf adding his own suggestions and Mungo listening attentively rather than making interjections as once he would have done. They had indeed pieced together a practical code of conduct for druids and pagan priests who were prepared to consider Christ's message, together with methods of handling their druidical superiors who might make objection. This, all agreed, was a major step forward.

Mungo managed to fit in a climb of a group of the Ochil summits near to Kinross, even though these were not to be compared with the Arran mountains.

It was in late May of 537 that the very grievous news reached Culross, and again by a messenger from Mormaor Nechtan, in this instance his son Prince Finan, now a young man of nineteen. Mordred mac Loth had taken the final step and broken out in declared rebellion against Arthur, and declared himself High King of the Britons in his stead. Not only that, but he had taken Queen Guinevere prisoner and had conveyed her under strong guard to Alyth, of all places, to Nechtan's alarm and consternation. What was to be done?

Serf required no elaboration on this to perceive its seriousness – and for Nechtan – apart altogether from the wider aspects and consequences of rebellion and usurpation, and for Guinevere herself. Alyth was in Fortrenn, if only just, a small township amongst the foothills of the Strathmore mountains, on the very borders of the mormaordom of Angus, renowned only for its great Pictish hilltop fort nearby. Why Mordred should have chosen this was a mystery, in Alba, and far outwith the Brythonic territories, and where he had no authority. Admittedly that fort was a most secure place to keep a special captive – but that could be said of innumerable other locations much nearer his own domains. It did not seem to make sense.

Young Finan said his father thought that Mordred had done this out of a set policy, deep-laid. Fortrenn and Angus mormaordoms had never been on good terms. If in his rising against Arthur, Mordred could use *Pictish* or Albannach allies, this could much strengthen his hand, particularly in the likelihood of rivalry for the high kingship from Morcant of Strathclyde, who was senior to him and had a much larger sub-kingdom. Angus was the next nearest mormaordom, after Fortrenn, to Strathclyde; and it had a new young mormaor, Bargoit. By imprisoning Guinevere at Alyth, in Fortrenn but on the very edge of Angus, he could ensure that no loyal supporters of Arthur, in the Brythonic kingdoms, could seek to rescue her; and at the same time inhibit Nechtan, Arthur's friend now, from doing so also, for fear of creating trouble between Fortrenn and Angus, of which there had already been stirrings. He could think of no other reason. But – Queen Guinevere was there, held secure, at Alyth.

Serf was nonplussed. No other explanation for imprisoning Arthur's wife in an Albannach fort occurred to him. But since he had done so, it must be out of considered policy, he agreed. As friends of Arthur and his queen, what could they do? Since Nechtan did not want to be embroiled, and it seemed with good reason.

It was Thanea who came up with the notion. Nearly all of Arthur's close friends and princelings were with him in Gaul – which was why all this was possible for Mordred. But King Lancelot, formerly of Northumbria, was not. He was a friend. And when Arthur did come back, Lancelot would almost certainly want his help to dispossess this invading Angle, Ida, and regain his kingdom. *He* might be prepared to help.

This was a possibility. But Serf wondered whether Lancelot would now have the means to do anything? It would require a fairly strong force, he imagined, to take this powerfully placed Alyth fortress. Now that he no longer had his kingdom, could he provide such?

Thanea thought that he probably could. The word was

that he was now in this place Yetholm, in the Cheviots, presumably some sort of summer palace, remotely situated as regards Bamburgh. He would not be likely to be there, an ejected king, without at least a fairly powerful bodyguard, and possibly quite a substantial body of men. Moreover, was he not one of the band of gallants who had reputedly been in love with the beautiful Guinevere?

All agreed that this was sound reasoning.

So what was to be done — since something clearly was required of them? A message sent to this Yetholm? They decided that more than any message was called for. Lancelot might have to be convinced, and warned as to the problems and difficulties involved. Finan also pointed out that although his father was sympathetic and would wish to help, he must not be seen to be actively taking part or co-operating, for fear of reprisals from Angus. So any armed approach to Alyth must not be too obviously through his land, implying his agreement. This might not be heroic but it was necessary.

Such requirement posed a problem indeed. How to reach Alyth without crossing Fortrenn? It was impossible, save by marching through Angus itself, which was scarcely to be considered. Finan said that he had been thinking about this on his way south and had come to the conclusion that it must be done most of the way by sea, or at least by the Firth of Tay. If a force could be sailed halfway up that firth, between Dundee and Perth, he knew of a little-used route across the Carse of Gowrie and up through the Sidlaw Hills, which would bring them to Alyth in about twenty miles. These hills were almost unoccupied, and the company traversing them would be inconspicuous — although the Carse of Gowrie was otherwise, and would best be crossed by night.

That might be so, the others accepted. But how to find vessels to transport the hoped-for force? Lancelot no doubt previously had shipping at his disposal, having ports at Bamburgh itself, Berwick-on-Tweed and along the Northumbrian seaboard. But these would now be all in Anglian hands. And north of the Tweed was only Eyemouth, before Mordred's own Lothian coast was reached. Eyemouth was only a small fishing-haven and unlikely to be able to provide many boats capable of quite a sea voyage.

Serf wondered whether the answer would not be to try to enlist the help of the east Fife fishermen. These, at Pittenweem, Anstruther, Kilrenny and Crail, were accustomed to fishing out beyond the Forth estuary into the Norse Sea, and therefore tended to have larger and stronger boats than the firth fishers, and so were capable of carrying a contingent of men the required distance and in the open sea. He had made many converts in these villages, and thought that he probably could persuade some of the boat-owners to co-operate, since it was all eventually in the cause of Christianity. And they had assisted in transporting Arthur's army to his defeat of the Saxon invaders at Abernethy, those years past.

This was acclaimed. How to proceed, then?

Serf said that he would have to go in person to the East Fife folk, to ensure speedy compliance, if possible. Mungo offered to go south to this Yetholm place beyond Tweed, to approach King Lancelot. But Thanea declared that she must go also. After all, Guinevere was her aunt by marriage, Arthur her uncle, and the wicked Mordred her half-brother. So she was very much involved. She knew Lothian best, and the approaches to the Cheviot Hills, whereas the others did not. Let them all go. Not Finan of course, who must return to inform his father.

Serf agreed. There would be no scows for horses, he feared, at those Fife havens, ferrying over to the Brythonic Lothian shores being no concern of theirs. He thought that they would have to try to find a boat and crew to take them to this Eyemouth, and hope to hire horses there. Even if it was only a small place, there ought to be farms around, with beasts.

All this would take considerable time, they recognised, so the sooner they started out, the better. Two days hence . . . ?

It was almost a sixty-mile ride from Culross to Fife Ness, the easternmost tip of the great peninsula, between the firths of Forth and Tay, by winding tracks, bays and headlands, more than they could cover in one day; so they halted for the night halfway, at Serf's diseart – good for prayers for the success of their mission – for the abbot was just a little concerned that this venture was not his usual effort towards saving souls for Christ and through Christ, but was in fact to initiate an armed sortie to attack a fortress. Mungo had no such doubts, nor had his mother. A Christian queen had been abducted by a pagan – that was good enough for them.

In the event, they found no real difficulty in either hiring a sea-going boat to take them to Eyemouth, nor in gaining the promise of quite a flotilla of craft to transport the hoped-for force to the Tay estuary – although how many would be needed for this remained to be seen. Serf's credit was high all over Fife by now, and he was especially popular with seafarers, always the most ready to listen to Christ's message. No doubt all would be adequately paid for their services in due course, as they had been in the previous case. Meantime, they were at St Serf's service.

So, horses left behind, the following morning early they set sail from Anstruther in a sturdy deep-sea fishing-craft with six oarsmen and a square sail. It was reckoned that Eyemouth was about thirty-five sea-miles away. With a westerly wind, by consistent tacking, they ought to be able to reach their destination in perhaps seven or eight hours, with little rowing necessary.

It made quite an enjoyable sail, strangely different from their Arran voyaging, much larger and longer seas with more rolling and tossing, but no real discomfort for good sailors, however set-faced was Thanea as they passed close to the Isle of May and out into the Norse Sea. She would never forget that island.

Thereafter they zigzagged down the Lothian coast perhaps four miles offshore, able to view those landmarks so familiar to her, the Craig of Bass, North Berwick Law, Traprain itself and all the long ranges of the Lammermuirs. Presently these gave way to high, precipitous cliffs for many miles, a fierce seaboard indeed; and then the land sank to more open bays and eventually to the one which marked the mouth of the Eye Water, a medium-sized river running southwards out of the Lammermuirs.

This proved to be a smaller place than Anstruther and the other east Fife townships, its harbour containing only some half-dozen boats. But these were fair-sized craft, necessary for fishing on this open sea coast. Disembarking, and making enquiries regarding hiring horses to take them to the Cheviot

203

foothills, still over thirty miles away it seemed, they were told that this was not the best way to their destination. Much better to go on in their boat down to Berwick, another ten miles, and there to turn in up the Tweed River, navigable for many miles for a shallow-draught boat, to take them much closer to their objective. Heedfully mentioning Yetholm and King Lancelot, they quickly perceived that these folk were loyal to their dispossessed monarch and hated the Anglian invaders – who, blessedly, had not so far troubled them thus far north. They became very helpful in directing the Anstruther boatmen as to their best course up Tweed, recommending that they ought to be able to get their craft up as far as Carham, with due care, from where it would be less than a ten-mile walk to Yetholm.

The visitors decided to spend the night here, with these good folk, since the navigating of the River Tweed would demand daylight and much care. These Eyemouth people were not Christian, but Serf forbore from seeking to teach, although he did say that *they* were Christian, and commended their faith.

In the morning they were not long in reaching Berwick, at the wide mouth of the great river. They did not go ashore here, for they had been told that this, a major seafaring place, was in Anglian hands. They proceeded directly westwards, upriver, suffering no interference, many boats to be seen. Now, of course, they had to use the oars, sails lowered.

For a mile or two the river was very wide, almost a small estuary, although with sandy islets; but thereafter it narrowed abruptly and began to twist and turn, although it still was no minor waterway. Now the current was quite strong, and the oarsmen had to work hard, and to watch out for shoaling, rocky spurs at bends, and sudden eddies. This was an odd experience for deep-sea fishermen.

They had been told that Carham, which they were making for, was about a score of miles up, but with all these bends and loops, and navigating difficult, it was hard to calculate distance covered. Passing one sizeable village on the north side, after a couple of hours of this, they landed and enquired – and were laughed at. Carham, they were informed, was at least another eight miles further up. This was Graden.

They found Carham at last, a riverside farmery and community, with a mill. Here they left their boat and crew meantime, and were glad to be able to hire three horses, little more than ponies. They were given instructions as to how to find Yetholm, some nine miles to the south, amongst the hills.

They had little difficulty in so doing, for not very far into the quickly rising ground they were in fact challenged by armed men, these obviously maintaining a lookout from a ridge, presumably for intruders. When Serf announced that they were seeking King Lancelot, suspicions evaporated, and one of their number was deputed to conduct the travellers to their master.

These Cheviot Hills were not unlike the Lammermuirs, grassy and rounded but steeper and with deeper clefts and vales. They constituted a belt, some forty miles by ten, of high, wild territory which had always acted as a barrier between the tribes and peoples of north and south.

The visitors were taken fairly deep into winding valleys and round hill shoulders, eventually to reach a somewhat isolated hill, by no means the highest thereabouts but, as it were, moated all round, on the east by a wider valley and larger river, and on the west by a loch and much marsh and associated streams. And not exactly on the top of this, on a broad shelf, they saw the green ramparts of an ancient fort; they had seen others, on the way, on heights, but this one was the largest. Presumably this Cheviot area had been important in far-off times. Within this fort's grass-grown perimeter rose an extensive hall-house, the walls painted white and gleaming in the sunlight. The only other buildings they had seen since leaving Carham were two rude shepherds' cottages. There were a number of lesser cabins and huts around the hall-house. It all made a strange sight in these surroundings.

They were not to see Lancelot immediately, for it seemed that he was out hawking, a favourite sport. But they were made welcome by quite a coterie of women, also strange to find in such a place, especially attractive women such as these – but then Lancelot had the name of being a ladies' man. One or two of them made quite a fuss over Mungo. For the company of a dethroned monarch, all seemed to be in remarkably good spirits.

205

Lancelot arrived in due course, himself cheerful after a good day's sport. He was quite the most handsome man Thanea had ever seen, in a dark and almost saturnine way, holding himself well, slender and supple. Needless to say he was surprised to see his visitors and to learn their identity, but greeted them cordially, courteously, and declared that he had heard much of them.

When they told him of their errand it was surprising what a change came over the man. Eyes flashing and fists clenching, he shed the image of courtly if somewhat superficial gallantry, and became the hot-tempered and combative man of action.

"Guinevere!" he cried. "The lovely Guinevere! And that scoundrelly Mordred! Here is shame. Dear God – disgrace! Treachery! That wretch dares! He holds her?"

"He does. A close prisoner," Serf said. "Holds her secure . . ."

"Not for long, he will not! Where? Where is Guinevere?"

"That is the strangest part of it. She is at Alyth, in Strathmore."

"Alyth? Alyth – but that is in Alba!"

"Yes. On the borders of Fortrenn and Angus mormaordoms."

"But – why? Why?"

"Nechtan of Fortrenn, who is Arthur's friend, thinks that Mordred is making an ally of Bargoit of Angus, the new mormaor there. And puts the queen at Alyth in order to ensure that Nechtan does not seek to rescue her."

"Then why not in Angus itself, man?"

"Perhaps he does not trust Bargoit altogether. Guinevere could cast a spell on him – as she has done on many! It is a very new alliance. But necessary, it seems, to keep Morcant of Strathclyde from challenging this rebellion against Arthur. Or using it to his own advantage. The threat of Angus. Always the fear of both Strathclyde and Fortrenn."

"This is a madness!"

"Perhaps, of a sort. But Mordred is no fool, whatever else he is. He has chosen to do this, of set policy, whatever his real reason. Guinevere is imprisoned in the great fortress at Alyth."

"Is she . . . ? Has he . . . raped her?"

"As to that we do not know. But . . ."

"I will have her out of there, if it is the last deed that I do!"

The visitors exchanged quick glances. They had come far prepared to convince Lancelot to try to do just that. It seemed that was not now necessary.

"You will?" Thanea exclaimed. "But — *can* you? It is a strong fort, or he would not have placed her there."

"I have my teulo, my three hundred. They should be sufficient." The teulo was the standard bodyguard of princes and great ones. "I may have lost Bamburgh meantime — but that was against ten thousand! I will take Alyth."

"That is what we had hoped for," Serf nodded. "But getting your men there will not be a simple matter of marching. Nechtan is concerned that any force does not seem to go with his blessing, or there may be trouble with Angus. So it will be necessary to go by sea, and up the Firth of Tay. Then a short march through the Sidlaw Hills . . ."

"But that is folly! To take three hundred by sea. I have not the ships. This Nechtan — is he a man or a mouse?"

"He has much to make him thus cautious. Both his Albannach neighbours threaten him, Angus and Atholl. He has ever to be on the watch for the Saxons. *You* know the danger of that! And now the Angles. But the shipping we have arranged for. East Fife fishing-boats, all deep-sea craft, will come for you. If you can get your men to Eyemouth, they will carry you on from there to the Tay."

"Ha! You have considered this closely, Prince Servanus! I think that you should have been a commander, a fighter, rather than a churchman!"

"I seek to fight in *Christ*'s cause, King Lancelot!"

"Yet you would have made a better King of Cantyre than your nephew. And made that kingdom fully Christian."

Serf bowed his head, silent.

Mungo came to his rescue. "There are many who can fight battles — like my uncle, Mordred! But not many who can turn great numbers to Christ-God. The abbot is converting all Fortrenn. He has brought Arran back to the faith. He even converts the druids . . ."

"Perhaps you are right, young man. But if your abbot was King of Cantyre, King Mordred might not have used this of Alyth and Angus. For he need not have feared a Strathclyde bid for Arthur's throne."

Thanea sought to curtail all this of inter-kingdom rivalry. "When can you move for Alyth, King Lancelot?" she asked.

"Give me two days to ready and muster my men. Another day to get them to Eyemouth. Guinevere must not be left to suffer one day longer than need be. Can your Fife boats be there by then?"

"Three days?" Serf said. "We have to get back there. Then they have to assemble from the various havens. Make it four."

"Very well. Four days hence, at Eyemouth."

"Then we must get back to Carham, forthwith, where we left our boat. This night. The long row down Tweed tomorrow . . ."

"My men will see you to Carham. You have eaten well . . . ?"

They did not delay, then, Lancelot's sense of urgency infectious. It was to horse again, seen off by smiling ladies and Lancelot's appreciative kiss for Thanea.

Three days later the flotilla of twelve boats left Anstruther for the thirty-five-mile sail to Eyemouth. Unfortunately the wind had changed to south-east, which enforced considerable oar-work at first. Mungo had volunteered to go with them, as link with Lancelot. They had little doubt that the king would be waiting for them.

He was, with his three hundred heavily armed Brigantes warriors, a rough-seeming company impatient to be off, and who packed the boats with over a score to each, the fishermen crews eyeing them somewhat askance. There was only a brief rest for these after their seven-hour voyage. The wind, however, was now in their favour, and the sails did most of the work, however overloaded the craft.

Mungo got on well with Lancelot – he was good at getting on with people – although their personalities were so very different, their outlooks likewise. Although Queen Guinevere's release was the object of this exercise, the king talked at length about Thanea, who obviously had much interested him.

It was almost dusk before they got back to Anstruther, an invasion of warriors which made a pronounced impact on the fishing community, especially on the women, a noisy and less than peaceful night following.

Although Serf sought to dissuade her, Thanea was determined to accompany the expedition in the morning. She did not look upon herself as a particularly adventurous or forceful woman – but as she explained her attitudes to herself, what she had been through in the past meant that little that might happen to her thereafter could frighten or put her off. Also, she pointed out, Guinevere, when rescued, would be glad of another woman's company. Lancelot certainly did not urge her to remain behind. Serf himself was going along, as was Mungo; that was never doubted.

The boats having been somewhat overcrowded, it was decided to involve a few more for what was reckoned to be about another fifty-mile voyage; so almost the entire deep-sea fleet of the East Neuk of Fife set out, Lancelot promising adequate recompense.

The wind was still easterly and the seas quite high, so that rowing was the order of the day for the first six or seven miles, until they rounded Fife Ness and could turn north-westwards and the sails go up. Not a few of the Brigantes were sea-sick, to their angry shame and the fishermen's delight.

They kept well offshore, avoiding the Carr Brigs rocks, and past Babbet Ness, to cross the wide bay of Kinkell with its turbulent shallows, and the mouth of the River Eden – another name for Mungo to remark upon. The shoaling, sandy shores beyond persisted all the way to the entrance to the Firth of Tay, where they had to skirt well east of the Abertay sands before they could turn into the three-mile-wide estuary westwards.

They could still use the sails here, the wind behind them. Those in charge were glad to see the firth widening fairly soon to fully twice its width at the mouth, so that, by keeping to the middle, their many vessels were the less likely to attract unwanted attention from the shores – which here seemed fairly populous, low-lying on the north side, more hilly on the south.

They found the firth very different from the Forth, much shallower, sand-banks everywhere, these tending to push the craft towards the south shore. Prince Finan had said that they should make for Errol, where there was a haven of sorts, about a dozen miles up. None of the fishermen had ever been here before; and although Serf had crossed Tay many times, it had always been further up, at or nearer Perth. So none knew these parts. It had taken them all day to get thus far; and although it was never really dark in May, visibility was by now restricted, and being forced towards the wrong side of the firth was unhelpful. They could have done with Finan's or others' local guidance. He had said not to land until well into the night, in order to avoid attention. Which might be sound sense in one way but difficult in another.

However, the firth quite suddenly began to close in again, and unclear as the dusk vistas were, they could see hills coming nearer on the north side. These would be the Sidlaws, behind the narrow Carse of Gowrie, which they had to cross.

Lancelot was growing impatient. The north shoreline, so far as they could see, was shallow and lined by reed-banks, no doubt deep mud and no place to effect a landing. He clearly thought that Serf ought to have obtained better directions. That man admitted that this was probably an oversight, but he had not realised that conditions would be like this, and complicated by the required poor visibility.

Mungo said why not send one of their boats as close in to the north shore as it could get, to prospect? He would go with it. If there was a haven at or near this Errol, surely there must be a channel through the sand-banks and shallows to reach it. Meanwhile, the rest of the fleet was to wait in mid-firth.

No one could think of a better course, and a call went out for the most shallow draught of their craft to come forward, and Mungo transferred to this. All sails were lowered.

His particular boatmen were not too happy about this venture as Mungo directed them northwards. Soon they were complaining about oars touching bottom. So they had to swing round westwards again. They kept up this process, nosing carefully landwards until it became too shallow and then turning upstream, one of their men in the bows using an oar as a pole to judge depth. Still none of the reed-beds were very close.

At length this man's soundings failed to touch bottom for quite some distance, and they decided that they had reached a channel of sorts, and might risk turning landwards. It was probably the mouth of some stream. Those Sidlaw Hills must be sending down drainage water in this direction, surely.

Creeping in, still with the water reasonably deep, they neared land. And there, presently, they found a timber jetty projecting. Whether this was the haven for Errol they did not know; but at least it was a landing-place. Thankfully they turned and worked their way back, in this deeper water.

Out in mid-firth again, how to mark this channel? The fishermen solved the problem by producing a sort of wicker basket on a rope, weighted with a stone and with a pig's bladder to be blown up, as marker-buoy, this for catching lobsters. Lowering this, and tying Mungo's shirt to the float to make it more evident, they rowed back eastwards to collect their fellows.

After that it was not difficult. Even in the half-dark, Mungo's light-coloured shirt was not hard to find. Forming single file, the others followed his boat up what, it was to be presumed, was an underwater burn-channel through the mud and salt-marsh.

They landed at the jetty, one boat at a time, for it was small and distinctly decrepit. Errol or otherwise, this was sufficiently isolated, and even three hundred of them were unlikely to be conspicuous. It would be nearly midnight by this time.

Serf and Lancelot had discussed the problem of their boats. None knew how long it would take to get to Alyth, nor how long any rescue attempt would require, from a defended fort. They certainly could not leave the boats and crews waiting here for days on end. Better that they should return to Anstruther meantime. They might well have to send for them again, later; but a horseman could cross the Fife peninsula from hereabouts, wide as it was, in a few hours, to summon them back. Moreover, Lancelot declared that, once Guinevere was freed, he might well be able to take her to safety by land.

So it was farewell to the fishermen, who might have a short rest before returning whence they had come. Now the northwards march for the rest of them.

The Carse of Gowrie here was some five miles wide. Finan had said to head for the Abernyte glen, or pass, through the Sidlaws – but where Abernyte was, from here, they had no idea. The only thing to do was to head north across the Carse, for the hillfoots, and then seek for a pass through the heights, Abernyte or otherwise.

211

That made for an awkward and ploutering march to the hills, for the Carse was undrained and full of pools, bogs and ditches, entailing much circling, dodging, falling and cursing, so that more than any five miles had to be covered. But eventually the firm ground beyond was reached.

Now to find a pass through the steeply rising slopes. Whether to turn left or right? This travel by night, in a strange country, was anything but simple.

Thanea agreed with Serf that Finan had indicated that Alyth was north of where the River Isla joined Tay – not the firth but the upper river – at one of its great loops. Since they must be none so far from Perth here, to the west, that must mean that they should turn right, not left, along the hillfoots. No one was in a position to contest this, so that way they went.

It was sunrise before the disgruntled, stumbling company were able to see a major gap in the barrier of hills. Whether this was the right one or not, they turned up it, to climb beside a well-doing stream. The glen rose, twisted and bent, but could hardly be called a pass. It seemed to be devoid of inhabitants.

It in time brought them out on to high ground, where they found that their burn issued from a small loch. Here, from a slight ridge, in the now strong morning light, they were able to see for great distances. Clearly a very wide valley was opening before them, with a mountain-mass far behind as far as eye could see. This must be Strathmore and those mountains the Highlands. So they must be fairly near their destination, and not far from the borders of Fortrenn and Angus. Where was Alyth?

Lancelot decided to rest here, by the loch, to eat and sleep. But they must, somehow, learn where they were and how they must head on. They could see two cottages on lower ground about a mile away, to their flank. Mungo offered to go down and ask for directions there, and Thanea said that she would go with him; a woman and young man would not arouse suspicions.

They found only women and children at the cot-houses, their shepherd and cowherd menfolk being already out on the hill. They learned that this area was called Ledcrieff, and that they were only some three miles from the ford of the River Isla where the Romans had established a camp to guard it, and a little community had grown up. Once they were across that ford, it was only about another six miles northwards to Alyth.

Lancelot decided, with only some ten miles to go, that their best course was to lie up here most of the day, then move by devious and if possible unseen ways at dusk again, to make a surprise attack on the fort in the early hours of the morning. If God was good they might well take the place without a great deal of fighting.

That was well received.

So there was much sleeping that day, in preparation for a busy night.

They moved off at sunset. The problem was to get across the Isla without creating suspicion or alarm, for it was a major river and apparently the only ford hereabouts was at this Coupar. However, as Mungo pointed out, even though they did arouse and concern the Coupar people, it was not likely that any of them would set off during the night to warn the garrison at Alyth, six miles away, which they could not know was to be attacked anyway.

A round-about route to the ford was probably not necessary. At any rate they reached the river without encountering any problems, and found the ford without difficulty, ropes on poles reaching across it, no doubt for safety in winter spates when the water would be much higher than it was of a May night. There were houses near the far side, but no lights showing therefrom. The company, silence enjoined, crossed the underwater causeway slabs carefully but without incident or much delay. A dog did bark at them from the village beyond, but that was as far as arousal went.

They knew only their general course now – north-eastwards; but since the Isla came down from that direction, they turned to follow it up, by a winding progression. This was satisfactory enough for a couple of miles or so, but when they came to another river joining theirs from the north, this proved less easy to cross, no ford apparent, and fairly deep and the current strong. There was nothing for it but to turn up its bank and hope to find a fording-place thereafter.

They had to go another couple of miles, with the river

213

unfortunately swinging away westwards, before they could find a practical crossing-place; by which time they were the more unsure of where Alyth might be. They thought that it must be no great distance off, but well to the east. The ground seemed to be rising again ahead of them – and their fort, they knew, was on a hilltop.

Lancelot said that there was nothing for it but to enquire at the first house they came to, however upsetting this might be for the inhabitants, at night. Mungo again volunteered, with Thanea, as the least likely to alarm.

They were not long in finding a cottage. The party keeping out of sight, mother and son went forward to knock on the door. A dog barked again, inside. They had to repeat their knocking before a man's voice came from behind the door.

"Who is there? What do you want?" came the demand.

Thanea answered. "Travellers. Lost travellers. We make for Alyth. But do not know the way. Nor where we are." She hoped that a woman's voice would reassure.

"You are at Aberbothrie."

"And where is Alyth from here, friend?"

Fears presumably allayed, the door was opened and a man wrapped in a blanket peered out at them, a dog growling behind him. Eyeing them, he pointed, north-eastwards.

"Alyth township lies yonder, less than four miles. Uphill. Why do you travel by night?"

"We became lost, at the river. To find a crossing. After we left the Isla."

"That was the Ericht. You should have crossed where the rivers joined."

"No doubt. But we missed that. How do we get to Alyth?"

"Up the braes ahead. You climb to a ridge. You will see a glen before you. With a burn. That is the Alyth Burn. The township is at the burnside."

"But . . ." Thanea hesitated. "It is a hilltop that we seek. With a fort."

It was the other's turn to hesitate. "Why? Why there? The fort."

"There is a lady there whom we go to see," Mungo said. Thanea wondered whether he was wise to say that.

"We have heard of her," the man said, carefully.

214

"Yes. But how do we get there?"

"It is a great fort. On Barry Hill. High behind Alyth. But you will not win into there at night!"

"No. But so long as we can find it. Behind the town, you say?"

"Yes. Almost two miles. There are two hills, together. The Hill of Laghail, to the west. And Barry Hill to the east. The fort is there."

"We thank you. We regret disturbing your rest."

"The lady in the fort is a great one, they say. Yet you travel on foot, by night?"

"We . . . left our friends to seek guidance," Thanea said vaguely. "A good night to you."

Back at the company, their information was welcomed and a move was made at once. It would be dawn in just over a couple of hours, so haste was of the essence.

It took them an hour to reach the Alyth Burn in its glen, east of the township, and almost another, passing a standing-stone on the way, to climb up to a high col between two summits, obviously the twin hills they had been told of. From here they could not see any fort, but it could well be close at hand, well above, on the right.

Lancelot decided to climb heedfully up, with a couple of men, to the top, to prospect, Mungo not to be left behind. There was a faint lightening of eastern sky. The nightfall would not last much longer.

Once over the brow of the hill, they could see the fort outlined against the eastern sky, the usual grassy earthen ramparts topped by a high stockade of timber, and inside a strongly defensive house of stone. It was all larger than most such forts, and clearly had been an important place once.

Lancelot studied it all carefully for some time. There would be guards on duty almost certainly, although they could not see any in this light. The main garrison would be asleep – and men slept deepest just before dawn. A distraction was what was needed, he told Mungo, some minor one, not to alarm but to draw the guard. Then a silent rush, to storm ramparts and stockade. Some of his men wore ropes round their middles, to surmount the stockade. Then to get the gates opened, from the inside.

He made it sound easy. What would they use for this distraction, Mungo wondered. Not to create alarm?

The king was pondering. What would cause guards to go to investigate, without arousing the rest of the inmates? Something simple but effective. A woman's voice, calling for help? The Princess Thanea's? That might serve. At the far side, the east side. Where the breeze would carry the cry. Then – attack from this west side . . .

They went back to the others. Thanea was perfectly ready to play her part. Serf and Mungo said that they would accompany her, in case any of the guards came down to her – assuming that there *were* guards on duty at this hour.

With no time to be lost the trio set off north-about round the shoulder of the hill. Reaching the east face, they started to climb. Lancelot had said that by the time they had got thus far, his people would have crept up to the brow, and be ready to advance.

Getting sufficiently close to be heard without being seen demanded some judgment. But, creeping and crawling up by declivities and banks, they found a hollow a mere thirty yards or so from the ramparts, and there crouched down.

"Now?" Thanea wondered, in a whisper.

They nodded.

Feeling distinctly foolish, she raised her voice to call for help, help. Pleas to come to her aid. She sought to make it somewhat quavery, as though weary and in distress. "Help! Come!"

Mungo actually laughed, but silently.

She had to keep it up for quite some time before there was any reaction, an enquiring shout from the ramparts. She continued to call. Was it just the one man she was distracting? How many would be apt to form a night guard? Would this be enough to do what was necessary?

They began to fear that it was not, for apart from another single shout from the fort nothing seemed to happen for a considerable time, Thanea's calls beginning to quaver indeed. And then, at last, there were results, and a sufficiency of them. Pandemonium broke out up there, shouting, yells, screams, thuds and the clash of steel. The trio, battle not in their experience, nor with any appeal to them, stared at each other, feeling somehow responsible nevertheless. But helpless.

What to do now? Nothing. Except pray. Pray that there would be a minimum of hurt and bloodshed.

They waited there, while the din and uproar continued, anxiously gazing towards the fort. They could see nothing of what went on beyond the high stockade. They could not tell whether the attackers were inside, nor who might be winning. Mungo was for running up to see, but the other two restrained him. There was nothing that they could effect which three hundred armed men could not, without them.

It was other running which yielded the first indication of results. Two men came bounding downhill past their hiding-place at no great distance off, in obvious panic, neither clad for war nor carrying weapons – so obviously not Lancelot's folk. Part of the garrison, therefore, and in flight. Further over, they saw another man, also running off.

"Praise God – these are not ours!" Serf exclaimed. "So they flee. Or some of them. It looks as though Lancelot is in. And gaining the advantage."

"Come!" Mungo pleaded. "Round to the other side. We must see what is happening. Not just stand here, while, while . . ."

Reluctantly the other two acquiesced. They moved back round the hilltop to the west side, closer to the fort now. The noise was still going on, but they imagined that it was lessening – and there seemed to be more groans than shouts now.

The light was strengthening. They could see ropes hanging down the stockade walls, but they could not see behind these. No men were actually in sight.

Then, further round the fort's perimeter, they saw a gateway. And the gate stood open. They made for this, Mungo eager, the others doubtful.

The first man they saw, unfortunately, Mungo tripped over, dead, just inside the gateway. It was a shock. He had never seen a slain man, and one still bleeding. He stooped, as though to touch, and then straightened up and hurried on, all but sick. Biting lips, Thanea followed him.

There were more bodies, some still stirring, groaning. One she recognised as of Lancelot's party. A piercing scream rang out from behind the stone house. Was fighting still going on there?

Uncertain what to do, they stood staring. Could they help any of the wounded? One man staggered to his feet at sight of them, and lurched off, bent double.

Then at the door of the stone building a man and a woman appeared – Lancelot with his arm around Queen Guinevere. Thanea, with a cry, rushed forward to embrace the other woman.

An emotional scene followed wherein, it fell to be admitted, death and the dying around tended to be forgotten for the moment, as they clutched each other and sought for words.

Lancelot, declaring that all was well, detached himself and went round the building and huts to see how the residual fighting was going, although with the noise abating, it seemed hopeful.

Guinevere, in a night-robe which revealed much of her magnificent figure, led Thanea and the others into the house – and even here they had to step over a body near the door, still with a dagger projecting from the throat. In the circumstances the queen was remarkably calm and lucid – but then she was herself a warrior chieftainess. She praised Lancelot and all her rescuers declaring that, yes, Mordred *had* raped her, earlier on – so she and Thanea had that in common. Here they had held and guarded her but had not molested her, no doubt afraid of Mordred's wrath. Now she need no longer fear that young man. And when Arthur returned . . . !

Thanea said that her half-brother's behaviour appalled her, savage, treacherous and unworthy. Was he here?

No, he had brought her here and then left her in the care of that man who lay near the door. Did Thanea know him? He was one of the chieftains from Traprain in Lothian, Aeadh by name, Aeadh of Stanypath.

Thanea gulped. Aeadh was the father of one of her friends at Monenna's school.

Lancelot came back. Fighting had ceased, he said, and the fort wholly in their hands. Casualties were not high, considering – clearly he was referring to his own people. There had been only the one guard on the gate when his stockade-scalers had gone in to it. Surprise had been complete, the garrison asleep.

Thereafter, with Guinevere dressing, Thanea and Serf took Mungo outside to see what they could do for the wounded, experiencing dire reactions at what they saw, the queen joining them presently. Mungo, getting over his initial upset at the sight of dead bodies and blood, went counting, and came back to announce that he made it twenty-eight dead, only four of them Lancelot's men, and fifteen wounded, again four of them their own. Apparently quite a number of the garrison had escaped through a postern gate.

The general consensus was that it had all been a great success – although with all the death around them, the non-combatants reserved judgment. At least the objective had been achieved and Guinevere freed.

With some of the garrison escaped, it was possible that there might be repercussions, a return attack, although Lancelot did not think this likely for some time. According to Guinevere, her captors had all been Mordred's men, and it was scarcely probable that any local chief of Angus would be eager to take up arms in what was no quarrel of his. And the Angus capital was a long way off, at Forfar. Nevertheless they would not linger overlong. To eat, and rest – there was ample food at the fort – and leave at dusk.

A discussion amongst the leadership resulted in the decision to attempt a landwards return to the south, rather than having to send for boats from East Fife. They were not so very far from Perth, after all, where they could cross Tay at the ford, the first such after the estuary. From there they could make for Stirling, where they would part company; Serf, Thanea and Mungo for Culross, the majority of the teulo for Tweed and the Cheviots, and Lancelot and Guinevere, with escort, for some haven on the Firth of Clyde. That would be best.

This plan, of course, aroused interest and speculation as to *where* the king was going to take Arthur's queen. Lancelot said that they had decided on Afalon, the Isle of Afalon, or Man as the pagans called it, the Isle of Apples in the Irish Sea. It was part of Arthur's high kingdom, but far enough away to be safe from Mordred's attentions. He would have to have a fleet to assail it – and he had no fleet, Arthur himself having almost all his ships with him at Gaul. Guinevere should be safe there; and they would send the High King word as to what had happened. Lancelot imagined that he would be back, to deal with Mordred and regain his wife and kingdoms, without undue delay. Meanwhile he, Lancelot, would look after Guinevere.

It occurred to Thanea to wonder whether, in fact, Arthur's wife would be so much safer, in one respect, with this Lancelot than with Mordred. But they seemed to be good friends, at least. She had heard of this Afalon – indeed it was famous in their Celtic mythology, the isle where the spirits of the departed were said to head, for final disposal. The Romans had called it Mona, but at some stage it had been renamed Man, after her familiar demon, Manannan, god of the sea. Strange that Guinevere should be taken there.

So they waited until the darkening, resting, and then started on their journey, so as to create the least possible disturbance again and give no reason for the Angus mormaor to make trouble for Nechtan. They agreed that they could find their way back to the Ericht and Isla rivers, as they had come, and follow the latter down to Tay and so to Perth, all this they calculated, without much difficulty, by night. Once south of Perth they were safely deep in Fortrenn, before reaching Manau.

Guinevere had quickly recovered her assured and queenly stance. She was graciously grateful to all; but none doubted where authority now lay, Lancelot notwithstanding. They buried the dead in the fort's ditches outside the ramparts, left the wounded as well cared for as was practical, and moved off at nightfall for Perth and their divergent destinations, mission accomplished – and another stage in Mungo's education effected.

17

Arthur's return was not long delayed, needless to say, although he had to leave much of his strength, indeed most of it, in Gaul, to wind up his campaign there. At Culross they heard that he was back, in the autumn, but with no details. They made a visit to Forteviot to learn the facts, for Nechtan was always well informed.

The news there was that there was chaos, all but civil war, in the Brythonic kingdoms to the south, sparked off by Arthur's return. Since he had little of his army with him, he was relying on an uprising amongst his peoples to oust and defeat Mordred; but although undoubtedly most of his folk were loyal and eager to rise, it was not so easy to form an effective host out of all the disparate entities and tribes, wide-scattered as they were. Mordred, whatever else, was efficient, and ruthless as a usurper, and had got rid of most of the leaders left behind from the High King's force in Gaul, which comprised of course most of his best lieutenants. And those who had sided with Mordred in his insurrection were now, not unnaturally, still supporting him for fear of Arthur's reprisals and due punishment. Not all might actually take up arms against the High King admittedly; but some, like the kings of Strathclyde, Rheged and Cantyre, pagans, were evidently not committing themselves as they ought to be doing but standing by, waiting to see who came out on top, making various excuses. So Arthur was not finding it easy to arouse and muster his undoubtedly prevalent support, especially with his Welsh allies preoccupied, as so frequently, with Saxon invaders. Carlisle, Arthur's capital, was firmly under Mordred's clenched fist; and Lancelot's Northumbria still very much in the hands of Anglian Ida. Nobody was quite sure, apparently, as to where Arthur was establishing his base, nor whether he had visited Guinevere on Afalon.

All this worried and concerned the trio from Culross. They

had no doubt that Arthur, in the end, would triumph, but that would apparently take some time. He might have to wait until he could bring his great and battle-hardened army back from Gaul and the Frankish wars.

Urging Nechtan to keep them informed, they returned to Fife.

It was late autumn before Finan arrived with more specific tidings. Arthur had chosen to set up his headquarters in the strategic area of the mid-Tweed valley, like the Romans had done before him, at Trimontium, the three Eildon Hills above Meall Ross, this with good reason, where he could act as a barrier between Mordred's forces at Carlisle and his kingdom of Lothian; also where Lancelot's people, in the Cheviot area, could flock to his standard; and where the Manau forces, which seemed to have remained loyal, could join him without too much difficulty.

Finan also brought word of his father's attitude. Although the Albannach mormaordoms were not involved in this Brythonic struggle, Nechtan, grateful to Arthur for his defeat of the Saxons at their one major invasion of Fortrenn, wished to help in some way. He would not send an army, but would place his men along the Fortrenn–Angus and Manau borders, where they would serve as a deterrent to any force Bargoit of Angus might send to aid his reputed ally Mordred. This was quite a notable gesture for the unwarlike Nechtan, and Finan was obviously pleased at it.

Mungo, now very much the young man, was agog at all this, and urged that they should all go and see King Arthur at this three-mountain place, go and welcome him home and encourage him in his struggle. Thanea did not take much persuading to visit her uncle; and she also would hope to see her brother Gawain, whom she expected to be with Arthur, whose side he seldom left. Serf was not so sure about it, not seeing quite what they could contribute other than mere good wishes, and doubting whether the busy monarch would have any time to spare for them. But he did not ban the project nor refuse to go along.

There was no disagreement about how to get to the Eildon Hills and Meall Ross rather than by crossing hostile Lothian – by boat to Eyemouth again, and then westwards south of the Lammermuirs, across the Merse country north of Berwick.

So it was off to Anstruther once more, two days later, to hire a boat. There they discovered that Lancelot had been as good as his word and sent handsome payment for the help given by the fishermen. So they had no difficulty in getting a craft and crew for this lesser venture.

That autumnal weather was not so pleasant for voyaging in the open sea in an open boat as had been conditions in May; but the journey to Eyemouth was accomplished without untoward incident. They spent the night at the fishing-haven, Mungo going to nearby farmeries to hire horses for the morrow. They said goodbye to their boatmen, after having arranged that Eyemouth men would sail them back to Anstruther in due course.

So in the morning it was westwards, mounted on sturdy garrons, up the Eye Water valley and over the rising ground beyond, grassy cattle country, quite populous in a pastoral fashion, land of the small Selgovae tribe, a people who alternated in adherence between the kingdoms of Northumbria and Lothian. Eventually this brought them to the Whiteadder, a quite major river, which they followed for some way until crossing to its tributary the Blackadder, the route given them at Eyemouth. This stream took them to the township of Duns, where they were nearing the foothills of a projection of the Lammermuirs, along these southern skirts of which they made their way, fairly easy country to travel, by Greenlaw and Gordon to Ersildoune. Here another great river of this land of rivers brought them down to Meall Ross, under the dramatic isolated triple peaks of the Eildons, the Trimontium of the Romans, these having been beckoning them on for many a mile. They had come about forty miles from Eyemouth.

The strangely named Meall Ross, the great headland, hardly to be looked for so far from the sea, proved to be in fact a mighty promontory of steep cliffs formed by a notably acute bend of the River Tweed, which they had now reached, and cutting a deep wedge through the foothills. But beyond this the great river entered a sort of small plain below the soaring Eildons. Here they found a large concourse of armed men encamped, many hundreds, Arthur's assembly place.

An elderly man, a young man and a woman aroused no concern here. Enquiries for the High King elicited the information that he was at present absent. He had apparently gone on some sort of pilgrimage, while awaiting the arrival of more men for his force, not very far away, to be sure, to a valley named Wedale, that of the Gala Water about ten miles to the west. Here there was a holy place called the Stow of Wedale, apparently, to which he was dedicating some relics brought back from Gaul. It was not known just when he would be back. He had been absent two days.

The travellers, used to riding long distances, felt that, as it was only mid-afternoon, another ten or so miles was not too much for their mounts nor themselves. They would go on to this Wedale. They had not heard of it, but apparently it was being called that, rather than Galadale as might have been expected, because many years before Arthur had won a very difficult victory there over a large Anglian force, and in gratitude to God had vowed to build a Christian shrine, the vow, or wed or wadset in due course fulfilled. So Wedale it was, a place for which the High King had a strong attachment.

They rode on up Tweed another few miles until they reached the inflowing Gala Water, up the winding valley of which they turned, probing deeply into green hills.

They were not long in reaching the Stow, or sacred place, where they found a company of about a dozen camped around a small stone chapel above the riverside. The first person they saw was Gawain. There was a touching reunion. It was years since Thanea had seen her brother. He was now beginning to show a little grey at the temples, but seemed more the warrior prince, experiences leaving their mark. For his part, he was greatly taken with his nephew, who was now looking much of the man he was going to be. He did not remark on Serf's evident ageing.

Arthur was in the chapel, he told them, superintending the erection of a statue of the Virgin Mary which he had brought back from Gaul for this shrine, to save it from being defaced by the heathen Franks. Gawain took them inside, where they found the High King on his knees, not actually praying but helping a local man to build a little stone platform on which to base the effigy of Virgin and Child, this attractively carved and painted. Thanea, who in her childhood had romantically prayed, like many another, that she might one day be privileged to emulate Mary and bear a son without having to be, as she thought, defiled by a man, gazed on this woodcarver's handiwork with somewhat wry admiration. *Her* experience had been distinctly otherwise.

Arthur was glad to see them, exclaiming at Mungo's development and anxious to express his gratitude for the major part they had played in the rescue of his Guinevere. Lancelot had told him of it all. He had sailed over to Afalon as soon as he had got back and learned of the situation. He had left her there meantime, in Lancelot's care; better there until Mordred mac Loth was duly dealt with. Thanea expressed her horror and shame over her half-brother's treachery, Gawain concurring.

Arthur presently showed them another relic which he had brought back from Gaul, a fragment of Christ's true cross which, he was assured, was genuine. He would have a silver casket made for it, and it would remain here beside the statue, for all time, as a token of his faith and gratitude.

They all took the grey-brown scrap of wood in their hands, in awe and reverence.

Outside, Arthur told them of his plans. He could not be sure when his army in Gaul would be in a position to return and join him, for they could not desert the Christian communities there until other protectors arrived, the Frankish invaders being fierce, ruthless and very numerous. He had sent and urged the High King of Ireland to despatch a force thither, in St Patrick's name, but whether he had done so, or would, was not known. So now he, Arthur, was trying to assemble a large enough host to defeat Mordred, no easy matter in the circumstances, with nearly all the natural leaders and chiefs still in Gaul, and Mordred having slain or imprisoned many who might have led resistance. He had promises of support from fair numbers; but Mordred held nearly all the forts and strongholds, and so was in a position to threaten would-be supporters in many areas. He had sent his secretary, Merlin, to Wales to appeal to the princes there. He was glad to hear of Nechtan's gesture.

Mungo wanted to know when the fighting would start. Surely once the famous High King actually drew sword, thousands would flock to his banner? Would not Mordred have to withdraw his garrisons from the forts, in order for them to face the battle, so that folk would no longer be threatened?

His great-uncle said that it was not so simple as that. Distances came into this. Many local chieftains and their men would be loth to go far from their own territories for fear of raids and reprisals, and not only from Mordred's supporters. So the chosen battleground would have to be selected with great care. In fact, the Welsh princes, if they could be got temporarily to forget their fears of Saxon invasion and come north for a brief, limited campaign, would probably offer his greatest source of trained manpower. Which in turn would affect the site of conflict, where it would be reasonably convenient for the Welsh and inconvenient for Mordred. Tactics and strategy were as important as numbers and armed prowess. In the circumstances, he thought that it might be best not to fight in this area at all, but to move south to Cumbria, possibly even as far as the great Roman Wall, where his Welsh allies could reach swiftly. Unless of course his own seasoned army returned from Gaul soon, when the entire situation would be very different. The winter would soon be upon them, not the best time for campaigning and marching through hilly country – nor for sailing armies across seas.

So it was all more complicated than Mungo, for one, had visualised. The young man felt somewhat disappointed, his hero Arthur's stature, for him, just a little diminished.

However, the High King's credit was redeemed that evening when, at Gawain's urging, he told them something of the Gaul campaign, his battles against the Frankish and Arian Visigoth invaders, victories and rescues of assailed communities. Although Arthur himself was very modest about his successes, Gawain detailed and extolled them. Mungo became lost in admiration again.

They spent the night at Stow, sleeping in the chapel after Serf held a dedicatory service for the statue and cross fragment. They would all return to Meall Ross in the morning.

Arthur further commended himself to his great-nephew next day when, under the triple peaks of the Eildons, Mungo declared that he just had to climb these challenging heights, and the High King announced surprisingly that he would accompany him. He admitted that he enjoyed climbing, on occasion, and that he did find this idle waiting period irksome, being a man for action. Serf had no such urges, and Thanea decided to stay with him and Gawain. So, dismissing the idea of an escort, the pair set out alone, well content, on a crisp October afternoon.

Arthur had done this before, to be sure; and offered as excuse for doing it again that he would have to decide which summit to put his beacon on. When Mungo asked what beacons were for up here, it was explained that they were for the swift sending of tidings widespread, and for the summoning of forces. A chain of beacons, set on prominent heights and hilltops, could send a message across the land, from sea to sea if need be, in an hour or two. He would require this when the time came to move his forces and call other groups to converge in an assembly area, here or elsewhere. He already had beacons erected on a number of prominent places. These Eildons could be seen from scores of miles in every direction, isolated as they were, ideal as a central point. There was an ancient Pictish fort on the top of the northern summit, a burial cairn on the middle one, but nothing on the southern.

Mungo said the obvious thing – should not the beacon go on the highest? To which Arthur pointed out that although the centre summit was the highest, because of its positioning it was not necessarily the one which would best be seen from all directions. It and its northern neighbour were so near each other in height that the latter could perhaps block out any beacon-fire in the centre one for quite a wide swathe of country to the north-east – the area of the Merse over which the travellers had recently come.

It was the northern hill which they ascended first, the one nearest Meall Ross, a quite steep climb, especially as they neared the top – although nothing to compare with Cir Mhor on Arran. The High King climbed well, even though rather less nimbly than his companion. He was now fifty-two, but very fit and active. His great-nephew did not have to do much pausing and waiting.

On the summit, from the ramparts of the old fort, the views all around were magnificent. Arthur pointed out that the very fact that the Picts had placed their fort here, not on the next and slightly higher hill, probably answered his question as to which was best for his beacon. Admittedly the view south-westwards was obstructed for a narrow segment by its neighbouring summit, but it so happened that there was only fairly low ground along that line for many miles, with no heights on which beacons would be placed. And the third hill was considerably lower, and would pose no problem.

Arthur pointed out sundry prominences, near and far, on which fires would be lit, naming them, and obviously entirely familiar with the wide terrain. He said that a beacon chain would extend all the way to Caerlaverock on the Solway Firth, where he had been born and where he intended to winter, assuming that his Gaul army did not arrive before that. There was a fine harbour at Loch Ryan, in Rheged, not far from there, where his fleet could make port – and from which *he* could sail if Mordred sought to capture him meantime. It was from there that he had gone to Afalon, or Man, recently, to see Guinevere.

They had to dip down quite sharply into a deep col before they could climb the second hill where, on the great mound of stones which constituted the burial cairn of some Pictish chief, they could see that indeed the hill to the north would have blocked out the light of a beacon here for quite a ribbon of country, including a prominent height, the Black Hill of Ersildoune, on which one of the nearest beacons was established a mere five miles away. Mungo was learning.

The third top was more easily reached, linked by something of a ridge, and the least impressive although its south side was the steepest. They did not descend this, after a survey of the vast panorama of plain and range, hill and forest and river valley, for Arthur said that the best and quickest way back was as they had come, only circling the tops to the south and not climbing them again.

On the way back, Arthur questioned his companion as to his plans and hopes for the future, and approved that the young man was determined to follow in Serf's footsteps and seek to bring Christ-Crucified to nations and peoples still pagan. Almost apologetically Mungo had declared that although he recognised that the faith required warriors like the High

King to protect its converts from their heathen enemies, so aggressive and fierce, he felt that this duty was not for him, that he must teach and preach and persuade, fight with his tongue and wits and convictions rather than with the sword. Was he wrong in this, selfish, craven even? He was told no, that he was right, right. Many could fight and battle; fewer indeed could effectively expound Christ's Gospel and convert. He must hold to his intention – and God would be with him.

Mungo was to remember that exchange for the rest of his life.

The Culross party said their goodbyes the following morning, wishing Arthur so very well, and departed on their forty-mile return to Eyemouth. Often on their journey Mungo looked back at the three peaks of the Eildon Hills, and pondered.

18

That winter was a notably hard one, and long-lasting, spring late indeed in coming, and when it did was wet, cold and miserable. Flocks and herds were decimated, the lambing unsuccessful and the ploughing and grain-planting direly delayed. Men declared that the gods were angry, and they sought the more urgently to placate them, sacrifices frequent, including human ones. The Christians taught and pleaded otherwise, to be sure, but it was difficult to convince that *their* loving God could not right this state of affairs for at least His adherents.

Serf, Thanea and Mungo, and Queen Eva and Finan also, with their colleagues, worked hard in atrocious conditions, seeking to see it all as a challenge. Their mission area was now so widespread that a great deal of their time was spent necessarily in travel, grim as the weather was, snow, storm, floods, rivers in spate and even hunger to contend with, for food was scarce everywhere, and as a result physical weakness not helping. Serf could not remember so grievous a period. And he feared for real famine thereafter.

In all this even Nechtan had little or no word of King Arthur and his doings. No doubt these conditions would be affecting him and his also – although, of course, the same applied to his enemies. But it did mean that, whatever was happening in Gaul, his army there would be unlikely to be able to return home while the storms lasted. There was certainly no news of great battles.

Whether as a result of the conditions, Thanea suffered a recurrence of her illness that so-called spring, to the anxiety of her son and friends. Now in his twentieth year, Mungo was very masterful about her taking Duncan the ex-druid's medicaments and remedies and resting. But his mother had proved herself ere this a woman of spirit, and was not to be coddled. In consequence, perhaps, she took a long time fully to recover.

It was mid-summer – if such it could be called – when Nechtan sent them the dire tidings. There had been a great battle, two of them indeed, on the Cumbrian–Northumbrian borders, at Camlann beside the Roman Wall known as Hadrian's; and although Arthur's forces had won in the end, he himself had been mortally wounded in a personal duel with Mordred, whom he had slain. Still alive, but undoubtedly dying, Gawain had taken him back to the Isle of Afalon, to his Guinevere. Whether he had reached there alive was not reported.

Stunned, devastated, his kin and friends at Culross wept.

Grieving, appalled, bewildered, they had to ask themselves – what now? Arthur had seemed all but immortal. What would happen to the high kingship, and all the kingdoms under it? Arthur's two feeble sons were presumably still with the army in Gaul; anyway, they would be useless to succeed their father. Who, then? And Lothian, too, would be without a monarch – although with his beloved uncle dead, Gawain would probably return to Traprain to rule there now. But he was not of the stature to make a successful high king. None could guess what the outcome of it all might be.

It was autumn again, and famine stalking the land, before sure word reached Serf, although rumours abounded. Arthur was dead, yes. Urien of Rheged, Owen's father, now nearing old age, had assumed the high kingship; but whether he would be able to retain it, or fulfil the task, was questionable. Lancelot, who might have made a bid for it, had failed still to regain his own kingdom and in consequence could not aspire to the senior position; he apparently was still on Afalon, with Guinevere. There was still no word as to Arthur's two sons.

At Culross they did not just sit down and pine and wonder, of course. They had God's work to do. But they were all greatly shocked. A light seemed to have been extinguished in their lives, the lives of all; and to some extent this had its effect on their living.

Serf undoubtedly was the most affected. Ageing anyway, he seemed to wilt somehow, to shrink in on himself. He did not lose his belief in any way, but clearly judged that Christ's cause had suffered a major set-back and that this must hinder

231

and limit his own work. He admitted himself to be weary.
Thanea tended to see it all rather as a test of their faith
that God's good and loving purpose would prevail, and that
meantime they must hold fast and work as before. Mungo, so
much the youngest, deemed it an actual challenge. He quoted
often those words of Arthur to him on the Eildon Hills, that he
was right, right, in his intention to do what the sword could not
do, to seek to teach, persuade and convert to Christ's Gospel,
to hold to that and that God would be with him. His elders
could by no means refute that, of course, nor sought to. Was
Mungo now to be the leader?

It certainly began to seem that that was to be so thereafter,
with the young man apt to take over much of the mission visiting and preliminary teaching. Thanea, her health improved
again, usually accompanied him. Serf by no means held back,
but Mungo very much took the initiative. In major matters,
to be sure, the abbot had to officiate; at baptisms, inductions,
consecrations and the like.

The inevitable happened, although Serf waited for Mungo's
twentieth birthday, the beginning of his vital twenty-first year,
to bring it about; the young man should now be ordained
priest. Mungo himself had never actually urged this, although
for long it had not been far from his mind. He had seen
ex-druids so ordained, and others who had been Christian
for years less than he had. But his comparative youth was
the governing factor, and he had spells when he well knew
his own unworthiness and inadequacy.

So when, on Christmas Eve, Serf told him what he proposed
to include in the next day's celebrations, Mungo was both
glad and apprehensive, unsure of himself but proud too, in
something of a humble way. A priest of the Lord – himself,
Mungo!

Thanea was proud too. Her son, so misbegotten, to be
admitted to the small company of the elect. Here was fulfilment
for her also. She knew a great satisfaction.

For so major a transition, the ordination was markedly
simple, mere words not the important part of it all. In
the middle of the Christmas service, after the consecration of
the bread and wine, Serf called Mungo forward by name to
the altar, and there before all, offered thanks for the faith and

dedication of this servant of Christ, proved over the years, by strong and sustained labours. Then he washed his head, brow and hands in holy water, a sort of second baptism to indicate a fresh start. Then the signing of the cross was followed by the laying on of hands, to confer the Holy Spirit, and anointing with oil. Finally a comprehensive blessing; and the abbot, taking the other by the hand, led him up behind the altar, and there, taking up the wine-chalice, presented it to the new priest with a bow, intimation that he was now competent and authorised to dispense holy communion. It was all as simple and basic as that, yet the authority implicit, undoubted. Mungo stood, trembling with emotion, afraid indeed that he might spill the precious wine, as Serf bid the congregation come and partake.

Thanea, by no means usually foremost in this procession, today led the way, in order to be the first to receive the sacrament at her son's hands, kneeling, heart full.

That was a very special Christmastide at Culross, despite the death of Arthur, disaster and famine. Somehow it seemed to signify, to that trio at least, that God's purpose and cause marched on.

19

In the year that followed, Mungo surpassed himself in activity and effort, all but exhausting his mother, whom he assumed would be his eager acolyte and assistant. He journeyed from end to end of Fortrenn and Fife, carrying the Word with enthusiasm, which undoubtedly he transmitted to others, so that results were highly encouraging and, it was to be hoped, enduring. It was his mother's slight fear that this, of all but sweeping people off their feet with his missionary zeal, might not stand the tests of time, temptation and trial. She hinted as much, but the last thing that she desired was to dampen his ardour – not that he showed any signs of that. There was no toning him down, much less halting him.

Serf rejoiced in it all, although he less and less accompanied the pair, spending an increasing proportion of his time at his diseart, in prayer and contemplation. Mungo was much interested in this, and concerned also. Not in the decline of activity, but in wonder at the old man's ability to adore wordlessly in silent worship for long periods, something which he himself could by no means aspire to. Serf had been a man in his fifties when he took Thanea in, so now he was in his seventies. He was not to be blamed if he was beginning to show it.

The situation in the late Arthur's high kingdom was meantime chaotic, Urien unable to hold the constituent realms together. Lancelot had made another attempt to win back his Northumbrian kingdom from Anglian Ida, but, with none of the other petty kings supporting him, he had failed, and was now said to be back with Guinevere on Afalon – whether they had married or not was unclear. Gawain had returned to Lothian to rule, but not from Traprain with its pagan and unhappy associations, having transferred his capital to Dunedin, under Arthur's Seat, with its mighty castle rock.

Twice he had come over Forth, from the haven of Leith, to visit his sister and nephew, and confessed that he was finding his task difficult indeed, with Mordred's legacy hard to disown and live down. Prince Owen was now ruling Rheged for his father, with what success they did not hear.

Fortunately Mormaor Nechtan was having less trouble with his neighbouring mormaors, the famine limiting aggressive tendencies. Also Mordred's death removed a certain amount of pressure from Bargoit of Angus. So missionary efforts in Fortrenn were not hampered. Thanea saw much of Eva and her young people.

In all his activities, the faintest of shadows was beginning to concern Mungo, and therefore his mother. This was that Serf was more and more evidently assuming that he, Mungo, was going to succeed him as Abbot of Culross and senior cleric of Fortrenn and Fife. And this was not that young man's intention and desire. He recognised ever more clearly how much sheer administration, supervision and pastoral care was involved in such a position, and this was not what he saw as his life's work. Not yet, at any rate. His urgent desire was to evangelise, to go out and convert many, peoples, nations even. He could not do that as Abbot of Culross, Serf's successor. He did not want to disappoint nor offend his old friend and mentor; but he was determined not to become tied down in administration, however valuable that was in holding together established Christian communities.

He did not assert this too strongly meantime, but it was much on his mind. Thanea understood. She wondered whether he should in fact go and seek to convert Lothian, and so help Gawain in his difficult ruling of a pagan realm; but somehow she herself felt strangely disinclined to become involved in that – and she wanted to accompany her son wherever he went. Lothian, her homeland, spelt darkness and fear for her now. Perhaps she should feel concerned to aid in the dispelling of that darkness; but within her she knew otherwise. The past had wounded too deeply.

So God's work proceeded, even though most of it was abbatial rather than evangelical, and another year went by without major change. Then, after a better winter, with spring upon them, there were sudden developments. Crises indeed, and quite unexpected. A monkish messenger arrived from Carnock, in Manau, to announce that old Fergus was dying, longing to see and say goodbye to his Culross friends, and asking to be taken to Cathures, in Strathclyde, to be buried beside his family and ancestors.

Such pleas, of course, could not be unheeded. They all must go, at least to Carnock, and at once.

They were too late. On their arrival at the tumbledown monastery, it was to find Fergus dead. He had passed on early that morning. But he had left a message for them. Would they take his body back to Cathures on the Clyde, where he had come from. But not only that. He had vowed, long ago, to go back to his birthplace and set up a cell or little chapel there, to continue St Ninian's work. He had never done it, for which God forgive him. But if at least his body could go back and something, even a mere cairn of stones with a cross be erected over it, as a little shrine, he might rest easier. Otherwise he would not so rest, he feared.

So – they were faced with a decision. To do as Fergus had pleaded? Or not?

Mungo, of course, was in no doubts, indeed eager. His mother was prepared to do it, Serf not so. Cathures, he reminded, was in Strathclyde, not so very far from King Morcant's capital, Dumbarton. With Arthur dead, Morcant would be less likely than ever to smile on Christians. The setting-up of a shrine there would be asking for trouble, trouble which they were not in any position to resist or repel. And it was a long way to carry a dead body. Fergus had lived his Christian life here; he was as well buried at Carnock as anywhere.

Mungo said no. A man's dying wishes should be heeded. And Strathclyde, where St Patrick was born and St Ninian had preached, should have at least a shrine of some sort. He did not claim that Serf, in his old age, was losing his drive and energy, but that was obviously what he thought.

They slept on it, that night.

Sleep did not change anything. In the morning, Mungo was for going on, Serf was not. But he did not dissuade his young friend from the project, especially when Thanea supported her son. Let them proceed, with the body, he said; but let

236

them not remain away overlong, for there was so much that needed attention on their own ground and he was not so able as he had been. Undoubtedly the older man did not realise the effect of those simple words on Mungo.

There remained, of course, the problem of transporting Fergus's corpse, stiff now. To tie it on the back of a horse would be difficult, as well as undignified – and Carnock monastery had only the one horse. An ox-cart would be the answer. But oxen were in short supply, hereabouts as elsewhere, most having been eaten during the famine. Besides which, much of the journey would be difficult for cart-wheels, with only mere tracks to follow. Mungo came up with the suggestion that a slype was what was needed, a shaft-dray or wheelless drag, on which they could strap the body. Two long poles, with cross-bars roped on. Would their horses drag such?

Serf said they would not. Horses had to be trained to shafts. These were riding beasts. They would refuse, bridle, pull against each other, especially with a man's dead body behind. They would sense it.

Mungo was not to be discouraged. Oxen, then, somehow. Surely somewhere hereabouts they ought to be able to find oxen to hire. There were many farmeries . . .

One of the elderly monks accompanying him, he went off to prospect, while the others wrapped up the earthly remains of Fergus in a shroud – no sad occasion Serf declared, for Fergus was infinitely better off where he had gone, relieved from the pains of his recent years. This wizened, withered husk was not important; the soul and spirit marched on, freed from its hampering weaknesses.

Eventually Mungo arrived back and in small triumph, leading two young oxen, little more than calves admittedly, but reasonably placid creatures and quite strong enough for the task – if they could be disciplined to it. He and the monks set about constructing a slype.

This at least was not difficult. Two long poles, previously used for building haystacks around, were produced, and short cross-bars bound at intervals with rope, to join them. Then handles were contrived at the butt-ends, to which to harness the oxen, while the other and pointed ends would just bump over the ground. The load would have to be very tightly strapped on to this sloping conveyance.

Amidst head-shaking from Serf and some others, the young oxen were led into position and tied to the handles, still mild and docile. Would they walk together, being led, and draw the slype? Taking a rope each, Mungo and his mother coaxed the animals forward.

They started at the first pulling, but when the contrivance began to bump and jerk them, one halted and so the other had to do so also, clearly off-put by this strange experience. Urging proving ineffectual, Mungo took both leading-ropes and told Thanea to use a stick to whack the creatures' rears. This joint effort worked and the beasts did move forward, approximately in unison. Mungo led them bumping slowly round in a wide circle on the grass, grinning his satisfaction. All was well. They had only to load Fergus on.

Thanea observed that it was going to be a slow journey.

In the circumstances they did not linger at the monastery. Serf accompanied them to the Carnock Burn, their first hurdle, with the young oxen reluctant to enter the water and having to be vehemently persuaded, and Mungo wondering whether the ends of the slype's poles might catch on underwater stones.

The parting there with Serf was quite emotional, the first time that they had separated on any major excursion, and the abbot not exactly disapproving but questioning the usefulness of the project. And it might be some time before they saw each other again. The young man's and the old man's divergent vision of what was the way ahead had never been so evidently exemplified, Thanea in the midst but having to hold to her son.

Using the two horses to lead the oxen across the ford, they got over after a considerable delay. Thereafter, Thanea mounted and leading the other horse, and Mungo afoot and leading the oxen by their ropes, they looked back often to wave to that beloved figure standing watching by the burnside.

It was a strange pilgrimage that they made, and taking quite a lot of getting used to, what with the oxen's slow and deliberate plodding, irritating at first, the ever-present feeling of the dead Fergus with them, and yet an atmosphere of aloneness tending

238

to prevail, missing Serf's presence. This last was strange, for these last months mother and son had taken many journeys on their own; but this somehow was different.

They reckoned that they had some sixty miles to go by the shortest route to their destination, Cathures; and at this walking pace they would be fortunate to cover ten miles in a day. They quickly learned that impatience was unprofitable. The oxen were patient, long-suffering and no trouble, but not to be hurried, taking their own deliberate gait. The slype proved effective, although the cordage fastenings tended to loosen, and had to be retied frequently; also detours had to be made to avoid narrow tracks, swampy ground, outcropping rock and other terrain unsuitable for such a contrivance, all so different from horse-riding. So, used as they were to covering long mileages in a day, they had to discipline themselves to a quiet pacing which, Thanea observed, might well be good for their souls.

The first part of their route was at least familiar, going south-westwards by the skirts of the great Tor Wood and the Manau Avon, and then the moors to Slamannan, even though it took them two days to reach that far, the first night being passed at Plean. And there, in a herd's rude cabin, Mungo revealed to his mother something of his hopes for this venture and the future. He desired, if possible, to do much more than erect any cairn as shrine over Fergus's body. This Cathures was deep in Strathclyde, indeed only some fifteen miles from Dumbarton itself, he reckoned, King Morcant's capital. That pagan monarch had been threatened with the wrath of Gualpian the torturer – a device of which Thanea and Serf had been a little ashamed, he knew well. Now he and his people should be brought to learn something of the true God and His power. St Patrick, from hereabouts, had converted Ireland; it was time that his own Strathclyde should begin to be converted back to Christ. He, Mungo, aimed to make a start at it.

Thanea had sensed, of course, that there was more to all this than merely conveying Fergus's corpse back to his birthplace. She did not disapprove – but indicated that this intention of her son's would take time. Would they return to Culross shortly, and seek Serf's aid and blessing on what must be a great and prolonged work?

239

No, Mungo said. Dear Serf would not wish it to be, would seek to retain them there, to have him administer the establishment. That was clearly his wish, but not his, Mungo's. He saw his task and duty otherwise. He had contrived this break of a set purpose. He would not be returning to Culross meantime. And he hoped that his mother would remain with him. Serf had plenty of disciples and converts to aid him. Culross Abbey would not suffer.

Knowing her determined son, Thanea did not argue. But she felt sad for Serf. So did Mungo; but it was a price which they all had to pay, he averred, for the greater good. Perhaps soon they should be informing him of their progress, busily preoccupied as they were.

Next day, crossing the high moorlands – which they found easier, strangely enough, than the low ground with its burns and bogs – they reached Slamannan, a dozen miles; and here, instead of heading south for Lanark and the upper Clyde, they turned westwards for Airdrie and Carmyle, passing out of Manau into Strathclyde.

It took them five days to reach Cathures, where the Molendinar Burn joined Clyde, and fresh water overcame the tidal salt, the river here some eighty yards across. The journey, after being trying to start with, tediously slow, became, for Thanea at least, quite pleasantly relaxing, a gentle, unhurried, drifting progress. Her son was less patient, but had to school himself. Fortunately the weather was not unkind. Less fortunately, the body behind them began to stink, and although the breeze was consistently westerly, carrying the smell away, at night it complicated their finding of places to lodge and eat, since people found it objectionable, and the corpse had to be left at a distance – yet had to be protected from dogs, carrion-crows and the like.

They found Cathures to be a small community, part milling, part fishing, largely under the sway of two brothers, Angwen and Telleyr, who ran the mill which gave the Molendinar Burn its name, and who proved to be kinsmen of Fergus, their parents, now dead, lapsed Christians. Mungo would not be long in going to work on them. Whether they approved, or not, of the body being brought back to where it originated, they raised no objection to interment in the family tomb, a hollow

240

cairn of stones. So Mungo conducted his first burial service, and took the opportunity to do some evangelistic work in the process. Whereafter he duly erected the required cross above the cairn, and blessed it, duty done.

By next morning, though, the cross had disappeared.

However, this was not the shrine Mungo had come to create. His aim was to build a chapel, not a diseart but a place for worship, however modest, his centre for endeavours. There had been a cell here, established by St Ninian, but it had fallen into ruin and its stones taken to build huts and walls. Thanea assumed that he would wish to restore this; but no, Mungo decided that a new start was called for. This site, however worthily begun, now represented a measure of failure to these people living around it. He would build afresh, and pray that this shrine would endure.

As always with that young man, intention was swiftly translated into action. He set about finding a suitable site forthwith.

His choice surprised even his mother. There was a stone circle nearby, abandoned and neglected, its monoliths reeling or fallen. No doubt it had been set up there because of the fresh and salt water confrontation, always held to be significant by the druids. Why now neglected was not stated. There was a spring close at hand. This was it, Mungo declared. Here he would build his chapel, with those drunken pillars around it, Christ superseding Manannan or whatever heathen god they were dedicated to. It had been a place of worship, however mistaken. They would make it so again, the true God triumphant over the false. Thanea, although she had dire feelings about stone circles and their rites, could find no fault in his reasoning.

She was set, there and then, to help in gathering stones, many stones. They would use the oxen and slype to transport them.

Fortunately, although the wide Clyde here was muddy-banked and unproductive of stones, the incoming Molendinar was otherwise, its sides quite steep and rocky. Here, over a few hundred yards, were stones of all sizes, in plenty. Mungo worked like any Trojan, Thanea contenting herself with finding, and acting slype-driver. Some villagers came to help, including the miller, Angwen – although his brother stood and mocked their efforts. Mungo wondered whether he it was who had removed the cross from Fergus's cairn. They learned that the circle site was called the Glas-cuil, or green neuk or favoured place.

Mungo had been at the building of Serf's chapel on the island in Loch Leven, his one-time paradise, and so knew sufficient of the basic principles of building in stone to construct the simple walls of a rectangular edifice, perhaps thirty feet long by twenty wide, rude and elementary, with two gaps for door and one window, but adequate for immediate purposes. It would take time to complete, of course, especially the finding of the wood and thatch for the roof; but a start was made. And perhaps they might get more help, once his teachings began to make an impact. It could then be enlarged.

There spoke faith. Let Strathclyde take note.

20

Take note Strathclyde did. It took only a few days to complete the wall-building and put a thatch on the chapel at the Glas-cuil; and one of those days a senior druid arrived, in company with the man Telleyr, demanding to know what went on at Cathures and why, very authoritative. Mungo was up on the roof, laying the reed thatch, so Thanea dealt with him.

"I am the Princess Thanea of Lothian," she informed the stern enquirer. "Sister of King Gawain, and niece of the late High King Arthur. This is my son, Kentigern." She did not hesitate to declare rank and status, knowing well its effect, when needful.

The other blinked, obviously impressed, Mungo watching from above.

"I greet you, Princess," she was told. "You are new come to Strathclyde? Does King Morcant know of this?"

"That I cannot tell you. We are Christians and come on a mission to this Cathures. Bringing back the body of one of our people born here."

"We were told that you were Christians, yes. And, proclaiming your beliefs."

"Yes. This formerly was a Christian place. Of Ninian of Whithorn. My son builds a chapel here."

"And preaches against the gods, we hear!"

"There is only one true God, friend. Him we serve. As did your late High King."

"M'mm. We believe otherwise in Strathclyde, Princess."

"Then you should be grateful for us bringing you the truth, Druid!" That came from the roof above.

"I shall tell the Chief Druid that you said so, young man."

"Do so, with our goodwill."

Their visitor, with a jerked bow to Thanea, stalked off.

Mother and son eyed each other. "It has not taken long," Thanea said.

"No. This is that Telleyr's doing, clearly. He has gone bearing tales."

"It would seem so. You think him actively against Christ's cause? That would be unfortunate."

"We will watch him. His brother Angwen is otherwise. Interested. I have hopes for him."

The very next day they had more visitors – none other than Morcant himself and some of his court. The king was now a man of early middle age, inclining to stoutness, florid, with a fleering eye.

"We meet again, Princess," he said, not dismounting. "Entering my kingdom, should you not have called upon me first?"

"If we had come visiting, yes, King Morcant. But coming as Christians, to bury one of our people, that is different."

"And to hold forth against our beliefs and teach your own!"

"Such teachings will serve you no harm, Morcant. Did not Prince Servanus and I tell you so those years ago, when we offered you Christ instead of Gualpian!"

The other frowned, but did not answer that directly. "What do you build here within this circle of our druids? Lacking my permission."

"Your druids, King Morcant, cannot think highly of this place, Glas-cuil, since they have abandoned it." Mungo had emerged from the interior. "Its stones were agley and fallen. We have straightened them, and made this a place of worship again. Does not that please you?"

"We do not seek Christians here."

"Then I say that you ought to. For Christians make better and more law-abiding subjects than do your pagans, King. We will prove it to you."

"If I allow you, young man!"

"I hope that you will, believe that you will." Thanea made that sound rather more placatory than her son had seemed to do. "We advised you well before, did we not? And you heeded us. We would wish to do so again."

"I need no help from such as you."

"No?" That was Mungo again. "Be not so sure, King Morcant. Your seat, the Rock of Alcluyd at Dumbarton, seems to stand secure. But God the Father Almighty in heaven can make the earth quake. Your rock could split wide open. Your granaries, yonder," and he pointed southwards to where, a mile away, a row of great barns stretched near the river-bank, "your royal granaries yonder look safe and secure also. But if Christ-God, who controls the tides and the rains, was to send a very high tide and at the same time rains sufficient to bring down this Molendinar in raging spate, those barns, so near the Clyde, could be swept away. And this part of your kingdom starve. Think on it, when you say that you have no need of aid."

Morcant, who had still not dismounted, took a deep breath and, suddenly snatching at his reins, wheeled his horse round and spurred off. His companions had to follow. One of them spat at Mungo as he went.

When they were gone, Thanea asked her son why he had used these idle and improbable threats to arouse the king so.

"Because, from what you told me, he is a very superstitious man. I have sown some seeds of doubt in his mind. Now he will ever be wondering, wondering. And if some ill does befall, he will remember what I threatened, and may do more than wonder."

"And is that the way to convert the heathen to the faith?"

"How would *you* do it better, with that man? He scarce knows the meaning of love, I judge. But he knows fear!"

She did not counter that. "So long as he does not, in his present anger, cast us out from here . . ."

That fear of Thanea's was not realised, at least. Morcant did not inflict his presence upon them, nor send emissaries, and they were left to get on with their chosen task, Mungo impatient to get the chapel built and finished, so that he could devote himself to his mission of teaching and converting. For her part, Thanea spent much time in another kind of converting, making one of the mill's former grain-stores, now empty and derelict, into a reasonably comfortable lodging for herself and her son, with the help of some of their new neighbours. They were pleased with the local reactions to their teaching. These people, of course, although they could not be called Christian, did not find their visitors' message wholly alien or strange, for there had been a Christian community here formerly, and although it had lapsed, the faith was not wholly new to them. Nor were most of them actively pagan, even though they accepted druidical theories and practices. So they listened to Mungo's teachings, and attended his meetings and services. Indeed that enthusiast went so far as to declare to his mother that such as these were not really his target; that he had come to convert the heathen, not the half-ready. But, admittedly, they would make a useful nucleus, a base, an established congregation around this chapel, from which he could go forth on wider, more challenging missions. One day he would probably turn this Glas-cuil into a monastery, not just a chapel.

Thanea urged him to be more thankful for their reception by these good people and not to look on them as in some sense unworthy of his best efforts.

In fact, Mungo came to find challenge enough here, for hostility developed, admittedly in only a small number but sufficient to provide any required threat. It was the man Telleyr who, the more his brother Angwen turned to Christianity, the more hostile he became. Almost certainly it was he who had sent word to Morcant. He found others, mostly young men, in the vicinity, who were prepared to oppose and obstruct the missionaries, and this they did by coming to jeer at some of the meetings, by telling others what fools they were, and even by seeking to damage the chapel, one night going so far as to set the thatch roofing alight. Fortunately the reeds were too green, as yet, to burn readily, and not much harm was done. But it caused Mungo to sleep in the building of a night, concerned. He asserted that God would punish these enemies of His cause.

Despite such hold-ups, and the inevitable structural problems for untrained builders, the chapel was at length completed, within its circle of monoliths, primitive necessarily but with its essentials of cross, altar – formed out of three of the standing-stones – scooped-out quern for corn-grinding acting as font, and a holy-water stoup out of a metal grain-measure at the door.

The dedication was to be a great event, for it was not only to be that but the first three full converts were to be baptised, these including Angwen the miller and his wife. This was a fulfilment indeed, a milestone on Mungo's chosen road.

So many of the local people came to watch, if not necessarily to take part, that much of the service had to be held at the chapel door in the open air. Mungo tailored it all very much as an evangelistic exercise, to interest, persuade and bring in others; so that his preliminary announcement, praises and prayers and address were very suitably delivered outside, he not failing to point to the stone circle monoliths as symbols of enduring worship, now reformed and given true meaning; the sun, to which the stones were aligned, equally God's servant with themselves. Even the baptisms took place in the open, using the holy-water stoup just within the doorway as font. Thanea had to act as acolyte and keep the shallow stoup refilled with water from the true font, her son being liberal in the washing process. The communion celebration had to be performed inside, at the altar, only the five of them receiving the bread and wine; but thereafter Mungo's address on the significance of what had taken place was delivered from the doorway with his typical enthusiasm and even some humorous asides deliberately introduced in order to emphasise the difference in Christian worship from the dire dread and threat of the pagan gods. He ended by declaring that he was giving this place, chapel, circle and spring a slightly different name from now on – instead of Glas-cuil, the green hollow or place, it was to be Eglais-cu, the Church's favoured place.

Angwen and his wife played their part thereafter by holding a celebratory feast at the mill, ample as to provision if modest in variety, only spoiled by the brother Telleyr hanging about and making sneering remarks, *his* wife partaking however.

That day's events were productive of much. It was not long before others came forward, prepared to be converted, to the missionaries' joy. Not only that, but the word spread around to neighbouring communities – and it was quite populous country, flanking the great Clyde, fertile and with the waterway convenient for transport, which was why the royal granaries were nearby. Interested or merely curious folk came to see what went on, some of whom waited to hear more.

Mungo, of course, needed no such encouragement to widen his efforts. He was eager to follow up any opportunity offered. When he was told of an aged Christian, a Welshman named Cadoc, crippled apparently and living at Cambuslang, a mere four miles upriver from Cathures, and who taught the Gospel there to anyone who would listen, he could not wait to go, his mother not to be left behind.

They rode next morning.

Cambuslang was a larger place than Cathures, indeed something of a cluster of villages and hamlets on the banks of a picturesque burn which entered the Clyde, where there was a wide green hollow under a ridge of modest height on which had stood a Pictish fort. Enquiries led the visitors to a cottage on the outskirts of one of the hamlets, where they found an elderly man, bent and lame but of some presence, hobbling about tending his beehives and extracting honeycombs. Being a beekeeper herself, Thanea took to him at once, especially so as his smile was warm, eyes at least young-seeming.

When they made themselves known, Cadoc declared himself most happy to see them. He had heard of them from others, and of what they were doing. He had wished that he could come and visit them, but he had no means of getting to Cathures now – he could not walk more than a few yards, for his sins!

"You are Christian, we are told. And teaching?" Mungo said. "We had to come and see you. That is good, good."

"Is it, young man? I am not so sure. But – you are kind to say it."

"Why are you not sure that it is good? Preaching the Word. Surely that is any Christian's duty?"

"That depends on the Christian, does it not? On what he is doing. Or on what he should be doing! If he is unworthy . . ."

"I do not understand you," Mungo admitted.

"You have something to tell us, I think?" Thanea said.

"It is a long story. Why should I inflict it upon you? You, who *are* doing God's work, as I hear." He had a lilting Welsh voice.

"We have come here to visit you. Tell us your story. And why you so doubt your own worth."

He sat them down on a bench before his cottage, and limping within, brought them honey wine and oatcakes.

"It is said that you are a princess?" he questioned Thanea.

"I was, yes. Daughter of Loth, of Lothian. Sister to Gawain. And this is my son, Kentigern. We call him Mungo."

"So! Arthur's Gawain? Well, I too was a prince. More, I was a king, once. In Wales. Better than any king, perhaps, an abbot! And now – I keep bees and make candles, that I may eat!"

They both stared at him.

"King!"

"Abbot!"

"Both, yes. I was Prince Cadoc of Glevissig, and was converted to Christianity. I was ordained, and established an abbey at Llancarfan, its abbot. Then my father died, and I succeeded to the throne of Glevissig, no great realm but sufficient. I sought to rule it for some years, but perceived that kingship was not for me. I was no warrior, and the Saxons pressed us hard. Glevissig needed a fighter. Also I felt that I was better an abbot than a king – although that could have been arrogant pride. But I could not go back to Llancarfan, for I had appointed a worthy successor there. I resigned my throne to one Mouric, the best of my warriors. And departed. Wales was in turmoil, with the heathen invaders – it still is – and more abbey-founding scarcely practical. But I wished to do God's work, *had* to try to do it. So I went across to Ireland, where Patrick's Church required assistance. And there, in Fermanagh, I founded another abbey."

He paused, shaking his grey head and looking self-deprecatory, while his visitors eyed him wonderingly.

"I laboured there, however unworthily, until the sickness struck me." He pointed to his twisted leg and side. "I had many small monasteries and cells to visit and care for. I could no longer do this, crippled. I could have remained in Ireland, but pined for my own Wales, and returned there. But all was different. I was the stranger now, I felt. So I came here, to Strathclyde. If I was to be a stranger, let it be in a strange land. And this was St Patrick's homeland. I had become a disciple of Patrick. So I would end my days where he had begun his." He shrugged. "And so I do question. Have I chosen wrongly, all along? Failed in my Christian duty? I could still be King of Glevissig, a force for good there? Although I could still be an abbot, using deputies, friars, but able to direct and teach. Instead, here I am, in a strange land, keeping bees and making candles, effecting nothing of any consequence. Can I claim that to be the good? Doing Christ's work?"

"I think that you undervalue yourself," Thanea said. "You have sacrificed much for Christ."

"But to what end?"

"Your sickness – you cannot blame yourself for that."

"Perhaps not. But have I misjudged how I should have acted with it? I fear that I have made the wrong decisions."

"We all do that," Mungo observed judiciously. "We all do that."

Thanea smiled. "Even you, on occasion!"

"But I have my mother to guide me!"

Cadoc wanted to hear details of their aims and endeavours. He had heard of St Serf. He much applauded Mungo's ambitions here in Strathclyde, and was admiring of their efforts in Fife and Fortrenn. He declared that however feeble *his* contributions must necessarily be, he would be anxious to help them in any way he could.

They left him, strangely affected by the man, his wry humility and attitude of self-criticism, the playing down of that he *had* achieved in the Christian cause. Thanea saw him as possibly a guiding and sometimes moderating influence on her impetuous son, in some degree perhaps acting as substitute for Serf. Mungo, typically, saw Cadoc's role more immediately. He would found another chapelry at Cambuslang, and make Cadoc its priest – he was an abbot, after all: the first subsidiary cell. There would be many others, to be sure, in due course; but this the first mission station out from Eglais-cu.

It was of no use to urge that one to hasten slowly.

21

In the event, they returned to Cambuslang sooner than
ever Mungo intended. Word came that the Arch Druid of
Strathclyde had ordained a great ceremony to coincide with
the harvest festival, or Lug Feast, Lug Lanfota being the
god of harvest. Actually it was to be a series of ceremonies
held simultaneously, in chosen centres all over the realm, the
principal one to be at Dumbarton, of course, but one to be at
Cambuslang, as a fairly large upriver community. It transpired
that King Morcant was childless, had recently remarried and
was anxious to have a son to succeed him. The Arch Druid
had decided that the Lug Feast was the suitable occasion for
a special supplication to the gods on Morcant's behalf, and all
his druid priests were to hold appropriate services.

Thanea, with all too vivid memories of druidical ceremonies,
would have made a point of avoiding Cambuslang then at all
costs; but not so her son. Mungo asked how could they fight
Satan if they hid themselves away from his works? They
must see what went on if they were to counter it all. His
mother had told him something of what went on, but Mungo
had to see for himself. Thanea, steeling herself, said that she
would go with him, despite all.

So, only some weeks after their first visit, they were back at
Cambuslang, and calling on Cadoc. That man told them that
the ceremony was to be held at sun-down in an amphitheatre
amongst the braes, and all people were commanded to attend,
in the names of King Morcant and the Arch Druid. Cadoc
had intended to disobey this order, his disability as excuse;
but when he heard that Mungo insisted on seeing all, and
offered his horse as transport, he agreed to accompany them,
although with head-shakings.

They had no difficulty in finding the scene of events, at
any rate, for as the August day declined, all the population

was on its way there, young and old, men, women, children and dogs.

The great hollow amongst the gorse-dotted braes proved to be already all but full, although an open space had been left in the centre. There was no stone circle here, but thirteen high poles had been erected, with material draped over and around them to form monolith-like tents, with a great altar in the middle. A profusion of resinous torches, raised on more poles, was ready to illuminate all when required.

Mungo found a place for them near enough the front to see all. The sun was beginning to sink to the low hills of Fereneze to the west.

They had not long to wait before a rhythmic clashing of cymbals heralded the arrival of a procession. It was headed by a robed druid and his acolytes and attendants, these bearing torches already lit. They were followed by two men and two women, roped together in pairs, with guards at their sides. Thanea caught her breath at the sight of these. Bringing up the rear were herdsmen leading a horse and a bull.

This procession worked its way slowly around the circle – and it was still light enough for the visitors to see that the leading druid was the same man who had called on them, with Telleyr, on that first inquisition at Cathures, no doubt the local dignitary.

Having made the circuit, the druidical party took up position in the centre beside the altar, whilst the roped pairs were led off into the tented contrivances masquerading as monoliths of a stone circle. The bull and horse remained available.

A blowing of horns commanded silence. Thanea could not hear what was said save for the odd word which came over to them, King Morcant's name being repeated. Clearly this ceremony was concerned with more than the harvest god Lug.

All were facing westwards, waiting for the sun to go down. The acolytes commenced a monotonous chanting. Although they continued with it, noticeably few of the crowd took it up. No doubt it was a hymn to the sun.

At last the sun touched the long line of the hilltops, and then slowly, so slowly, sank. When it was half hidden, the chanting changed in tempo and volume and, as the last fiery gleam of it vanished and only the glowing sky remained, a great shout went up, and the druid raised arms high in a kind of ecstasy.

All was now changed to activity. A dark heap near the altar proved to be of wood, no doubt of oak and rowan, the sacred trees, and this was lit from one of the torches, obviously previously soaked in resin, for it blazed up immediately. The many poled torches were then lit, to bathe all in their flickering, ruddy light, and from one of the tents a cauldron, heavy with water, was brought to hang from a trestle above the fire.

The crowd waited, expectant.

More horn-blowing, and the horse was led forward. It would be a mare, for the fertility it represented. The druid drew a sword and went to the fire, to heat it in the flames. Then turning back, he brought it in a sweeping upwards slash to the animal's neck. As the mare reared, pawing the air, screaming, the attendants went to work with daggers, ripping open the belly and drawing out the heaving, steaming entrails.

The creature took a long time to die; but even before its limbs ceased to kick, daggers were cutting flesh from the haunch, and lumps of this were taken to the cauldron over the fire and tossed in. A small piece, raw, was given to the druid, who chewed at it before spitting it out.

"Fertility rites for Morcant," Cadoc explained. "He is supposed to bathe in a mare's blood's broth. No doubt he will be doing that at Dumbarton. Here, I think, there will be a substitute."

Sure enough, acolytes unslung the cauldron and carried it steaming to the druid, while one of the roped couples was brought out from a tent, now man and woman naked. They were led to the druid who, using a scoop, splashed the scalding broth over the substitute. Perhaps it was meant only for the man, but it reached the woman also, and there were yells of agony.

"This is damnable, utterly damnable!" Mungo exclaimed. "It must be stopped."

"I fear . . . that you will see . . . worse than this!" his mother said, a restraining hand on his arm. She did not tell him that a substitute for the king would not be allowed to live.

"I think that Morcant's bathing will be less onerous!" Cadoc observed grimly.

The sobbing, unhappy couple were taken back to their tent, and the bull was led forward. The cauldron was returned to the fire, acolytes refilling it.

The procedure was the same as for the mare. The sword was heated and the animal's throat slashed open. But unlike the mare it did not rear and scream but stood wide-legged, head drooping, rocking but upright still. The attendants pushed, but to no effect, and eventually had to get down on hands and knees to slit open the belly, for the beast's legs were short.

There was a change as far as the druid was concerned. He chewed some of the raw beef cut from the still-heaving animal's shoulder, and when it eventually collapsed, he took another piece to the cauldron and merely dipped it in, then anointed his brow and wrists with the purely symbolic broth. He returned to the altar and climbed thereupon, to lie flat on his back.

The cymbals clanged and the chanting arose.

"I have heard of the bull-sleep," Cadoc said. "This must be it, or a gesture at it. Supposedly the druid, sleeping, dreams the fate of whoever the sacrifice is for. In this case, Morcant."

"May he perish miserably! And his druid also!" Mungo declared. Which perhaps was not entirely Christian.

The alleged sleep was a very brief one, for very quickly the druid sat up, climbed down from the altar and, raising hands high again, shouted something incoherent.

"What now?" Mungo demanded, anger shaking him.

Thanea forbore to tell him. Those two roped couples had not been brought here merely to splash water over, even scalding water.

"I fear . . ." Cadoc began again, but did not finish.

The druid gestured and the acolytes went to the tents, cymbals beating, to bring out the four naked men and women.

The first pair were led to the altar, and the druid picked up his sword, to go to the fire to heat it.

"No! No – he will not!" Mungo shouted. "No, I say!" And

254

leaping forward, he pushed headlong through those in front of their stance and went running out into the great circle of flaring torches, crying aloud.

Thanea could not let him do it alone. Biting her lip, she jerked a word to Cadoc and hurried out after her son.

People stared in astonishment.

The druid himself had turned to stare, beside the fire, sword in hand. Mungo raced up to him, in a fury of protest and anger.

"No! You cannot do it! You *shall* not!" he cried. "These are God's children. You shall not harm them."

The other sought for words, and raised the sword threateningly at the interrupter.

Without hesitation Mungo leapt at him, ducking to one side to dodge the wild sweep of the weapon, and closing, smashed down his fist on the druid's forearm. The sword dropped to the grass.

As the older man staggered back, Mungo stooped to pick up the weapon, and brandished it. "Let them go. These people. Let them go, I say!" he yelled. "In the name of Christ-God, let them go!"

The other shook his head, clutching his hurt arm. Clearly he was at a loss, this all beyond any experience of his. He called out something incoherent, but gestured towards his henchmen and acolytes.

Thanea had come up. "They have daggers!" she gasped, warningly.

"But this – the only sword!"

Some of the attendants were coming forward to their master's aid, if somewhat uncertainly, others still holding the roped couples.

"Back!" Mungo commanded. "Back! And untie these people. Do as I say – untie them. Or . . . !" He waved the sword at them.

Two still came on, and the torchlight gleamed on the steel of their dirks.

"Mungo, they do not heed! You cannot . . . !" Thanea exclaimed.

Her son turned to the druid, and menacingly thrust the sword-point at him. "Back, all of you," he cried. "Or this man suffers! Come no nearer. This sword is sharp. And longer than your dirks! I can use it."

That told. The two men halted, hesitant, while the druid cowered.

Mungo ran forward towards the pair of henchmen. They stepped back promptly. Pointing the sword at them, he ordered them to drop their daggers. These acolytes were of the priestly sort and no warriors. Their dirks fell to the ground.

"Take them," Mungo jerked back to his mother. "The daggers. Cut the ropes of these captives. Cut them free." He turned back to the druid. "You," he ordered, "begone! And take your folk with you." And without waiting to see whether he, and the sword, were obeyed, he ran over to the altar itself, and clambered up to stand on it. Thereon, holding the weapon aloft, he raised his voice to its highest.

"This wickedness and folly is over!" he cried. "Christ-God abhors it. Will have no more of it. Savagery! For false gods. Away! Home with you all. Christ-God the Almighty comes to Strathclyde! Away, I say!"

Thanea was cutting free the two naked pairs of their cords.

Chaos ensued. People shouted and surged. Some came into the circle, others streamed away as ordered. The freed captives raced off, to disappear into the crowd. The acolytes, seemingly leaderless, did nothing very positive, certainly did not seek to tackle the man with the sword.

That man, jumping down, gestured at the unhappy druid, ran to the nearest of the torches and snatched it down from its pole. This he took back to wave in the druid's face, pointing away with the sword. Torch and weapon were too much for that priest, however expert he was with sacrifices. He turned and hurried off into outer darkness, clutching his arm. Mungo's furious blow had been a heavy one.

Thanea came to her son. "We can . . . do no more . . . here," she panted. "Let us be gone, also."

Drawing a deep breath, he nodded, the tension suddenly leaving him. He cast the torch from him. "I will keep this!" he said, waggling the sword. "The Sword of the Spirit, which the gospels speak of!"

"Scarcely that! It will have slain many, ere this."

256

"No doubt. But even such may be redeemed, God willing."

They had difficulty in finding the lame Cadoc in all the confusion and darkness, for many of the torches were now extinguished and the fire dying down. When they did come on him, he was loud in Mungo's praise, declaring him to be the sort of young man he wished that he had been.

Thanea, whilst admiring her son's courage and driving force, was less sure of the ethics of it all. Was this how Christ's message of love should be demonstrated? As she recollected, the only sword Jesus had referred to was the one he ordered Peter to put up after he had struck off the high priest's servant's ear. Admittedly they had saved the lives of those human sacrifices, but . . . he that taketh the sword shall perish by the sword! No?

Both men held otherwise. That sword had been all but put into Mungo's hand. Nothing else would have saved those unfortunate people. Moreover, a great blow had been struck for Christ's cause this night, Cadoc felt sure.

They conducted their friend home to his house, and rode on beside the Clyde's dark waters to Eglais-cu.

There would be repercussions, of course, they knew well.

22

Repercussions there were, but of more than one sort. Mungo's name began to resound throughout Strathclyde. Many undoubtedly, probably the majority, were critical of what he had done, but not all by any means, human sacrifice not appealing to all. But none could deny the courage demonstrated by one man and a woman, the challenge, and the blow struck against druidism.

That last was emphasised the very next day, when the Arch Druid himself arrived at Cathures with three of his senior priests, angry men all – but, it was to be noted, King Morcant did not come with them. They made their wrath very clear, confronting Mungo and Thanea at the chapel.

"You have insulted the gods," they were told. "You have offended against all in this kingdom. You have desecrated the altar to the sun. You deserve to die!"

"If we deserve to die, then Almighty God will undoubtedly slay us, in His own good time. But your sun, and ours, will not. See – it smiles on us!" Mungo pointed upwards. "Nor will, nor can, any of your other imagined deities, products of fear and fevered minds. You, Druid, who worship the sun, tell it now to strike us down! Or Lug. Or Gualpian. Or Manannan. Or any of them."

"Do not mock, fool!"

"I do not mock. I challenge! You are Chief Druid, are you not? Then bring down the wrath of your supposed gods upon us."

"I can bring down the king's power against you."

"But you have not done so. Because King Morcant fears. He is less sure than are you of your false gods. If even you are sure? You but use the threat of them for power."

"I have sufficient power, as you will see!"

Thanea intervened. "All power comes from Almighty God,

whether we admit it or not. Arthur, your late High King, and my uncle, the most powerful man in all Britain, acknowledged it. King Gawain of Lothian, my brother, admits it." This bringing in of her royal kinship, although Mungo deplored it, Thanea knew to be most effective, giving men pause. "I ask you to mind it."

That produced no reply.

"If King Morcant sent you, go back and tell him that we wish him no ill. Indeed we wish him and his whole kingdom well. And shall work for its well-being, under Christ."

The Arch Druid snorted. "Enough!" he jerked. He raised a hand, wrist gold-encircled. "I hereby curse you! Curse you both. In the name of the great sun and all his lesser gods. Curse you! Curse you! Curse you! Know it, know it well. You are accursed now and for ever!"

His companions repeated the formula, and they rode off.

"How do you feel to be accursed of all these non-existent gods, for ever?" Mungo asked, then, smiling.

"Their cursing in itself is nothing. It is their hatred that I grieve over. Hatred is . . . evil."

"It must go down before love. Can you love these?"

She wagged her head. "I can but try," she said.

No further visitation materialised from Dumbarton meantime.

They went to see Cadoc a few days later, Mungo buoyed up by all the interest and acclaim aroused by the Cambuslang incident. Cadoc was full of it all also, recounting still more talks of its effect on the ordinary people and even on some of the lofty. He said that the druid concerned, one Manus, was in deep disgrace and was to be removed from his charge.

Mungo expounded on his plans. Cambuslang was to be the second charge of his mission and Cadoc its priest in charge. They would build a chapel, near his house, so that he did not have much walking to do, a fairly large one in the hope of a large congregation. And from here they would proselytise further up Clyde.

At first the older man was distinctly doubtful about this, or at least about his part in it, declaring the task and responsibility beyond him, with his age and infirmity. But Mungo would not take no for an answer, asserting that Cadoc could do all that was necessary perfectly well without moving far from this spot, preaching, celebrating communion, baptising, burying. He was a priest – and where was he to find another priest to serve the charge? He prevailed, of course.

The site of the chapel, at least, proved to be no problem. The hut in which Cadoc stored his hives and honey had once been a cottage, the twin of the present one. Now more or less derelict in one of its two chambers, it still had stone walls and roofing of a sort. This would serve as a basis for the chapel, saving much stone-gathering, although very considerable restructuring would be required. They would build another hut for the bee equipment, and take down the walling between the two rooms to make a fair-sized whole. Later they could add to it.

So, as so often with Mungo, design was swiftly translated into action. Work began, almost there and then. Well satisfied, mother and son returned to Eglais-cu, Cadoc promising to spread the word.

For the next week or two, then, they spent more time at Cambuslang than at Cathures, and to good effect, in building both chapel and congregation. Mungo was able to set a day for dedication – they decided to name the shrine after St Serf – and hold the first baptisms, a round dozen of them.

But all was not progress. Their absences from Eglais-cu held their own penalties; for on one occasion when they had been away for two nights, they found their chapel there ravaged and damaged, the altar overthrown, the font defaced and the holy-water stoup battered out of shape. Fortunately there was nothing which could not be rectified or replaced. With many of the ashamed villagers helping, they washed and scrubbed the place clean, and re-blessed it. Angwen admitted that he feared his wretched brother Telleyr and his gang would be responsible; but there was no proof. Mungo asserted that God would punish those who deliberately defiled His sanctuary, although Thanea believed that this was not the right reaction, however natural, and said so.

They had no further attentions from the Arch Druid, although they did wonder whether he might perhaps have put the desecrators up to their mischief, as some attempt to fulfil his cursings.

The inauguration of St Serf's at Cambuslang was a great success, again the ceremony having to take place outside, even though the late autumn day was chilly and grey. Mungo insisted on Cadoc conducting the service, after he himself had done the dedicating. No doubt, once again, many who came were there to see the young man who had so dramatically broken up the Festival of Lug ceremony, and to examine what he was trying to put in its place; but there were sizeable numbers who took actual part, whole families, and not a few who stayed behind afterwards to ask questions. Mungo was never wholly satisfied, but he was well pleased with the occasion, and impressed with Cadoc's handling of the service.

So now for fresh fields of endeavour. Where next to turn?

That decision was made for them, and in a strange fashion, the rogue miller Telleyr the cause. He was, in fact, dead. He and two of his friends had apparently gone marauding by night to a farmery in the vicinity of the village of Rutherglen, where there were two young sisters who took their fancy. There they had assaulted and injured the father and taken the girls and had their pleasure of them. But returning in the dark, no doubt drink-taken, they had all three fallen over a cliff-like bank of the Polmadie Burn. Two of them were only badly bruised, but Telleyr himself had broken his neck.

This provoked a great stir, of course. With few mourning the man, possibly not greatly even his now Christian wife, the general attitude might have been that here was natural justice. But no – it was remembered that Mungo had said that God, *his* Christ-God, would punish the desecrators of the chapel at Eglais-cu; and this proved that Telleyr had indeed been responsible, as was suspected. So the curse had been fulfilled – although it was in fact no curse.

Profound was the effect. The people, reared in the pagan tradition, saw Mungo now as a wonder-worker, a powerful wizard-priest come amongst them, and his god to be feared, the terrible one.

This upset Mungo, not so much the death as the reaction to it, Thanea even more so. They sought to counteract it all, even going so far as to offer Christian burial for the man, to his wife and brother, as indication of God's love and forgiveness rather

261

than His harsh judgment and vengeance. This was accepted gratefully, and they interred the body near to Fergus's, to the wonder of the community.

But it was the other community which now beckoned Mungo, Rutherglen where the girls had been raped and their father assaulted. Reports reached Cathures that there was a major excitement there, a belief that the same man who had made a nonsense of the Cambuslang Lug Feast had now prevailed on his god to visit Rutherglen and punish its enemies. They were much aroused and concerned. What next?

The missionaries, of course, saw it as a duty, but also an opportunity, to go and reveal the truth to these people, to have good come out of ill.

That was their next priority, then, and a challenging one indeed, for Rutherglen was a much larger place than Cambuslang or Cathures, providing the greater opportunities; and even though the attack on the farmer and his daughters had taken place well outside the township, the word was that the entire community was much exercised by it all and eager to see the wonder-worker and hear his message.

There would almost certainly be a resident druid at a place of this size, which could complicate missionary work. Thanea suggested that it might be wise to go and see such a functionary first, a sort of courtesy call, to explain their intentions. It might not do any good but it surely could do no harm. Mungo assented.

They did find a druid, one Malduin, and his house, the largest in the township, below a mound surmounted by a stone circle. He proved to be a youngish man with fiery red hair and a less stern demeanour than was usual with his kind – indeed a spontaneous smile was apt to appear, which the visitors got the impression that he was at pains to suppress. Also he had a notably good-looking wife, whom they saw first, and who seemed prepared to be friendly.

When the visitors identified themselves as the Princess Thanea and her son, from Cathures and Eglais-cu, the druid's incipient smile of welcome stilled to a carefully masked expression of interest and some required disapproval. The wife was not so burdened, fine eyes widening but no frown developing.

Mother and son had discussed procedure in advance, and Thanea spoke first, advisedly.

"We come to Rutherglen in friendship," she said. "Christians, we preach love, kindness, care for others – and would ever seek to show it in ourselves, however inadequately. We wish you and your people only well."

The druid inclined his head but carefully said nothing.

"We wish your agreement for us to speak to your folk here, if we may. To explain away certain . . . misapprehensions which we have heard have arisen. Over the sorry matter of the rape of those two young girls, and the injury of their father. We are concerned that wrong impressions may be dispersed."

"That was ill done."

"Yes. But good may yet come of it."

"Good? Good is not born of evil."

"Are you sure?" That was Mungo. "Why then do druids sacrifice their fellow-men and women? We abhor that. But wickedness, hatred, pain *can* produce the opposite, in men's revulsion to it. Good which otherwise might not have come about."

"So . . . ?"

"We hear that the folk here are blaming the death of the man Telleyr, of Cathures, on a curse laid on him by my son here, in the name of our Christ-God. This is not so. There was no such curse. And Christ is the God of love, not of vengeance."

"That man deserved to die. The others with him."

"You say so. Others say so. Even we might wrongly be moved to say so. But our God would not. He would forgive, whilst hating what was done. That is, if the man repented. Perhaps even if not. We wish to make that plain," Mungo asserted.

The wife, who had been listening, spoke. "But he *was* killed. And they say that you said that he would be."

"No. I said that God would punish whoever desecrated our Christian chapel at Eglais-cu. Only that. God can punish without killing and pain. By causing regret, anger at self, remorse for the deed done and which cannot be undone. I did not curse him. As a Christian, I am a man of peace."

"Then you *should* have done," the woman declared. "As my husband truly says, those men deserved to die for what they did. If not to your shrine, to those girls. They savaged and soiled them. Innocents." She turned on Thanea. "Can you say otherwise, a woman, Princess?"

"Rape is vile, yes. But . . . *I* have sought to forgive the man who raped me! Sought, if not altogether achieved!"

"You? *You* were raped? A princess?"

"Yes. And by a prince! This is the result!" And she gestured at her son.

The other woman stared at her. "This is the truth?"

"It is. Not something that a woman would lie about, I think."

"Then, then . . ." The other turned to her husband. Clearly she was much impressed, moved. "*I* would not forgive!" she declared.

"If you were Christian, you would try."

The druid shook his head. "I say that you talk with two tongues," he said. "You speak of love and forgiveness and friendship. Yet you it was, we hear, who ruined the Lug Feast at Cambuslang, threatened Druid Manus with a sword . . ."

"The sword he was about to slay his fellow-men and women with, friend, had I not stopped him."

"They would be transgressors."

"Are not we all?" Mungo demanded. "We all transgress God's laws at times. Even your gods' laws, I think, sore as they are. No? See you – we do not come here in enmity, to interfere with or spoil true worship. We come to proclaim better, fuller worship, not of the sun or moon but of God Almighty who made the sun and moon and all things created. And He is the God of love and kindness and forgiving. *You* are a worshipper. You teach, as well as offer sacrifices. You teach more than dread and fear and vengeance, do you not? Wonder? Trust? Gratitude? Obedience? These are good. You are halfway to the true worship of God! We came to proclaim the rest, the Christian message."

"And we are very well lacking it, I say! We require none of your teaching."

"Yet you lack love. And love is joy. Can you deny it? You have your wife, and love her? Children, perhaps? Friends? Yet which of your many gods is concerned with love? None. Only power, terror, threat, pain. Can you in truth worship such? Or only fear them?"

The other man was silent.

Not so the wife. She nodded a lovely head. "*I* could worship a god who loved and was kind," she said.

"We all could, and should." That was Thanea.

"We have gods of fertility and harvest and weather. All under the all-seeing sun," her husband insisted, eyeing her.

"Do any command love, forgiveness, even friendship?" Mungo asked.

Again he got no reply.

"So – our God Almighty, the Creator of all things, is unique as well as supreme. We, however unworthily, bring Him to you all here. To that end we have come."

"To do what?"

"We will hold a great meeting. Invite all to attend. You also, we hope. Explain, teach, answer questions. Then, if sufficient pay some heed, set up a chapel, as we have done at Cathures and Cambuslang."

"To work against me! To hinder my teaching and lessen my authority?"

"Not so. You would have men and women to worship. So would we. To heed more than just earning their daily bread and seeking their pleasures? So say we. So we do your work for you, not against you. Only, we tell of the great God, greater than the sun, which is only a fire in the heavens, lit by God for our comfort and to help feed us. We can, I say, work together. Other druids have learned to do so. And senior ones."

"They have . . . ?"

"Yes. Know you of Duncan of Dumyat? Duncan of the Ochil Hills. A notable man, guardian of notable and sacred things. He is now Christian. As are others."

Druid Malduin looked at his wife, clearly at a loss what to say.

The woman nodded again. "I think that we should come to your meeting, Princess."

Thanea recognised when enough was enough. "Do that," she said. "And, if you will, tell others."

They left the pair and went to spread the word throughout the township that the man Mungo and his mother, who had disrupted the Cambuslang Lug Feast, and had protested to God about the rape of the farm girls – that was how they put it, carefully – would address all who were interested that late afternoon, one hour before sunset, in the common-grazing pasture. Let all come, they urged.

They need not have worried about attendance. Rutherglen was sufficiently aroused already to ensure that most of the population would be present once they were informed. In fact, the problem was to clear a large enough open space at the pasture-land, in the centre of the assembled crowd, and to find something to raise them high enough to be seen and heard by all. In the end, Mungo had to go and collect their horses, tethered nearby. Mother and son, mounted on these, managed to gain the height and space they required. It did not take long for Thanea to spot the beautiful wife of the druid not far off, and two children with her. There was no sign of the husband, but that was not to say that he was not discreetly somewhere in the dense and noisy crowd.

Gaining silence, what with children shouting and dogs barking, was a problem – they could have done with a pair of druidical cymbals – but at length they could make themselves heard. Again Thanea spoke first, explaining that in fact they had not cursed Telleyr of Cathures but only said that God would punish the deliberate desecration of His chapel. So the miller's death must not be blamed on them, or on their Saviour, who would not so direly punish any. Life here and hereafter was what they had come to tell of, life and love. Which was why they had tried to stop the slaying of the human captives at the Cambuslang festival. Love, kindness, compassion, friendship – that was their message. Now her son would tell them more fully.

Mungo did that, with eloquence, vehemence and even a touch of humour where not inappropriate. And he had the attention of all, children and dogs being shushed and skelped to silence. He told them what was intended here, a mission station set up, a chapel, perhaps more than one, conversion and baptism. And he ended up by boldly declaring that the Arch Druid himself had come to Cathures, those days ago, especially to curse them, in the name of the friendly sun which was now setting yonder – and the sun had continued to smile on them as it had done on all, the servant and tool of God the loving Creator.

Thanea hoped that this last would not too greatly trouble and put off the Druid Malduin.

The intended question-and-answer session thereafter was not a great success, for after an uncomfortable silence when Mungo ended, somebody at the back shouted something uncomplimentary and was thereupon shouted down by most of the others, which tended to produce quite the wrong attitude and atmosphere. This was followed by sundry calls, all at the same time, which of course could not be answered effectively, so that Mungo had to wave all down and to signify the end of the session by dismounting.

However, thereafter people did surround the pair, asking questions, this without having to raise voice in public. In general, these were ready to agree with most, if not all, that had been said. Not all questions were really to the point or relevant, but at least the interest was there. Mungo announced that they would hold small meetings in houses and barns, where folk could come closer to it all and talk more freely. Many said to come to their houses.

These invitations were followed by another, unexpected. Pleased, even elated, by the reception of their efforts, they were moving off when the druid's wife, with her two children, came to them to ask where they intended to spend the night. They said that they had thought to ride back to Cathures, barely five miles, and come back next day. She told them that this was unnecessary. There was ample room in her house, and they would be welcome. They accepted gratefully, wondering, however, what her husband would have to say to this.

On the way thither, leading the horses, on which they had mounted the children, to their delight, the woman told them that her name was Nessa, and that she was the daughter of a distant cousin of King Morcant's. She said that she was much interested in their message, and believed that Malduin her husband might well be so also, even if he was less prepared to say so, in his position. He was really a gentle man and had always disliked and shrunk from the cruel and harsh side of druidism and sun-worship. Often he had told her so, and avoided the performance of it wherever possible. There had

267

been no human sacrifice at the Rutherglen Lug Feast, only the mare and bull deaths. She thought that he could not but respond, in his heart, to their Christian declaration of love and kindness. If they talked with him, privately, they would probably find that they had much in common. Obviously a strong-minded as well as a handsome woman, this Nessa clearly was concerned for her husband, not so much perhaps for Christian doctrine as for his peace of mind.

When they reached the druid's establishment again, and found good horses stabled there and a byre of milk-cows, and in the house itself fine plenishings and every sign of plenty, it was evident that this Malduin was a man of means, whatever else. The wife Nessa explained that his uncle had been the Arch Druid of Strathclyde before the present one, and that he had been destined for the priesthood all but from birth.

Malduin arrived soon afterwards, as his wife and a servant were setting out a meal; and whether he felt it, he showed no sign of surprise at seeing the guests there – no doubt knowing his wife. The spontaneous smile was not long in manifesting itself, especially when Mungo's gift for humorous comment likewise was evidenced. They had an enjoyable repast in good company, religion scarcely mentioned save in the rather comic reactions to it which had arisen.

But afterwards, with the children put to bed, while the women talked women's talk before a peat and log fire, the men did get down to serious discussion on ethics, faith and worship, Mungo by no means having it all his own way, although without any major disagreements. He did stress Christ's teachings, how utterly new and different they were from all that had gone before in all mankind's experience, His emphasis on love and forgiveness at all costs, something man had never so much as thought of previously. He had initiated a completely new way of thinking and living, so that His birth was the supreme turning-point in man's history.

It was late before they all sought their beds that night, Mungo and his mother far from dissatisfied.

In the morning they started on their round of the houses and sheds of the township, to talk and teach and answer questions which had not been put the day before. Families fetched in their neighbours and friends. The missionaries were soon over-full of proffered hospitality, but well pleased. To their surprise, presently they were joined by the woman Nessa, who accompanied them on their further visits, not actually addressing the folk but, by her presence, and as the druid's wife, greatly furthering their acceptance and in consequence their claims. Even so they had some rejections, to be sure, but no contumely. Later, in the druid's house again, they agreed that it was the best day's missionarising that they had ever experienced.

Malduin was friendly but still not committing himself.

Mungo had spotted a disused barn, which he now suggested could be turned into a chapel, large enough to hold three or four score worshippers. The druid made no objection. But presently he disappeared, and came back for the evening meal with another man, older, heavy-built, slow of speech but direct of gaze. This proved to be another druid, wearing his white robe, Ferchar by name, from neighbouring Cathcart. Mungo was to be further tested, Nessa patently disapproving of this development.

Thanea supporting him, he had no easy time of it that night, for this Ferchar, however slow of speech, was not slow of wits nor determination. His probings were searching and detailed, and he followed up each answer with further consequential points. Malduin sat silent, heeding closely, although his wife went off to leave them to it. Thanea joined in only occasionally. She was on the whole proud of her son's reactions and rejoinders, and could almost hear Serf speaking through him.

The main sticking-point proved to be human sacrifice, together with this of life after death. They all, the sun-worshippers, accepted the latter, but differently. The druids held that in such life hereafter men and women would change, for better or for worse, become new inhabitants of this earth, according to the gods' wills. They might come back as finer, more highly esteemed folk, or they might revert to animals, even birds and reptiles. So the sacrificed ones might indeed gain from their deaths. And evil-doers not come back at all, perish for ever. What said the Christians to that?

Mungo declared that Christ taught that we survived death, but remained *ourselves*. Entered a better, fuller life, this present life but a preparation for the next. That those who *tried* to do well, in whatever degree or success, would advance in eternal life, towards bliss. So might the ill-doers, God being ever forgiving; but at a slower pace, having to labour towards it.

The older man was not convinced.

Thanea ventured an interjection. "You, Druid Ferchar, clearly are a man of your own mind, a man of thought and care and decision. You will have lived a full life, I think. You have grown not only in years and stature but in experience and testing and decision-making, as all must do, in greater or lesser degree. You, the *you* into whom this has developed, are a *character*, different from every other. Is that to mean nothing? Gone when you die, blown out like a candle? Would you desire it so?"

The man stared at her, as did Malduin. He took his time to answer. "I . . . think . . . not," he said.

"I did not believe that you would, a man of your wits and character. So – we are none so far apart. You will go on. I will go on. We all will. As Christ teaches. And His sacrifice of Himself on the cross was the price He paid to ensure that we learned it."

There was a long silence. Then Ferchar rose from his bench and made a slight bow. "Princess, I thank you," he said quietly.

Thanea usually knew when enough was enough. She also rose. "It has been good to talk with you," she said. "Now we will seek our couches. And pray to the God we believe will order our affairs, in love, hereafter. Come, Mungo." It was long since she had summoned her son to bed thus.

He stood, and nodding to the others, followed her out without a word. Almost wonderingly he eyed his mother's back.

In the morning there was no sign of either Malduin or Ferchar. Nessa accompanied the pair on their continuing round of visits to groups and families. Again they were, on the whole, well received. On their way back they had another look at the disused barn, and Mungo began planning how best it could be adapted for their purposes. Much labour would be involved, but surely, with all the interest shown in this Rutherglen, sufficient help would be forthcoming.

On reaching the druid's house they found Malduin there. He did not mention Ferchar, nor the previous night's deep discussion; but when Mungo spoke of the proposed chapel, and getting help to build it, the other shook his head and pointed. And he pointed upwards.

They looked that way, to the mound which rose above the house, on which the stone circle was sited.

"There," the druid said simply.

They all stared at him.

"That is the place of worship. There build your shrine."

Their indrawn breaths were eloquence enough.

That brilliant smile flashed at their wordless astonishment. "Come," he invited. "We shall go up and see it. There will be sufficient space."

Mother and son eyed each other almost unbelievingly. Nessa clapped her hands. "Come," she added her urging.

Even Mungo, normally so forthright, hardly dared to ask the essential question. "You . . . you say this? The chapel, there? You mean that, that you accept what we say? That you accept Christ's message?" Some of his breathlessness could be attributed to climbing that hill, of course.

"Some of it, yes. Some of it. This of love and forgiveness and what happens after death. Not all, perhaps. But enough that we may work together."

"Work together!" Mungo was not at his most coherently vocal. "Work? *You* will work with us? In this of, of . . . ? You, a druid!"

"I am the druid, yes. And will remain one. But much of what you teach makes sense to me. Answers much that I have questioned and long pondered over. We can work together, druid and Christian. *I* teach these people to worship. So do you."

"Yes, yes! Glory be – yes! We work together, here."

Thanea, panting over the ascent as once she would not have done, asked, "Your position as druid, Malduin? This will not endanger it? Cause you trouble? With the Arch Druid."

"I think not. I have spoken with Ferchar, who is senior priest for these parts. He is coming to see it as I do. He believes that I shall not suffer for this. And if I do, I can live without the Arch Druid's favour!"

"So say I!" Nessa agreed. "I am of Morcant's kin. And Malduin's uncle was Arch Druid. We think little of the present man."

Up at the stone circle they had no difficulty in deciding just where the chapel should be sited and approximately its dimensions, pointing it towards the east – as indeed was the thirteenth monolith, taller than the rest, aligned for the sunrise. Mungo's delight was almost exuberant, and infectious, his gratitude to Malduin and his wife vehement. From this prominence, as they gazed around, all Rutherglen was spread below them. Up here, the Christian chapel would not exactly dominate all, but be the most evident feature of the township. And within that sacred circle, its impact would be the more effective.

That evening was a joyful one in the druid's house, with Mungo hardly able to wait to get busy organising assistant builders and materials.

He found no difficulty about that, next day, having indeed to restrain volunteers, although many were required, especially for the task of transporting heavy stones and timber up to the summit of the mound. And when they got back to the said mound, there was a tall cross erected upon it, the cross-bar bound with rope, clearly Malduin's doing. Heart full at the sight, Mungo named it Cross Hill, there and then.

They decided that this new charge should be dedicated to the Virgin Mary, on the urgings of the two women involved.

That same night Thanea had a return of her kidney pains, dormant over these last years. It passed, but was perhaps a warning. All, it seemed, could not be joy unbounded.

23

Now the missionaries were busy indeed, with the three charges to supervise as well as the building to see to. In fact, Mungo began to fear that he could well become so involved in overseeing and administration as to have to neglect his prime duty and mission, the converting to Christianity – as he had felt had become Serf's problem.

There were other problems than finding time for everything that had to be done. His mother was feeling less than well, and although she tried to keep up with her so-active son, she knew that meantime she was becoming of less help to him than she would have wished.

Then there was the matter of finding a priest in charge for St Mary's, Rutherglen. Since it was a much larger community than either Cathures or Cambuslang, Mungo was tempted to move over there himself, as his base, especially with the co-operation with Malduin to think of, and what they might achieve together. But he was loth to leave Eglais-cu, his first charge and foothold in Strathclyde; and Thanea supported this attitude. But Rutherglen did require a resident priest – and where were they to find one? Mungo thought of requesting Serf to send one from Culross; but that might take long enough to arrange.

It was his mother who came up with the suggestion. Their miller, Angwen, was the most dedicated and effective of their converts here at Eglais-cu, a sincere and enthusiastic Christian. Why not have him ordained priest? He had not been long converted, admittedly – but then neither had Christ's own disciples when he turned them into apostles. Cadoc, an abbot, could do it, no doubt giving Angwen some especial teaching first. Angwen had a son, nearing twenty, who could manage the mill for him well enough. And he would be a most suitable choice to go to Rutherglen, would he not? The brother of the man whose attack and death had precipitated all this upheaval there. An example of Christian forgiveness in action, good coming out of ill. If Angwen would do it . . . ?

Mungo warmed to the idea at once. He himself, of course, would continue to keep a close watch on the situation at Rutherglen; but Telleyr's own brother as missioner and shepherd there, seeking to compensate for the wrong done to that community, would be a telling gesture. He and Cadoc would give the miller the instruction required:

He went off to see Angwen forthwith.

That man, sorting grain with his son, took a deal of persuading, after his first shock of surprise, seeing himself as utterly unworthy and unsuited for priesthood. But with Mungo to deal with, his battle was lost almost before it started. That younger man said that if all priests had to be worthy of their calling, the Church would be without almost all its ministers. He himself was unworthy. They all were sinners. But God had to work with sinners. And the sinner was the better able to cope with other sinners, since he knew their temptations, problems and weaknesses.

Angwen's wife, a committed believer, came to help, and together they convinced a very doubtful recruit to the ministry.

Cadoc took almost as much persuading as Angwen – not over the latter's suitability but over his own to consecrate any priest. He had done so, of course, many times, in Wales and in Ireland, as abbot – abbots as well as bishops could consecrate priests, in the Celtic Church, as Serf did. But he had been inactive for so long, neglecting his abbatial duties and failing in his responsibilities, that he felt quite inadequate to perform this ordination, even though he was now admittedly acting as a priest again, in a very lame and halting way. Mungo, needless to say, swept all that aside. Once an abbot always an abbot, he declared. The Church needed something from Cadoc which only he could effect. Was he going to fail Christ's cause in this? He had the undoubted authority, whatever his self-doubts. How else could they get a priest?

Unable to answer that, Cadoc succumbed. And he agreed to give Angwen a course of instruction, to add to Mungo's.

So activities multiplied.

They decided that the ordination should take place on All Saints' Day, and at St Mary's Chapel at Rutherglen itself, and before as many people as could be persuaded to attend – thus making the greatest impact. How they would get Cadoc up the hill remained to be seen, but God would ensure it. They had three weeks, and much to be done, and not only at Rutherglen, although that chapel had to be finished and ready.

Thanea sought to do her share, however handicapped meantime by her physical weakness.

The great day dawned, and reasonably fair as to weather for the first day of November. Surely never had there been a more doubtful and reluctant ordainer and postulant, however enthusiastic the organiser of it all.

When the party from Cathures, via Cambuslang, arrived at their destination, they were astonished to see the crowd which surrounded the Cross Hill, climbed its sides and thronged its top. There were many hundreds waiting, clearly more than the population of Rutherglen, so the word had been spread around the district – which of course was all to the good, even though it might present organisational problems.

They had to work their way through the ranks of people even to reach the foot of the hill, Mungo leading Cadoc on his horse. There, getting the older man down, he called for volunteers to carry him up. There was no lack of these, and amidst much perhaps unsuitable hilarity, the officiating celebrant was hoisted aloft.

At the summit, Malduin and Nessa awaited them, and surprisingly Druid Ferchar also – whether to support, or to watch critically, remained to be seen. Although he did not smile, nor did he look hostile. Greetings were exchanged.

Those crowds posed a problem indeed. Mungo had anticipated that he would have to hold the ceremony in the open air; but if all present were to see something of it, let alone hear, especially those down on the level ground, some extraordinary proceedings would have to be adopted. They could hardly stand on the roof of the chapel, ridged as its thatch was; anyway, Cadoc could never get up there. So some repetition of part of the service would have to be performed at the perimeter of the circle, if all around were to see at least enough to establish the occasion as memorable. Mungo asked Malduin what *he* usually did in such circumstances, to be told that never had he had to hold a ceremony before with so large a gathering.

It was important, of course, in all this, that the essence and solemnity of the ordination should not be lost in the need for display. So the vital parts would be conducted at the chapel door, and the parading done afterwards.

First, then, Mungo, backed by Thanea, Angwen and Malduin, made a shouted speech, or rather two speeches, for he did it from opposite sides of the mound, raising his voice to its loudest and most penetrating, heralded by the clanging of the druid's cymbals. He declared that this was a very special and significant occasion, on a very special day, the formal establishment of Christ's Church at Rutherglen; also the appointment and ordination of the first local inhabitant and convert as priest, and his induction as minister to this congregation of St Mary's, Mother of Christ, all present to bear witness. That convert was none other than the brother of the man who had so grievously transgressed against this community by his attack and rape, Telleyr of Cathures. He was no Christian, but his brother Angwen was. And Angwen had now come here to seek to make recompense for the injury done, by bringing them services of Christ's forgiving love, and requiring of them the forgiveness which he preached. Here, then, was a demonstration of their loving faith. Let all perceive and understand it, in goodwill. Here was the reverse of human sacrifice and vengeance.

Mungo did not go into any details of the ceremony, which would not be understood anyway, but added that Druid Malduin, whilst maintaining his druidical position, saw no real conflict in worship between them. He then signed for the cymbals again, and ragged cheers rose from such as had been able to hear him.

Then they returned to the chapel door, and Mungo, no longer shouting but slightly hoarse, went through an abbreviated version of his consecration service for sacred buildings, blessing holy water and then sprinkling it on altar, font, door lintel and walling. This completed, he handed over to Cadoc.

That man, however dubious, revealed nothing doubtful in

his contribution, simple as he made it all. After a brief prayer for God's blessing on what was done, and the occasion at large, he called forward Angwen and there informed him that he had been chosen to minister in Christ's name to this community, and would do so hereafter with all his soul, spirit and strength, knowing his own unworthiness but also the very great privilege of so doing. Then he had the ordinand kneel, and declared that, using his abbatial authority of Holy Church, he would anoint Angwen mac Kenneth with the oil of gladness and salvation, blessed in advance, in the name of God the Father, the Son and the Holy Spirit. This he did, from an ampulla which he had brought, on the kneeling man's head and brow. Handing the ampulla over to Mungo, he proceeded to the laying-on of hands, declaring that thus the Holy Spirit descended upon Angwen, who was now duly ordained and confirmed as priest in Christ's Church. Arise, Angwen mac Kenneth, and serve your flock faithfully hereafter.

It was as simple but assured as that, however uncertain the new priest looked as he rose, not knowing quite what to do next. To help him, Thanea stepped forward to kiss him on the cheek, and Mungo came to punch his shoulder in congratulation, the others looking on bemusedly.

After that it was merely a matter of escorting Rutherglen's minister round the lip of the Cross Hill, outside the circle of standing-stones, and waving to the crowd, pausing every few paces to raise hands in blessing and make a sign of the cross, Malduin contributing with a rhythmic clashing of cymbals.

That concluded the ordination ceremonies. But Mungo was not finished yet in his emphasising of the day's significance. He had heard of a locality in the neighbourhood shunned by the people, not far indeed from the farmery from which the two girls had been abducted and raped. It was a green hollow in rising ground to the south, where a spring or well rose, said to be accursed and to transmit sickness, gout, even leprosy to anyone foolish enough to dip so much as a finger in it. Indeed the proximity to the said farm was linked by some with this hollow, as regards to its grievous happenings. Mungo had decided that this was a suitable objective for a demonstration of Christ's power over pagan follies – although even Malduin was doubtful over the wisdom of this proposal.

277

There was almost a mile to go. Down on the level ground again, Cadoc carried once more and then set on Mungo's horse, Mungo once again addressed the throng. He announced their errand to the Tobarmallachd, the accursed well, and said that God Almighty would remove any evil from it, if evil there was, as divine token of the day's importance. He invited all who cared to see good triumph over ill to accompany them.

This produced something like consternation amongst his hearers, alarm at the least. There was much head-shaking and exclamation, even amongst those inclining to Christianity, Malduin stroking his chin uncertainly. Oddly, the druid Ferchar seemed interested. As a sort of reassurance, Mungo added that after they got back there would be a meal, a modest feast, for all, on the common grazing near this Cross Hill.

Even so, when they set off, not more than a score of the crowd followed Mungo's party, none looking entirely happy.

Thanea could have ridden, but chose to walk with the rest, although she found it tiring in her present state.

There was nothing off-putting nor ominous about this Tobarmallachd hollow when they reached it, amongst the green braes, just a reedy bottom, through which water seeped rather than ran, from a spring. Eyeing it, Mungo turned and smiled to the company, touched Angwen's shoulder and then walked forward, followed by Thanea and not very confidently by Angwen. Cadoc heeled his horse on after them, and, after a moment, the woman Nessa came also, almost at a run.

At the well, Mungo walked round its soggy margins. Then halting and raising a hand dramatically high, he exclaimed, "In the name of God Almighty the Father, the Son and the Holy Spirit, I declare this water pure, unsullied, free from any ill or hurt, indeed now blessed." And he made the sign of the cross over it, this repeated as he walked round it again.

Stooping, he cupped up some of the water in his two hands, and drank it. Then he washed his hands in it, and ended by bathing his brow with it. He stood back, and looked at his mother.

Thanea also drank and washed. Steeling himself most evidently, Angwen did the same. Nessa peered at them, as though to convince herself that they were none the worse for it; but when Thanea helped Cadoc down from the horse to drink his

278

share, the druid's wife rushed over and scooped up a little to put to her lips.

There was much murmuring and exclamation from behind them.

Mungo called out, "This water is pure, excellent, and now blest. In token of which I now call upon Angwen mac Kenneth, your priest, to use it for holy baptism. Who will come forward to be the first he baptises into Christ's faith and care?" He was taking a major risk here, and knew it; but he had Cadoc's ampulla to put some of the water in. This he bent and did.

There was a long, almost quivering pause, as folk eyed each other. Then, with a gulp, Nessa edged closer, but not in any rush this time.

It was Mungo's turn to sigh with relief. He handed over the ampulla to Angwen.

That man, biting his lip, took the couple of paces over to Nessa. Glancing back at Cadoc, he spoke falteringly. "Do you . . . do you . . . renounce sin? And repent – aye, repent? Repent past sins, woman? I say . . ." He paused, clearly searching his memory, "Do you put from you all . . . idolatry? The worship of false gods. Accept, accept Jesus Christ as your saviour?" He looked back at Cadoc again, who nodded.

Nessa also nodded, words not coming.

"Then – I baptise you. With water, this water. In the name of the Father, Son and Holy Spirit!" That came out in a spate, as he splashed the ampulla's water over the woman's brow and hair. "Be Christ's good servant until your life's end. And thereafter." With obvious relief, he handed the empty ampulla back to Mungo.

Smiling now, joyfully, that young man turned back to face the company. "This is Christ God's day!" he called. "Will any others come forward? Wish to accept Christ on this most important, wonderful occasion? Opportunity indeed – what opportunity! Come, I say!"

Again it was a woman who, after a moment, stepped out, elderly but head held high. And behind her, more hesitantly, came an older man, no doubt her husband. There was some nudging, and another couple made a move. That was all – but it was sufficient.

Mungo did the baptising for these four, poor Angwen having had enough of trial for one day. That over, and happily, with congratulations, Mungo called on the watchers, almost in challenge, to come and at least drink from the purged well. Some dared to do so, but not all. Amongst the drinkers was Druid Ferchar; and with such example, together with that of his wife, Malduin could not but do the same.

Thanea it was who questioned Ferchar. "You, friend, how see you all this? It does not trouble you? Offend your beliefs?"

"No, Princess – I am interested in what is done. This, of curses and fears and foolish dreads, is not any true part of our religion. It belongs more to sorcery and witchcraft. You Christians are right in this. The people are misled and should be corrected. *We* should have done it, but have failed in this. As in much else, I fear. I do not accept all that you teach, but much I agree with."

"I am glad. You do not resent our coming, then? See us as enemies?"

"I see you as bringing some reform. Our druidical faith has become debased in some measure. In need of reform. All faiths tend so to sink. I see druidism using some of *your* teachings to aid it to recover much that it is in danger of losing."

"Only *some* of our teachings? But not all, not the principal ones?"

"I accept that the sun is not a person, as you claim that your God the Father is. It is the symbol of power and force, which mankind requires to survive. Such force cannot create itself, so I accept that there must be a creator, a maintainer and orderer of all. That far I do go with you."

"Then we are well on the road to agreement, friend."

"Thus far, yes. But I cannot accept that this Jesus Christ, a man who lived and died, is the son of the creator, any more than we all may claim to be."

"Yet you accept His unique message of love and caring and forgiveness, His revelation of God's nature, purposes and methods? None other has ever so taught and revealed. He changed the world's thinking and understanding. Can you deny His authority?"

"I do not deny it, Princess. But nor do I wholly believe in it. Not yet."

That "not yet" was, in a sense, a partial victory with such a man. Thanea had established a rapport with this senior druid in a way which her son had not. She was satisfied, meantime. They would, she hoped, speak again.

Mungo was congratulating Nessa on her courage, convictions and acceptance of baptism, and Malduin on the wife he had, and the influence for good which she would exert, in *his* work as well as Christ's. Without actually saying it, he inferred that it would not be long before Malduin too would be a candidate for baptism.

With the daylight declining, it was time to head back for Rutherglen and the celebratory meal – which Nessa and her husband indeed had had a large hand in organising. It was going to have to be held by torchlight, and they would require bonfires to keep them all warm. No doubt, however, the crowd which had so signally failed to accompany them to Tobarmallachd would be preparing for that. It would be very different from their druidical torchlight occasions.

In the event, the feast on the common grazing was a great success – for feast it was entitled to be called because of the festive spirit prevailing, even though the provender was ample rather than rich or varied. Religion, of one kind or another, was scarcely mentioned thereat – but the story of the well-blessing and its consequences lost nothing in the telling, even though some of the company did not fail to keep an eye on the drinkers of that water, to ensure that there were no delayed effects.

It had been an All Saints' Day to remember, Thanea and Mungo agreed, before they slept.

24

That winter also was memorable, in more ways than one, the inevitable increase in missionary activity and supervision ensuring that – for Ferchar permitted a proselytising effort in his own bailiwick of Cathcart, much to Thanea's satisfaction, despite her own inability to be as active there as she would have wished. She had real hopes of Ferchar; and if he actually could be turned Christian, what might not be possible in this entire area of Strathclyde?

But it was the weather, and its consequences, which made that winter of 542–3 so memorable for all, worse than that of 537. Never could even the oldest remember conditions so bad, rains and winds and storms all but continuous from late November onwards. The effects were grievous, as well as spectacular, unpleasant and trying. Rivers rose, the low ground grew flooded, stock was drowned, barns were swept away, and waterside mills could not function. These were not the best conditions for converting folk to Christianity. What was their God the Creator up to?

Christmas, the Feast of the Nativity, was partly celebrated by trying to anchor new thatching on the three chapels' roofs, no easy task in gales, and reed for the thatching hard to come by, being mainly under water in flooded areas. A test of faith, Mungo called it – others naming it otherwise.

And in the weeks which followed, hunger began to rear its ugly head. Much of the oat harvest, stacked in yards or stored in barns, was swept off or submerged. Cattle, sheep and poultry were lost. Larders and stores were emptied or their contents ruined. Mills could not grind what grain there was available. The druids' beseechings of their various gods were unceasing. Christians did some praying also, with famine confronting them.

Thanea and Mungo could not but be concerned, whatever

the strength of their faith, distressed for hungry and suddenly impoverished folk, millers who could not mill, farmers, cowherds and shepherds who found themselves unemployed. And Cadoc's house and chapel, set in fairly low ground, were both flooded, although not demolished. Fortunately the other two shrines were safe, being set within stone circles, which were always erected on heights, although Mungo watched with some apprehension as access to their Eglais-cu establishment became difficult, so that he had to have a sort of causeway of stones created over the sodden ground to reach it.

The Molendinar was roaring loud and brown and the Clyde itself running high.

Then one morning in early February, after a particularly wild night, more widespread damage was evident, many folks' homes being inundated and having to be evacuated to move in with more fortunate neighbours. The word was brought to Eglais-cu – the range of royal granaries to the south, on the bank of Clyde, was gone.

Mungo and Thanea did not fail to remember the former's remark to King Morcant, two years before, that if God so willed, the Rock of Alcluyd at Dumbarton could split open, and these granaries disappear into the Clyde. There had been no earthquake, so the palace rock presumably remained secure; but the King's grain stocks had indeed been dispersed.

This had its impact on more than the royal commissariat, for it so happened that some proportion of the stored oat-bags had been washed up on the river-banks as the tide receded, and the local folk were not slow in learning of this and rescuing the grain – and not for the monarch's use. Much searching and carrying went on, and the effect of salt water on oats discussed.

In the midst of all this Thanea and her son were astonished to have a special visitor, who had come far despite the extraordinarily difficult travelling conditions – surprised and grievously saddened. For it was the monk Bran, a colleague from Culross, who came to announce that Abbot Serf was dead; and to urge Mungo to come back to Fothrif and take over the abbacy.

Apparently Serf's death had come very suddenly, although his strength had been failing for long, suddenly and unexpectedly without any prior serious illness, his stout heart evidently just having had enough, and perhaps his soul seeking the different challenges which lay ahead in a better life?

Mungo and his mother were direly upset. They blamed themselves that they had put off going back to Culross to see their old friend, whom they both looked upon as father-figure. They had been just too much caught up in activities here, too busy. Serf would not have disapproved of that, the Lord's work; but they knew some guilt, nevertheless. Now it was too late. Too late even to take part in funeral obsequies, for the abbot had been buried before Bran had left. They grieved, but for their own loss, not for Serf himself, who would have gone on to infinitely greater fulfilment than had been possible for him in his declining years.

As for the request that Mungo should take over the Culross abbacy, and charge of all its missions, there was no question of him agreeing to that. His place, he declared strongly, was here in Strathclyde, seeking to turn this important kingdom to Christ, not going back to all the supervisory duties in Fife and Fothrif. Surely there were others in Serf's community who could take over the abbatial tasks? What about Bishop Gabhran, of St Serf's isle in Loch Leven? He would make an excellent abbot. Thanea did not attempt to persuade her son otherwise, although personally she would not have been averse to going back to Culross and the quieter life there, where she had found so much joy and satisfaction in her life, or even to the island in Loch Leven itself, near to Forteviot and her friend Queen Eva. But she realised that her son had his own challenges to meet, his own life to live; and she was certainly not going to leave him to it.

So the monk Bran went back eastwards alone, disappointed. It all seemed like the end of a chapter.

Only two days later they had another visitor at Eglais-cu, King Morcant himself, with a hunting-party; hunting and hawking being, in present conditions, more than any mere sport and pastime, a valuable source of food, for the creatures of the wild seemed to know better how to protect themselves against storm and flood than did the domestic ones. Morcant was in angry mood. From his horse's back he pointed at Mungo, ignoring his mother.

"You! Wretch! Evil sorcerer! You shall suffer for this.

Destroying my granaries. You and your devilish Christian god! It was your doing, your cursing. All the store of grain gone, lost. As you threatened. You shall suffer for this, I say!"

"I did not curse, King Morcant, that day," Mungo gave back. "I did but say that Almighty God *could* split your rock at Alcluyd, *could* wash your barns away. If He so chose, with your worship of false gods offending Him. He could do much more than that! He has not damaged your rock palace, I think? Be grateful for that, and turn away from your idolatry and seek His forgiveness, and worship Him."

"Fool! Do not deny your ill-will and cursing. You and this mother of yours. I could have your life for this!"

"No doubt you could – but will not! Lest worse befall you."

"I can drive you from my kingdom."

"You could do that also, yes. But how think you that God Almighty would judge that? When we are seeking to make *your* kingdom His? Heed His warning, King Morcant. And think how excellent it would be for you to share the reign of Strathclyde with the All Highest!"

Thanea put in her word. "Think of it, Mórcant. No longer needing to fear Gualpian. Nor Lug. Nor Manannan. Nor any of them, and certainly not the sun. No more fear. But blessing, in a joint kingdom with God the Father."

The other glared at them both, finding no words to cope, uncertainty vying with his anger, a man of many fears. After a silent moment or two, he jerked something incoherent, frowning and shaking his head, before waving to his followers to ride on.

These were not all so dread-conscious as was their lord. One, a young man of hot eye and hatchet-like, dark features, reined his horse over close to Mungo and suddenly kicked out at him with all his force.

The blow knocked Mungo off his feet so that he fell to the ground, the other hooting a laugh.

"Tell your supposed Christian god to look after you better, knave!" he shouted, as he spurred away with the others.

Raising himself on an elbow, Mungo called after him, hotly. "And you! Tell Him to look after *you*, unbeliever! Who strikes His servant!"

Thanea, helping her son to his feet, ascertained that he was not hurt, save in his feelings. As she shook her head over him, he unclenched his fists and, from glaring after the retiring horsemen, looked at her and actually mustered a smile.

"I know it, I know it!" he declared. "Forgiveness! I must forgive. Give me just a moment or two and I shall forgive him. I *think*!"

She squeezed his arm.

Others who, standing by, had watched it all, were eyeing the pair doubtfully. Mungo waved to them.

"Am I not the fortunate one? To suffer, even a little, in Christ's cause!" he asked, and fetched a laugh. "Let us be sorry for that man and his like. One day, perhaps, they will learn."

As it transpired, the learning from that incident was not all one-sided. It took only a day for the news to reach Cathures. The young man who had struck Mungo had been thrown when his horse bolted, only an hour or two later, when charged by a wounded wild boar, and was thereupon gored by the boar's tusks and died that same night. And his name, it seemed, was Cathen, and he was a grandson of King Loth, son of Mordred, and therefore nephew of Thanea and cousin of Mungo, on a visit to Strathclyde.

All the kingdom rang with the story within days, Mungo's name on all lips – the second death attributed to him.

He and Thanea were greatly concerned. This was not the reputation they wanted for him, a man to be feared, who could bring down the wrath of God on offenders against him. It could perhaps influence King Morcant and the Arch Druid and suchlike, for good, admittedly; but that was not the message that they had come to expound, the nature of a loving and forgiving Creator and His self-sacrificing Son. Mungo began to blame himself for those last words he had hurled after the retiring horseman, in his angry reaction, his own cousin although he had not known it, about telling God to look after *him*, the unbeliever, who had struck Christ's servant. Those onlookers had heard this, and now all heard of it, or versions of it, no doubt improved upon. And what had been but an involuntary spurt of resentment became a dire cursing.

286

In his teachings and talks thereafter Mungo sought anxiously to proclaim otherwise, to emphasise that it was indeed no curse nor threat, that he had meant no harm to the man, that accidents were always happening, and especially on such as boar-hunts, and that God did not exact that sort of vengeance, that only a terror attributed to the false gods. And so on. He was by no means wholly successful in his efforts to absolve himself. And he was aware that the more he so declared, the more he was assuring King Morcant that it was safe to assail him and his mother. He could not have it both ways.

That winter, then, was memorable indeed.

25

The grim winter passed, but its effects did not, for inevitably hunger continued, the lost harvest and stock animals not being replaceable until a new season fulfilled itself. So there was much distress in the land. And it so happened that the Cathures and Eglais-cu folk were distinctly better off than most of their neighbours, this because of all the rescued grain from the washed-away royal granaries, a situation which did not fail to arouse comment, if not envy, whether or not it reached King Morcant's ears. And this had the effect of further enhancing Mungo's reputation for being a useful friend to have, since apparently his God looked after His own. This, no more than the deaths of Telleyr and the Prince Cathen, was not the message the missionaries desired to proclaim, but it did gain them ever larger hearings.

Besides consolidating in the already established areas of Cambuslang and Rutherglen, mother and son were now busy in the Cathcart and Pollock communities, where the druid Ferchar was not only allowing them to operate but supporting them, if not quite so actively as was Malduin – possibly because he had no wife to egg him on. Here too they were permitted to erect a chapel within a stone circle, as symbol of co-operation in worship. So now Mungo had four chapels to superintend, and was looking for more. He came to the conclusion that the widespread hunger was in fact aiding their mission, folk conceiving the all-but-famine as a sign that the powers above, of whatever name, were displeased with them, and possibly the Christian message worth looking into.

Such an attitude did not extend so far as Dumbarton and Strathclyde's monarch, to be sure. Morcant *was* seeking to ameliorate the food shortages in more than appeals to the pagan gods. Dumbarton had always been the main port of Strathclyde, a sheltered and capacious haven, and much trade was based there, especially with Ireland – for the north Irish coast was only a score of miles from the mouth of the Clyde estuary. The winter's storms did not seem to have affected Ireland in the same degree, and there was no famine there. So Morcant was importing food across the Irish Sea, grain and cattle, a costly process. He was said to be a very angry man, in consequence.

This Irish connection, although none of the imported provender came to Cathures, undoubtedly the last place that Morcant would allow it to reach, did have a reaction there, in a quite unlooked-for fashion. A visitor arrived one day in May, and from Ireland, an important visitor – a bishop no less, come over on one of the grain ships. And come, it appeared, specially to see Mungo, although he had come via Cadoc at Cambuslang. Astonished, that young man was still more astonished by the explanation.

Cadoc was responsible. Concerned about Mungo's problems over the provision of priests for his ever-growing missions, he had sent a message over, in one of the ships, to his old Irish abbey, requesting this Bishop Cathal, one of his own former assistants and friends, to come to Strathclyde and make Mungo a bishop, so that he himself could ordain new priests.

That young man was utterly bewildered and overwhelmed by this development. How could he be a bishop, at his age and lack of seniority? He had been a priest for only four years. He was in truth only a novice in Christ's cause, however active. It was ridiculous. Cadoc must have lost his wits. He had said, more than once, that Strathclyde needed a bishop, but never that Mungo himself should be that.

The episcopal Irishman did not see it that way, at all. Age had little to do with it. Faith and works were what mattered. And the respect of others. Had Christ chosen His apostles and disciples by age? Abbot Cadoc had written that Holy Church here grievously needed a bishop; and he, Mungo, was apparently the obvious, the only choice. So let it be.

Thanea at least was pleased, proud of and for her son.

They now had to go to Cadoc, of course, at Cambuslang. He proved to be nowise apologetic about his initiative in this matter. It was for the good of them all, and for Strathclyde. Priests they must have if the good work was to proceed. And he himself was a broken reed. Mungo would make an excellent bishop, indeed had been acting the part, save in this matter of ordaining priests.

The younger man still doubted. And how was it to be done? What preparations were necessary? And were not *three* bishops required to consecrate another to the episcopate?

Bishop Cathal said that three were usual. But in special circumstances one would serve. He had consulted other bishops in Ireland, and they had given their support and authority. For here, these were sufficiently special circumstances. Mungo was all but single-handedly seeking to convert a whole nation. He should have this aid and prerogative, and deserved it.

With all so minded, even his mother, Mungo acceded.

As to procedure, there was some discussion. Although the so-questioning candidate would have elected to have a brief and private ordination, he recognised, as the others proclaimed, that the cause of mission might well best be served by making a major event of it all, with maximum promulgation. That would undoubtedly imply having a ceremony at Rutherglen, much the largest of the communities so far involved in their campaign, even though Mungo would have preferred it at Eglais-cu, where it all had started. So – the word to be spread abroad. A great gathering at St Mary's Chapel on the Cross Hill at Rutherglen in two days time – for Bishop Cathal was anxious to return to his duties in Ireland as soon as possible, it seemed.

Thanea was busy indeed in the short interim, making a new white robe for her son to wear on this auspicious occasion, his old one being somewhat tattered and torn. The Celtic Church clergy did not go in for elaborate robes and vestments, nor dress distinguishing between the various orders of ministry. Only the pastoral staff, the crozier or shepherd's crook, marked out the bishop and abbot – and Mungo was sent out to find a suitable length of wood, a slender bough with a hooked end, to serve. He privately wondered what he was to do with this, and judged that it would be something of a nuisance to carry about with him.

The chosen day dawned fine, fortunately, for of course this celebration would have to be held in the open also. Bishop Cathal was much impressed with the size of the crowd which had assembled at Rutherglen, and equally so with the dramatic site of the chapel on its hilltop. He admitted that he had never conducted a service within a stone circle before; nor had he ever known druids to be in attendance at a Christian ceremony – for Ferchar had also elected to attend, from Cathcart, with not a few of his people. Getting Cadoc up the hill again added to the unusual and especial nature of the occasion.

When all was in readiness, they went through a similar performance to that of the previous dedication service, parading round the hilltop to the clash of Malduin's cymbals, with pauses to wave. This time Mungo made no speeches, but instead they sang a psalm, to the rhythmic beat and clang, to Cathal's bemusement, although presently he did begin to beat time with his crozier. Then back to the chapel door, where bishop and candidate went through their ceremony.

Necessarily it was a simple one, as Mungo desired, for of course he had already received the washing, anointing and laying-on of hands, for priesthood, and there was no point in repeating this. Cathal merely made an announcement as to the importance of the occasion and the worthiness of the man before him to be raised to this notable position and office, then said a prayer. He then placed his own cloak round Mungo's shoulders, intoned a blessing, and declared that in the name of the Holy Trinity he was a bishop of Christ's Church, with all the authority and responsibility that office carried with it. Thereafter he handed over the pastoral staff which Mungo had produced and trimmed, held meantime by Cadoc. So the thing was done. The child unlawfully conceived in the Lammermuir Hills those twenty-five years before, was now Bishop of Strathclyde.

After due congratulations, the procession formed up again to encircle the hilltop twice, with the psalm and cymbals again, this time Mungo holding high his crozier, actually a piece of an oak branch with the required handle, and waving it towards the cheering crowds.

Down they went, to mingle with all, in distinctly holiday mood. It had become that sort of occasion.

Despite the food shortages, Malduin and Nessa had contrived a celebratory festivity of sorts. There was little in the way of provender, save for netted fish from the Clyde and wildfowls' eggs, hard-boiled, of which there was no lack that breeding season. However there was liquor in abundance, honey wine by the barrelful, for the bees at least had not failed them; and fermented, that can be potent stuff. As a result the occasion developed and became vociferous and noisy to a degree, all in the best of spirits. Whether the new bishop's cause was thereby advanced by all the enthusiasm evinced was a moot question.

There was no complaint from the official party, at any rate.

Mother and son went back to Eglais-cu that evening with a new problem to consider – the finding of suitable converts to turn into priests, a matter for much deep consideration and prayer, although already some possible names had come to mind. However they would not rush this, they decided. The way, they believed, would be shown to them.

26

The year which followed was both productive and the reverse, great advances on the mission front but troubles elsewhere. The first was possibly largely responsible for part of the second, with King Morcant and the Arch Druid clearly becoming worried about the rapid spread of Christianity, and demanding that something should be done about it; even though they neither of them came directly to Mungo or his mother.

It was Ferchar of Cathcart who came to Mungo one day when he was teaching at Pollock. "My friend," he said, "I have had a visit from the Arch Druid Dungal. He is most concerned over your successes in advancing your faith. He sees it as threatening his own direly, and therefore his authority. He believes his position and power endangered, and so threatens in turn. And with King Morcant's support, he says."

"Who does he threaten? Me? And how?"

"He threatens all who take up your Christian faith, in whatever degree. Or who allow you to teach it."

"He does! So-o-o! Then you, Ferchar, are threatened? And Malduin also."

"Yes. Although for myself I do not greatly fear. The Arch Druid is not in sole authority. There is a council of druids, on which I sit. Malduin also. We have our friends. And Dungal is not well liked. I think, towards us, he will but threaten. But others, the ordinary folk who turn Christian, he may be able to harm. With the king's help."

Mungo frowned. "That is bad, bad. Those who come to us must not suffer. Or fear to suffer. They must not be persecuted. That would be most serious, grievous. And myself? And my mother? Will he move against us?"

"I think not directly. But by injuring your followers. I have heard that the king fears that you can bring down trouble upon him. Have already done so, he believes. He will restrain Dungal from assailing you meantime. But for how long, who knows?"

"You, Ferchar? Will you now forbid my mission in your Cathcart, and here in Pollock?"

"No. I see you as doing me no harm. You indeed make my work the easier. I am not myself prepared to turn Christian, but I do not see myself in conflict with you. I do not accept your Christ as the son of an all-high god. But in much else we see alike. And I am not afraid of Dungal."

"I am glad of that. But I am concerned for others."

"Yes. You will continue with your teaching?"

"I must. But if others have to suffer . . ."

"Aye. That is the price to be paid. Others paying it."

"I will go see King Morcant. And this Dungal, if necessary."

"Think you that will serve anything?"

"It might. I can play on Morcant's fears. As we have already done. How much control does he have over the Arch Druid?"

"In some matters, much. In others, little. In religious observances he has little say. But where his people are concerned, in their lives and the laws he lays down, he is supreme."

Thanea was not with her son on this visit to Pollock. She had intended to accompany him, but that morning her pains had returned, and she could by no means ride the distance. This was happening not infrequently these days, and was worrying them both, not only the pain but its weakening effects. She was still a woman of but forty-three years, but at such times she felt so much older. And concerned that she was not able to help Mungo as she had done, the more so now that he was a bishop and his responsibilities increasing.

When she had heard of his intention to visit Morcant at Dumbarton, she was urgent to go with him; her birth, her links with the late High King and King Gawain apt to tell with Morcant; and the memory of that first encounter, with Serf and herself, his yielding over the threats of Gualpian the torturer, a source of pressure. At first Mungo would not hear of it, for if riding to Pollock had been more than she could face in her present state, the journey to Dumbarton, fully fifteen miles, was out of the question. But when she suggested that they should borrow a boat and row down Clyde, he changed his tune. Many of the Cathures families had boats, for the fishing. They should find one without difficulty.

So next morning, the bishop and his mother were rowed downriver, past the villages and communities of Haugh of Kelvin, Whiteinch, Iochar and Dalmuir. Mungo had never made a point of seeking to convert the people thereof, over a feeling he had that the nearer he got to Dumbarton the more unproductive his task would be, the more enmity aroused. And there were innumerable other areas to tackle to south, west and east.

They came in sight of the soaring rock of Alcluyd on rounding a bend of Clyde off Kilpatrick, although it was still five miles ahead, with the river now widening rapidly into an estuary. They wondered about their reception.

Manoeuvring their boat amongst the large trading vessels moored in the re-entrant below the great palace rock, Thanea and Mungo landed, leaving their two oarsmen to wait, to make their way to the outer gates at the foot of the steep ascent.

They had some difficulty in passing the first gatehouse, the guards eyeing the less than handsomely dressed pair unfavourably. But Thanea, adopting her most lofty and royal style, as princess and aunt of the late Prince Cathen, gained them entry. King Morcant was in residence, they were told.

Now they had the steep ascent to mount, taxing indeed on the woman, with both wondering why the palace should have been sited up near the top of the rock, entailing all this climbing and descending each time its royal denizens left the premises — although, of course, it would make a magnificent viewpoint for the Kings of Strathclyde to survey much of their realm without leaving their house.

The site inevitably made for a strange and scattered establishment, for there was no single spot level enough on which to base a large house. The result had to be more in the nature of a hillside village of different-sized buildings, of both stone and wattle and daub.

Actually the visitors did not have to enquire as to the king's location, for they saw a group of men holding an archery practice or competition on a shelf of the rock. Archery was a fairly new introduction for the Celtic peoples, used for sport rather than war, perhaps the only helpful benefit obtained from the Saxon invaders.

Morcant, bow in hand, was not long in spotting the new arrivals, and his glare was anything but welcoming. However, this had been anticipated. At this stage, Mungo wisely left the talking to his mother. He did bow slightly to the monarch.

"What is this? What mean *you* by coming here, trouble-makers!" Morcant demanded. "I have not sent for you."

"We come for speech with you, Morcant mac Coledoch," Thanea said. "It is necessary, we think, in present circumstances."

"Why should I speak with you or your son, woman? Save perhaps to denounce you as enemies of my kingdom."

"It is because you say the like that we have come. To assure you that we are *not* enemies of Strathclyde. Friends, rather. We wish your people only well. Have indeed brought many of them well, benefit . . ."

"Cursing, rather! You, you have laid curses to the death!"

"It ill becomes you, I think, Morcant, to speak of cursing, you who have been under the dread of it all your days, believing that your own father died of it. I say that he did not, but no matter. *We* do not curse. We seek to bless, in Christ's love and forgiveness. It is of such that we come to you today. Blessing, not cursing."

The other eyed her, unspeaking now.

"Better that we speak alone, perhaps?"

"I wish no speech with you. I have nothing to say to you. Save that if you are wise, you will leave this my realm of Strathclyde!"

"I think that you speak now with the voice of your Arch Druid!" That was Mungo. "His is the curse of this kingdom. We come to advantage it, advantage *you*."

"Fool!"

"Morcant," Thanea all but pleaded now. "Hear us. Before these others, if you so will. But better privately, I think. Dungal thinks only of his own power and benefits, as Chief Druid. He sees us threatening that. Yet other druids see Christianity differently. They see it as *helping* worship in your people, not hindering it. Making your folk better subjects, more law-abiding, more kindly, better workers. Christianity is not against kings and lawful authority, only against the wicked teachings as to imagined gods, cruelty, human sacrifice . . ."

"Yet you sacrificed that miller. And your own nephew, Cathen. No doubt others also."

"No. These deaths were no sacrifices. Accidents only. The one drunken, the other engaged in dangerous boar-hunting. You must have known scores of such accidents and not attributed them to Christ's vengeance. He does not work His will that way. But by love and kindness. That is our message to you. Do not support Druid Dungal's threats against all who heed us. He does it for his benefit, not yours. Our Christian converts are your best subjects. Other druids see it so. We are no threat to you."

"You lie! There has been naught but trouble since you came. You and Servanus of Cantyre threatened me long ago. And you continue to do so. You mock the gods. There has been famine – *your* god, if he did not ordain it, did not halt it. You had my granaries swept away, costing me dear. I say that you are unwelcome here. So go – before I banish you from my realm. Or . . . worse!"

"If you attribute so much power to our God Almighty, ought you not to fear Him, at least?" Mungo demanded. "Not further injure His cause. Would that not be wise . . . ?"

Thanea still believed that not the best attitude, however effective it might be. "We suffer from hunger also," she interrupted her son. "The granaries were swept away by storm and flood, not at *our* behest. Indeed we seek to fight hunger here in Strathclyde, earthly hunger as well as spiritual. We have sent to my brother, King Gawain, for wheat grains. You will know of wheat? It is grown in our Lothian. You do not grow it here, we learn, only oats. Wheat is better than oats, better feeding for men and women, more grows in the same space, twice the weight. When the wheat grains come, and are planted, your people will have much more to eat. Is that hurt or ill-will, King Morcant?"

The other dismissed her intervention with a wave of the hand which held the bow. "Enough!" he jerked. "Leave me while still you may! I will not have my kingdom perverted and estranged from the gods. Those who continue to follow you will suffer for it – that I promise you! Heed it – and go!" He turned his back on them.

Mungo was raising his voice again, when his mother laid a hand on his arm and gestured away. There was nothing more usefully to be said, meantime.

Sadly they began the descent of all those steps.

On their way back up Clyde, they discussed what their course should be now – although it was mainly Mungo's talking, for his mother was feeling very tired, weak, not only from the climbing of the rock. That interview seemed to have taken a lot out of her. She was grievously disappointed in herself, and knew a great lethargy.

Mungo's contention, needless to say, was that somehow they must keep on with their missionary labours whatever the challenge. But the threats that it might be their converts who would pay the price, before themselves, was daunting, even to that determined young man. The thought of people like Angwen and his wife, Nessa, and even old Cadoc, being persecuted, perhaps even slain, become human sacrifices, was not for contemplation. But what could they do to avoid it?

It was not often that Mungo did not see his way before him reasonably clearly – and his mother doubtful as to what advice to give him.

Next morning he went to consult Cadoc and Malduin. He went alone, for Thanea, after a night of pain and a kind of fever, kept her bed.

Mungo did not get a great deal of useful guidance from his friends either. Cadoc said that, for himself, he was not greatly concerned for his freedom or his safety. He had lived his life, less than fully and successfully, but he was thankful that this last year or so he had been able to redeem his failures a little. Becoming a martyr of sorts in Christ's cause might even be a fitting end! But he was much alarmed and worried for others, those who had heeded the Christian teaching and were likely now to suffer for it. Was Mungo to have their sufferings and possible deaths on his conscience? He did not know, he did not know . . .

Malduin was rather more positive, if not really much help. He believed that Mungo and his mother would not personally be assaulted, though they might well be banished; Thanea's background as sister of the King of Lothian ought to save them from the worst of Morcant's spleen. And the Arch Druid would not risk going directly against the king's interests. But there would be a campaign against the converts, and such as inclined that way, almost certainly. How severe, it remained to be seen – but Dungal was much worried, clearly, and would go to great lengths if need be, so long as he did not run counter to the monarch. He, Malduin himself, and Ferchar, had been warned; but he did not think that Dungal could effect much against them, because of their positions. He and his council could declare them in breach of druidical standards and practices, but he did not see that they could do much more than that. Ferchar was very senior, and had many friends on the council – of which they were both members. For himself, his wife Nessa being kin to Morcant would almost certainly tell.

Mungo went back to Eglais-cu little the more sure of the course to be pursued.

27

In the event, Mungo carried on with his missionary work more or less as before, but without actually seeking to establish any new charges or extend into new areas. He was waiting to see what developed. Although he had one or two possible candidates in mind, he did not in fact create any new priests, feeling that this might well seem to be a further provocation – for no doubt the Arch Druid would keep himself well informed. This attitude, this careful limitation of his appointed task grievously irked him, but seemed the wise course meantime.

In his modified labours he did not have the active help of his mother, morally supportive as she was, for Thanea's sickness and pains were all but permanent now; and although she bore it all with exemplary patience and fortitude, she was unable to stir far from their home at Eglais-cu, and had no physical energy to call upon. She had little doubt that her illness was going to be fatal, but did not say so to her son.

Mungo, needless to say, was greatly worried about her – and she grieved that this added anxiety aggravated his other problems. She sought to continue to encourage him, but herself was much concerned as to the effects of his continuing ministry on others. She gave the situation intense thought and prayer.

Mungo had not long to wait for the proofs that the threats of Dungal and Morcant were not idle ones. On a morning, calling at Cambuslang, he found the chapel roof burned, the interior desecrated and Cadoc also bed-bound, battered and bleeding. He had been beaten up by a gang of thugs the previous evening. They had not said who had sent them, only that decriers of the gods must learn the error of their ways; but that was sufficient. Cadoc was philosophical about his injuries and hurt – he would recover – but he was fearful for others.

He had reason to be, for at another house nearby where a young man lived who aided Cadoc in his services – not a priest but a deacon of sorts, one of the possible candidates for priesthood – he was found to be savaged also, his injuries worse, for he had put up a fight. His young wife had been stripped naked and assaulted.

Angry and much upset, Mungo consoled them as best he could.

He rode on to Rutherglen, his mind seething, and fearing what he might find there, with Angwen and the others. Actually there was nothing amiss. Whether this was because of Malduin's presence there, or not, they could not tell. But obviously Cambuslang was a warning.

Telling Thanea all this thereafter, she reached out to take his arm.

"Mungo, my dear, it is as I feared. I have pondered long on this, and sought God's guidance – as, I am sure, have you. This is only the beginning. We have to school our minds to accept the situation. Our work here, for the time being, must halt. God's purpose in it is unclear to us – but sure it is that He will not wish His innocent converts and believers to suffer. And for no end, for it is not as though they, or we, can prevail against the powers of the kingdom. Resistance will avail nothing, that is clear . . ."

"We cannot just tamely accept! Give up all that we have fought for. Christ's cause here abandoned! Never!"

"Not abandoned, no. The seed that you have sown will not die, will come to harvest one day. But meantime, as I see it, there can be no more of the sowing. Not here. A kind of winter is upon Strathclyde. But spring will come again."

"What would you have me to do? Nothing? Sit idly here?" He all but glared down at his mother's lovely face, drawn now with pain and weakness, but none the weaker in character for that. "I cannot, I will not, do that."

"What *can* you do, Mungo? You can rebuild the Cambuslang chapel again, yes – although I do not advise it, since it could, and would, be destroyed again, and mark defiance. You can go round our people, telling them – what? That they must bear the wrath and punishment of their king and his pagan priests? That all will be well, one day. Meanwhile, suffer!"

301

He stared, silent.

"That will not serve, my dear. More unmerited suffering and violence on our people will not forward God's cause. I think that you must go away, Mungo. Leave here for a spell. Let the seed you have planted lie in this bitter blast. Until a warmer air comes, as surely it will. And it will spring to life again."

"Leave? Flee! Desert all? Is that what you would have me to do? Like any craven!"

"No. None would ever think that of you. But when one is confronted with an insurmountable barrier, one must surely seek a way round it. To stay staring at it gains nothing. If you go, meantime, I think that Morcant and Dungal will be satisfied, believing that they have won in this, and will cease their persecutions. You will have told all our people to hold on to their faith. That you will be back – for you are still Bishop of Strathclyde. They must trust to God's enduring love. His purpose will not fail because of this enmity of the men in power here. This is a testing time, yes – for them and for you. But faith will triumph. You will come back, and go on to greater things. And meantime you can serve God elsewhere."

As well as this so positive and urgent advice, something else got through to Mungo – the emphasis on you, *you* all the time, not we or us. He charged her with it.

"You speak of *me*. *I* will come back. I, I! What of you? There are two of us. We do all together. Do you think to stay here? While I go? Surely not!"

She mustered a faint smile. "My body may stay here, Mungo. Not *me*. See you, my dear – we should not shut our eyes to this. I will not live much longer – not in *this* life, that is. I go to a better one, of that I am sure. I have recognised this for some time, now. This sickness has become much worse and will not go away now. It has hindered me from aiding you, surely. So let us accept that. You will go, and my spirit and love and care will go with you, wherever."

He gazed down at her, tight-lipped, wordless.

"Dear Mungo, this cannot come as any great surprise to you, surely? You have seen me failing, my strength going, my becoming of so little use to you. It has been getting the more evident for some time. I have known it. Have not you?"

He shook his head, afraid to speak. He *had* known it, of course, even if he had not admitted as much to himself, shut such perceptions away from his mind.

"Do not take it too hardly," she urged. "*I* do not. We accept and do God's will – that is sufficient. So it is you who will go from here. And return, its bishop!"

Gripping her shoulders, and at last permitting himself to perceive how frail they had grown, he took a turn away from her, and back, seeking to school his voice.

"You, you are brave! As I am not. We have always been . . . together. We . . . this is hard, hard to consider, to bear. We are more than just mother and son. We are a, a unity . . ."

"We can remain a unity, Mungo. In spirit, in *me*, the real me, I shall always be with you, never fear. Wherever you go, always."

"That, yes. God help me! But . . ." He jerked his head, as though to master his emotions, change the direction of his thoughts. "You say to go. Where? Where am I to go once I leave here? Back to Culross? Would you have me go back to Fothrif and Fife?"

"You could do that, my dear. But I think that is not best. You are Bishop of Strathclyde. Made that by no seeking of your own, even though you chose this field to labour in. You were made that for a purpose, I do believe. There is much of Strathclyde, more than this area. It extends far to the south, right to Rheged and Galloway, a large kingdom. Dumbarton is at the very north of it, because of the port, the Clyde, and the rock of Alcluyd. Morcant and Dungal dwell *here*. But your bishopric is not only hereabouts, surely. You could go to other parts of it, and convert there, where the Church's enemies would probably not see you as so much of a foe and danger. Or go further south still. To Cumbria, Arthur's land. Even to Wales. Or Ireland. The gospel needs to be preached far as well as near. No lack of working-places for Bishop Mungo. Until you hear that you can come back."

"Aye – when? What is going to change here? To allow me to come and resume my work here, where I belong."

"I think . . . I think that it may not be for so very long." Thanea was clearly becoming exhausted by this so serious talking, persuading. "I was considering Morcant that day at

Alcluyd. He is not the man that he was. He has grown gross, heavy, slow, thicker of speech. Ferchar says that he has the gout. He limps a little. When he waved that bow at us, he winced. That is gout. And gout can kill. Morcant may not live so very long. And Dungal is elderly. Morcant is unlikely to leave an heir, an evident heir, despite the sacrifices and appeals to his gods. So there could be great changes here, in none so long a time. And for the better, we pray. You could return."

"I do not know . . ."

They spoke a little more, but with his mother's strength obviously draining away, Mungo called a halt, telling her to rest. He had more than enough to think about, on his own. But of one thing he was sure – he would not leave Eglais-cu unless his mother was fit enough to travel with him. Was she right about her time being so short? Could she tell? His heart sank at the thought.

He took some of her advice, at least. He did not repair the Cambuslang chapel. He went the rounds of his charges and people, talking not preaching, talking to groups and families and individuals, seeking to explain the situation, how they should react to it, that it might be best for him to leave them for a time, if this would halt the threats against them. He emphasised that they must have faith in Christ-God, who would not allow His work to die. They must keep up their devotions, meet frequently for prayer and worship. It was not certain that he would go, not yet; but if he did, he would return.

His reception varied, some alarmed and fearful, some reassuring, most prepared to do the best they could to maintain the faith – although a few did want nothing more to do with it, or him, as too dangerous. He was sad for these, but understood.

Malduin and Ferchar both agreed that it probably would be wise for Mungo to leave the area for a while, that this would probably more or less satisfy the persecutors. They would do what they could among their fellow-druids, especially those on the council, to counteract Dungal's enmity; but with King Morcant supporting him it would be difficult. If only the High King Arthur had still been alive . . .

They were not the only ones to think of that. And his successor, if that he could be called, Urien, formerly of Rheged, in fact Mungo's grandfather, blew neither hot nor cold, useless to the cause of Christ whatever else he achieved.

So now there followed a most curious period in the life of Thanea and her son, an interlude, not of inaction, for Mungo continued with his visitations and teaching, even giving Christian burial for one old woman who died suddenly. But he did not conduct any services in the remaining chapels, although he did, as it were privately, in houses and barns, to groups and families. He deplored having to act thus, but was persuaded to do so by his mother, Malduin and Ferchar. For himself, he would have gone right ahead with his mission; but almost certainly it would be others who would pay for his defiance, and that he must not tolerate.

So they waited. Waited for what? Waited to see what would transpire – with Mungo never admitting that he was waiting for his mother to die, whatever her own frank and positive attitude. For it was obvious that she was failing fast. She seemed to need to sleep much of the time, but awake she was remarkably cheerful, at least when her son, or others, were with her.

The days grew into weeks without anything being resólved.

28

It was well into the summer when there was a significant development. Of all things, it was a joyful occasion, a wedding, which brought it on. One of the Cathures young women, one Shona, a relative of Angwen's wife, and a devoted Christian like her spouse-to-be, was most eager to be married in the chapel at Eglais-cu, where they had both been baptised and confirmed. Mungo felt that he could by no means refuse this request, that he *must* not; but advised that only a small company of kin and neighbours actually attend the ceremony, however many might gather to celebrate the occasion afterwards. And Thanea, who was friendly with the bride, decided that she would, and could, attend, however poorly she felt.

The brief but happy service was nearly over, with the couple duly wed and kneeling to receive the final blessing, when there was a commotion outside, shouting. Then men burst into the chapel, many men, wielding clubs and staves.

Pandemonium followed. The intruders laid about them indiscriminately, beating men and women alike, their leaders making for the bridal pair near the altar, yelling. With their blows they felled the bridegroom to the floor and began to tear the clothing off Shona.

Mungo rushed forward to her aid, and was beaten back. He tried again, and this time was grabbed, punched and hurled against the stone walling, winded. Thanea, who had been sitting on a stool at the font, rose and, protesting, went to the bride's aid as she struggled with two men intent on entirely disrobing her. She threw her arms around the younger woman, to protect her. But she was roughly wrenched away and struck viciously. Choking, she fell to the ground beside the groaning bridegroom.

Shona, hysterical and now wholly naked and mishandled with it, was left to sink down beside her husband, reaching out to him, while Mungo came staggering across to his mother, panting, to kneel and take her in his heaving arms, gasping his anxiety.

Chaos prevailed, bawling chaos. For not only the wedding guests were struggling to get out but the intruders also, for smoke was beginning to fill the chapel. During the assault, somebody had set the thatched roofing on fire.

Mungo somehow managed to pick Thanea up and lurch with her to the doorway, while Angwen and another man, injured as they both were, came to the aid of Shona and her husband. Somehow they all got to the doorway and out, through the thickening smoke, the roof crackling above them.

There they were greeted by a jeering party of fist- and club-shaking men, shouting further threats and making obscene comments on the bride's unclothed person and her husband's present inadequacies to take advantage of it. Their objurgations were presently lost in the roar of the fire, and they turned away and left, laughing.

Thanea, barely conscious, was carried to her house, Mungo beside himself with worry and rage, the former considerably outdoing the latter. He put his mother on her bed. He sought to revive her with honey wine. Then he knelt to pray over her. Only incoherences were effected.

Presently, with Thanea between unconsciousness and sleep, he went to see how others fared. The bridegroom was the worst injured, his collar-bone broken by a club's blow. Shona, clad again after a fashion, was tending him, in dire state of mind but recovered from her hysteria. Angwen had chest pains, hoping that ribs were not broken. Others with various injuries, all relatively minor. Mungo sought to comfort and sustain faith.

The chapel was a smoking ruin. Obviously word of the forthcoming wedding had gone beyond Cathures' community, and some ill-wisher had informed the authorities.

Mungo did not know what to do for his mother. There were no practitioners of the healing arts at Cathures; besides, these tended to be druids and much of their devices little more than sorcery and witchcraft. He knew a little of herbal remedies, but did not think any of them valid for this situation. He sat at Thanea's bed all that evening, holding her hand and talking to her every now and again. But, although she tossed and

307

jerked sometimes, her eyes remained closed and she answered nothing.

Later he moved his own couch near to hers, and laid himself down to sleep, or to try to, his mind in turmoil.

Sometime in the night he wakened to a sound. It was his mother's voice, weak but lucid.

"Mungo – hear me, Mungo," she was saying. "I am . . . going now. You hear me? I am going, I know. Not leaving you. I will never do that. But going on. On . . . to the next stage. Of our journey. Near you still, I believe. But not as I have been."

A pause, as he rose.

"Loving. Loving you always. Aiding you, if God wills. My time . . . has come . . . to move on."

He was kneeling at her bedside now, holding her hand, choking back tears, and mumbling the broken words which were all that he could produce.

"My dear, do not weep for me. I am . . . the happy one. Pains almost over now. Good, good ahead of me. I go to better things. Closer to our Maker. Our redeemer and friend. And Serf." Her voice was sinking. "Joy for me . . . save in that I . . . am not to be . . . at your side. Above you, perhaps? But not . . . but not . . ."

"Yes." That was all that he could find to say. "Yes." Mungo, the eloquent.

"You . . . now. You too go on. Leave me here, Mungo – but come back. One day." That was only a whisper now, but somehow urgent. "You have . . . work to do. Great work. And you . . . will do it. Chosen to do it. From that day . . . In the Lammermuirs! I, I have been . . . blessed. All unworthily. I . . . I . . . go. Till you . . . join me . . . again."

Thanea spoke no more.

Mungo did. He found voice after a fashion. He talked to her, told her of his love, praised her life, assured her that he would do as she said, would go, but indeed come back, faith and care, *her* care, sustaining his efforts and labours. Whether she heard him or not there was no knowing. It was dark and he could not see even whether her lips moved. He held her hand throughout in both of his.

How long he knelt there he did not know. But after some

time the hand within his gave two little grips, slight but distinct. That was all.

Later he realised that his mother no longer breathed. That had been Thanea's farewell. To fare well, indeed, she and he.

Mungo sank over her, and let the tears come.

Postscript

Mungo did go on, and to great things in Christ's cause. He left Clydeside soon thereafter, once he had taken leave of his friends, seeking to arrange for worship to continue in private, and assuring all that he would return. Since he would go southwards, to cover the rest of Strathclyde, Cadoc urged him perhaps to go as far as Llancarfan in Wales, and to visit his former abbey to see that all went well there. He had left unfinished business at Llancarfan, and it would ease his last days if he knew that his former charge was being cared for.

Mungo did go to Wales, after journeying and preaching the length of Strathclyde and Cumbria, pausing for quite some time in the mountain lands of the latter and converting numbers. But the authorities at Carlisle proved to be hostile, and he headed on. He found all well at Cadoc's former abbey, and went on to Menevia, to meet the renowned St Dewi or David. There he was greatly welcomed, an extra bishop and a vigorous one. He and another young priest, Asaph by name, became St David's assistants in that man's major task of turning all Wales to Christ, in the face of unending heathen Saxon penetration.

Mungo, or St Kentigern as he was known in Wales, remained in that land for years, awaiting word that he could return to Strathclyde and his spiritual responsibilities there, without hurt to his people, making his headquarters at Llanelli. It was eight years before, at length, he could return, with news that Morcant mac Coledoch was dead, and the new king who had succeeded, Roderick, far-out kin, was not formally Christian but not antagonistic, indeed reported to be interested.

So it was back to the Clyde for Mungo to resume what he saw as his life's work, back to his mother's grave and Eglais-cu – which in due course got called Glasgow. There he established good relations with King Roderick, and laboured abundantly and successfully.

St Columba meantime had come over from Ireland, to the vast task of Christianising the Picts of Alba; and these two valiant warriors for the faith, working in parallel, eventually met, and are reported to have exchanged croziers, their pastoral staffs, in a significant gesture of mutual co-operation and regard. What was to become Scotland was firmly on its way to Christianity before Mungo rejoined his mother for new endeavours.

NIGEL TRANTER

CHILDREN OF THE MIST

'Our race is royal,' was the proud claim of the MacGregors. Yet for all their history and fighting qualities, they were a small clan and their lands too close for comfort to the great Clan Campbell.

So by the end of the sixteenth century, the heritage of the new young chieftain, Alastair MacGregor, was a poor thing indeed. Not only was much of the land lost, but their principal threat, Black Duncan of the Cowl, Campbell of Glenorchy – as clever as he was unscrupulous – had the ear of the king . . .

'Tranter's style is compelling and his research scrupulous. He reaches down the ages to breathe life into his characters'
DAILY TELEGRAPH

'A magnificent teller of tales'
GLASGOW HERALD

HODDER AND STOUGHTON PAPERBACKS